AS MANY NOWS AS I CAN GET

AS MANY NOWS AS I CAN GET

SHANA YOUNGDAHL

Dial Books

Dial Books
An imprint of Penguin Random House LLC, New York

Visit us online at penguinrandomhouse.com

Printed in the United States of America
ISBN 9780525553854

10 9 8 7 6 5 4 3 2 1

Design by Cerise Steel
Text set in Gamma ITC

FOR BETH, MY OAK.

"Life is not easy for any of us, but what of that? We must have perseverance and above all confidence in ourselves. We must believe that we are gifted for something, and that this thing, at whatever cost, must be attained."

—Marie Curie

MINE GULCH BRIDGE · GRACEVILLE, COLORADO

"I want to feel everything—what it's like to be that heron, or those clouds, and to jump off that bridge." David's eyes were steady as a bird's as he pointed upriver to where the old metal bridge glinted in the late afternoon sun. I smiled. I'd known people who'd jumped from it, but I'd never considered it. Too risky. Yet, in that moment, feeling like I could control the earth's rotation, I grabbed David's hand and we ran. Behind us we heard the others emerging from the forest to stack firewood on the sand. David pulled up on the guardrails, and steadied himself on a piling. I climbed up next to him. My bare toes gripped the railing as I swayed. David reached for me. Our fists laced together above the water.

"Ready?" he said. I wasn't. But he'd already stepped into the air, so a millisecond behind him, I stepped off the bridge.

NOW

LEAVING ALBANY, NEW YORK

I don't remember meeting David Warren. That's just part of growing up in a small town—some people are part of the landscape
from the beginning. For many of them, this mountain-in-the-
background or oak-tree-in-the-front-yard kind of permanence is
just fine, unquestionable. There's little change in their location
relative to you, and they travel at predictable speeds. Hannah—
my best friend from before I can remember—is like that, depend-
able like an oak in the front yard, always there. From the time we
could toddle we were together: in the preschool sandbox; holding hands on our first day of elementary school; in fourth grade,
exploring the trails behind my house and pretending the lookout
bench was a one-room school; by middle school, taking cookies
to our blue-haired ladies at Christmas. I have no first memory of
Hannah, but that doesn't matter. She was at every birthday party
from one to eighteen. We grew together until it was time to part,
and I left her standing in my front yard certain she'd be waiting
there when I returned.

Still, there isn't anything I could conjure from the dry mountain landscape of Graceville, Colorado, that might explain my

friendship with David Warren. And so not remembering how I met him is like a black hole.

I asked my mom if she knew when I met David. I was hoping for some story like how we were kids at the park and he knocked me down with a hug but then threw sand in my eye, but Mom said she met his parents in childbirth class.

My roommate, Mina, thinks life in utero is like being behind a curtain, and that babies actually learn much more about the outside world than we give them credit for. She says this is why newborns turn their heads toward their mothers' voices seconds out of the womb. Mina is probably right about this because she's nerdy about things like developmental psych. It makes me wonder if David and I could have been communicating even then.

I bet he called out to me at those birthing classes:

"Hey! Scarlett! Does that breathing calm you?"

And I answered in the secret language of those not-yet-born, "I get more room to kick when she exhales."

David laughed. "Ah, getting cramped in there?"

"Of course! What about you?"

"I can't wait to get out," he said, and elbowed his mother's uterine wall for emphasis.

"Yeah, me too."

That's it. That's how I met David Warren. Both of us in utero, cramped as hell, waiting for the right time to drop into position, to escape.

NOW

APPROACHING THE PENNSYLVANIA STATE LINE

Einstein rocked our conception of the universe because he proved time is not static experience. In other words, there's not just one NOW to "be here" in, as the bumper sticker of the Subaru Forester in front of us for the last seventy-five miles asserts. Instead, there's a *now*-continuum depending on speed and light.

To tell my story, I need to lead you through a series of my "nows," but I can't start at the beginning—my birth nineteen years ago, or even when David and I stepped off the bridge up Mine Gulch Road and everything changed. I can't start at one "now" and travel straight to this one, where I am en route to an internship in California, because by the time I finish, I won't be here anymore. Motion continues, and though time feels linear in some ways, that's just another way common sense fails us.

As we pull over, the Subaru we shared a now with for seventy-five miles disappears. All the traffic on I-90 appears to be speeding by, but to the people in the cars, nothing is moving. Their radio is still there; their drink doesn't move relative to where they sit.

My roommate, Mina, tucks her bobbed hair behind her ears and opens the door to the hum of the interstate. To all those cars whizzing by, it looks like the cows and fields, and Mina, poised in her platform sandals as she clicks a photo of the WELCOME TO PENNSYLVANIA–PURSUE YOUR HAPPINESS sign, are speeding past. And when Mina gets back in the car and accelerates like a banshee into Pennsylvania, it'll be us speeding through the landscape. My point? Motion and time are relative.

"How's it coming?" Mina twists to buckle in while peering at my laptop. "Motion and time? What does that have to do with anything?"

"Relativity has everything to do with everything!"

"Relatively speaking," Mina says, all puppy-eyed.

"Stop." I laugh and elbow her away. "I need to get back to work."

"Stopped." She turns to the wheel and guns it onto the freeway.

Mina jokes when I bring up relativity because she thinks it's absolute, complex nerd-territory, but I've always thought the idea shouldn't be that complicated. It's really a lot like memory. What I need to tell you about David Warren—there's no linear way to tell it. It's more like time is this vast honeycomb, and inside each tiny cell is one moment. To tell my story right, I need to hop forward and back through the past few years. And maybe that's the truth of time after all.

Given that, there are a few things you should know about David Warren.

First, David Warren was the longtime best friend of my first love, Cody Martinez.

THREE YEARS BEFORE THE BRIDGE

GRACEVILLE AREA UNIFIED HIGH SCHOOL · GRACEVILLE, COLORADO

Hannah peered into my locker mirror. Her green shirt turned up the color in her ever-changing hazel eyes. She shook out her sandy hair. "You look excellent," I said. We were sophomores and slightly less nervous than the freshmen buzzing through the hall. I closed my locker and turned to see Cody Martinez appear out of the crowd, six inches taller than he'd been in June, tan from a summer with grandparents in New Mexico, black hair flopping across his dark eyes.

I fell against my locker as he stepped toward us. Yes, Cody-my-first-love, there is no story without him. Cody-my-first-everything. Cody, who stood and half smiled at me as he said, "Hey, Hannah. Hi, Red."

My breath caught. My cheeks burned. I looked down at my red tank top.

"Cody, can you just drop the tacky name puns, please? You know she hates that," Hannah said, tugging on her backpack straps.

"No, I . . . don't mind," I said.

"Since when?" Hannah slipped one strap of her bag off and dug in the back pocket.

"I've mellowed this summer."

"Yeah?" said Cody, one eyebrow raised.

"Um, teaching science to little kids *definitely* mellowed you out," Hannah said.

"I was great with the kids! You saw!"

"Did you know the vein in your neck twitches when you get angry?" Cody had his finger pointed millimeters from my ear. I had never been so aware of the distance between us. The bell rang. "Well, off to pre-calc we go," he said, pulling his hand away and swiveling on his squeaky sneakers.

"Yes, let's," Hannah said.

I dropped a few steps behind Cody to watch his loose-legged walk and whispered to Hannah, "The vein in my neck twitches?"

"Yeah."

"Is it, totally ugly and disgusting?" My eyes were on Cody as he disappeared into the crowded hallway.

"'Course not, don't be silly."

I touched my neck. "That vein is going to be *all* I think about today."

"Come on, Scar, hop on the Zoloft like everyone else."

"Uh, supportive much?"

"Well, you were diagnosed! Do something about it." Her voice was gentle and pleading and exasperated all at once.

"It's not severe." I met her eyes.

I think it worked, because she smiled, then said, "*Seems* bad if you're thinking about your *vein* instead of six feet of Cody Martinez suddenly all up on you."

I grinned. I couldn't stop grinning. "The research on SSRIs and developing brains is mixed," I said, still grinning.

"I'm not even sure what you just said, except somehow it wasn't about Cody."

I swatted her shoulder.

"If you're really worried about your vein-twitch, just stop wearing ponytails." She gave mine a tug, then went for my hairtie.

"Stop! I want it up." I pushed her off. "No Zoloft. I'm going completely Zen this year—deep breathing. No anxiety. Ever."

"Zen? Scar, you must be ill. You're, like, immune to religion."

"Not the religion part. The breath control."

"Okay?" Hannah opened her hands in a sort of confused surrender.

"Research shows breathing can grow gray matter in your brain, *Hannah*."

"You know what? Studies show prayer can too, *Scarlett*." She smiled and pointed a frayed nail at me. Then: "Got any ChapStick?"

"No."

"It *is* kind of amazing, isn't it?"

"What, that I never carry ChapStick and still you ask every day?" I said.

"No, that's just my optimism. I *meant* how much someone can change over a summer."

"Yeah," I said. "Hormone development." I tried to walk faster to keep my eyes on Cody.

"Elevated testosterone production," Hannah said.

"My limbic system is going into overdrive," I said.

"Well, keep it together; eat some chocolate." She handed me a mini chocolate bar, melted slightly from her jeans pocket. "I need your help to get through pre-calc this year."

As we stepped into the classroom, David Warren stood and shouted to Cody, "You didn't call when you got back!"

"Just got back yesterday," Cody said, pulling David into one of those chest-bump dude-hugs before sitting down at an adjacent desk. Cody Martinez. I'd known him most of my life, and he went away for a summer and returned as a person I suddenly wanted to be near. Always. All the time. Right then.

"Scarlett!" Hannah hissed. "Sit next to him! Don't just stand there."

I sliced my eyes to her, and probably the vein in my neck twitched too. I tried to breathe slowly through my nose as I slipped into the desk next to Cody. I thought, *Inhale 1, 2, 3. Hold. Exhale 1, 2, 3, 4.*

And so, with one toss of his hair and a bad name pun, Cody Martinez had suddenly become the brightest object in my universe. My North Star. My Polaris. It wasn't long before Cody and I were together. All the time. And we were happy, mostly, for over two years.

KAMPGROUNDS OF AMERICA · ERIE, PENNSYLVANIA

The first step in the scientific method is to ask a question. For example, why is it that when you grow up in Colorado, people think you must like camping? Or why do some people from upstate New York think camping is putting up a cheap tent between RVs? Or that campgrounds should offer heated pools and pygmy goats to pet? Yeah, these aren't questions I care enough to research, so I'll get to the real one: At what point did I stop being a planet in orbit, held in place by familiar forces of gravity? And after the cosmic collision that followed, after I cut myself loose, cast myself off, made myself alone, will I ever return to my old orbit?

Can I? Do I want to?

TEN MONTHS AGO, EARLY AUGUST

THE RIVER AT MINE GULCH BRIDGE · GRACEVILLE, COLORADO

The best swimming spot near Graceville is a beach reached by a twisting, five-mile dirt road. We always parked on the far side of Mine Gulch Bridge and followed a path a half mile upstream to where the water spreads out wide, flanked on one side by a pebbled beach, and the other by smooth granite rocks that wait as warm rewards after swimming across the river. That night we were drinking a bottle of Jack Daniel's that Rage stole from his dad. We swam and took swigs in turn as shadows crept across the bank. When the bottle was empty, and just before the tree branches were swallowed into darkness, Hannah leaped up and said, "Time for firewood!"

Her boyfriend Rage stood, ran his hand over his bleached hair, adjusted his sagging swim trunks, and started toward the trees, reaching out and catching Hannah's hand as he did. I was feeling slow, a kind of weighted-by-sand drunk. Instead of jumping up to help, I lay back on my elbows.

"Scarlett and I will collect downstream," David said, moving to his knees.

"Whatever, just get some wood," Hannah called, disappearing into the trees, tugging Rage behind her.

David spun the empty bottle in the dirt.

"You really collecting wood?" I asked as he settled himself down to watch the bottle slow. He reached into his jeans pocket. The bottle stopped, its long neck facing the river.

"No," he said, pulling out a pack of cigarettes, opening it, and tapping out a pre-made joint. David didn't smoke. He just acquired a pack of cigarettes once and handed them out to the smokers so he could keep the box for joint storage. He flipped open his silver Zippo, lit it, and took a long drag before passing it to me. While holding the smoke in his lungs, he spoke. "I didn't want to share with everyone," he said, sounding like an exhausted frog.

"You're stingy," I said, taking the joint, inhaling, and passing it back. On the other side of the river, a large, thin-necked bird stood among the reeds. "Look."

"Nice," David said, and took another drag.

"Heron or sandhill crane?" I asked as we both gazed at the bird swaying slightly in the breeze.

"Great blue heron—you can tell by the bluish head coloring. And also, sandhill cranes only migrate through this part of Colorado, but great blues are here all year."

"Right, forgot." I watched the bird's unwavering eyes. "Biology's not my favorite."

He tapped off a little ash. "Ah, but you sure can memorize for a test."

"And forget it two weeks later. How do you even remember all this bird stuff?"

"I'm a Junior Ornithologist," David said. He pointed to himself and smiled wide.

"Oh come on. That was an award in sixth grade."

"I like birds. But I especially like it when the smartest girl in Graceville doesn't remember that sandhill cranes have red on their heads."

I ran my fingers across the pebbly beach. "Are you really telling me that you stayed interested in birds just to prove you're a smarty-pants?"

"No need to prove it to anyone but you, Scarlett, and there'll be so few chances to one-up you after we leave," David said, roach clip in hand.

"You'll find a way."

"A guy can try," he said, placing the roach at his lips. I watched the final embers glow.

"So now are you going to tell me?"

"What?"

"Why you care so much about birds," I said as I watched the heron. The combination of pot and alcohol was making me feel like the speed of the earth's rotation had increased to such a degree that I could see it. I spread my palms into the bank to try and stop the sensation. Through the motion I could hear David's voice.

" . . . a way of understanding the world. I mean, if I take the time to notice the little differences in a bird, define its shape, its location, give it a place, find it in a book, describe the color, categorize it, then I can feel like I get it. I need as many ways of understanding the world as I can find."

I stared at the heron. "I get that. Like figuring out the math of things."

"Yeah. Exactly." His fingers traced arcs in the sand. "So thanks to your calculations, Scarlett, I know I've been on the cover of point-seventy-seven percent of the *Graceville Times* published since my birth."

"And I know *that* is a great blue heron and not a sandhill crane," I said.

We sat then, listening to the river, the crickets, the stumbling sounds of Hannah and Rage as they hunted for dry wood in the forest behind us.

If I breathed slowly, the spinning waned.

"Do you think we'll still do this in a few years?" David asked.

"What, smoke weed? Of course. This is Colorado. We make weed history. We don't just give it up on our twenty-first birthdays when it's legal."

"That's not what I mean," David said, licking his lips. "I mean we've worked so hard to get to this summer, where we've earned the right to spend a Monday night up here not worried about the morning. We can't lose our scholarships for anything at this point. You could probably stop showing up for Step-up to STEM and everyone would still think you were the best public servant in the world just for coming up with the thing."

"I don't know about that."

"Bet it wouldn't matter. Graceville decided about us a long time ago. It doesn't matter if we drink or fuck as much as the kids who won't set foot in a classroom for the rest of their lives. We've been given this big pass, but how long does it last? You know, when we leave here in a few weeks, we've both got to start over, to convince everyone wherever we go that we're worth it. We've got to work our way back to a day like today, where we get to forget everything and just be in the world. Enjoy the weed for itself, not just as medicine to help us later through our cancers and chronic pain."

I was not entirely sure I was liking the fight I was having to keep the earth's rotation under control, or the direction of this conversation. But I didn't say it. "D," I said instead, "it doesn't sound like you're enjoying things *now*."

"I am. I'm just aware," he said looking at the river.

"It's not just stress that causes cancer," I added. Right then the great blue heron lifted into the sky, its thin body seemingly released from gravity, its beak heavenward, like it was diving into another life.

"I know, Scar—*Silent Spring*, genetics, and blah, blah." He waved his hand in the air. "So what's your plan? You going to cure it? Is that how you're going to earn your days-like-this?'"

"Ha. *Ha.* I could ask the same of you," I said. After Cody's mom died of cancer, our entire friend group had been plagued by questions of who was going into medicine. As if the loss of her should motivate us to action. As if we'd want to watch more people die. Or spend our lives delivering that kind of news.

"You're the one into genetics," I said. "Go invent synthetic cancer-fighting genes or something."

"Ah, no, but I might figure out how to splice the shark's anti-cancer gene into human DNA and save us all." David smiled and leaned back.

"Oh, shark-humans! There'll be no fallout from that."

"It's no different than making an edible apple, Scarlett. Our world is one big splice."

"Maybe," I said, realizing that the immediate effects of pot and alcohol were waning, and I felt like I could again move my hands without the earth tilting too quickly.

"Do you know what I want?" David said, looking suddenly straight into my eyes, and what I saw in his face was like I'd caught rare footage of a strange beast. He'd never looked at me so intently before. I don't think anyone had.

"I want to feel everything—what it's like to be that heron, or those clouds, and to jump off that bridge."

NOW

The second step of the scientific method is research. David would tease me for getting all metaphorical right now, but if a return to my previous orbit *is* possible, I have Mina to thank. She is currently dashing off to help feed the goats—yes, there *are* actual pygmy goats at this campground. Mina—I met her on my first day at Colwyn, trying hard to not see David Warren everywhere I went.

NINE MONTHS AGO, SEPTEMBER

COLWYN COLLEGE · WATERTOWN, MAINE

My body felt heavy as I shut the cab door and stood at the edge of the Colwyn College campus for the first time as a new freshman. I inhaled salt from the foggy air. It wasn't cold. Still, the skin on my bare arms broke out in goose bumps. Through the mist, a guy in a red hooded sweatshirt like David always wore strode toward me across the green grass. He was tall with David's brown hair. For a second I thought David had come to Colwyn to make things right. It wasn't logical, so I wasn't surprised when the boy in David's sweatshirt came closer and I noticed his rounded nose, the opposite of David's sharp Roman one, and twinkling blue eyes unlike David's deep brown. Not-David also had freckles and a comparatively bony build. Still, I stared.

"Can I help you?" he said, his voice resounding. He had a large Adam's apple that bobbed as he spoke. He was very much Not-David.

"Oh, I'm no, I'm new?" I said.

He pointed to a banner on his shirt that read *I Can Help*

and *Colwyn Residential Advisory Council.* I bit my tongue. The acronym—CRAC. Whoops.

"I'm Welcome Week staff. Check-in is that way—just follow the signs. Most things are closing up for the night, but there's someone there for late arrivals. You already eat? If not, you'll have to hustle to get through check-in and make it to dinner."

"I'm good, thanks."

"You come from away?"

"Colorado."

"Cool, my family spends Christmas at our place in Vail."

"Must be nice," I said. He grinned at me, missing the insult. So-Completely-Not-David.

"Yeah it's great. You ski, right? Where you from?"

"Graceville."

"Where?"

"Western slope, two hours out of Denver."

"Hmm." He rubbed his round chin. "Never heard of it."

"No one has. Little town, you know, one without a resort."

He smiled. Oblivious. "Well, if you're from Colorado, you should consider going out for the ski team. It's icy here, but there're some decent hills nearby."

"Okay, yeah, I might. Thanks," I said, pretty sure I didn't want to be on a ski team with a bunch of resort kids.

"See you around, uh—what's your name?"

"Scarlett."

"Nice to meet you, Scarlett. I'm Harold," said Not-David,

holding out his hand. I let go of my suitcase to shake and my bag fell over, bumping his shoe. "Looks like you're missing a wheel." He righted the luggage and tipped the handle toward me.

"Oh, yeah. I am. Thanks," I said, and waved as I walked in the direction he'd pointed, feeling the weight of my backpack as my suitcase rattled across the brick sidewalk. I thought, *I'm going to school with people who have second—or third—or fourth?—homes in Vail.*

I'd managed to get my busted bag up the steps. Balancing it now against my leg, I jiggled the key in my dorm room lock. The latch clicked and I stepped forward just as the suitcase toppled in front of my foot so that I stumbled headfirst through the doorway into a short, brown-haired person—Mina—crashing into her and sending the large plastic box in her hands flying. It followed a swift trajectory to the floor. *Crack!*

"Oh my god I'm so sorry!" I said as Mina's mouth fell open in horror. She dropped to her knees and looked up at me, ashen-faced, and said:

"So much for my plan to greet you with some Dickinson."

"What?"

"'I'm nobody, who are you? Are you Nobody too?'" She said it like it was blah, blah, blah, punctuating each word with a tiny hand-wave.

"Um, I'm Scarlett. Your roommate?" I was utterly confused. I stepped back and pulled on my backpack straps. Mina stood up in the wreckage around her feet. The top of her head reached only to my shoulder.

"Right, yes, of course, but that was the Dickinson I'd planned to welcome you with."

"Huh?" I said.

"Emily Dickinson. The poet."

"No, I—I don't read poetry," I said.

Mina tilted her head. "But didn't you in school?"

"Shel Silverstein in third grade."

"Really? That's too bad. Well"—she paused—"there's time. More now because I guess we won't be listening to records."

I winced. "That's a record player?" I looked closer at the thing that had landed upside down.

"It was." She got down on the floor again. "I'm not sure what it is now."

"Oh god I'm really sorry, I'll replace it, I was just trying to—" What? Walk into the room? "I'll replace it," I said again. "Really."

Mina waved. "Don't worry about it. It sucks, but accidents happen, right?" She sounded like it was some universal truth, like sometimes people smash your record player, oh well. I shook off my backpack as she said, "I took this bed against the wall. I hope that's okay. I thought maybe the window was nicer and you'd want it, but we can switch things around, move the furniture or whatever. It's totally cool."

"No, this is perfect. I love windows," I said. I dropped my backpack to the floor.

"My parents just left. They really wanted to organize with me, but I said, guys, my roommate isn't even here yet and she might, like, have an opinion about the room."

"Maybe they should have stayed. You might still have a record player."

Mina made a sound close to laughter. I tried to smile. It felt like work.

"It was maybe stupid to bring it, but I've been collecting records since before I was born."

"I—uh—how can you collect before you're born?" Poetry. Records. These words. I'd broken her record player and she'd given me the better bed.

"My dad's a major nerd. He started a collection for me as soon as the little pink plus appeared."

"Huh. I've never even played a record."

Mina just shook her arms like she didn't know how to respond.

I carefully leaned my suitcase against the wall before flopping onto the bed, not bothering to dig through my bag for sheets or a pillow. I stared at the ceiling.

"So I'll have this dresser and you can have that one?"

"Sure," I murmured, eyes unable to follow where she was pointing. "I'm wrecked from all the travel, I guess. I think I need a nap. It's nice to meet you. I'm really sorry about your record player. I'll . . ." I just wanted sleep. Maybe if I slept I could curtail my socially awkward spiral.

"Do you want help making your bed or anything?" Mina said.

"Thanks. I'm good." My eyes were already closing.

"Right, you should rest." I think I heard relief in her voice. Of course I did. I broke her record player! I closed my eyes. The world went blissfully black.

When I woke up, the sun was low in the sky. Mina was gone and exactly half of the room looked like it had been lived in for years. The cracked record player sat on her dresser, a lesson in gravitational force. Her record crates formed a nightstand. A blue tapestry hung above her bed and next to it, pictures of her family. I stood to inspect them: Mina with her parents on the beach; smiling with a pair of old people; a black-and-white of her dad, stubbled and young, in front of what looked to be some kind of historic building with a large white rotunda; one of Mina as a toddler laughing with a dog by a lake. A fan stood guard over her laptop next to a desktop bookshelf where she'd set some novels, Bob Dylan's biography, Emily Dickinson's collected poems.

All I'd brought for decorations were a framed family photo and two posters I'd owned since fifth grade. I extracted the posters from the slightly flattened tube in my suitcase, examining their tattered corners and new creases. As I tried to smooth out the black-and-white of Einstein holding a puppet of himself, the door opened and Mina walked in on tiptoe.

"Oh, you're awake!" she said, dropping her heels to the

carpet. "Einstein—cool. Also, do you like what I've done?" She gestured to her half of the room, then gripped her hands behind her back, released one to point to my other poster unfurled on the bed. It was a headshot of Marie Curie and the quote *Nothing in life is to be feared.* Mina tapped her bottom lip. Her nails were a deep, glimmering purple. "So one's saying"—she pointed at Einstein—"that science is fun, and the other"—Curie—"that science is serious?"

"Oh—no—uh, I don't know?" The question caught me off guard. "I've just had them both, like, forever."

Mina cocked her head to the side, and then launched herself like a panther onto my bed, narrowly missing Curie's head.

"What are you doing?"

"Not to worry—I have not crushed Madame Serious! I'm just helping," she said. "It's not easy to get a poster straight on your own."

"Okay," I said. When I didn't move, she took the poster gently and held it straight. I reanimated and began pressing tacks into the wall. Once both posters were hung, I set my picture frame next to the lamp on my desk. Mina stood at my shoulder, looking at it.

"You look just like your mom," she said.

"Really? People usually say my sister, Jessica"—I pointed— "but we only share DNA from our dad. That's Katelyn. Niece extraordinaire." In the picture, Katelyn was smiling, wearing my cap and gold ropes. Mom, in the same sundress she wore fourteen years before to Jessica's graduation, held Katelyn's shoulder, and Dad towered behind us, flashing a wide, toothy smile.

"I'm an only child. Maybe that explains the pre-birth record-collecting. My dad was forty-five when I was born and a tad excited. Which reminds me, I think the record player might still work. It kinda looks like it does? But I didn't want to try because you were sleeping. Let's see if there's still potential to have the best sound system in the dorm . . ."

"Okay," I said, pulling my Einstein biography out of my bag. I was about to set it next to the picture when David's graduation photo fluttered out. Mina picked it up off the floor and raised her pencil-enhanced eyebrows.

"Boyfriend?"

"Yeah," I said. And for a second I didn't even realize I'd lied.

"Cute," Mina said, handing it to me. I tucked it deep into the book as Mina placed a record on the turntable and dropped the needle.

The sound that came out was shrill and fast, and then the voices sang.

"The Chipmunks?" I asked.

Mina shook her head. "Nope. The Kinks on a broken record player."

LEAVING KAMPGROUNDS OF AMERICA · ERIE, PENNSYLVANIA

I didn't start writing this in Maine. Or as we drove through New Hampshire. Or as we crossed the entire state of Massachusetts and arrived in Albany, where we spent our first night with Mina's family in their book- and record-lined Queen Anne home, complete with a wide porch and seed boxes bursting with springtime buds lining the windowsills. I didn't put one word down, even though Mina had bugged me to start writing from the minute I'd strapped myself into her leather passenger seat in the Colwyn parking lot. I had time, I'd said—there was a lot of country to cross. But I knew I was delaying. I never wanted to write this. I might not have started at all if it weren't for the stop at Mina's house. That and the fact that I pretty much have no choice.

On Mina's porch, three fat cats made their way around our ankles, but we didn't have a chance to reach down to their wet noses before we were bustled inside to a front room rowed with records. "You weren't joking about the listening room," I said to Mina.

"Arranged Armstrong to Zappa," her mom quipped, pulling me gently from so many square shelves and surround-sound into a formal dining room. A reclaimed wood table was set with mismatched china. Mina's mom, a rounder version of Mina with hair dyed a brilliant purple red, loaded our plates with steaming veal, fingerling potatoes, and sautéed spring greens. "Most people call me MJ," she said, touching the square beads of her necklace. "But I'll respond to Madeline Jean, Maddie, or Mina's mom," and when she said this, her face broke into dimples and the tip of her nose flushed. Mina shook her head and tucked her dark hair behind her ears. Her dad came in, pointed to himself, and said, "Rick, for Derrick," then started filling our glasses with red wine. Mina read my surprise but matched her mom's dimpled smile. She took a sip and rolled her eyes heavenward. "God, Dad, this is really good."

"I didn't know you drank," I said.

MJ's smile bubbled into a small giggle.

"Min!" her dad said, his hand going to his gray-stubbled chin. "You don't drink at Colwyn? Why do you think we're sending you to college?" If not for the tic of his eyebrow, I would have thought he was serious.

"No way! They drink shit!"

"You spoiled her," MJ said, wiping her eyes, humming a last laugh.

"Oh come on! There's got to be at least some beer snobs at Colwyn. I just had a student in my office waxing poetic about pilsners. I had to cut him off after thirty minutes."

Mina picked up her napkin. "Dad, you would think I was insufferable if I got into beer."

Rick swirled his wine. "Just don't be afraid to get to know people. Relax. Make friends." Mina raised her hands in my direction, like *See exhibit A.* Her dad winked at me. "You girls could bring your own bottle."

"She does. Of seltzer," I said.

"*See?* I do go to parties," Mina said, then paused unfolding and refolding her napkin. "Sometimes."

I raised the glass to my lips and tipped it up. I swallowed slowly.

"Wow, I think I maybe get wine now," I said. Mina's parents

smiled. I could not imagine my parents setting out wine for Hannah and me. Ever.

Mina cleared her throat. The table was quiet, expectant. "So, I've got a new poem for you, 'Small Frogs Killed on the Highway,' by James Wright."

Rick set down his wineglass and leaned back.

"'Still, I would leap too, Into the light, If I had the chance,'" she began. I watched her father nod, saw how his eyes became both more and less focused with her words, how they radiated some feeling. I understood now why Mina didn't rebel against her dad's insistence that she memorize poetry. I remember my father looking at me like that exactly twice—when I gave my graduation speech, and again at the airport as I left for college. If there'd been an easy way to get that look from him, if I could have just memorized a poem like Mina did, I'd be a vast repository of verse just like she was.

"'Across the road, tadpoles are dancing on the quarter thumbnail of the moon. They can't see,'" Mina recited. "'Not yet.'"

Sitting at their long table, sipping expensive wine, my first alcohol in months and months, and watching her dad's eyes, I thought about my parents and that little town I came from, where I don't think anyone ever feeds their family veal with fingerling potatoes and sautéed spring greens.

I promise I haven't forgotten the story of what happened after David and I jumped from the bridge. But before I can get to that, you have to know something else about David Warren.

David Warren = Asshole

I have several examples that can support this claim, but I know I left you—us—in midair, plunging toward the river. First, though, before we go back there, let me give you this one from our senior year—eight months before the bridge, the leap, the untethering of one orbit, the pull of another.

EIGHT MONTHS BEFORE THE BRIDGE

GRACEVILLE, COLORADO

I never knew what to expect from David. Except that sooner or later he'd act like an ass.

Graceville's Winter Town Tree Event was supposed to be a "nondenominational" annual lighting of a "holiday tree." It drew just about everyone in town into the cold to sing together. Because choir and AP physics were offered at the same time, David and I gave up singing for science senior year. And so, for the first time since kindergarten, we were not freezing with our friends in black-and-white concert clothes, but in the audience, appropriately attired in sweaters and jeans, listening to the mayor speak.

The tree-lighting was supported by people who'd bought colored bulbs in honor of those "no longer among us." Blue bulbs cost twenty dollars; yellow, thirty; green, forty; red, fifty. Clearly, reality didn't reflect what was actually purchased, because after the crash that tanked the economy and closed Tidal Force Plumbing's doors for good, the tree would have been *entirely blue*. And then what would we have done? Had the school choirs, now diminished because families fled town, *Grapes of Wrath*-style, sing "Blue Christmas" by Elvis, and we'd all go home crying?

No. Not helpful.

Even now, our town's sloth-paced economy was obvious in our reduced size. And if you opened the tree-lighting program and counted, which I did, you'd see the ratio of blue to red lights still wasn't right. I'd just finished the math when David arrived, pushing his grandfather's wheelchair to the front row. He kissed his grandpa and whispered something to his mom, who smiled and waved at me as David walked my way.

"So, Scar"—he stood next to me, facing the dais, rubbing his hands together in the cold—"what's the ratio of blue to red at this, our last tree-lighting?"

"Fifteen to one," I said, looking up from the program and opening an arm for a quick side-hug.

"Hmm, wasn't it *seventeen* to one last year? What's your analysis, Doctor?" He turned to me. "Does this reflect the modest economic recovery we've been seeing nationally?" David held his fist under his mouth like a TV reporter's mic, then tipped it toward me. I leaned in.

"It might, except it appears that fewer bulbs were purchased overall—so maybe the rich are just getting richer and the poor, poor enough they can't afford any lights at all."

"Well, that's a grim outlook for some, and great news for others." He said this back into his mic-hand. "But it's always nice to assess this situation with you, Dr. Oliveira." He dropped his hand to my shoulder before stuffing it into his pocket.

"Weird to not be doing this backstage." I pointed to where the high school choir was gathered. Cody blew a kiss at me, and Hannah copied him with much exaggeration. "I guess it's just the sacrifice we make for science," I said.

"Speak for yourself. I hated choir."

"Really?"

"Yeah, I only sang for so long to make me look well-rounded on college applications."

"What? Mr. Stallman tried to get the physics schedule changed so you could stay in choir!"

"That's what Mr. Stallman wanted. No one asked me," David said, watching the choir take the stage.

"Huh. Guess it worked out for you. I miss it. Especially when they sing the new songs. But it's physics."

"It is the supremely best class ever," David said, grinning.

"Yeah, but not because Ms. Henderson is hot," I said. Ms. Henderson was a new hire—right out of school, probably only twenty-two, and the focus of much "admiration" from the boys.

David laughed. He looked at me, then away. "She's a good teacher, but I'm not into those sensible skirts. They should be short, really short."

"You're an ass."

"That's right, they should show just a bit of ass."

"No wonder Melissa dumped you."

"Why do I need a girlfriend? When it's so easy to see a little bit of ass?" he said, gesturing to the choir where a few of the girls were shivering in miniskirts.

"I repeat, you're an ass."

"Not a bad thing to be." He looked big-eyed as Melissa Mahoney reached down for something. "My point is demonstrated," he said, gesturing to how Melissa's skirt showed just the bottom of her butt's curve while she adjusted her heel.

"Shut up, you ass. They're going to start soon." Choirs from Graceville's three schools were arranging themselves on the stage next to the tree, moving like penguins in their concert attire, flashing trained, tight smiles.

"Come on, Scarlett, I only said that to piss you off," he whispered. "I was kidding. Wanted to see the vein twitch."

"That doesn't work anymore. I'm a trained breather," I whispered back, but to be sure, I counted my inhales and exhales.

"That's what you think," David said, nudging me with his elbow.

"Shut up, and frankly, I don't believe you."

David crossed his arms. After that we listened to the concert, twenty minutes of winter songs, and a short speech by Mayor Hernandez, who ended by inviting everyone to join in with the choirs to sing "Joy to the World."

David leaned over and whispered to me, "How is this non-denominational?"

"One nation under God?" I offered, and noticed suddenly

how red and weepy his eyes were. "D—you're stoned out of your mind."

"Let Earth receive her king," he responded.

I laughed, but my eyes flashed to Cody and then back to David as I sang along. "Let every heart prepare him room."

See? Kind of an asshole, right? But maybe not the only one.

TEN MONTHS AGO, EARLY AUGUST

THE BRIDGE AT MINE GULCH · GRACEVILLE, COLORADO

It was only seconds. But my memory of the drop is long: the water reflecting the last pink light, my feet and David's speeding toward the blue, and then the sudden slap of cold water, and the pressure of the current mid-river, stronger than we'd imagined. It pulled our hands apart and pushed us downstream until we swam to an eddy, and in the shallow water we gasped and laughed so hard we fell into each other's arms, fell into the darkness, tugged off our wet clothes, and there in the warm summer air discovered how two bodies can undo each other, slowly, in a way neither of us had expected, or known before. Even if the act itself was not new, something about it was.

Yeah. So I did that with the sexist ass. Why? I don't know, chemicals are weird. And people are complicated. Right now, though, I have to say I'm more concerned about what you're thinking about me. I mean, I know that girls who are comfortable with their sexuality are judged. Especially ones who are comfortable (okay, kind of comfortable) with the reality that they slept, knowingly, with their friend who is an ass. So, let me say right now, not that it matters, but David was only my second, and Cody, well, I really loved Cody.

But since actions speak louder than words, you should know some things about the summer and fall of junior year.

TWO YEARS BEFORE THE BRIDGE

GRACEVILLE, COLORADO

Our sixteenth summer was supposed to be fun. We had cars! Well, to borrow, anyway. Cody and I were together and things were great. But then Cody's mom, Teri, got sick again. She'd had a bout with breast cancer when we were eleven, and five years later her doctor discovered a new lump. Cancer is one of those things that's never better the second time around. Teri's sickness drew a heavy shadow across our summer.

When Teri fell asleep on the couch, Cody and I would sneak off to his bedroom to make out. There on his blue comforter he'd kiss my neck, and I'd breathe in his scent of pine body spray and sweat. We'd lie there, his hands up my shirt and mine pulling on his belt loops.

One July afternoon, I said, "Do you want to?"

He paled. "Of course, but my mom's right there!"

"She's sleeping, and anyway you're a teenage boy, how long do you think we're going to take?"

He blushed as I rubbed my hand over the lump in his jeans. "I just don't think I can with her right out there. What if she needed something? What if she got up and opened the door?"

"Cody, she's not going to open the door on us. Do you think she wants to see what we do in here? I mean, she's your mom. She changed your diapers."

"Gross. Stop it!" He shooed my hands away, pushing a pillow in my face.

"It's just, you know, I don't think she'd mind. You could probably talk to her about it."

"Uh, no thanks." He threw the pillow on the floor as I laced my fingers between his. "Not everyone has a"—and here he would let go of my hand to make air-quotes—"*sex-positive* nurse for a mom."

"Oh, come on! Do you think I really want to celebrate my 'sexual debut' with her? She'll probably buy me donuts like she did when I got my period. Not happening."

"Scarlett, you know I really, really want to, just not here. Not if she might need me."

"Okay," I said, a needle of guilt in my belly for wanting him like this when I knew Teri was sick and he was sad. It was gross of me. I ran my hands down his arms and he nudged my temple with his nose, tugged a wisp of my hair. He was right. We could wait.

"When are you starting the birth control or whatever?"

"Told you—I already have a prescription for the ring. I can start it right before we decide . . ." Then I kissed my way up his collarbone to his mouth. "And we can use condoms for backup like we talked about. I know you have some already—"

"Jesus, Scarlett."

"*What?*" I said, "You don't need to be embarrassed about being prepared. It's sexy." My hands moved back to his belt loops, and I pulled myself on top of him to press my weight in. "Feels good, doesn't it?"

He answered with a kiss.

The summer passed. The first week of September marked our one-year anniversary and Teri came down with a cold that caused her to rasp so much she needed to spend a few days in the hospital with breathing support. Cody was terrified. But the doctor assured us this was not the end. So on our anniversary, Cody gave me a silver necklace that looked like a DNA double helix encased in glass, which he said was "for the remarkable modern art of not reproducing while mating" and we unbuckled our pants and joined the world of grown-up relationships. We quickly discovered that sex, unlike cancer, is better the second time, and the third time and the fourth and fifth and on and on.

It was only a week later when I came home to find my mom, still in her scrubs, drinking a glass of wine in the immaculately clean kitchen, the three silver, sealed packages that kept my rings next to her glass. "Scarlett, I know what these are," she said.

"Well, you *are* a nurse." I leaned over to greet her with a peck on the cheek.

"Why didn't you talk to me about this? I always said you could. I thought you'd come to me when it was time for your debut, like your sister did." Her eyes were glassy, wet, about to spill. Oh god.

"Mom, don't be—don't be *sad*. I didn't do it to hurt you. Jess is— We're just different. And sex—it's kind of a private thing. I don't want you talking to me about your sex life with Dad."

"Okay." She took a deep, composed breath, but a tear escaped anyway. "I just thought you would talk to me about this."

"Oh Mom, *why*? Because of all the great books you gave me about the magic of my body? I'm grateful to know about my clitoris, but that doesn't mean I want to explain my relationship to mine with you."

"Jesus, Scarlett, I'm trying here."

"Well"—I made my voice gentle—"stop."

"Okay." She looked at me. "Just one thing."

"What?"

"This was just as much your choice as his?"

"Oh Mom, you know Cody! He's not a manipulative shit. If anything, I wanted it more than he did, or at least I'd wanted it for longer than he did. He kept putting me off."

She traced the counter tile's grout with her finger and raised her eyes to me. "Did you manipulate him?"

"Mom!"

"Honey, I want you to have positive sexual relationships."

"Mom, stop. I do. It's great. You want details? The first time was not so good, really fast in fact, but the second time we tried some different positions—"

"Scarlett."

"What? I thought you wanted me to talk about this with you?"

"Well, not in that tone."

"What tone?"

"That I'm-going-to-try-to-shock-you-now tone."

"Seriously Mom, you *just* asked, and now you critique how I'm going to talk to you about it?"

She reached over to take my hands in hers. I let her. "I'm not shocked, sweetie. I'm glad the second time was better, and that you're experimenting. I just want you to know, if you want to talk, or have any questions, you know I'm here."

"Thanks. I think I'm good for now," I said, but I squeezed her hands. She smiled. Her eyes still glistened in the corners.

And that was that.

I know that some girls would have loved a mother like mine. Hannah was always coming around to talk sex with my mom. Her parents' view was "ask no questions," because she wouldn't need to know anything about sex until after she was married anyway. But Hannah, while fully down with the sweet Lord, takes a much more technical view of virginity than her parents would, so she'd often sit at the table and quiz my mom about all things sexual. While they talked, I read about physics. I liked being able to hear their laughter in the background as I tried to understand exactly how a black hole stops time.

NINE MONTHS BEFORE THE BRIDGE, NOVEMBER

GRACEVILLE, COLORADO

Hannah's family lived in one half of a duplex owned by friends from their church who, for years, had struggled to sell the property, or at least rent both halves. This failure of our local economy meant we were allowed to hang out in the still vacant unit downstairs, provided we followed the rules. Or, at least, didn't get caught breaking them.

And so we gathered one November night to cram for an exam we'd done zero prep for. To make up for not doing our assigned reading, we divvied up the chapters to create a practice test. Hannah passed out blankets and we kept our hats on; the heat was just warm enough to stop the pipes from freezing. We'd just begun reading when Rage said, "I've got something to keep us focused," and he pulled a bag of weed from his pocket.

"Rage on!" Cody shouted, and dove for the bag.

"Quiet!" Hannah shushed.

"Right, sorry," Cody said, and then added as if in explanation, "David smashed my pipe yesterday—the wasted bastard."

"Totally your fault." David pointed at Cody. "Who leaves a glass pipe sitting on a table anyway?"

"Um, who throws a basketball inside?" I said, having witnessed the incident.

"Who can't catch?" David narrowed his eyes, but a smile fluttered there too.

"Whatever, D." I rolled my eyes. "So, who's got some equipment?"

"Rage, don't you?" Hannah said. "It's your weed."

"You know what I say—pot is for sharing, why spend money on paraphernalia? Who's got us covered?"

"Not me," I said. "I would never buy the stuff. But I don't need to—I hang out with you stoners."

"They aren't stoners," Hannah said. "Stoners wake-'n'-bake."

"I guess you don't sleep over at Cody's," I said to Hannah, who looked away. Hannah said I should talk with Cody about getting it together after Teri died. There was partying and *partying,* she said. But every time I tried to bring anything up, a cold lump stuck in my throat. The boys were okay. We all partied some. We weren't like Melissa's brother, who blew his college fund on bags of cooked Sudafed.

"Hannah, you got something hidden around here?" David said.

"Naw, I don't keep anything around." Hannah twisted her hair up into a bun with the pen she'd been using to write our study guide.

"Yeah, her parents would go ballistic if they knew," I said.

"What do they think happens here?" David asked, and then yawned. When he covered his mouth, I thought—I can't be sure, but I thought I saw him slip something onto his tongue.

"Homework," I said, eyebrows raised. "It's called trust, David." My voice was flat. David swallowed hard.

"Mom *did* ask why Rage is called Rage," Hannah said.

"What'd you say?" Rage was holding the bag of weed up to the fluorescent lights, the bleached tips of his hair glowing in the brightness.

"I said it was a joke, because you're so against partying," Hannah said.

I rubbed my arms. Even through my sweater I could feel the goose bumps. I thought, *David's probably on antibiotics or something.* Cody told me they weren't doing pills that much anymore.

"Man, you've got her good," Rage said, leaning over to kiss Hannah's temple. She blushed. I looked at Cody. Examined his eyes. He kissed my cheek, calm, normal. I breathed.

"Hannah, that sounds like a lie to me. Not a very Christian thing to do," David said, taking the bag from Rage.

"Whatever, D. I don't think Jesus was against weed."

"Well, you're the one who's read the Bible," David said.

"Right, so drop it," she said, and David dropped the weed onto the table, smiled.

"Okay, okay." I eyed David. "What's important here is that Hannah's mom trusts us all. Thank god."

"Yeah," Hannah said. "We get to hang out *here*. Where we probably won't get busted and kicked off the track team."

"But if you got kicked off the team, that would just be more time for you to hang out with me and Cody," Rage said, smiling.

"No, if she got kicked off the track team, she could cover Step-up to STEM while *I* was at practice! God, that would make my life easier. Those new volunteers are kinda flaky. Should I call the cops, Han?" I waved my phone.

Hannah's face went flat. "You know if I got kicked off the track team I'd never be able to leave the house again, even for Step-up to STEM." She pulled the pen out of her thick hair and stuck it between her teeth.

"If Hannah's parents knew about any of this, it would be"—Cody ran his finger under his throat—"for all of us."

"But they do not," Rage said, "and I take that as a great reason to get very high in order to assist with my understanding of separation of powers in this great free country of ours."

"Thank you, Rage, for refocusing this study party. Now, how is it that none of you overachievers has a pipe?" David pointed his finger at us one by one. We shook our heads again. "And I'm out of rolling papers, so it's time to get creative. Let's see, kids, I need two plastic cups, a straw, and some tape."

"That," said Hannah, "we definitely have." She disappeared upstairs and came back down with the cups, tape, straw, as well as a box of glitter glue and colored markers.

"What I Learned in High School," David said, smiling. "How to build a bong out of just about anything."

"Engineering 101," I said, snuggling into Cody's side.

That night we built the Graceville High Spirit Bong out of blue plastic cups, and since Graceville's colors were blue and red, we decorated it with red glitter glue. David wrote in red Sharpie along the side, *To Eliminate Some Brain Cells of Graceville's Finest!* and we all got so stoned, it looked like the world was made of flip-book pictures. We laughed and quizzed one another about the powers of the executive branch until just before midnight, when we had to appear at our own houses to get six hours of sleep before the big exam. As I recall, Hannah and Rage brought in B's on that one. Cody, who always struggled when he put things off, got a C; I knew he'd have to knock that off to make it through engineering school someday.

David and I both took home A's. Which reassured me he was just fine.

KAMPGROUNDS OF AMERICA · TOLEDO, OHIO

Before, I memorized facts for my exams. Before, school was a game I knew how to play. Before, I could stun adults with knowledge of light speed, turn their cheeks pink when they noticed the lightbulb on my shirt and read the words under it: *Physics Turns Me On*. I appreciated the attention I got for informing people that the space station orbits the earth 15.54 times per day. I liked their shock when they noticed the formulas I scribbled all over my paper-bag-covered books because most think the equations of rotation and velocity look like another language. Before, I could speak science, and Graceville knew it. Everyone. Especially David.

David Warren and I lay naked on the shore and looked up at the sky. He tapped my hip with his finger, then kissed the bone. Everywhere he touched me pulsed with electricity. He didn't say "You're star-lit Scarlett" like Cody would have, just to annoy me. He didn't say a word for a long time. Finally, he said, "Scarlett, what are the odds?" I threaded my fingers through his while I worked out my calculations. But I couldn't decide what numbers to use. What was the probability that David Warren and I would end up like this? Together, naked on the bank after stunning each other with some previously unrecognizable physical chemistry that seemed to tackle us as we were in free fall and led us to this moment: David and me under the stars, exhausted and reeling.

"What do you think are the determinates?" I asked, raising my head and touching the hair falling around his eyes. "How long we've known each other? Divided by the number of people in Graceville who we might find ourselves attracted to—or an average between the two percent of the population I'd find attractive and the thirty-four percent that you would?"

"Hmm, you think you're that much more selective?"

"I'm entirely selective."

"So you'll need to factor in a selectivity ratio."

"I'm guessing we had somewhere between a point-zero-zero-one percent and one hundred percent chance of ending up here."

"That is quite a range, Scarlett."

"Isn't it? Fairly all-inclusive, I'd say." We listened to the night around us. Something landed in the water. Leaves rustled in the breeze.

"I like all-inclusive. That's what I want. I want it all." David splayed his arms out to the darkening sky. At that moment, I knew what he meant.

"I feel like we could do almost anything," I said, "like maybe reach up and grab those treetops."

"You know, that's just a consequence of your altered perception," he said.

"Maybe. But sometimes, I feel like I can sense my elements, like I'm physically aware for the first time that I'm made up of atoms, just like the horizon," I said.

"Damn, I am good," he said, "I made Scarlett Oliveira think the horizon is made of atoms, when everyone knows it's a visual perception depending on perspective."

"You dickwad, I meant it metaphorically—like the edges of everything we see disappearing in the distance. That's what it feels like. Elementally it all pretty much comes down to the same stuff, just in different combinations. And human beings—we aren't that different from the trees. Well, we are, but some parts of our DNA look similar."

"Mmm . . . biology. It's just the combinations—what's turned on, or off, that matters." David's voice was thoughtful.

"Exactly," I said, and bit my tongue, not entirely sure what I'd just admitted to.

"The only combination I'm interested in right now is Scarlett and David," he said, and kissed me. When I finally pulled away, I felt his eyes move past me. "There they are," he said, "the stars burning themselves toward extinction, or maybe already extinct and we can't even see it yet."

"Actually, the ones we can see are *just* burning themselves to extinction. There's only a few dead ones in the Andromeda galaxy that we can see with the naked eye, so most of those are active stars," I said.

"First you were all metaphor, and now you're the literal one?" David said before kissing me again.

Then we heard the others calling, and I felt a trickle of reality like cool water down my spine.

"David, I'm on birth control but, are you—have you—you know—been checked for stuff?"

David grinned. "I'm clean, and maybe not as bad as you think."

"Really?" I said, unconvinced.

"David! Scarlett! Where are you guys? David? Scarlett? D?" Hannah and Rage were calling from the bridge.

Our swimsuits were wet, heaped on the rocks. We pulled them roughly over our skin, and suddenly nothing felt right, the sand on our bodies was rubbing, uncomfortable, the darkness too black, a mosquito bit my neck. David grabbed my hand as we walked up the riverbank in the darkness.

"We're here. We're all right," we called. When the bonfire came into view, I dropped D's grip. I didn't look at him.

Hannah ran to me and put her hands on my shoulders. "What the hell?" she said, shaking me a little so that drying clumps of her hair swatted me. "We saw you jump, and Rage and Cody jumped the bridge before, so we figured you were all right, but then after a while we realized time had disappeared and you guys hadn't come back— You scared the hell out of us."

"We were just talking physics," David said, and let his arms swing loose at his side.

"Oh. My." Hannah pressed her forehead into mine. "You are so stoned. Your eyes are like Red Hots."

"Real nice, D. Only shared your joint with Scarlett?" Rage grabbed David around the neck, holding him in a quick headlock before releasing and crying, "Dammit, now you got me all wet too!"

"Because I forced you to attack me, Rage," David said.

"Male aggression always has a price, Rage." Hannah spun away from me and ran her finger down Rage's undefined biceps. Rage was soft, his muscles hidden since dropping off the football team junior year, but still powerful.

I don't remember exactly what happened next, except that no one imagined the reality. No one would have guessed. David played it cool, and I must have too. The boys left together and Hannah drove us to my house. We made my one a.m. curfew. Mom as usual was reading in her room until she heard the lock click in the door.

"I'm home and Hannah's sleeping over," I called.

"Okay, there's half a pizza in the fridge," Mom said. We ate the pizza and a bag of chocolate chips. We laughed. It was almost normal, except every hair on my body was electric, wired, like our house was the highest point around in a thunderstorm, and the earth was gathering its electricity in response to the clouds. Everything looked the same, but the air around me was charged, and outside an unstable wind blew.

Truth is, I might not be obsessing about any of this if things had turned out differently. See, the other thing you need to know about David Warren is this: David Warren is dead.

SIX WEEKS AGO

COLWYN COLLEGE · WATERTOWN, MAINE

I'd been doing homework when my phone pulsed. I remember the sun was almost down because there were streaks of golden light across my bed, so I had to shield my phone to read Hannah's name on the screen.

"Hannah! Hey!" I said, surprised. She always just texted.

"Scar, I have something to tell you," she said with a slowness that sounded practiced. "David's gone to God."

"What?" I said, "He converted?" But as soon as it flew off my tongue I knew it was the wrong thing to say.

"No, Scarlett. He's gone. Dead. In heaven or—"

I'm not sure if the line crackled, or if we were silent a long time or what exactly. But in my memory, there is a line of static almost as if blue lightning flashed through the room. Eventually, I must have said, "Don't worry. David didn't believe in hell. There's no way he could end up there." I heard Hannah's deep wail, but a strange calm swam around me. The dorm had never seemed so quiet. Hannah caught her breath.

"How?" I asked.

"Overdose." I can still hear how this word lingered in the air, floated into my room, a dark gray cloud. In my memory, that was right when the sunlight disappeared from the sky, and in the courtyard, the trees became black shadows against a white sky as the world began its slow fade. My lungs tightened, and I heard her voice very far away.

"This is the second death I've heard about from Facebook. Maybe there's something to your crazy shunning of social media. I mean, it's David. Why didn't people wait till, like, phone calls could be made? At least with my great-aunt it was kind of a mistake because I didn't call Mom back earlier in the day."

Hannah babbled on as I opened the window above my bed. The spring night was freezing. There were still piles of snow in the corners of the courtyard. I took long gulps of air. The phone cut in and out. Cell reception is a problem in Graceville and in Maine. It's also possible that I only recall a bad connection because that's how it felt—unreal, impossible, a hum growing louder, like an angered hive ready to swarm.

"Scarlett, are you okay? Because I'm all wigged out. I came straight home when I heard the news. Rage is meeting me at the duplex tonight, which will be its own kind of weird, but whatever. We're all in shock. Can you come back? Please. No one is sure yet, but Mom thinks the funeral will be on Sunday."

As she spoke, I felt myself split from my body. In my memory, I'm watching myself on the phone at the window, paralyzed in my blue cotton sweater. I must have managed to murmur "No." I know I said, "I haven't heard from David in months."

"Because you guys were on opposite sides of the country, Scar. It wasn't personal."

"Maybe not," I said.

"Scar, he was like one of our oldest friends. Even if—look, I know you had that thing with him that you won't tell me about—but whatever that was—it doesn't matter. You know he'd want you there. And even if he wouldn't, it's not about what the dead want. Isn't that what Cody's dad said when Teri died? The dead don't get a choice. Let it go. I want you here. Come home."

My hands shook. Hannah knew there were things I wasn't telling her. Of course she did. And she didn't care. I wished I could hug her then. For so long. Let her grief slide onto my shoulders. Cry mine onto hers. But all I could say was, "I wish I could come home, but you know I can't afford to."

There was a long pause before she finally said, "I know." Her voice cracked. "I just wish you could."

I don't remember what we said after that. Maybe I just listened to her cry, maybe I told her I was glad she called, that I was happy not to hear about this from a text.

I remember feeling at first like his death was far away, happening in a world I wasn't part of. In Graceville, Mom said the snow was already gone, but probably nothing was growing yet. I imagined the town looking barren and brown. Everyone in shock at how David, who once seemed so capable of everything, who appeared so together, had actually been falling fast. David, who when he started to spin, had an amazing way of not caring what anyone thought. Not even me. He embraced chaos. I guess I thought David was just spinning in circles until he dizzily dropped. I didn't think he wouldn't get up. I guess no one did.

I wanted a drink. A long, powerful smoke, and even though I never really took pills, suddenly the idea of one that might stop me from feeling like I was shrinking sounded good. But I knew I wouldn't do those things. Not anymore.

After I hung up with Hannah, I turned off the lamp and watched light from the courtyard split the room in two. I couldn't stop myself from imagining that Hannah was lying because she worried the longer I spent away in my private New England college, the snobbier I'd become, that this was some tasteless ruse to get me home. But as much as I wanted to believe that, I knew she would never joke about this. I did the only thing I could then. I put on my running shoes, and even though night had already arrived, I jogged out the door and onto campus, careful to slow in the pools of darkness between the streetlights so I wouldn't slip on any ice hiding there. I went off campus and into town thinking in a mantra that matched my steps, *David is dead. David is dead. How can David be dead? David is dead. David is dead. How can David be dead?* At the edge of town, I climbed the hill, the one ships' captains used to live on. These giant houses all face the ocean and have small decks at the top—widow's walks, they call them—where the women would stand looking out to sea waiting for their men to return after a storm on the ocean. I looked out at the black pool that was the

Atlantic. Black like I imagine space. Dark as our ever-growing universe. Impossible now for me to find David anywhere, and yet he couldn't be gone. Energy doesn't disappear. I kept jogging as my breath clouded around me. My legs beat a slow march. *David is dead. David is.*

Mina's out taking a picture of the WELCOME TO INDIANA, CROSS-ROADS OF AMERICA sign. She's doing most of the driving so I can write this. I need to finish before we get to California. Because isn't California the classic American place to leave your past behind?

I know, I'm contradicting myself. I've already claimed the past is just as real as the future, but given the limitations of being human, I can't get to the past except by remembering it. And that remembering—call it "grieving," call it "obsessing"—is because David Warren died. Or maybe not just because he died. Because of what he was: this lightning bolt that struck me. And no one is really the same after that. If they survive, they're likely to have popped eardrums, a concussion, chronic dizziness, insomnia. For me, it's like there was a blue line in my vision, a flash of David Warren, and I never saw anything the same again.

One thing about death that I didn't realize before is that each one is compared to the other, but none of them leave the same-shape scar. So when I think about David being dead, I think of Teri's death, Cody's mom. It wasn't just the loss, though; it was what she left behind. A cabinet of pills for Cody and David to enjoy. Her death. His death. And the orange pill bottles that link one to the other.

"Anyway," Cody's mom, Teri, said to me one day as she passed me the vaporizer, "if I'm going to die, I might as well have some good giggles with my only son and his smarty-pants girlfriend while I can."

I laughed. "So, the real reason you let us get high with you is just to keep him around the house?"

"Whatever works," she said. "Plus, this stuff has lower THC than whatever you'd buy"—she flapped her hand toward the window—"so maybe I'm also protecting your young brains."

"Is there conclusive evidence that it's THC that impacts the brain?"

"Scarlett," Cody said, and exhaled slowly, a cloud of steam passing from his lips. "You can do research later."

And so we passed Teri's last months at Cody's house, getting high, watching TV, cooking pot brownies, laughing. My parents were glad I'd taken so much interest in helping. If Cody's father was worried about the group of teenagers he returned to in the evening giggling with his sick, stoned wife, he never let on.

It was as if all that mattered was we'd figured out a way to be together, to smile in the face of the terminal prognosis.

Sometimes when Cody and I would emerge from his room, we'd find Teri awake on one of the blue couches. "When I die—" she'd say.

"Mom, stop. You're not going to die." Cody leaned back in the recliner, the silver vaporizer in hand.

"I'm sorry, Cody, but I am. Just not today."

Cody would look light-years away after that.

One time I remember her saying, "When I die I want you to celebrate right. Scarlett, you be sure that they don't do any of that weeping at my gravesite shit. Have them reserve the botanic gardens. Serve wine and good coffee. Order twenty trays of the best desserts from Sweet Sense and have music and dancing. Got it? No religion, no graveside umbrellas." After the celebration, Cody and his dad were to spread her ashes up one of the 14,000-foot climbs she'd never scratched off her bucket list.

A month later, when she actually died, I tried to make it happen exactly as she wanted, but Cody's dad compromised her plan. I can't complain. I wasn't really family. Some of her ashes were interred in Graceville Cemetery, the rest scattered on a mountaintop like she wanted. There was a short graveside service followed by a reception at the botanic gardens.

Our friends gathered together, sipping coffee and eating desserts, trying to figure out how to act at a funeral, shivering in the late-October chill. Cody and I secretly passed around the last of the pot cupcakes we'd made for Teri, the ones she couldn't eat. There was music, but nobody felt much like dancing, although some of the small kids did. It was like a wedding where everyone thinks the bride and groom have made the biggest mistake of their lives. We all stood around trying hard to live out the command to celebrate.

A screen on one side of the garden showed movies of her life. Our only way of peering back in time. I kept close to Cody, holding his hand, letting him drop his head to my shoulder when he didn't want anyone to see his tears. His uncle snuck Baileys into our coffees, saying, "If there ever was a time to drink, kids, it's now."

When Cody was starting to have trouble standing, David helped me load him into the car that Hannah, our designated, drove. When she stopped at the town's one light, Cody lurched for the window but still spattered vomit all over himself. Hannah pulled into the gas station, and David and I rubbed Cody clean with thick, blue paper towels. David got Cody back in the car, where I buckled him in and held a bag over his lap. Hannah navigated to Cody's, a white Victorian with a front porch and a historic plaque next to the door. Plugging her nose, Hannah helped to get Cody's arms around David and me, then opened the front door as we heaved him up the steps.

Cody's arms were heavy on my shoulder. He lifted his head and said, "I'm fine. Don't worry. I got this," then took a few steps on his own and fell onto the painted porch. "I'm so messed up—god. Sorry. I'm—" He got to his knees and his words tumbled together. "Thanks-Starlit-I-love-you-the-best-ah-shit." Before he was standing he curved into himself. "I'm going to—" I put the bag to his mouth while David held Cody's trembling back. Then we dragged him between us through the front door held wide by Hannah.

"You got him from here?" she asked, fingers still over her nose.

"More or less," I said.

When we finally maneuvered him inside and into bed, I stripped off Cody's vomit-covered T-shirt and dumped it in the washing machine. "I'm sorry," Cody said again as we propped him on his side with pillows under his head.

"It's okay, man," David said. "It's okay."

In minutes Cody's eyes fluttered shut. David and I decided to stay the night. We wanted someone to be there when he woke up. We weren't counting on his dad to offer any more than a glazed "Hey" to his grieving, hungover son. David and I, we were the kind of best friend and girlfriend Cody could count on.

David plopped down in a blue recliner at one end of Cody's oddly rectangular room. It was probably once part of the living room but someone built a wall, and now there was a bed at one end and some cushy chairs and a coffee table in front of a large-screen TV at the other. I swung around in a gold corduroy bucket chair, where I could keep an eye on Cody and make sure he didn't get sick again. I don't remember what David and I talked about exactly, but I do know we didn't stop until the sun started to whiten the blinds. I think it was mostly about Teri. When I finally tried to climb in bed with Cody, I peeled back his blue sheets and began to nudge his leg over, but the stench of alcohol and vomit was enough to make me gag.

"What is it?"

I felt sudden heat behind my eyes, the ache of tears in my nose, and pressed my fingertips to my eyelids. "He reeks so much, I can't lie there. I won't be able to sleep. He's completely wrecked."

"Here," David said, moving over in the recliner and motioning to the seat.

"David, I'm not snuggling up with you."

"Who said anything about snuggling? I'm giving the recliner to you." He stood quickly and stretched out on the floor with a pillow he'd yanked off Cody's bed. Was David trying to hit on me then? Was he actually such an asshole that he would hit on his best friend's girlfriend, right after that best friend's mom's funeral?

When I woke, David was gone and Cody was dry-heaving into his trash can. I held his shoulders. Later, we went into the living room to find David had left a bag of pastries and two large coffees from Colorado Beans, our favorite study spot, the only coffee shop in town.

Would an asshole do that?

After Teri died, there was no excuse for getting stoned on a school night, no more reason to laugh as we gathered at Cody's to cook brownies. So instead of getting stoned, I tried to just be there, to spend time with him. I slept at his house a lot, studied with him. But I also put more energy into cross-country. Running helped with my own grief. I ran. I planned for college. My mom offered to bring Cody along on our college tour that spring because his dad's grief response was to work so much he didn't even seem aware he still *had* a son. For spring break, we flew east to visit MIT, Boston College, and, for an excuse to extend the trip for a day, Colwyn in Maine. Mom wasn't exactly thrilled that we were applying to all the same schools, even though she'd invited him on our tour. But she didn't lecture me about it. She just got very quiet whenever the subject came up. She would chew her lip and nod and then plan dinner or tell me the latest news about my niece. It was clear enough she thought college meant I should move on from Cody.

Cody and David took the rest of Teri's pain pills and split them up, swallowed their escape. Since Mom's a nurse, I've been warned plenty about prescriptions. The boys knew I didn't want anything to do with that, and we didn't talk about it. I remember how let down I felt when I saw Cody, heavy-eyed in his gold-backed bucket chair, and David stretched out on the recliner. I knew it wasn't going to be a good night for conversation, or sex, or anything, because I was not in their strange new world. I would leave, or I'd pull out my copy of Walter Isaacson's Einstein biography to reread. There were times when I wanted to yell at them, to say, *You guys are so lame right now, and don't you know this is* dangerous? But something clogged in my throat. The words limp, even in my own head. I stayed mute. I figured Teri's prescriptions would run out quickly. Then it would all be over. I didn't realize Teri's prescriptions were long gone, and whatever they were swallowing now was depleting their savings accounts.

As spring melted into another hot summer, and Step-up to STEM moved from after school to all day, Hannah and I would finish with the kids and catch up with the boys for a few hours before heading home to laugh and watch movies. Sometimes Rage stayed with us, other times he disappeared with Cody and David into the night. I guess we all hung out less and less, but by the time I noticed enough to start to worry about Cody, fall came around again, and he was back, prepping college applications at my house and getting cheered on by my parents every time we pressed SUBMIT on the online forms. He'd stay for the meals Mom cooked, new recipes from her favorite public radio cooking show, and my dad would talk soccer with him. Those nights, around our dining room table, I hoped Cody had returned to me. But a text from David meant he'd drop a kiss on my cheek, promise to call the next day, and head out the door. It was like feeling a chill. I was relieved to have him around again, but I felt our heat dissipating. I told myself as long as they were planning for the future and still showing up for school, everything must be okay. Their grades were okay. True, Cody's had wavered. I told myself it was grief.

Maybe, though, I didn't say anything because I'd thought of

Cody as my brightest star, one to navigate by. But I'd gotten that wrong. Cody was more like a star many light-years away that had already burned out, and I had no idea that, for him, the fire was already dead.

A FEW MILES INTO INDIANA

"What you writing about now?" Mina says. She turns on her blinker and checks over her shoulder to gun it around a Buick with Iowa plates.

"College acceptances."

"Scarlett, that's like eons ago! Pick up the pace. How are you going to get done?"

"Well, I'm going to continue to write till my carpal tunnels are completely filled with scar tissue and my fingers are claws on this keyboard."

"Fine, but—what do college acceptances have to do with anything?"

"Um, how do we know each other?" I say, slapping her elbow. "Also, Cody dumped me over them."

"I think the better way to phrase that is Cody's insecurity resulted in him not being able to handle your success," Mina says, taking her eyes of the road to give me a full-dimple smile.

"I'm so glad I got a therapist *and* a roommate this year."

"Not a therapist. Now get to work, *mon ami*."

"I'm *trying* to work. You're interrupting me with your compassionate French!"

A few days after we built the Graceville High Spirit Bong, Cody and I sat at my kitchen table while Mom zested oranges for one of her new recipes, waiting to log in to our MIT applications and find out the results. MIT tops the list for most aspiring engineers, and Cody was no exception. It's also home to the number one physics department in the nation. On our tour, we'd stood in front of the busy student center, watching all the smart kids bustle around with their book bags and coffees. Cody leaned in and kissed me. He said, "This is where I want to wake up with you every day."

But that December, in my orange-scented house, I reread the blog post that announced there had been 8,915 applicants and only 500 offers extended to students from 489 different high schools across the globe. That wasn't many from the same school. Odds were low there would be one from Graceville High, let alone two. My palms were so sweaty, my fingers slipped on the keys.

"You ready?" I asked Cody.

"Yeah. You want to go first?" he said.

I pulled out my ponytail. Hid in my hair. Breathed. Tugged my hair back up and looked at Cody. "Maybe we should log in at the same time—you know, from our own computers?"

"You sure?"

I inhaled. Counted *1, 2, 3. Exhale. 1, 2, 3, 4.* "Yeah. But, wait. Mom! We're looking at the MIT results."

"I'm right here!" She turned to the table with a towel in her hands. Cody opened his computer and sat down next to me. Mom dropped her hand to my shoulder.

"You sure you don't want to wait until Dad's home?" she said as I clicked to the log-in screen.

"I don't think I can. I've been waiting all day. Also, I'm not sure if I could deal with his pity face when I don't get in."

"You don't know yet what face he'd give you." She pointed at my computer screen.

"Odds aren't in my favor, Mom. There were almost nine thousand applicants." I glanced at Cody. His teeth were deep in his lip.

"Ready?"

Cody said, "I am."

"Me too."

"Okay, go."

I entered my application code and hit SUBMIT. Immediately, "Congratulations! Welcome to the Massachusetts Institute of Technology" popped up. I felt like I was floating. Mom squeezed my shoulder and squealed.

"Honey, this is amazing! I'm so proud of you." I was about to hug her when I remembered Cody. His eyes were down. I touched his shoulder. He shook his head. All the excitement I was feeling drained away, emptying me. Like I didn't deserve to be happy if Cody didn't get in too. My gut churned.

"Just denied," he said, closing his computer and standing up. I knew that meant he wasn't one of the thousand students who were offered a chance to reapply during regular admissions.

"Oh Cody, I'm so sorry," I said, my hand reaching for the hem of his T-shirt.

"That's tough," Mom said, stepping toward him and lightly touching his shoulder.

"It's—it's okay." Cody's voice wavered. "Congratulations, Scarlett. I'm happy for you."

"Thanks," I said as he kissed my cheek.

"I'm going to go, all right? David wanted to meet up."

"I thought you were staying for dinner?" Mom said. "I'm trying a new recipe I think you'll like, orange-glazed chicken."

"Maybe next time?"

"You never said anything to me about plans with David." I studied him.

"I guess I forgot, sorry." He smiled and pulled my ponytail.

"Ow! What—"

"Sorry. Just teasing."

"Be careful," I said. He slipped his computer into his bag and my stomach flopped. "David" meant pills for forgetting.

- - -

After that day, Cody and I looked up our acceptances separately. I was getting admitted to my schools, but how could I celebrate? Cody got one rejection after another. Maybe he wasn't as strong academically. He struggled when we crammed, but what really hurt him were the low grades from the semester after his mom's death. And that burned. It wasn't fair. He was grieving. He'd gone through something most sixteen-year-olds don't have to. He shouldn't have been punished for it. So every time I got another acceptance, it was like my belly was full of bees. I dreaded telling him.

At first it was just awkward between us. He didn't wait at my locker in the morning. He didn't come to our usual lunch table. So a few weeks after the MIT news, I went by his house. He stepped out onto the porch like he wasn't even going to let me in.

"Cody," I said stomach buzzing, "I know this is hard for you. No—I *don't* know. I can't. With your mom, and—" I tugged my hair up, squeezing handfuls of it, and let it drop. "But I'm trying. You can talk to me."

"Scarlett—" When he sighed and looked down at the chipping porch paint, all the bees in my stomach seemed to sting at once. I clenched my fists. "I don't really want to talk to you about it," he said. "Your grades are perfect. You started Step-up to STEM. You went to state for track. I play on the second-worst soccer team in Colorado and my fucking mom died. It wasn't exactly easy to keep my grades up. Admissions reps said they'd understand, but they lied."

"I know," I said.

"You don't." Those two words together had never sounded so hard. But they throbbed. I rubbed my temple.

"You're right. Come here." He took a breath but still folded himself into my arms, and I held on to him while his shoulders shook. I snuggled my face into his neck the way I had so many times before, trying to pretend I didn't know how much was gone from us.

I whispered, "You'll get in somewhere great. I know." My frozen breath hung in a cloud around us.

He pulled back, but I held on to his fingers. "No you don't, Scarlett." He dropped my hands. "I don't know what I was thinking, applying to all the same schools as you. My grades aren't as good. I didn't volunteer like you did. Why didn't I just apply to some school that I could actually get into? God, why didn't I help with Step-up to STEM?"

"You *wanted* to apply to all the same schools as me," I said quietly. "And you didn't apply to Colwyn. You thought it was second-rate."

"I bet I wouldn't have gotten in anyway. You hear from them yet?" His voice wavered just slightly on the last word. I looked down.

"No."

I felt his eyes on me. "You've gotten in everywhere else, though." My silence was all the answer he needed. "Jesus. Really? Who does that? Who gets in everywhere? It's just not fair," he said. "The system's fucked." He took a step back inside the house. "You should go home. I'm going to hang with David."

"Why can't I hang out *with* you and David?"

"Scarlett, go home. I want to be alone."

"With David?"

"Just go."

"Okay, whatever. I get you need your guy time. But, David can be—" I shook my head. "Just call me later," I said, and walked to my dad's car, crunching through the thin layer of snow.

Maybe because Cody and I had been together for so long, and because after Teri's death we kept our trajectory, I wasn't worried about this fight. But he continued to avoid me and by the second week of winter break, he'd stopped calling or texting at all. He didn't come with us to take cookies to our blue-haired ladies at Graceville Retirement Center on Christmas Eve, didn't even show up to the New Year's party at Hannah's duplex, though everyone else was there. I got very drunk and ended up sleeping in the hallway outside the bathroom with a blanket I vaguely remember David pulling over me as he asked if I was okay. Hannah told me later he made sure I was sleeping on my side so I wouldn't suffocate myself if I puked, and he sat there with me until just before dawn, when she kicked all the boys out of the house so her family wouldn't know they'd stayed all night.

I didn't get up until well into the afternoon. I had a crushing headache and my stomach groaned. I heaved bile into the toilet, and then scrubbed the bathroom for Hannah with a bandana tied around my face so the cleaning products didn't make me vomit again. You might think I was cursing my stupidity and vowing to never drink so recklessly again. But actually, it felt good to be wretched. Like I deserved it. Because Cody had disappeared, Teri was dead, and I was the one getting rewarded for what? Having not lost my mom? Having the entirely useless ability to memorize information and regurgitate it on a test? Didn't I deserve some pain for the fact that I hadn't lost a damn thing? My parents loved each other; they even still owned their home while my friends' families had lost theirs. My parents kept their jobs while kids who came to Step-up to STEM after school went home with nothing but the extra snacks I gave them for dinner.

On January second, we returned to Graceville High and Cody still didn't talk to me. He only nodded from across the room. When I finally confronted him at the end of the day, it was on the school's frozen lawn just after the bell rang. David was walking with him.

"Cody," I called. He didn't stop. David looked at me and turned to Cody, making a gesture I couldn't quite see. "Why are you avoiding me?" I yelled. Cody turned, his lips in a straight line. David pushed his shoulder in my direction. "Come on, Cody. What the hell. We've been together over two years and you suddenly stop calling, stop answering my calls, my texts, you miss the New Year's party? Are you seriously dumping me this way?"

Cody looked at his sneakers, half sunk in the melted snow. He kicked the sidewalk and said, "I guess."

"I guess? How can you guess? Either you're dumping me or you aren't. It isn't something that you think you, like, maybe, *might* be doing."

"Yeah."

"Yeah, what? Say it. Cody, I deserve a sentence from you at the very least." My hands were shaking. I was probably yelling. I'm certain the vein was popping. I didn't even care. Didn't try to breathe. I wanted to feel this anger. He turned his back. He didn't say anything as he walked toward the school's stone wall.

"You're a dick. What are you afraid of? That I'm smarter than you? I always expect that kind of sexist bullshit from your prick friend here, but not you, you fuckwad," I screamed. People were staring. I remember sweating even though it was beginning to snow.

"Come on, Scarlett," David said, "let me give you a ride home." He gestured toward his dad's old blue Volvo. I eyed him accusingly.

"Did you know about this? Did you?" I said. "You're best friends."

"Scarlett, don't make me violate the code of brotherhood," David said.

"You're an ass."

"Maybe sometimes. Not now," he said, putting his arm over my shoulder and walking me to the car. His voice was so quiet and calm that I let him steer me like some disconsolate widow. He opened the car door. I climbed right in.

"You want to go home, or . . . ?"

"Or, I think. Definitely or," I said.

"All right." David started the car. As we drove out of the parking lot, he raised a hand at Cody, who was now leaning against the rock wall that edged the campus. I looked away.

David drove out of town and up Mine Gulch Road. The snow was falling harder now, but it wasn't cold enough to stick to the ground. He parked on the far side of the bridge and we got out and stood on it, looking down to the dark water below.

"I always make a bet with my brothers," he said, "about when the river will freeze."

"Not yet," I said, leaning farther over the railing. Along the banks where in the spring and summer foam gathered, there was ice, but the center flowed freely.

"No. My guess this year is never, but it might still happen." We were quiet and in the silence, I looked at the water, felt my eyes blur, and wet warmth on my freezing cheeks. David held on to the metal rail of the bridge with a bare hand. After a while he said, "You know, Scarlett, I know you shouldn't ever say this kind of thing about your best friend—"

"What?" I pressed my sleeve into my eyes.

"Just"—he hesitated—"just that if you're dating someone who's smarter than you—you're supposed to value that about the person, not resent it."

"But—"

"Look, it probably isn't fair that I say any more because Cody is my man, but you've got to know that I think he's being a total dickweed."

"Thanks, David," I said, and put my arm around his back. We stood there looking at the water for a long time.

"Want some?" he asked, pulling a pipe out of his pocket.

"Sure." David held the lighter to the pipe for me, shielding the flame from the snow and the wind. After we smoked we stood there again, our arms around each other's backs, the snow falling around us. It felt like we were two very old people, people who'd known each other forever, holding on in silence, watching how the snow fell on the river and melted, appearing to leave no trace.

When the sky began to darken, we got back into his car and drove home, listening to one of his mixed tapes. The Volvo only had a tape deck because the car was older than us, so David collected tapes. But he didn't like albums—he liked personal mixes. He got them from people's parents, and sometimes from garage sales and thrift stores. I held up a black cassette with *The Golden Age* scribbled across the side. David looked at it and said, "That one has lines from famous films between each song. It's one of my favorites. Put it in." I did and immediately heard "I'm mad as hell and I'm not going to take it anymore!" followed by a cheery song with a chorus about how "your flag decal won't get you into heaven anymore" and then just as that ended someone said, "What do you need a fake ID for?" and the song "Don't You Forget About Me" from *The Breakfast Club* began. I'd seen it a thousand times with my mom, and every time, she pointed out all the things she thought were sexist, and every time, she teared up at the end. My eyes were dry as we listened, the volume crackling as David drove me home.

I went straight to my room. My mom came in and sat next to me, quietly, on the bed. She wasn't surprised. She'd noticed how long it had been since Cody had called. She'd noticed I hadn't been staying there. I knew she'd been waiting for the inevitability of this, and her kindness added heaviness to my chest. She sat there with me and said, "I'm sorry, sweetie." I was silent. "It's so hard." I said nothing. "Heartbreak is the worst." As she started to rise, she placed her hand on my leg; the familiar weight of it felt good. "Stay on birth control anyway," she said. "It's easier to do it once you've done it before."

"Mom!" I said, turning against the wall and pulling my leg from under her hand.

"I'm just saying."

"I'm not going to start sleeping around just because my boyfriend of over two years dumped me," I said, eyes on Einstein's and Curie's black-and-white faces above my bed.

"No, of course not. I know you make good choices. You know I don't worry about my nonprofit-starting wunderkind, but . . ."

"But what?" I turned back to her and sat up, feeling the vein in my neck bulge.

"You just never know who's waiting around the corner."

"Way to comfort your heartbroken daughter, Mom—tell her to be safe when she continues to put out."

"Sorry, Scarlett. I know it sucks. I'm just trying to be realistic. There's nothing wrong with continuing to have sexual relationships."

I moaned. She shook her head. "Anyway, I can't share a tub of ice cream with you because of the lactose. You're not even talking to me. What can I do?"

"Well, you don't need to endorse a rebound."

"I wasn't."

"Could you just beat him up or talk some sense into him? I don't know."

"Oh, honey," she said, shaking her head and moving back to the bedside. She took my foot in her hand and began to rub the arch slowly. "I'd love to light his car on fire and throw him into a canyon, but I'd be no good to you in jail."

"And I'd resent you for killing him anyway," I said, kicking my feet away from her, up onto the wall and re-tearing the taped corner of my Einstein poster. "But thanks for having my back."

So my not-an-asshole boyfriend was suddenly an asshole, and his asshole best friend was suddenly not an asshole. I guess people are complex, made of matter as we are, full of energy, always ready to create friction.

As if to prove himself a complete jerk, before January ended, Cody was kissing Rachel Higgins, whose cascading brown hair somehow always looked perfect, and whose only flaw was she believed the earth was six thousand years old. Every day they stood making out at their lockers. I had to watch it, and it made my stomach turn. His hands deep in her apparently unmessable hair. Her arms around his waist. Hannah, Rage, and even David were mad at him. For a while I thought it was the kind of thing we'd seen happen when parents divorced. And Cody was such a spectacular shit that I scored all the friends. But I knew he still talked to David. I could tell he missed us. And I could tell he was jealous. We had our plans coming together. David was going to Stanford, a feat only one Graceville graduate before him had ever achieved. I surprised everyone, even myself, when I turned down MIT for Colwyn College. They offered me a big scholarship and I couldn't justify the better name in the face of so many zeros I wouldn't have to take out in loans. Hannah was going to Fort Collins, and Rage was headed to the University of Denver with scholarship money in hand.

My only consolation was that I heard Rachel was hoping for some unaccredited Bible school in the sticks. I knew Cody wouldn't follow her there. David told me that Cody was in the middle of some late applications to places like College of Santa Fe, Luther College, and St. Olaf. I felt bad for Rachel. I couldn't help but think Cody was dating her because he knew whatever he did next year would be better than what she was going to do. I almost told her. I almost stopped her in front of her locker to ask if she felt suspect of a guy who suddenly dropped his girlfriend of two years. But I let it lie. It wasn't Rachel's fault. I was a heartbroken mess, but I was also the jackass who'd dated someone capable of dropping me because he was afraid I might be smarter than him. He was probably worried that if he kept on with girls like me, he was on track to be a stay-at-home dad in the outer suburbs. Why did I fall for that shit? What was wrong with me? I didn't know then that I probably had Rachel to thank for getting Cody clean. When his late-night drives with David stopped, so did his drug use. I didn't realize that his disappearance from our friend group had a lot to do with peeling away from David's doomed trajectory, and maybe not much to do with me at all.

In my now, Mina is buying cherry Coke from the Come-N-Go. The sun is so bright it appears to be burning down the fields where small green heads of corn peek up through the reeking fertilizer. There is a deep funk to the humid air that we can't seem to shake even with the windows rolled up and the AC on high. If dead people can miss things, I wonder if they miss even this. Because I know that my smelling this funk right now is the difference between David Warren, Teri, and me. Whatever they are now, whenever or wherever they are, they can't smell this. They are gone.

Teri knew she was dying; she got to imagine what her memorial would be like and give instructions, but when someone dies young and suddenly, there's none of that. It's not unfair. The dead don't care even if the living do. David didn't care that there was a rash of head-shaking and Bible-thumping after his death. Of course there would be; he was one of Graceville's most beloved sons, gone semi-mysteriously and too soon.

And I'm not just talking him up because he's dead. David was a local celebrity. At the time of our graduation, David Warren was named in 426 newspaper articles, 398 of those from the *Graceville Times,* leaving 28 articles to larger local and state papers. This means he averaged a mention in the paper 1.97 times per month from the time he was born. Given that the *Graceville Times* was only published 3 times per week, that means David Warren appeared in roughly 13 percent of the local papers. He graced the cover 24 times, or .77 percent of the time. Considering that there were only one or two appearances in the paper per year before David started preschool at the age of four, by high school, he was noted in the paper almost weekly. I'm not a stalker for knowing these figures; I just remember the binder his mom put out at his graduation party.

TWO MONTHS BEFORE THE BRIDGE

GRACEVILLE, COLORADO

The binder was black with card stock pages where each honor roll announcement and intellectual or athletic victory was carefully clipped, dated, and glued. Occasionally a handwritten note was scrawled—something cute David said. On being on the county's winning soccer team in second grade: "Soccer used to be played with heads. We don't do that anymore. Too squishy!"

Hannah and I arrived at the party together. We wore thin summer dresses but despite the late afternoon heat, David appeared in a long-sleeved white button-down shirt and linen pants. His body and face had changed, but I couldn't help noticing the similarity with the outfit he'd worn when our fourth-grade robotics team won the state championship and David, not I, was pictured on the front of the *Graceville Times*.

As I stood looking through the binder and noting David's transformation from baby to boy to graduate, I noticed also the yearly articles about robotics from third through twelfth grade. Cody and I were in a few of these clippings too, like the last one, seven months ago, weeks before I got dumped. There were sports clippings and scholarship announcements, and on the back page, a picture of David from that day's paper with the headline "Graceville High Graduates Ready to Take on the World." David leaned against the GRACEVILLE HIGH sign at the front of campus, backpack hung on one shoulder and his arms splayed wide as if he were embracing the world. The article featured an interview with him about his plans at Stanford and then went on to mention anyone from Graceville with notable plans after graduation. Hannah, Rage, Cody, and I were all included. The binder stood on a dictionary stand next to an easel of portraits and seemed to prove, along with the busy house that hummed with guests, that though he'd missed the valedictorian podium—narrowly, to me—he certainly won the love of the town. The memory book, so unlike anything my mother would even think to do, riveted me. I read it, taking notes on my phone and making calculations. Next to the binder was a guest book; I wrote: "I might have won the GPA race, but I certainly didn't grace the cover of the *Graceville Times* .77 percent of the time in the last 18 years. You win."

I stood in front of his portraits. The one from the yearbook—a headshot of David in a black T-shirt that profiled his rather large nose—was familiar. The others I hadn't seen. In the center of the poster, he stood outside next to a tree in jeans and a blue T-shirt, unruly waves of brown hair falling mid-ear. His arms were crossed as he leaned against the tree. I noticed for the first time he was actually the kind of guy girls find attractive—six feet tall, dark-eyed, muscular, a bit tan. David, I thought, David is kind of a looker. I peered at him across the room like another person had been laid over the David-who'd-always-been-there—the confidence in the way he held his head, his wide-legged stance. When I caught his eye he boomed, "Girls! You don't come to greet the graduate first?" and strode across the room.

"We're college women now, David," I said, and tapped the end of his nose. "And anyway, why weren't you sharing this sexy shot with us? I didn't know you had it in you." I pointed to the photo.

David laughed. "You're the only girl"—he paused and fake-coughed into his hand—"*college woman*, who's missed it, Scarlett. I'll get you a wallet size of it if you like. Mom ordered a million."

"She didn't order a million," I said.

"No, Literal One," David said, dropping his hand to my shoulder. "I think it was thirty-two."

"And you would give one-thirty-second of those to me?"

"Mom can't fit all thirty-two of them in her wallet at the same time," David said.

"You're so generous, D."

"I know," he said.

"Hey, did you know, you appeared in the local newspaper three hundred ninety-eight times?" Hannah asked. "Scarlett did the math. You've been in the paper like fifteen percent of the time."

"Thirteen," I corrected.

"Really, is that all?"

"Humble much?" I said.

"You have no idea how humble you keep me, Ms. Twenty-Thousand-Dollar Scholarship."

"Twenty-*five* thousand," offered Hannah.

"Oh pardon me, Ms. Twenty-*Five*-Thousand-Dollar Scholarship."

"It's renewable, so really it's a one-hundred-thousand-dollar scholarship, over four years," I said.

"Well, Ms. Valedictorian of the One-Hundred-Thousand-Dollar Scholarship, may I get you a drink?"

"Sure."

Then he leaned close to my ear and whispered, "The punch on the left is spiked."

"Ah, good to know you're not trying to get me drunk without my knowledge."

David took his hand off my shoulder and stepped back. "Come on, Scarlett. Not funny."

"Really? After all the things you say to me?" But I smiled a little. "For all of your dickishness, D, you know I wouldn't hang out with you if you were rapey."

David rubbed his eyes with thumb and forefinger, like he couldn't believe I'd just said that.

"Anyway, you know I'm not an easy drunk," I added.

David opened his mouth, but it was Hannah who said, "Nope, you're just easy."

"Thanks"—I turned to her—"Ms. Blow Jobs for Jesus."

"I won't dignify that with a response," Hannah said.

I slipped my arm around David's waist as we crossed to the drinks table.

He passed me a spiked punch filled to the brim. "Scarlett, I'm glad to know you don't think I'm actually the scum of the earth, but you should know I'm wise enough not to tangle with my intellectual superior," David said, eyes on the punch as he filled his own cup. I knew we were both thinking of that winter day on the bridge after Cody dumped me, when he raised his glass and said, "Cheers."

"I'll drink to that."

He took a long swig and said, "Cody's already been here, so hang out as long as you'd like."

"I'm not allergic to him. We can be in the same room." I lifted the cup to my lips immediately.

"No, you can't," Hannah said.

"Well, not if he has Rachel surgically attached to his face," I said.

"Which he always does," Hannah said, holding her cup to her lips and gazing out the window behind me. "Look, Rage's here! Grab him a glass, Scar, and refill yours, you drunk. Let's meet him in the yard."

"Rage!" I shouted over the heads of David's brothers and some other kids I vaguely recognized from Step-up to STEM—cousins maybe?—who were running around the yard with squirt guns. "You must come see how well-documented David's life has been in the local media!"

"Please! Save me from another doting mother's memory book." He kissed Hannah's cheek and turned to me. "You a two-fisting swinging single, Scar, or is that for me?" he said.

"How'd you know it wasn't just fruit juice?" Hannah said.

"David and I made plans, babe," he said.

And so we passed graduation night in David's yard, drinking spiked punch. When at three a.m. David's dad shouted from the back door that we'd better "shush our ruckus" or he'd be sure we were all "locked up," we waved to David and piled into Hannah's car to wait for my dad to pick us up.

When Dad arrived, he pretended to scold me. "In my day, Scarlett," he said, "the valedictorian didn't get bombed."

"Maybe Graceville High was more challenging then," I said.

"Or maybe you just had a boring valedictorian," Hannah said.

"Or maybe you weren't cool enough to hang out with the valedictorian, so you don't know," I said.

"*Cool* isn't the word I would have used, but yeah," Dad said. "It was a good party then, for Graceville's Golden Boy?"

Everyone knew. David was golden.

The wallet-size graduation photo David gave me later that night is still tucked inside the pages of my Einstein biography. It's the only print photo I have of him. I have other pictures; I could order more, but I won't. It's enough to pull him up on my screen sometimes and see all that captured light.

Now, I realize David was probably flirting with me at his graduation party. Now, I imagine his obituary glued on the last page of his mom's memory book. Now, I picture his final appearance on the cover of the *Graceville Times*. It's true, David had this thing about him, this energy, and people wanted to capture some of it, be near it. But it probably had something to do with his district attorney dad too. The DA's son shone, and I'm sure this led to even more whispers when David was discovered dead in the Volvo six weeks ago.

The day the news broke I avoided texts from my mom. When we finally talked, the conversation went something like:

"Scarlett, I have some sad news for you." I winced. She sounded like she was reading from a script.

"I know. David is dead." I kept my voice mechanically steady. I counted my breaths.

"You heard?"

"Hannah called."

"You okay?"

"No. Not really," I said, and thought, *Inhale 1, 2, 3, exhale. 1, 2, 3, 4.*

"Okay, because I know this is really hard. Are you okay?"

"Mom. I just said I'm not okay. But I'm not going to, like, swallow a bunch of pills and let Mina find me in the morning."

"So you're okay?"

"No Mom. I'm not. Are you okay?"

"Right, I guess I'm not. I've known David since he was a baby, and maybe I wasn't happy with some of the decisions you two made, but he was a great kid . . ." She spoke in past tense. The room blurred. My fingernails dug into my palm. The counting didn't help this time. I let out a low groan. "Oh honey, do you want to come home? I could figure out a way to cover your ticket."

"No!" I took a breath. "I do want to, but I can't, finals coming up, I've got this major project for bio, and I'm working more at the tutoring center because it's crunch time."

"Okay . . . but you can change your mind."

"Thanks, Mom, but I need to be here."

"It's good to be focused on school, Scarlett. But this is actually a time when you can give it a break. You can come home."

"No, I can't. But thanks."

"So, you're all right, then?"

"Not really, but you aren't either."

"I know. I just can't—" Her breath caught. I imagined her eyes looking out the window, on the sad Colorado mud. "If it were you sweetie, if you— You know you can talk to me about anything, right? You promise to call if you need anything? Or if you change your mind and want to come home."

"Mom?" I shivered. I missed her. But I felt so far away. I wished I could press my face into her sweater. I wished she could make everything feel better like when I was little.

"Yeah?"

"I love you and I'm not coming home, but I'm not going to overdose either. I promise. I'm the cleanest college student you've ever met. I'll see you in six weeks. Seriously, I'll be okay."

"I love you, honey, and I'm sorry. He's just—it's so sad." I could hear her fighting off tears. I took a deep breath and felt the room come back into focus.

"I love you so much, Mom, but I gotta go—it's almost dinnertime." As if I could eat. I hung up the phone and opened my computer. I found the first article in the online edition of the *Graceville Times*.

> *Man Found Dead on Mine Gulch Road Former GHS Track Star*
>
> *The body found early Thursday morning in an automobile at the side of Mine Gulch Road has been confirmed to be David Warren, age 19, of Graceville. Warren had returned to Graceville in December to live with his parents during a leave of absence from Stanford University, where he was studying biochemistry. Warren was known for his academic strengths at Graceville High School, where he graduated second in his class. At GHS he was a leading member of both the soccer and track teams, and president of the Robotics Club. An autopsy is pending. No foul play is suspected.*

I wondered as he sat in that darkness if he remembered how we'd jumped the bridge together. Did he remember that night in August on the bank? Did he think of me at all? Did he see another heron? Was he conscious until first light? Or was it in blackness that, as my mom would later suspect, the crushed pills swallowed him? Did the night press into his car as he took out the keys and the interior lights automatically faded out with him? I tried to think of him dead there, or dying there, but my thoughts kept slipping into how alive he was, how he pulled his arm around me the January day Cody dumped me and I cried as snow fell around us, how in August as we jumped from the bridge our hands intertwined until the current split us apart and we came together again on the bank. I tried, my hands on my belly, to force myself to think of his car, was it running, was there a mix tape in the deck? Did he slump against the door, the window? When they found him, was he already blue? Were there still piles of snow around the bridge? Did a crocus bloom in the mud? What did he see? I wondered, but my mind kept slipping— It wasn't real. Couldn't be. David was in the water and under the stars and inside me forever and never again.

The obituary did not recount the autopsy or toxicology report. It read:

> *David Warren of Graceville died Thursday morn-*
> *ing in Grand County. David is remembered as a star*
> *academic and athlete at Graceville High School, where*
> *he was admitted to the National Honor Society, led the*
> *Robotics League twice to the state championships, and*
> *was a cherished member of the soccer and track teams.*

He is survived by his mother, Madeline Warren, his father, Paul Warren, brothers Solomon, Joseph, and Marcus Warren of Graceville, grandparents Saul and Patricia Warren of Minot, North Dakota, and many aunts and uncles. He is preceded in death by his grandmother Constance Hayes and grandfather David Hayes. A service will be held at Graceville Community Church, Saturday, April 11, at 4 p.m., with graveside visitation to follow.

When people die young, the circumstances are never good. And the district attorney can ensure the salacious details of his son's death don't make the paper.

Still, people will talk. And talk is unthinking, ugly. It doesn't ask what any of us could have done differently, how we might have helped. It tsks and tuts and whispers *This boy failed*. Talk cares nothing about what would have mattered most to David—the birds, the music, the shape of his darkness.

Now, I'm thinking about all the other people who were sad or lonely, grieving or lost, who have driven this road. How we are connected by our sadness, our joy, our subatomic particles.

Now, my freshman year of college is over. Even if the last two years smashed me out of orbit, and I don't know what's ahead, somehow I'm here. Now. I'm writing this.

TEN MONTHS AGO, AUGUST

GRACEVILLE, COLORADO

After the night at Mine Gulch, David and I never said *Don't speak of this,* but it was understood. We didn't text. We didn't see each other. I convinced myself that this was just a strange thing that happened, an end-of-high-school, end-of-the-summer, drunken mistake. I figured when we met again, we'd be just Scarlett and David, friends since before we could remember. David-and-Scarlett-of-the-landscape.

I told myself this for three days and I almost believed it despite the fact that my mind kept sliding back to him. But on the fourth night after the bridge jump, I was startled awake by a knock on my open window. Hannah and I had an agreement that she could show up at my house anytime in the night, so instead of calling the cops, I raised my head to the screen and peered out. I didn't see Hannah but David, pressing his palm to the glass and pointing to his car on the street.

"Scarlett," he said, "I've found a garden full of moonflowers."

"Don't get all full of shit, D," I said, though my hands were shaking, and at that moment, I wanted to go anywhere he did.

But I made my best disapproving face and said, "It's three a.m. Some of us were sleeping."

"So wake up and come on, Scar. Come see."

"I don't know, David. It's—"

"Calm, calm, calm," David said, and pressed his mouth up to the screen. "I'm talking about life. LIVING. Come out, see the moon while you have time, witness the flowers that bloom at night before we jump that big corporate train and leverage our college debt with investment plans and car payments. Before everything is . . ." He stopped and stepped back from the window. I felt a wave of cold. I shook as I unlocked the screen. My rational nature was throbbing against another impulse, like I was a leaf caught in an unstable wind. I felt like I could barely move and like I couldn't stop moving. Like being inside a barrel rolling off a cliff—I chose to get in, and now I had to hold on to the sides, stay rigid, because I gave up control over my speed and direction the moment I did something as asinine as step inside a barrel.

The screen bent as I lifted it over the crank and slid it down between my bed and the wall. David dropped his hands on the sill. I shivered. We were lucky—David and I—our families had weathered the recession more or less unscathed. Though cuts to my father's pension and paycheck loomed, his job was secure. And Mom, she was in one of the few growing industries. David, Cody, and I were the only people I know who were allowed to look at colleges out of state, and Cody only because his mom's life insurance and social security were paying for his education.

"I just need to get dressed."

"You don't need to get dressed for this," David said, eyeing me braless in an oversized T- shirt, one of Cody's that I still slept in. I hoped he didn't recognize it.

"Just hold on," I said, turning to grab a dress from my closet. David and I knew our friends were jealous that we were moving farther than Fort Collins or Denver. I couldn't complain about plane rides when Hannah would have loved to go anywhere out of state. I knew I was lucky to have parents who could help me, but even with my scholarship and loans, my mom had said, "I'm glad I love my job, honey, because I'm never going to retire." Nope. David was right. We were not free. We were not on the cusp of an exciting open road. Even if that's what our parents and teachers wanted us to believe.

With my back to the window I slipped off my T-shirt and slipped on my dress, smoothing the built-in shelf-bra into place.

"Thanks for the show. Next time, could you dance a little?"

"You're gross, David Warren."

"No, I just know how to annoy you," David said. I grabbed my phone and bag, and slid out the window. After I was out, I cranked the window mostly shut, leaving it open enough to reach an arm in when I got home.

David pulled me to him as soon as we were in his car. We kissed long and slow so the spruce and sweat scent of him filled me up. His hand gripped mine and I wanted to move it everywhere at once but then our kiss ended and he pulled it away and set it on the steering wheel. I felt dizzy. I had that sense again like electricity was gathering below and above me, like I was waiting for lightning to strike.

"Sorry—I wasn't trying to be an ass," he said, turning the key but looking at me. "It's just, do you have any idea how beautiful you are?"

"That is a much nicer thing to say than *dance a little,* but if you really want to watch me get dressed while dancing, maybe you could just ask politely and not like some jackass."

"And what would you say?"

"No, but at least I wouldn't be sitting here wondering why I just got in the car with an ass at three a.m."

David drove in silence through the split-level houses of our *Brady Bunch*-style neighborhood on the north side of town, and wound through the mostly shuttered downtown with its wooden sidewalks and once brightly painted storefronts. They'd lost most of their luster since Tidal Force left and the specialty stores shut down. The hardware store, Colorado Beans, and Sweet Sense were the only long-standing businesses in the four-block Old Town now. The rest were gone. We rolled through the one stoplight, and passed Cody's dark house. Everyone sleeping. David turned onto the strip that ran the south edge of town and fed into the highway. There were a few new developments out here, built just before the economy self-destructed. It was a new kind of ghost town—these neighborhoods that never had people living in them long enough to plant trees. David parked at the end of a darkened cul-de-sac. He led me by the hand through a gate into the one landscaped property with a pool, a kidney-shaped shadow in the moonlit yard.

"I've been watching," he whispered. "No one here. I think this was the demo house for the neighborhood and that's why they bothered with the pool, grass, trees." He gestured around with open arms, as if he could hold the universe there. Then he turned to me and grinned in the moonlight before pulling his T-shirt over his head, yanking off his shorts, and diving into the water. I watched his feet kick patterned splashes as he swam from one end to the other without coming up for air. Moonflowers climbed a wooden trellis and hung down over reclining deck chairs. David treaded water and raised his arm to point at the moon.

"Almost full," he said.

"Well, nothing's perfect." I dropped my dress before diving in to swim next to him. I stopped treading water just beyond his reach. I could hear his breathing and the little splashes our hands made. He floated backward so that his legs rose up under mine. I inhaled and took a stroke away from him and floated on my back to gaze at the stars. "There's that whole universe again," I said.

"Yep. There's everything. Don't you just want to swallow it up?" David spit a stream of water into the sky. "Here we are in the vastness."

Did I know what he meant? I saw the stars, the moon, felt water and skin, and somewhere as if from very far away I heard David whisper something incoherent about our atoms interfering, cellular reorganization, the simple ways we are all this or that constitution of carbon, hydrogen, and oxygen, the mystery and mistake of it all, how little boundary there really is between body, moon, sky, water. All of us made up of carbon forged in the bang that created the universe. All of us that elemental.

I moved to David, encircled him with my legs. I didn't say a word. I thought there would only be the water, David, the universe, and me. But turns out it's easier to have sex in a pool in the movies than in practice. I ended up pushing him over to the stairs and laughing as we kept bumping our knees on the concrete or splashing each other in the eye. When we finally slipped from the pool, we lay naked on lounge chairs until the moonflowers began to tighten their white buds and the bird-chorus began. We didn't talk as we dressed, just watched the darkness break into a low, gray light and listened as a few cars started in driveways unseen. David was right, the house was empty, but the neighborhood was far from abandoned. As we slipped out the side gate, we heard a voice call after us. We slammed the car doors and careened onto the strip toward the freeway. David drove with one hand on the steering wheel and one tight on my thigh.

"I could keep driving," he said as he neared the turn toward my house and looked at me, his grin breaking his sharp features into the smooth curves of still boyish cheeks.

"Go on." I raised my arm out the window and we headed deeper into the mountains.

And when he got to the freeway, he said, "I could keep driving."

"Go for it," I said. "Go on."

And we did.

NOW

LAKE COUNTY, INDIANA

Maybe it's impossible not to connect our experiences to one another in a really linear way. But Einstein gave us another approach to thinking about time. When one of his best friends died, he wrote, "For us believing physicists, the distinction between past, present, and future is only a stubbornly persistent illusion." Maybe this thinking and his studies helped him through his loss? For me, it lets me imagine time like a flipbook—each image still there but only moving because we turn the pages to see it. Some people would say that we return in our memories to important events because they've brought us to where we are today, but I think we flip back because they're still happening. The past is not gone, it's just not being witnessed. One flip and I'm headed out on the road with David ten months ago, another flip and I'm in this car with Mina today, another, it's eight months ago, and I'm sweating through college orientation. All these nows happening at once. And if all our nows happen at once, then death—it's just a scavenger hunt through time.

COLWYN COLLEGE · WATERTOWN, MAINE

Colwyn looked like every vision of New England ever captured on film, and had been used as a set for several. Maple trees lined brick walkways, bronze statues of statesmen with swords dotted the quieter corners. At the north edge of campus, a clock tower proudly displayed time in Roman numerals, and below it, an ornate, now nondenominational chapel opened its doors for things like orientation. I wanted to be excited; I'd been dreaming about college for so long. I imagined myself across campus, working in the wide-windowed labs as the trees turned orange. But inside the hot chapel, I felt terrible. Maybe it was jet lag. Or my body detoxing from the last month. Either way I was exhausted. And second-guessing my choice. Because really, who passes up MIT? And I missed home. Mom's cooking and David. David.

The orientation-week events, where we'd played get-to-know-you games with M&M's while wearing expensive school merchandise and standing around trying to figure out what to say, included a weeklong competition between majors. It was a scavenger hunt. And I didn't know if I was more relieved or resigned to learn that the peer leader for physics was Harold-who-is-not-David.

He led ten majors, like a group of kindergartners bobbing around without our parents, out the chapel doors and into the eye-slicing brightness. I saw Mina gathered under a beech tree with the psychology majors, her arms loose and mouth open, chuckling. I thought I could pick out the sound, but then realized I didn't know her laugh, and might not even recognize her voice if she called to me across the grass. I thought about the incoming class of physics at MIT. How it was at least five times bigger. How I wasn't there.

"As you know," Harold-who-is-not-David was saying, with a voice almost like David's, "majors compete against one another to win." He paused. "Physics has never won. This year, I'd like to change that."

"Is it possible," I said, feeling dizzy and cranky but trying to smile through it, "that physics majors do not care about a scavenger hunt that will not solve any tangible problem or serve as the groundwork for any major discoveries?"

"No," Harold-who-is-not-David said, and his face shifted. Suddenly he looked older—how did he do that? "This is your new cohort. They'll be your lab partners, research team, and study buddies for the next four years, or longer. This scavenger hunt is where you'll start the friendships that'll build your career. Any one of you could be the next Stephen Hawking or Freeman Dyson."

"Actually," I said into the silence that followed this speech, "that's a bit hard for three of us." I looked at the other girls.

Harold's cheeks paled. He dropped his eyes to the sidewalk, raised them. "Sorry," he said, his fingers rubbing together, pink climbing his cheeks. "You know what I meant."

"Mm, that only men have great minds?" The words slipped out. My own cheeks flamed.

"Not at *all*." He looked directly at me this time but turned even brighter.

"That's what it sounded like." What was I doing? This guy was a senior in my major. I squeezed my hands into fists.

"I know, Scarlett. I'm sorry." He put a hand in his hair, like David's but shorter, then dropped it back down. "But all of us probably agree gender imbalance in STEM is a real thing and would like to see it stop. I would, even if sometimes I put my foot in my mouth."

A fly landed on Harold's T-shirt. The breeze died. The silence dragged. The bright spots on his cheeks lingered.

"Scavenger hunt!" a boy in a white button-down called.

"Right," Harold said. "Scavenger hunt. So first, you need to find a book in the library."

The fly launched from Harold's orientation-issued shirt, its drone filling another awkward pause, and flew straight at my ear. I swatted it away. I should have just shut up. Instead I said, "Harold, there are over two hundred sixty thousand volumes in the Colwyn library. How are we supposed to find something if we don't know what it is?"

"Ah." Harold tapped his temple. "If you can recall the approximate number of books in the library, you can figure it out, with help from these clues: One"—he held up a finger—"all of your challenges will be somehow related to science and mathematics. And two—" He paused, noisily unfolding a paper, and read, " 'The Nobel prize, she won it twice—no other can compare. But what she did *isolate*, ultimately signed her *fate*.' "

"Okay, you ruled out nothing with the first clue," I said, "and the second makes it pretty clear it's a book about Marie Curie." To my surprise the kid in the white button-down laughed so suddenly, the soda he was drinking came out his nose. It felt good to make someone laugh. But I still felt awful, like my individual arm hairs had lives of their own. Like breathing was impossible.

Harold-who-is-not-David tapped his temple again and said, "Good. I can see this team might be our best yet. A clue will be taped to the correct book."

And so our illustrious cohort, ten physics first-years, trooped off to the library, where I secretly hoped to find a corner to curl up in and sleep straight till winter break.

Colwyn's library was the crown of the campus. It sat on a little hill in the center, its height accentuated by marble stairs leading to heavy oak doors. Inside, spiral staircases climbed into the stacks. As we walked in, a girl who'd been typing on her phone held it out for us to see, on the screen, a page of call numbers with "Curie" listed as subject or author.

"This way," I said, figuring that if I took the lead I could get this over with faster. Harold did have a point about cohort and all. I would try. We wound up the spiral staircase to the library's second floor and down the stacks. Sure enough, attached to a yellow volume I hadn't read called *Radioactive* was an envelope marked *Physics*.

"Here," I said, peeling the clue from the book and handing it to the girl who'd found the call numbers. "Read it?" She shook her head and her black hair swished along her shoulders.

"I will," said the kid with the soda and the button-down. "'It's elemental. Can you guess what around here was pounded best to make a vase, or crock, or plate? Hurry now or you'll be late.'"

"God, who wrote these rhymes?" I said, leaning back against a shelf.

"Probably Harold," the kid offered.

"And how many of these are there?"

"No idea," he said. "Don't you want to win?"

I tried to smile but it probably looked scary. I shrugged. "I'll play along."

The girl who'd held up her phone looked sympathetic maybe. She half nodded from under her bangs and tilted her screen to us again. It showed the periodic table. "Here," she said, pointing to Tin, 50 Sn.

"Tin," I said. "Oh, you're good!" She smiled, a cherry-lip-gloss smile. "Is there something at Colwyn made of tin?" I looked around at nine half-interested, slightly shell-shocked faces. "Let's split up to find this thing. Who wants to work with me?" The kid in the white button-down raised his hand. "Okay, um—Bert," I said, reading his name tag. "Bert and I will head toward downtown. The rest of you fan out toward the other edges of campus."

"Where?" the girl with the phone said, slipping it into the back pocket of her jeans.

"Good question"—I read her name tag—"Courtney. Let's go outside and figure it out."

The impossibly bright light of the quad momentarily blinded me. I stood blinking at the beech trees as their leaves flipped over and over in the breeze, white to green, green to white. I heard a cough, realized I'd been staring, took a deep breath: *Inhale 1, 2, 3. Exhale 1, 2, 3, 4.*

"Okay," I said, "first, let's exchange cell numbers." When we'd finished squinting into our phones, I lightly touched Courtney's shoulders to point her south, toward a statue of a man in a three-cornered hat. "I'm not trying to gender separate, but the reality is we're going to need to stick together the next four years, so Courtney and"—I read the name tag of the girl with a pixie cut—"Sora, start by going that way in search of tin."

Courtney shrugged at Sora and said, "Well, at least she didn't put us together because we're the Asian girls."

The world spun away from me. "Oh my god." My face burned. "I wasn't—I—"

"Actually, I don't identify as female anyway," Sora said. "I prefer they/them pronouns."

"Oh, sorry!" Courtney said, and my own apology skidded in feebly after hers.

"You didn't know," Sora said, and walked off. Courtney turned to catch up.

I watched them go. I tried to shake off the stupidity of myself. I nudged two guys in matching Colwyn T-shirts west toward the campus café, and then sent the last pair east toward the gym.

Bert-in-his-button-down and I turned north. "Where should we start?" he asked.

"You know, if we split up, we would cover more territory," I offered.

"But we just did split up?"

"Yeah, but downtown is big and might hold more prospects for locating tin. I'll head toward that downtown church."

"Which one?"

"The white wooden one on all the postcards."

"Right."

"And you head—" I said, realizing I had no idea where much of anything actually was at Colwyn or in Watertown.

"Toward the stone church on the northeast side?" he said.

"Okay." I was completely unaware of where that was.

Once Bert was out of sight, I turned toward my dorm, checked for texts from home and, finding none, slogged back to my room, lay down on my bed, and fell asleep. *Jet lag*, I thought, *is serious.*

When I woke up, there were four texts on my phone. I hoped one was from David. All four were from Bert. "No luck here." "Still looking for clues." "Nothing yet." "Any news there?"

I texted, "Still looking," and walked out to the campus cafe for a coffee, hoping to end the feeling that I was about to fall back asleep while standing. Courtney was sitting in a corner booth. I sugared my coffee and stood next to her table.

"Hey," I said. She eyed me from under her bangs for a second. I couldn't decide if she wanted me to go away or if she was trying to decide how to respond.

"Where's Bert?" she finally said.

"We split up. Downtown's big. Where's Sora?"

"They ran into their roommate and went to get high."

"You didn't join them?"

"Not my thing. You find anything?"

"Nope, not yet. Any ideas?"

"Just this," she said, pulling up a map of the town on her phone. In the center was campus, to the east the ocean, and in the west a large green space called Tinners' Park.

"Ah! You're brilliant! But what happened to the slackers who were supposed to go west?"

Courtney shook her head.

"Well, what are we doing?" I said. "Let's go."

"We need to be at that history lecture in fifteen minutes," Courtney said. "Let's just meet everyone there? It'll save us time if they found it and forgot to tell us."

"Good idea," I said. Courtney smiled but ran her eyes to her phone's screen. The conversation felt over, so I gazed down at mine, taking a seat across from her without looking up. I flipped through Instagram, where Hannah had posted pictures of her dorm room at State. She was rooming with this girl Natalia from Graceville who ran track with us and had gone to her church. Natalia was all right, but we'd never been close. I felt a prickle on my neck as I remembered Hannah doubled over with laughter, chocolate smeared on her face, red-eyed at two a.m., eating brownies straight from the pan. Was she doing that with Natalia now? And would Natalia help Hannah study by making up stupid songs? My sister posted a picture of my niece heading to PreK with the caption "Obligatory back-to-school photo." David appeared to have erased his account. I searched for Mina and clicked FOLLOW.

Occasionally I looked up at Courtney, but she kept her eyes on her phone. Oh well. I wasn't awake enough to make small talk anyway. I sipped my coffee and thought of David. I searched for messages from him on my phone—he wasn't a big texter. He'd just show up instead of communicating a plan. I thought of how he looked the last morning I saw him before we both left Graceville, the dawn breaking across his face.

"Hey," I texted. "How's it going?"

It was the first of my unanswered texts.

NOW

THE ILLINOIS BORDER

Mina pulls the car off the highway again to photograph the WELCOME TO ILLINOIS, LAND OF LINCOLN sign.

"Can I snap it out the window for you?" I ask. Traffic's pretty thick, and I'm not interested in any more dead friends.

Mina drops out the door with an air-kiss, digital 35-millimeter in hand as she says, "I only make it *look* easy." She appears to lean against the wind as she takes the picture. My arm hairs rise. This thought settles over me: David will never take another picture again.

Mina opens the door and hands over the camera to see if I approve the shot.

"Looks good, but I bet I could've gotten it out the passenger window. Or are you still afraid to let me touch your things?"

"You did break my record player." She stretches over the steering wheel. "But this, I have to do for myself."

I pull out a Red Vine from the pack. "So you're saying it's not all about me."

She flashes her half dimple and accelerates into Illinois.

Once we'd driven long enough that David had stopped saying "Should I turn around now?" we settled into a kind of mesmerized quiet as we flew through the uncrowded highway, winding through campgrounds and trail signs, our windows open, mountains dropping shadows around us.

"We could follow the Great Divide all the way down," David said. "Then maybe split off to see the temple in Coba. It'd only take a few days." He held his phone, steering with one hand and typing into his map app with the other. "Forty-eight driving hours, actually."

"Oh, only forty-eight?" I asked, knowing David was full of shit again. We'd turn around before night came.

"A mere forty-eight hours separates us from where the Mayans made love, ate chocolate, sacrificed."

I looked at David, at his curls drying in the cool air and the contours of his face in the still blue-ish morning, and I understood how magnets seized together. I leaned toward him. I thought about Step-up to STEM, and Mom, who'd worry.

But it was our last summer. And David was aglow in the morning sun, smiling. "Come on! The Great Divide! The crest of the mountain that divides the flow of rivers east and west. Scar, don't you see? It's so accurately a story of us, it's not even a metaphor."

I slipped my phone from my bag, texted Mom a quick "At Hannah's."

I looked at David sideways and tapped his knee with mine.

"What—you don't like being compared to a watershed? Come on, dear Scarlett, creative thinking is important to the scientific mind. Haven't you read all about that?"

"No 'dears,' David. It's just me."

"Just you?"

"Yeah, just Scarlett."

"Just Scarlett," David said slowly, like he was exerting extra control to get the words out in one long even tone. "Just Scarlett, who is about to flow east and away from me while I flow west."

"So we're just riding this crest together for a while," I said, and ran my finger down his ear.

David leaned into my hand but kept his eyes on the road. In Graceville, the night had been clear and cool, and the morning too, but now the earth's rotation had brought us into the full force of day. Even as we twisted through these high mountains, there was a sudden and heavy heat.

"Just Scarlett," he said again, shaking his head and placing his hand on my knee.

"Yes, just Scarlett. Just part of the landscape."

"You're not even *of* the landscape, Scarlett. You're from somewhere else entirely."

"Oh god, don't start with that starlit crap."

"There might be reasons why people tease you with celestial references."

"Well"—I smiled and ran my finger along the softness of his ear—"I'm not orbiting anything but the sun. And I'm not 'my own sun,' if that's where you were going."

"We, dear Scarlett, are orbiting all kinds of things."

"You mean one. The sun."

"No, I mean the forces that will eventually consume us."

"So, the sun again?" I scrunched up my nose.

"Scarlett, I know the sun is going to vaporize the earth when it supernovas. You told me like six hundred times in third grade and I had nightmares about it for weeks."

"You did?"

He nodded.

I looked at him. His eyes steady on the road. Faint stubble on his chin. I thought of David shaving.

We rode for a while in silence.

"So what forces are you worried about, then?" I asked. "Money?"

"No, more like not living up to what Graceville thinks we are, not doing all the things they've said we would."

"I never thought the guy who appeared on the cover of the paper point-seventy-seven percent of the time would be worried about that," I said. "Because despite not being valedictorian, you were still the newspaper's graduate to watch."

"Scarlett, you know that has more to do with my dad than it does with me."

"I've never believed that. I figure it's just sexism. Pure and simple."

David shook his head. "Maybe. But what does your dad do?"

"You know he's a fireman. You've known that since preK when he brought the fire truck to school and you refused to get out of the driver's seat to let the other kids have a turn. You threw such a fit, Ms. Mendez had to take the rest of us inside while my dad called your mom to come get you."

"What can I say, I've always loved driving," David said. "And you got to sit in fire trucks all the time. I was always so jealous that you got to ride with your dad in every Fourth of July parade."

"Um, David, you totally could have come with us. You still can. You need a plan for next Fourth of July? I'm sure my dad will let you ride along."

"Funny, I'm not so obsessed with fire trucks anymore."

"That seems healthy."

"I know it was always a joke to you guys, but it was real to me. The district attorney's oldest son was one to watch. I had a 'responsibility' to our town, and Dad loved to remind me every day in every way."

I touched his knee, thinking about how it had always seemed

so easy for David Warren. Everyone loved him, everyone knew he was smart, knew his name, knew that he was headed to Stanford. We always joked that David was a golden boy. But now his face was more serious than I'd ever seen it.

"There is no way to live up to their expectations."

"Whose? Your dad's or the town's?" David didn't say anything. "Are those the forces that'll consume us? Not living up to people's expectations?"

"Or worse, our own."

"You really think that?"

"I don't think. I know."

"Oh come on, you won't disappoint. Anyway, your metaphor is wrong." I pressed his arm with my finger. "We'll slowly move away from Graceville and watch it from farther and farther away until we are in stasis—so more like the earth and moon than the earth and sun."

"We are each entitled to our own hypothesis, Scarlett." He smiled, and the flash of insecurity seemed to whip out the window. "You're probably right, you always win in the end. That's why you gave the valedictorian speech, not me."

"I didn't *win* my GPA, David. You got an A-minus in AP history because you decided to experiment and do no work."

David laughed. "True."

"Yeah, you sat in the corner at our cramming parties building marshmallow people with toothpicks."

"Well, somebody needed to help you understand the battles

you all were learning about for the first time. Marshmallow figures were the way to go. I don't know what the rest of you were doing in fourth grade when I read all that stuff."

"Reading stuff normal fourth graders read."

"Yeah? Like biographies of Marie Curie?"

"Yeah," I said.

"Not normal, Scar."

"At least they were the ones written for fourth graders."

"Look, not my problem that you weren't riveted by history texts at nine. Anyway, I got the minus on a technicality."

"The technicality being you did no work."

"When you put it that way, Scar, the A-minus is pretty impressive."

"I actually always thought so."

"Wait, did you just admit you were impressed by me?"

"I said getting an A-minus was impressive considering how much you *didn't* do. Big difference."

"No, I don't think there is. I think you just admitted you were impressed. You know what? I'm going to turn around now and drive back to Graceville just to tell everyone that I impressed you with my A-minus." David started to pull the car onto the shoulder. I was suddenly seized with a desire to not turn around, ever.

"I was not impressed by your A-minus," I said.

"You were, you just said it. I impressed you. Now I'm going to tell everyone."

"Come on, D. Even if I was impressed by you, which I wasn't, no one would believe it," I said, running my hand up his leg. "Ninety percent is not impressive." I leaned over and whispered, "Anyone ever give you a blow job while driving?"

His face went pink. "Um, no. No, they haven't."

"Would you like that?"

I watched his jeans bulge at the idea.

"Uh, yes. Yes, I would."

"Okay. You'll admit I'm not impressed by you."

"That sounds like you are bribing me with sexual favors. I'm not sure how I feel about that. I think it might be abusive," he said. I raised my eyebrows and moved my hand to the waistband of his jeans to rub my thumb on the metal button.

"Okay! Okay! Scarlett Oliveira is not impressed by me at all and never has been whatsoever."

"That's the truth," I said, kissing the hairs below his belly button and unzipping his pants. "Kind of."

Whatever tape was in had loud, screaming rock on it, and with my head down near the speaker I could hear a long-repeating riff. I was aware of David's arms above me, hands clenched tight to the steering wheel. I remember trying not to bump his elbows or the wheel with my head. The music filled my ears as I listened for his low moan.

After, he said, "Man, I feel like . . . You are . . ."

"Impressive?"

"Very. Very impressive."

"Good job not getting into an accident."

"Where have you been all my life?"

"Across town," I said.

We drove in silence again. After a long while David said, "This is what I want to do, this, before the random mutations catch up with me. I want to live my flawed best every day, going fast down the highway with—"

"But that's just it," I said. "We can't do this again. Ever." The air wasn't working again and the heat swam around the car. I unrolled the window.

"Maybe it's possible to find time for things like this—maybe the summers," David said.

"Summers are for internships and jobs."

"Stop, you're growing my cancers."

"Shut up. The only random mutation you'll ever have is something almost everyone else wants." I stretched my arm out the open window into the warm morning air. My hair was dry now and separating into thin strands in the wind.

"Scarlett, a Romanesque nose is hardly a mutation. It's presentation, you know that."

"I was speaking of your IQ and your ability to use it in order to do very little and still bring home praiseworthy grades, not your obvious relation to the statue of David."

"Also, as you know, not a mutation, but you have discovered the secret of my name."

"Really?"

"Yep, when I was born my mother looked at me and said,

this boy will look exactly like the statue of David. And hence, my name."

"Ha."

"You got me—it was actually that my gaze was fixed in the direction of Rome."

"You were born in Graceville."

"One can certainly gaze toward Rome, even from Graceville."

"The human infant can only see twelve inches at birth."

"Twelve inches toward Rome."

"Twelve inches from your mother's breast to her face."

"Let's not talk about my mother's breasts. Let's talk about what you did earlier, or maybe my nose."

"I'm not sure I have much to say about either."

"You're still unimpressed?"

"I've always been impressed," I said. David smiled but didn't say anything. He turned up the music. For a while we just drove. He took the curves fast. The car was loud; there was a constant sound of wind even when we closed the windows. The air conditioner worked sporadically, and the heat swelled. On big hills the engine worked so hard, David turned up the stereo so we could still hear the music.

We listened for miles, then he said, "So what's up with you and physics anyway? What about it moves you or whatever?"

"Physics moves everyone," I said, rolling my eyes.

"My bad," he laughed. "But really. Why? It's not, you know, the sexiest of future plans."

"It's not? Shit. And you know the sexy factor was always

something I considered when thinking of how to change the world. I better rethink." I leaned out the window. "Help me! I've just been told physics isn't sexy! Get me some modeling auditions pronto! I'll save the world with my lovely smile." I flashed David my cheesiest grin.

"Sweet Scarlett, you're too short and you know it."

"Damn, all five foot six inches of me will have to resort to my backup plan of astrophysics."

"And in ten years I'll say, 'Remember Scarlett? You know she's literally a rocket scientist now.'"

"I can't believe you don't think that sounds sexy."

"Actually, I do."

"Well, it's better than pole dancer."

"Well, maybe," David said.

"Come on."

"Okay. You're right."

"So at our ten-year reunion, they'll nod when you tell them what I'm up to and say, 'It doesn't take a rocket scientist to figure out that she was destined for that.'"

"And I'll say, 'She's really just a bomb-builder, but did you know I successfully introduced the shark's anti-cancer gene into the human genome?'"

"But they won't because everyone is freaked out by shark genes even if you say you're going to use them to cure cancer."

"See, you'll win in the end, Scarlett. With your belief in the nuclear-energy dream, the clean green future. Is that what makes it your thing? Is it?"

I looked down. My nail polish was peeling. "That's part of it."

"So?"

"So what?"

"What's the other part?"

I cupped my hand to the wind and moved it like I was swimming through the hot air. Finally I said, "I can't believe I'm going to admit this, especially to you."

"Oh my god, you killed somebody and so you're devoting your life to a better future because you are in deep guilt for the pain you've caused?"

"I was going to bare my soul."

"Sorry, I don't want to discourage you from baring anything."

"Ugh," I said, shifting toward the passenger door, "don't be an ass."

"Couldn't resist. Sorry. Go ahead."

"Okay, so when we were little kids, most people would talk about wanting to be teachers or firefighters or something like that."

"Right, like me. I wanted to ride in those cool trucks all the time."

"Exactly. Well, I heard that astrophysicist was a job from somewhere, maybe from my sister watching Bill Nye the Science Guy. I didn't know what it meant, but I liked the sound of it, so when people asked what I wanted to be when I grew up, I said astrophysicist, and from the reaction of the grown-ups I knew it was impressive. People thought it was cute. Some would call me ambitious, or tell me how smart I must be, and how hard I would need to study. I guess I figured if I were actually an astrophysicist, everyone would think I was smart. So I studied. And now, here I am headed to major in physics." David watched the road and pressed his foot to the gas. The car began to shake as it neared seventy-five miles an hour. He punched the brake back to sixty-five going into a curve, then turned to me.

"It's not bad to want people to notice you're smart, Scar. Why do you think I'm going to Stanford?"

"Um, because it's a really good school."

"But there are lots of really good schools, and only a few that everyone in the world *knows* are really good."

"Tell me about it, I'm the girl who turned down MIT."

David tugged his hair. "Was that because you wanted to be an astrophysicist but have no real passion for physics?"

"No, it's not that. That was about money." I shook my head. "You know, after I started saying I wanted to be an astrophysicist, people got me books on science and astronomy, and physics for preschoolers. Then Dad got our telescope and Mom made sure I read all the Magic Tree House and Who Was? books about scientists, and before too long, I started to like it because it's cool. Legit cool. 'Cause of the number of things we use every day that wouldn't be possible without our understanding of physics—cell phones and watches and—god, almost everything."

"I know. I took physics with you this year, remember?"

"I wasn't sure you were paying attention."

"Ha. Ha."

"When my dad surprised me with Einstein and Curie posters on my eleventh birthday I remember thinking it was the best present ever. I'd read so much about them that I asked my teacher if I could do an extra report so I didn't have to pick one over the other. Remember how Curie created those X-ray trucks during the First World War? You know how many people are alive because of her? It's crazy."

"Was that about the time you won the science fair with that project about electric conduction? All that stuff about Einstein coming to his great ideas because he played with electricity as a kid?"

"The very year! You remember that?"

"Of course I do. I worked so hard on my cat-breeding simulation and came in third."

"Really? Who came in second then?"

"Second went to that kid Joey Trujillo. He moved away later that year, I think."

"Oh Joey, he was so cute. I can't believe I almost forgot about him and his perfect teeth. Who has perfect teeth in fifth grade? The rest of us had, like, half our grown-up teeth partway in, but Joey's smile, it was perfect."

"I didn't think I'd get to have another reason to be glad Joey moved away."

"He'll probably end up your roommate at Stanford. You'll need a new rival with me across the country."

"You were never my rival," David said.

"Come on. That's like saying my love for physics is fake. It isn't, but it started out as a way to get a reaction, which turned into motivation—"

"For every action there is an equal and opposite reaction?"

"Maybe—if you're going to apply the third law to human behavior. Problematic, though, because the third law only applies to two objects, and human behavior is way more complex. But I do love how science allows us to do so much that a hundred years ago wasn't even possible. Like, this road—because of physics, engineers could design curves through the Rockies that we can drive at up to fifty-five miles per hour."

"You'll notice I can take them at sixty-five."

"Yeah, you just did. But if that Winnebago drove that fast, it'd probably tip over."

When David saw the Winnebago, he swerved into the oncoming lane despite the double line and pressed his foot to the floor. There was another curve ahead and so we couldn't see the black Land Rover until it was laying on its horn and pulling onto the shoulder to avoid us. The Winnebago slowed, and David cut over so quickly I was pushed toward him by the force of it.

"You like motion," he said. I was scared, yes, but also excited. Alive. I felt every follicle. Imagined myself down to the smallest atom humming with motion, exhilarated by the avoided.

"I do."

"And you like this too," he said, running his finger up my thigh and along the line of my underwear. I slowly exhaled, rolling back my head as he pulled his hand away and flipped open the glove box. The fireflies inside my skin flashed. Whatever zoomed between our bodies, whatever biophysical connection we had was like nothing, nothing I'd encountered. He flipped open the glove box, and a cell phone fell out. He shuffled it under some papers and pulled out a carved wooden container and handed it to me. Inside were two small white pills. "Ecstasy. You, me, moving along the Great Divide."

"It's all I've got today," I said. I'd never swallowed pills before, though I knew the boys did. Prescriptions, mostly, but sometimes other things. My mom had warned me well. Prescriptions were dangerous and anything, anything could be ground up and pressed into a white or colored pill and sold on the street. Because of this, you could never know exactly what it could do to your brain. That August morning, I was aware of what I shouldn't be doing. I just didn't want to care. For once. At least for a while.

We swallowed the pills dry.

NOW

CHICAGO SKYLINE TO THE NORTH

Funny to think how all those months ago, David was hypothesizing about the forces that would consume us. I thought he was talking about both of us, I thought we were a pair, the bright stars of town running together, two comets racing across the sky. I didn't realize we had different orbits. Not really, anyway. Not yet. Now I remind myself that I need to breathe.

I close my eyes. Blink them open. Traffic is thick. Mina grips the steering wheel hard, her eyes laser-focused as she weaves in and out of lanes. I inhale the sweet scent of asphalt steaming from a summer rain. On busy interstates like this, I think about how if one person looks down at their phone at the wrong second, the impact of that one small move reverberates through the lives of so many. It makes me dizzy. Like looking at the stars makes me dizzy, like thinking about all those worlds. All that possibility. For beauty, but also mistakes.

NINE MONTHS AGO, SEPTEMBER

COLWYN COLLEGE ORIENTATION · WATERTOWN, MAINE

I didn't want to go to the official first-year welcome, but I had to. I was going to be called to the stage because of my scholarship. And ever since I got to Colwyn, I just kept thinking that the scholarship was saving me money, but it kept me from MIT, a school, as David would say, the whole world knows is good.

I showered, slipped on my blue dress, the one that comes down to my ankles and has an open back. I tried not to think about how David hadn't answered my text as I spun my wet hair into a bun, trying to keep cool in the humid air. Instead I thought about the weather in Maine, how the day before it had been cold and foggy; I wore a windbreaker when Mina and I walked to town. I dabbed on lip gloss and some light brown eye shadow to counteract how much I wanted to crawl into bed and sleep for an eon. Mina wore short, tight navy pants that matched her yellow-and-navy-striped halter top and three-inch yellow platforms. Even in heels, she was shorter than me.

We gathered in the auditorium. No AC. Students folded their programs into fans. Mina leaned over and whispered, "My face is melting!" and pointed to the black eyeliner now seeping onto her cheekbones in black comet trails.

"I thought you were crying because you're so happy to be here," I murmured in her ear. Mina smiled. I suddenly became aware of what was being said on stage. The provost, in a tan skirt and fitted blazer despite the heat, said:

"Among the promising incoming class is one standout student, Scarlett Oliveira, who should inspire us all. Scarlett is from Graceville, Colorado, a small town deeply impacted by the recession. The town's largest employer, Tidal Force Plumbing, closed, and many residents lost homes to foreclosure. As the community's population plummeted, young Scarlett felt powerless. One night, upset because her best friend lost her home, Scarlett's father challenged her to find a way to help. He told her he was given a voucher for free daycare when Scarlett's sister was young, allowing him to complete his firefighter training. So with assistance from her parents and friends, Scarlett worked with Graceville Parks and Recreation and opened a free-to-low-fee after-school program with a STEM focus. Before long, Scarlett wrote and received a grant from the Colorado Commission for Sciences, and the program expanded. Today, Step-up to STEM is all-volunteer-run and serves one hundred students every week during the school year in its after-school program, and six hundred fifty students in its summer programs combined. Last spring, Scarlett presented at the national youth leadership conference, where she trained others to set up sister programs in their own communities. The community-centered nature of this project, combined with Scarlett's excellent academic record, has earned her the Wallace Hartford Memorial Scholarship for Service in Science and Technology, a twenty-five-thousand-dollar annual scholarship for each of her four years at Colwyn. Congratulations and welcome, Scarlett Oliveira. We're glad you are one of us!"

There was clapping. Lots of loud clapping. I rose through waves of heat to the stage, where I shook the provost's hand. I could see sweat dripping down her neck toward her tan suit. I touched my damp hair. It was so hot; it looked like everyone in the room was dissolving into streaks like Mina's makeup. Everyone was waiting for me to say something, to be the clear-headed leader they'd all been told I was. But the world became dark at the edges, the faces mushed together until they were just a pinprick in the center of my vision. *Am I a leader?* I thought as my knees hit the stage. Then everything went black.

Someone's hands were on my shoulder. The room echoed with "Ohhhh!" sounds and the provost saying, "Scarlett, Scarlett? Are you okay?" I tried to nod my head, but I couldn't seem to control my body. I sensed myself being lifted and placed on something sticky and cold. Then lifted again. After a while, I felt something cool on my forehead. I blinked and the world became a white dot that widened. My vision was still frosty, but I could tell I was lying on a gurney.

"Do you know what your name is?" a woman in a white coat perched on a rolling stool asked.

"Scarlett," I said, taking in the shape of the room and recognizing the student health center.

"Scarlett, do you remember what happened?" She rolled closer to me.

"Yeah, I blacked out?"

"Has this happened to you before?" the nurse asked.

"No, but I do get dizzy sometimes. Anxiety."

"Do you take anything for that?"

"No. It's mild. I control it with exercise. And breathing."

"A serious attack could cause you to faint even if you haven't before. They said you were being honored. Were you nervous?"

"I guess."

"Were you sweating excessively?"

"It was so hot—*everyone* was sweating excessively."

"AC down again. Timely. How much water did you drink today?"

"I don't know, a glass."

She pinched the skin on my fingers.

"It could be anxiety, but you're also probably dehydrated. The two combined could certainly result in passing out. Everything else looks fine. We could take you to the hospital and put you on a saline drip, but I'd rather you just drink something here. Are you ready to sit up?"

"I think so."

"Take it slowly." She handed me a plastic cup. Whatever it contained was gray and fizzing. "Electrolyte water," she said. "Where are you from?"

"Colorado."

"Drier out there, easier to remember to drink. You can stay here as long as you like, and I'll have Public Safety give you a ride to your dorm when you're ready to leave."

"Okay. Thanks."

When I got back, I didn't go to dinner. I asked Mina to sneak some rolls in her bag. I went to sleep.

The endless orientation scavenger hunt continued the next day, when we found a clue that made everyone but me giggle: "If you go and copulate, remember: Give one of these to your mate."

"So, the health center?" I said to the flushed faces of my teammates. "Or where else do they hand out condoms?" The group squirmed and stifled their giggles. "Seriously, you guys can't handle talking about where the condoms are?" Everyone looked down. "I'll go then."

Sure enough, at the front of the health center was a jar of condoms, and taped to the side was a clue labeled *Physics*. Someone, obviously from another team, had defaced the envelope with *How'd you nerds figure this one out?*

Really? I thought. *I could have gone to MIT, where my major would be respected. Instead I'm here where people think studying science is nerdy?*

I was about to take down the clue when I suddenly froze. Condoms. I hadn't used them in the last month. I'd stayed on the ring like Mom suggested after Cody and I broke up, but I didn't remember when I last took it out. Why couldn't I remember what I'd done? My arms prickled as I realized I should have had my period already. Had I put in a new ring and just skipped my period? Did I never take it out? I looked up at the girl in the office chair in Student Life. "Where's the closest bathroom?" I asked.

"Just down the hall, on the left," she said.

I went into a stall and felt for the ring. Not there. A wave of cold washed over me. Shaking, I pulled up the calendar on my phone where I usually marked my cycle. Nothing. Maybe I wrote it on my wall calendar? I walked past the clue taped to the jar of condoms in Student Life, holding my elbows all the way to my dorm room. I looked closely at the calendar, and by now my heart was beating so fast, I thought my atoms might separate and I'd explode right there, taking the school and most of Watertown out with me. There was no little *p* written in the corner of the calendar, no sad face. Nothing at all to suggest I'd just had a period that I was forgetting about. I opened my drawer, a pack of three rings still sealed in their box. I didn't have one in, and I wasn't bleeding. I should be if my hormone ring wasn't in there. That was the deal, ring for three weeks and take it out to bleed. If you really want to skip it, just put another ring in, but that always creeped me out, so I didn't do it. I wondered how, or if, I could have completely forgotten to slip a new ring in during the worst possible month in my personal history to forget. Could it have fallen out? It never had before. It wasn't designed to, but if it did, when? Why couldn't I remember this incredibly important detail?

My phone buzzed. I thought, *David,* but it was Courtney asking if I'd found the clue. I switched it off. I thought of what I would say to David if he did finally text: "You know how science made family planning possible? Turns out this young scientist forgot her birth control all last month. Wanna guess the results of our fertility experiment?"

I texted: "David?"

Then I lay in my bed, looking out my window at the sky peeking through the mask of maple and beech trees. And as I waited for the text that would never come, I thought about how my new landscape seemed so small, just this little bit of sky through the trees, compared to that wide, western blue, flanked by mountains and rock and winding roads. That road trip with David is like a dream I'll maybe never stop returning to.

TEN MONTHS AGO, AUGUST

NEW MEXICO/COLORADO BORDER

As we crossed into New Mexico, golden dust rolled across both sides of the highway, the world shimmered with heat, and from the stereo came a smooth voice singing, *If I ventured into the slipstream, between the viaducts of your dream . . . Could you find me? Would you kiss-a-my eye?* Maybe it was the pills, maybe it was the song and how it reminded us that everything we'd known our whole lives was about to end, and we would soon be far apart. Maybe it was the sun glistening across the desert, but I felt outside of time, like I'd entered a moment I'd been in before and could return to someday if only the light and the music were right. *To be born again,* the song said.

Through the windows came the scent of sage. The sky was a blue usually reserved for Instagram-filtered photographs, dotted with puffy clouds. I held my phone out the window and took a picture as the song ended and David pulled onto a scenic overlook.

"You radiate," he said, and stared at me. I watched the movement in his dark eyes, and when David ran his finger along the line of my veins, the rough skin around his thumbnail scraped my arm and a surge of energy gathered under the cloud that was David and me. He reached his palm up and placed his hand on my cheek. Heat pulsed there. It was like drawing fire from his skin.

"Heat," I said, "causes motion," and moved closer to his body. Our lips touched and I felt his warmth transfer to me.

I suppose cars sped by us and the sun glinted off the windshield. Inside the car, we burst into each other like we'd taken off our bodies to become elements mixed together. There was so much texture, my cotton dress lifted up, his hands sliding my underwear off, the sticky leather of the seats, his breath in my ear.

Later, when we walked into the sage, David looked up, pointed at a power line with a large nest on the top. In it perched a princely bird. "Red-tailed hawk," David said.

We watched it. It watched us. Then suddenly, it swooped down, caught something in its talons, and returned to the nest.

David shook his head. "A bloody, beautiful life." I hooked my fingers through his belt loops and leaned against his sweating back, brushing my lips against his neck.

"The beauty of survival."

David didn't answer. He pointed to a trail leading out from the overlook into the desert, away from the highway.

"I want to know where that goes," he said, walking farther into the sage, Coke bottle in hand and white T-shirt like a sail or a flag of surrender, billowing behind him like he was something to run toward, something to follow.

As if possessed, David walked quickly into the sagebrush and scrub pine. The path cut down from the highway into the valley below, then turned and started up a different ridge. We didn't talk. We listened first to the whoosh of cars and the flap-flap of my flip-flops, the low hum from the sage. It must have been some insect, but it sounded operatic under that bright blue sky. Sweat pooled on David's T-shirt in growing orbs, and I struggled to keep his pace. Eventually I just followed him. He stopped at the top of a plateau, and when I caught up to him, I leaned into his back, felt his warm dampness, his body's attempt to control heat.

"Scar," he said, looking out over vast dregs of Colorado to the north, the yellow expanse of New Mexico to the south, "when you're all grown, when you're working sixty hours a week to afford a nice car with roof racks for a canoe that you never have time to paddle, and you're walking around in your modestly hemmed skirts, will you promise to remember this? Right now. Right here. This?" He pulled some piñon needles off the tree next to him, crushed them between his fingers, inhaled, and then held his hands to my nose. The scent, soft and sharp at once, a mix of cardamom, nutmeg, orange peels—it filled me up. "When you smell this, will you remember?" I raised my eyes to his, those amber pools. I may have stood there and stared into him for hours. I don't know. His eyes were like a leaf-pile blowing in the wind. So much motion, layers of brown flecked by gold, then splashed by a wave of green, every shade of the earth spinning together.

"I won't forget, and I don't think I want a canoe. Boats freak me out. And anyway, you'll know me. We'll meet back in Graceville at the tree-lighting or something and you'll be one of those West Coast rich guys with five-hundred-dollar jeans and a white T-shirt, really hip glasses because instead of going into Frankenstein monkeys you'll actually go into computers and be like the new Steve Jobs or something and everyone will—"

"Want to do cocaine in my car?"

"Well, that wasn't what I was going to say." At the time, I wasn't sure if David was asking me to do cocaine in his car, or saying that in the future people will *want* to do cocaine in his car. I didn't ask because I was suddenly crazy, mind-numbingly thirsty. I drained the water bottle David had pulled out of his trunk, and then grabbed the bottle of Coke from his hand. I swallowed. It burned.

"What the hell *is* that?"

"Jack and Coke." David took it back and downed the rest in one long swig.

"Shit, David."

"What?"

I squinted at him. "Nothing."

I don't know why I didn't say anything—me, typically the DD Police, the hider of car keys, the matron of road safety. But it felt good somehow to risk everything. To stand in those dry mountains and toss my life to the wind.

We followed the trail farther, and David said, "You know, if I make it big with the Frankenstein monkeys I'm going to single-handedly purchase all the red lights and throw off your long-standing economic analysis of the town of Graceville."

"You wouldn't dare," I said.

"Just you wait," he said, "just you wait."

Eventually, my mouth was so parched, I thought it was filled with dust and began worrying I would choke. We headed back to the car and stopped for water at the next gas station. David drove in a daze through northern New Mexico. As we wound through the high desert we spoke little, lulled by the hum of the engine, the relief of sex, and the resplendent hue the drugs imparted to the world around us. We were diamond encrusted. We were jewels in glimmering sand.

And then there were sirens.

I watched the big cop in the rearview mirror step wide-legged up to the driver's window. He tipped up his glasses like an actor in some bad cowboy movie to stare hard at David, then me, then David again.

"Good afternoon," he said.

"Afternoon, sir." David smiled.

"License and registration?"

"Scarlett, could you hand it to me? It's in the glove box." I tried to smile but only the edges of my lips turned up. I was nervous the cop might see David's little box of colored pills, and I worried my fear would give us away because my hands shook when I passed David the folded pieces of paper that had been covering up a cell phone. I wondered why he had two.

"Where you headed today?"

"To visit my big sister at UNM."

The cop nodded. "Did you know you were going sixty-five on that last curve?"

"No sir. I didn't, but I'll be sure to slow it down. I'm just a little nervous. She hasn't met my girlfriend, and you know how big sisters can be. I'm distracted. I know it isn't an excuse, officer." When David smiled, I'm pretty sure the cop fell in love.

"All right, hold on a minute," the cop said, and went back to his car. All I could think about was David's blood alcohol level. What was it right then? I rubbed my wet palms across my dress. I looked at him sideways; he winked. I wondered if the X could come out in any test the cop could do right then. I wondered why I didn't know these things and if David did. How was he so calm? How was his speech not slurred? Was it possible he wasn't drunk from the Jack and Coke? How could that be?

"Don't worry, I got this," David said.

The cop came back to the window, looked me over. "You sure you want to meet this guy's big sister?"

"Yeah." I smiled and put my hand over David's on the gearshift, a gesture I'd seen my mom do to my dad.

"All right, well here's a warning. Slow down and be careful.

Big Sister wants to meet this girl, not see pictures of her bent up in the wreckage of your car."

"Yes, sir." David reached up and touched my cheek and said, "I wouldn't want to put her in any danger. Have a nice day, sir."

The cop lowered his sunglasses. David started the engine.

"What—David? How did you do that?"

"Never underestimate the power of a Roman nose, a reasonable lie, and a pretty girl. Right now, we're untouchable."

"Maybe," I said, feeling like I had a molten core. David was right—we felt untouchable, outside of time and consequence. And as much as I wanted to keep going, as much as I wanted to live in that place, to believe we were somehow, for a moment, cut free, I knew it was wrong. We were being given a pass, one we didn't deserve, and for a lot of reasons—the Volvo, our clothes, our whiteness.

David kept the car within the speed limit for at least another ten minutes until we stopped for gas. I bought chips and more water because the pills that made everything seem so electric also depleted me of salt and made me feel like my mouth was full of cotton. I went to the bathroom and retrieved my phone from the depths of my bag. One message from Mom saying to have fun and fourteen texts from Hannah from the last two hours. Shit. It was Sunday afternoon. We were supposed to meet at Colorado Beans to go over the week's Step-up to STEM lessons. Instead I was on a trail with David inhaling dust and piñon, high on ecstasy, while Hannah and the others waited for me in Graceville. Instead of texting back, I called.

"Where are you?" she said, picking up the phone.

"What you don't know can't hurt you," I said.

"Scar, are you being hyperbolic or irrational?"

"Both?"

"Come on, Scarlett."

"I'm—" My mouth was so dry it was hard to talk. "I'm in New Mexico with David. We're driving the Great Divide. It's a parting ritual or whatever."

"A parting ritual? With David? What?"

"Come on, Hannah, you know we're both going far away."

"I almost hate you right now."

"I know, but will you continue to love me like a neighbor and cover until we're back?"

"Yes, but only because Step-up to STEM is important, and because I do love you."

"You just said you almost hate me."

"I love to hate you."

"Thanks."

"And I have to tell Rage because you're supposed to be working with him, remember?"

"Thank you—for being so forgiving, Han. I know I suck right now."

"Did you just admit Jesus has some perks, Scar?"

"You're free to interpret my words any way you'd like so long as you forgive me."

"I will, if you tell me one more thing."

"Yeah?"

"Nothing's going on with you and David, right?"

"Hannah, that's disgusting," I said, trying to keep my tone even. "David's like my brother. We've been friends forever."

"I know, but—"

"Hannah, when people are your friends since forever, you go a little wild when you're, you know, about to not see them for a long time."

"Ouch, so you're not doing something wild with *me*, and instead I have to run Step-up to STEM for you because, in case you're forgetting, I've always been here too?"

"I know you have."

"Helping to put the pieces back together," she muttered.

"What?" I said.

"Look, Scar, you're being selfish. I know you and David both get to go far away to school, but I'm the one who has *always* been here, and now you leave me to plan Step-up to STEM without you?"

I thought about Hannah the day I didn't get into jazz band in ninth grade. How she got her mom to bring her over with a whole pan of brownies. Food from a family that barely had any. My stomach burned. She was right. And what did I do for her but help her with her math sometimes, let her crash at my place when she wanted to hang out with her boyfriend late?

"I'm sorry." I was.

"You should be. You suck."

"But you do forgive me?"

"Of course I do. Just understand that *I'm* going to miss you too. Tell me you're being lame, and come back soon, and stop being an idiot."

"I'm lame. I'll come back soon. Can't promise about the idiot part."

"And tell David he sucks."

"Will do."

"And text your mom."

"I did," I said.

"Again."

"I will. Thanks, Han."

Hannah hung up and I stood there staring at something brown wiped in an arc across the tile wall. I flinched as a sudden headache bloomed and pulsed behind my forehead. *God. What did that pill do to my brain?* I pushed the thought away, used a paper towel from the dispenser to open the door, blinked through the bright of the parking lot, slid into the car next to David, and said, "Drive on."

NOW

LASALLE COUNTY, ILLINOIS

"Red Vines are the best straws," Mina says, biting off both ends and slipping the candy into her cherry Coke.

"Yes, and so much better for the environment," I say, and bite off the ends of my own.

"Did you know I wondered if you were a serious food snob, and that's why you weren't eating much in the dining hall? I thought you were freaked out that Colwyn wasn't local and organic." She glances at me sideways, sucking soda through her candy straw.

"I would love food services to be local and organic, but—"

"You were too busy hating food."

"All food but crackers. What else did you think about me? That I was a record-player-breaking, science-nerd-menace bent on falling asleep in the middle of every conversation we'd ever have?"

"Pretty much," Mina says, and accelerates like we have to pursue the Iowa State Line at cosmic speed or be toast.

EIGHT MONTHS AGO, OCTOBER

COLWYN COLLEGE · WATERTOWN, MAINE

So while everyone else at Colwyn walked around in packs and laughed with the ease of friends who took baths together at playdates, I cocooned myself in denial. It took all my energy to lie there in that strange bed, in my room with the industrial white walls, to look around and know what I'd done. A month after orientation, it was clear my dizzy spells were growing. But instead of floating outside myself, my vision went black. I told myself biophysical reactions to new situations happen. Anxiety. Breath control. Transitions are hard. Depression can cause people to not want to eat, to need sleep like a drug. It wasn't a problem I'd had before. Was it now? Or could I really be—

On the day Mina found me retching into our trash can, she looked through her heavily mascaraed eyes at me and said, "Okay, out with it, are you bulimic, pregnant, or just depressed? Because I know you aren't hiding vodka bottles around here, and besides, if alcohol was the problem, you might have come to a party with me. But seriously, whatever the case, I can walk you down to the counselor or give you a ride to the clinic, whatever,

I don't judge. But clearly, Scarlett, you need some help." Her words were on a roller coaster, fast, focused.

"Um, maybe, both?" I said, and heaved.

"Both what? Bulimic and depressed? They kinda go together."

"The other thing," I said, holding on to the plastic rim of the trash can. My stomach flopped.

"Shit." She got on her knees next to me. "You're not sure?" She reached her hand up as if she was going to smooth my hair behind my ear but then let it drop.

"I never took a test, so I guess there's a chance I have some terrible disease that makes me dizzy and exhausted and hate food."

Mina clapped her hands together. "Oh good! Just a terrible disease. Tell you what," she said, "I'll go get you a test tonight and then we can figure out if we need to plan for your life of breathing machines and hospital stays or if the cause is more temporary."

"Temporary?" I said. "A solar super flare would also be temporary but would knock out all Internet communication and destabilize nuclear reactor sites and—"

"And my guess is humanity would ultimately be just fine. Whatever it is, you got this," Mina said. "You're the girl who started that STEM program that's everywhere, teaching today's youth about the dangers of super solar flares."

"Solar *super* flares," I said, but my heart wasn't in it. My eyes burned. My nose began that fizzy ache. I was the girl who started an after-school program with its own nonprofit status that was expanding to sixteen sister locations, sitting in my dorm room wiping puke from my lips. How could this be me?

Mina handed me tissues and picked up the trash can. "Right. I'm gonna wash this out."

When she came back, I'd settled on my bed, pillow in arms. She dropped down next to me and scooted back so her head bumped the bottom of my posters.

"Watch out for Einstein," I said. She inched her head lower so it rested below the poster. "You know, people say he could work with a baby on his knee."

Mina tipped her head to me. "But he did not, ever, have to give birth," she said. I must have paled. "Sorry. You know I was serious when I said you got this." She touched my arm. "Even if it *is* a terrible disease."

"Whatever it is, I guess there's probably a possibility for research."

She reached over and squeezed my hand.

Later that night, dressed in a trench coat and glasses, Mina said, "I'm going incognito to buy the test."

"Um, Mina." I examined her getup. "You really think a baby-blue trench coat and glasses that look like they came straight out of my grandfather's yearbook are going to make you less noticeable?"

"No," she laughed, "less *identifiable*. Of course, if you *want* people to know about this, come with me. You know that's fine, right? This is about what *you* want."

"What I want is for no one to know about this ever. Even *I* don't want to know about this."

"Which is one way to end up going into labor in a bathroom somewhere."

"What?" I said. Mina was not usually so macabre.

"I just mean, you don't really have a choice—to know or not."

"That appears to be the case." I inhaled.

"So, can I borrow your sneakers?"

"They'll be like four sizes too big for you!"

"Even better!"

"You'll trip."

"Scarlett, I can walk in six-inch heels! I'm sure I can make it into the drug store and back to my car in too-big running shoes."

"Here they are." I dangled them by two fingers. Mina pulled the laces until the tops puckered.

"Just sit here. Relax. Mistakes happen to everyone." Yes, Mina had peer leader training in high school. It was something we had in common. Unlike me, she did it because she liked it. For me, hearing kids' problems, kids I didn't know very well, was like trying to calculate gravitational force between two objects without knowing the mass of either. I hated that I couldn't actually *do* anything for them. I stayed at it because I knew I had a choice to listen or not. It didn't feel like enough but maybe it was the best I could do. Still, I always wanted a solution. A fix. An answer for them.

Mina returned with the test and read the instructions to me. I lay on the bed with my hands over my eyes. "It says here, the first pee of the morning is best because it'll have the most pregnancy hormone. But if we don't want anyone else in the bathroom . . . the best time to take it is probably about four a.m., after the late-nighters have gone to bed and before the crew team is up for practice."

"How do you know that?" I said, sitting up and looking at Mina, the instructions flopping between her purple nails.

"I am a woman of many mysteries," she said. And I suddenly realized I didn't know when she slept, or studied, or if she partied, and with whom. I'd been so exhausted, I'd barely bothered to get to know her at all in the last month. Beyond talking a bit about high school, ordering her a new record player, and listening to her explain to me how it worked and what the best albums were for the changing season, we hadn't talked all that much. She *was* still a woman of many mysteries.

I set my phone's alarm for 3:58 a.m.

Sure enough, when we got to the bathroom, it was empty.

"I'll wait here," she said, handing me the white stick. She'd even taken it out of the package. I felt this weird surge of gratitude at the sight of it and almost started crying again. Instead I focused on lining the seat with paper. I sat down. Inhale. *1, 2, 3.* Exhale. *1, 2, 3, 4.* "Remember to place it mid-stream," Mina said from outside.

"Like I'm launching a boat?" I grunted. "Head for the high water!"

"You really have not spent much time in boats, have you?" Mina said, leaning on the stall door.

"Not really."

I suddenly missed Hannah so much, my chest hurt. I remembered her crying in the bathroom in sixth grade—she'd gotten her period for the first time and was unprepared and terrified. I hugged her and went to my locker for pads. After that day, we shared locker combinations just in case one of us didn't have what we needed. It's funny, I know lots of people love the privacy of their locker, but I always felt better knowing Hannah could get into mine. Not until David did I ever hide anything from her. But now, if I were in Graceville, it would not be Hannah handing me the test. Most of the time, our differences didn't matter. But something in me ached all the more knowing, as I stood in that stall, that this time it would.

I was supposed to hold the stick for five seconds under a stream of piss and then wait to see if the blue minus sign or pink plus would appear.

Turns out I didn't need to wait five seconds. As soon as the thing was wet, it emerged: The pink plus. It darkened and darkened before my eyes. Maybe it was only confirming what I'd known for weeks, but it was different somehow to have that pink ink confirmation. And a witness. This was more than me now—a secret that threatened to move toward the outside world.

I capped the test, steadied myself against the blue stall door, took a deep breath, and pushed through to Mina. I held the stick out so she could see. She looked like she was about to ram a fawn with her car as she said, "Oh shit." Then she opened her arms and I stepped into them. For a long time, we stood awkwardly hugging under the white lights. When I loosened my grip, she took the test from my hand, dropped it into the deep pocket of her zebra-striped robe, and walked me back down the hall to our room.

The door clicked. "What will you do?" she said. I was quiet, Mina half coughed. "Are you going to do physics with a baby on your knee like Einstein? Because I'm not sure babies are allowed in dorms." She chewed her lips. I think she was serious. I almost smiled. "Sorry," she said, "I'm getting ahead of myself. What about your boyfriend?"

I shook my head, nodding to the Einstein biography where David's picture lived. "He's not my boyfriend. Not really. It's"—I put my hands up—"complicated." My cheeks burned. I couldn't say more. Not yet.

"Well then." She squinted at me, and I felt myself transforming in front of her from the silent roommate, science-nerd, to secret-bearer, slut. "I won't judge you whatever you do." Or maybe she thought of me as just a nice girl who'd had an accident. She added, as if to clarify, "Abortions don't mean you're going to hell or anything, no matter what those Colorado Christians say."

I smiled. Mina knew that for some, there is no choice in choice. For Hannah, an abortion would never be okay. Ever.

For others, it would be the obvious choice. For me, the decision loomed. I was too responsible for unplanned pregnancy, period. But the plus. The plus. The plus.

"You know this is Maine. They don't shoot up clinics here," Mina added, as if that was what I was worried about. The look on my face must have been enough, because she went silent. I sat down on the bed, drew myself into my knees.

After a long time, I said, "Mina, I don't know what to do."

She crossed the room in two steps. "Well, I'm good at plans, so you're in luck. Most people think there are three choices in this situation, but most people are not as creative as me. Sure, you could go the abortion, adoption, or mothering route, but I think it's best to link any experience to your own life path and goals. Right? So"—she paused and picked up some stress clay from my dresser—"maybe we could pitch you to be the first pregnant woman sent into space?" The tip of her tongue appeared between her lips.

I smiled a little. "Sign me up for experiments in zero-gravity childbirth," I said.

Mina lobbed the stress dough at me. I caught it.

"See," she said. "You got this."

But did I?

Okay, David Warren was my first love's best friend, an asshole, and is dead. David and I went at it for most of August when I thought I was on birth control but wasn't. Then I found out I was pregnant. Given these facts, one might deduce that David Warren caused this situation. And he may have. But to really understand how the fact of my pregnancy seemed to suck me into a black hole, I need to present all the research. Even the parts that make me squirm. You can't just overlook some facts because they make you uncomfortable, right? What kind of scientist would that make me? So, I'll tell you now: David Warren wasn't the only possible father.

TEN MONTHS AGO, AUGUST

GRACEVILLE, COLORADO

A few days after David and I returned from the Great Divide, my parents went to Colorado Springs for the night to see my sister, Jessica, so David, Hannah, Rage and I gathered in my parents' living room for one last little party. We'd only been sitting around a few minutes when David looked up from his phone and said to Hannah, loud enough that I would hear, "Cody might stop by later to say hi before we all disappear."

"Oh really," Hannah said. "He thinks he can just roll back into our lives? Why does he think Scarlett will let him in?"

"He's probably figuring someone else'll get the door. Plus"—David paused and his voice flattened—"he broke up with Rachel." My spine straightened and when I looked up, David's eyes burned into me. I hoped Hannah was so surprised by this news she didn't notice David's look.

"I told Rachel forced conversion never works," Hannah said.

"You talked to *Rachel* about *Cody*?" It was out of my mouth before I realized I said it. David's eyes were needle sharp. I dug my nails into my palms.

"Come on, Scar, you know our parents are old friends. I can't hold Cody against her. But I wasn't encouraging."

I crossed my arms. Tried to shake them loose. David slouched. Eyes ablaze. He cleared his throat. "Speaking of forced conversion, Han, you know how Cody's going to St. Olaf, right?"

"Yeah," she said, glancing at me. The air in the room had thickened.

"Well, Rachel said she was thinking about it a lot, and the fact that he chose to go to such a liberal Lutheran school must reflect poorly on his morals."

"Sweet Jesus," Rage said, "as if going to St. Olaf is the thing to make you question Cody's morals."

"Language, babe," Hannah said, winking at Rage.

"Sorry, sweetie, I try to scrub the blasphemy from my mouth before we hang out, but some of it always clings there."

"With the taste of holy—"

"David," I said, well aware that the pink of his cheeks meant whatever he was going to say next was offensive.

"What? Hannah proves her Christ-like nature every time she hangs out with us. We're the prostitutes and thieves Jesus befriends," David said, moving a curl out of his eye and holding my gaze a beat too long.

"Yeah . . ." There was a hint of a question in Rage's voice as his eyes darted between us before narrowing on David. "It's true—while you've been drooling over Scarlett, I stole thirty-six dollars and four pills from your coat pocket," he said, flashing a bit of green. David suddenly looked away from me and launched himself on Rage. "Give EVERYTHING back, you asshole."

"Chill, D—" Rage shoved him off easily. "I was joking. That's my cash."

Hannah crossed to Rage, touched his frosted tips. Something passed between them. They glanced at David and then, like I'd seen her do a million times before, Hannah flashed her milk-white teeth and said, "Let's play a game, you heathens."

Everyone settled around the oak coffee table to play I've Never. Rage put his feet up on the fireplace hearth, his head in Hannah's lap as she lounged across the floor.

"I'm not playing," I said.

"Why not, Scar? You afraid of what you might have to drink to?" David asked.

I tried to fire back at him with my eyes. "No, I just don't want to drink tonight," I said, yanking out my ponytail and letting my hair fall over part of my face.

"Why not?" David raised his eyebrows, but his voice was cold. Such an ass.

He wasn't exactly wrong, though. If Cody came over, I wasn't sure what it'd be like, to have them both there—Cody, my first love, and David, my what? My crash? I watched his fingers twitch. I shook myself deeper into my hair.

No one knew about David and me. I didn't tell Hannah because I couldn't find the words for it, and also because I didn't want to deal with her judgment or joy. I had enough of both myself. We never said it was secret. I guess I assumed David was still Cody's best friend, even if that was strained. And announcing a late summer fling with me was probably not a great way to mend their friendship.

I sat across from David, sinking deeper into my hair, feeling his anger scorch the room. My own simmered. After a few rounds, the game had gone from "I've never gone climbing" or "I've never gone on a seven-day canoe trip," to sexual acts. Of course.

It was David's turn.

"I've never done, or taken it, up the bum, for Jesus or otherwise," he said with a smile at Hannah, who stuck out her tongue.

"You're an ass," she told him.

"Ass is what I'm talking about, Hannah," David said as Rage made a big show of lifting his shot glass to his lips and tossing it back, confirming that he'd achieved this act, which David had not. In response, David lifted his own glass and said, "Oh my god! You OWN her! Way to go, man." Rage turned red. I rose to leave the room. Behind my back I heard David say, "Hannah, you didn't drink."

"You're disgusting," Hannah said. She must have thrown something in his direction, because the next thing I heard was glass shattering.

"Nice one, Han," David said.

"It's your fault. If you weren't such a shit, I wouldn't have thrown anything at you."

"Violent acts," said David, mimicking the voice of a teacher, "can never be blamed on anyone but the perpetrator."

"You think you're the victim here?" I said, turning back to the room to face David.

"Yeah," Hannah said. "Not only did you talk about sex as an act of ownership, but you managed to completely offend me, my religion, and my choices, which by the way, David, are none of your freaking business."

"Well, they are if you agree to play this game," he said, smiling. "And anyway, we're one big happy family here. We're Graceville's Finest."

I couldn't find the words to continue the fight. My heart was thumping. "Who's going to clean up the glass?" I said.

David raised his eyebrows at me. I ignited the planets in my eyes. Rage jumped from the couch, still pink, and shrank under Hannah's stare. "I got it," he said. "Where's the vacuum?"

"Thanks, Rage. Hall closet. Bags for the glass are under the sink."

"I'm sorry, Han," David said. "I wish all good girls were like you. But alas, many are less liberated. You can talk to Cody about that."

"David," I said. He flinched.

"Hey, this might be our last party," Rage said, turning on the vacuum.

"Rage's right. I'm crossing lines again." David's voice was loud, but somehow smooth over the vacuum's hum. "Forgive my assholery, and let's keep playing. Please."

"Fine," Hannah said, but her eyes were on Rage as he straightened from unplugging the vacuum. "As long as you know you're a jerk, David Warren."

"Proudly," he said.

"Okay, my turn," Rage said. "I've never"—he cleared his throat and sat up pretending to straighten an invisible tie—"had vaginal intercourse with anyone in the room." Hannah crossed her arms.

David drank.

In my memory, even the music stopped as Rage looked to Hannah and then to me. "Scar's the only one not playing! OH MY GOD, you guys—spill it!" Rage said.

"Holy crap, does Cody know? Holy crap!" Hannah said, sitting bolt upright and looking straight at me. David half smiled, then said with an affected drawl, "Secret's out, Scar."

I wanted to scream, to tell them all to grow up, to get out, I wanted to swear in their faces. But maybe all of the breathing paid off in that moment. Because I didn't say a word. I just continued to walk into the hallway. I took deep breaths. *1, 2, 3. Hold. Exhale. 1, 2, 3, 4* and repeat. All the way to the bathroom. I locked the door behind me and turned on the hot water. All I wanted was to get to college, to get away from my friends, who I suddenly felt such hatred for that I'd bitten the inside of my lip bloody from holding it all in. I spat red into the sink, waiting for the shower to heat up. David's comment about Rage owning Hannah, about sexual acts implying ownership—I thought about the blow job I'd given him while he drove. I'd done it because it seemed exciting and slightly dangerous. I'd done it because I'd wanted to. Did he think I did it because he *owned* me?

Right then, I felt our friendship vaporizing. I told myself, These are just the people in this little town who have always been here. I didn't choose them. We are friends only by default because we've been in the same place at the same time, and that time is almost done.

But time is never done, is it? The past happens. It's still happening. And because we're human, we relive our memories again and again and again as our only way to fold time backward, to unbend the illusion.

I undressed, thinking about college. We all were leaving. Our relationship with Graceville would change forever. I'd slip farther and farther away from everyone like a shirt lifted over my head. Like the moon, I'd drift from Graceville until I reached a safely observable distance. The steam rose from behind the shower curtain. I stepped in. I stood under the water and let it massage my shoulders. I looked at my body, my dark hair clumped around my breasts, my hands smooth, nails clipped short, my toes painted Posey Pink, my stomach flat but certainly not a muscled washboard, and my arms thin as spindles in contrast to my thick and muscled legs.

I heard a knock. I pretended not to hear, leaning my head back under the hot stream. Then another. Then three rapidly. I put my head out of the shower and shouted, "Puke in the kitchen sink for all I care, just clean up after yourself." I was about to pull my head back in when I heard a laugh that made me suck in a quiet breath, then:

"Did they piss you off, Starlet?"

Cody. The vaporous room was like a dream. I turned off the water, wrapped myself in a blue bath towel, and went to the door, opening it a few inches. Cody leaned into the crack, pushing the door in, pushing toward me. Cody. I could smell his coconut shampoo. I could almost taste his skin. "Hey, I'm in the shower," I said as water ran down my legs and puddled at my feet.

"No, Starlet, you're out of the shower," he said, playfully pushing me back into the bathroom and closing the door behind him. Cody. Beautiful, calm, Cody.

"Don't call me Starlet. You know I hate that."

"Okay, Red."

"That's worse and you know it."

"You're scarlet, Scarlett," he said, reaching up to rub my cheek with his hand. "Red as a beet."

"Beets are purple."

"Whatever. You look beautiful." And he kissed me. And then I learned how easy it is to do something once you've done it before, even if you've told yourself you wouldn't. Because when I felt his kiss, it was like going back in time, stepping into that sticky honeycomb. The world felt so fragile, like it could split in two along the Great Divide. I thought, time can be like that. There are moments when it feels like everything known of the world is disappearing, and a new reality fills in, as if painted on a canvas, one where everyone you know and love is leaving.

It felt for a moment like Cody and I could return to the time we were together, the shower steam rising to carry us back there, to December and before. And the recent past would just disappear. But I knew what was happening was goodbye. It was short, terrible, and sad. Too quickly he was buttoning up his jeans. And after, he leaned in, kissed me, and said, "I know what happened between you and D, and I'm not mad."

I gaped at him. "And so you came down here to what? Reclaim me?" I spat my words at him. I think I was shaking.

"Scarlett, no—I—"

"Don't say another word," I said, and dressed without meeting his eyes. I pushed past him and walked to the living room to give David a piece of my mind, but he was already gone. He had taken advantage of my absence to find his car keys and drunk-drive to some guy's house to buy whatever pill was on hand. Asshole. Stupid me, for even thinking he'd still be around. Stupid me, for falling back into Cody. Hannah and Rage were on the couch, a laptop between them, drunk eyes heavy. They barely looked up at me.

"Come on, Scarlett, why are you so pissed?" Cody grabbed my arm. His grip was too tight.

"Because you're a jerk," I hissed. "You don't own me. We're not together and won't ever be again. Get out of my house." I peeled his fingers off my arm and pushed him toward the door. He stumbled backward a step and his eyes widened.

"Scarlett?" he said, his voice slow and abnormally steady.

"Get out!" I screamed.

"Scarlett, I'm—"

"I said get out! You can't do this. You can't come here after dumping me for some girl who thinks the earth is six thousand years old and make up by acting like you own me. I'm not a possession. I never was. You might have had me, for a second, with your voice, but what happened is never going to happen again. Get the hell out of here."

Hannah and Rage looked up. After what felt like a long pause in which Cody did not open the door, or make any motions to leave, Hannah cheered, "Way to tell him, Starlet!" her voice deeply slurred.

"Don't call me that," I said. I turned away from them, my friends wasted on the couch, my ex-boyfriend staring at me with—what? Confusion? Anger? It was five a.m. and the sky was turning white. From the open windows was the too loud chorus of squawking birds.

I walked quickly to my room, shutting and locking the door behind me. Cody followed and knocked once, twice, probably three times. After a while I bet he hammered the pressed wood with his fist. Maybe he even got the butter knife to jimmy the lock. I don't know. I slipped on my shoes, popped out the screen, and climbed through my window just like I'd done the night I left with David. Once alone in the cool air, I crept through the landscaped yard and out the side gate. I ran up to the bench where I always stop to stretch, where Hannah and I used to play as kids, our one-room schoolhouse. The sun was coming up, making the red dirt appear to glow orange. I touched my toes once and turned up the trail. I ran.

"So you know Newton's Third Law, right?" I ask as Mina flips on the blinker.

"No," Mina says, and glances at me. "Nice face, Scar. Don't judge—you didn't know Emily Dickinson, remember?"

"Okay, but the third law? Every action has an equal and opposite reaction?"

"Oh yeah, sure. That one. It's like—the difference between how you felt looking at your SAT scores compared to the pregnancy test."

"Ha. Pretty much. Or maybe that was more like, Pregnancy: The Black Hole."

"Pregnancy: The Exploding Sun," Mina says, a small smile sneaking around her eyes.

"Pregnancy: The Interstellar Collision," I say.

That's how it felt. It didn't matter that I worked so hard to get to college, or that I created Step-up to STEM. Everything would dissolve around this one gigantic mistake.

EIGHT MONTHS AGO, OCTOBER

COLWYN COLLEGE · WATERTOWN, MAINE

A few weeks after I'd taken the piss-test, Mina made me an appointment at the clinic to officially confirm the pregnancy, and then she drove me to it. I let her.

Her car wasn't a fifteen-year-old beat-up Ford like Hannah had saved for with money from her job at the grocery store. It wasn't even like David's dad's well-kept Volvo. Mina's car was a Jeep with a skylight. It seemed to say "Welcome" as we slid into the all-leather seats. I buckled myself in and Mina handed me a sticky note with a number on it.

"I know, I know," she said when she caught me looking at her. It was the first time I'd been with her in her car, and I must have had a weird look on my face, because she said, "I'm so short I should be in a booster seat."

"Not what I was thinking."

"Were you worried about the airbags? They're a real danger to women of my stature."

"Nope."

"Well, what was the weird look?"

"Probably just my stress-face."

"Okay, well," she said, sounding not entirely convinced, "call this number, tell them that you want all your explanation of benefits documents sent to you here, and not at your parents'."

"My what?"

"You're on your parents' insurance, Scar. They get a letter, or email, or something explaining what the charges are. You don't want them to see 'pregnancy test' or anything, right? Unless you do. That would be okay too? But I think it's better they find out from you. Not their insurance company."

"It's better if they never find out."

"Why?" She put up her hand. "Don't answer that now. Call the number."

"Right. Thanks."

When I hung up, she glanced over and said, "Why don't you want them to know?"

"Because—because I don't screw up like this. Ever. It isn't me."

"You mean, it didn't used to be." I couldn't read her tone. But the reality of her words hung there.

Finally, I said, "Well, they can't know it is now."

"You sure about that?"

I didn't answer. Everything would relate to this one mistake for the rest of my life if I told them. That wasn't happening. Out the window the trees were bright red and yellow. Then the wind pulled the leaves down so they drifted and skittered across the street.

After a while Mina said, "I can't imagine being, you know—"

She took one of her hands off the steering wheel and gestured at her stomach.

"Me neither," I said, "but here I am."

"Right, but I've never even—" Mina's forehead turned pink. Her dimple flashed.

"You haven't?" I said, staring at her red lips and cute outfit.

"I kissed this guy once—" This time the dimple stayed.

"*Once?*" I covered my mouth with my hand. "But you're pretty—and—"

"Doesn't mean I go to orgies all the time," Mina said, and snapped her gum.

I couldn't tell if she was mad. I tugged my sleeves into my palms and took a deep breath. Mina was a woman of mystery.

"I didn't say orgies," I offered after a while. "I just thought—everyone who wasn't religious probably had. Or at least, you know, almost."

"Well, you learn something new every day, don't you?" Mina said, slowing for a stop sign.

"I wasn't trying to be a jerk."

"You weren't. Not really. Most of the time I'm okay with it. I'm not wired for hook-ups. I'd like a boyfriend. You know, movies and hand-holding. I'm not saving myself for anything except someone special." She looked in the rearview mirror and reapplied her lipstick.

"He was special," I said, my voice small.

"Oh god! I didn't mean—" She squeezed the steering wheel. "I'm sorry."

"It's okay." I felt suddenly hot. I hadn't explained everything complicated to Mina yet. "I mean, they were special. Cody. And David." I let their names hang in the air.

"Oh." Mina tapped the steering wheel. "That must be hard. Not knowing."

"Yeah," I said. Non-judgmental Mina. "You know what's really freaky? It's how despite myself, I'm interested in what's happening to my body"—and as the words came out I realized how much I liked them—"because all of these cells are reorganizing inside of me. Did you know my blood volume is expanding?"

"Your blood volume. Really? Then, you're like—what? A one-woman biology lab?"

"More like a fucking public service announcement," I said.

"You're not a public service announcement."

I shook my head, thought of David, his pillboxes, the texts he hadn't answered. And I thought of me. Pregnant. Driving to the doctor. I breathed slowly through my nose. "We're all biology labs," I said. "Just look at the stuff that lives under your fingernails. You've seen that, right?" Mina nodded. "Good. So, did you know Einstein had a daughter no one knew about?"

"Oh, god, Einstein again. You can't secretly raise a baby in our dorm room, Scarlett, even if you *could* do physics with it sitting in your lap. I really think it's against the rules." Her hands tightened on the steering wheel, but her mouth twitched toward a smile.

"That's not what I was thinking."

"Good."

"I know what the logical choice is," I said, "and it's something I'm not against at all. I just— It isn't the kind of thing I ever thought I'd do."

"Scarlett, that's kind of the point. It's not anyone's hope to be in your situation, like 'I'm going to go get knocked up today so I can go get an abortion, yippee, cross that off the bucket list.'" She plonked her head against the headrest and rolled it to face me for a second before turning back to the road.

"Yeah," I said. And I knew she was right. Abortion seemed like the right choice, the thing most girls like me would do. It was what Cody and I agreed we'd do, if it came to it, if all our modes of protection failed. Why was I so curious about not just what David would say, but what it would be like? Feel like?

When I thought about actually being a parent, though, my curiosity flatlined. Because Mina was right: I didn't want to do physics with a baby in our dorm.

Mina was looking at me.

"What?" I said. "Eyes on the road."

"Adoption agencies will cover your medical expenses," she said.

I didn't want a baby. But could I have one and not raise it? Could I get away with hiding something so big? Could I feel this and let it go?

I exhaled. "How do you even know about medical expenses?"

"I was a candy striper at home."

"A what?"

"Sophomore year, I started volunteering at the hospital. I

had this injury"—she made a blah, blah, blah gesture with her hand—"and because of it, I wanted to be a doctor. Until I was a candy striper."

"Okay, what injury?"

"Just a sports thing." She flinched. "Anyway, I talked to people drowning in medical bills. I met this woman who was freaked out because she was pregnant again and the last time she had a miscarriage, she couldn't afford the bill for it. It went to collections and ruined her credit."

"Oh man."

"Yeah. Sucks. She had insurance too. Since then, I've wanted to be a therapist, but lately I've been thinking lawyer. I'm either going to help people recover from the damage the system has done to them, or I'm going to sue the system on their behalf."

"Don't therapists take insurance?" I said, cocking my head.

"Yeah, but at least then I can help them process their payment issues."

"Insurance is sort of the last detail on my mind, so, thanks," I said. The fact that Mina was thinking about these things, that she knew about them and cared, it was like a weight lifting off me.

She slammed the brakes. "Stupid lady! Don't you know how to merge?" she yelled at the RAV4 that had cut us off, then cut off someone in the left lane and sped away. I held tight to the door handle. Mina shot her eyes to me and flashed a smile. "Just trying to distract you from all of the 'wow I guess I really effed up' preggo-emotions."

"Thanks, mortal fear will do that. Could you speed up? Go

yell at that lady? Why don't you rear-end her? Then maybe I'll have a miscarriage and this whole drive will be unnecessary."

Mina didn't say anything.

"I guess," I said, "nobody thinks miscarriage jokes are funny. Probably they're really unfunny if you combine them with car-crash jokes."

"Probably," she said, flicking on her blinker and swerving into the left lane.

"It's just, like, I got hit by this local gamma ray burst. You know, like anything could destroy me right now. How can I be pregnant?"

"Um, the only thing I understood about that was the final question."

"Local gamma ray burst—it's one of the great cosmic disasters. Could threaten life on earth by wiping out our ozone. Happens in seconds. So, like, my egg got fertilized and boom. I'm just open to all this ultraviolet radiation."

Mina loosened her fingers on the steering wheel and her shoulders dropped. "That's kinda poetic," she said, pulling into the clinic parking lot.

When we got inside, my hands were so sweaty, they left fingerprints on the plastic clipboard the clerk in a jack-o'-lantern headband handed me. I sat down in an uncomfortable chair to fill out the papers. I read, *Date of last period:*_____.

That blank space was a black hole. I could almost see the light disappearing into it. I held my pen over it. I looked at the calendar on my phone. July 30? August 5? 10? In the end I wrote *August 1-15?* And brought the board back to the clerk in cat-eye glasses.

Mina flipped open a magazine. "Horoscopes!" she said. "We're going to read all of them." She gestured to the pile on the yellow plastic table.

"Come on."

Mina shook her head. "Many a literary giant was fascinated with the occult."

"Because they didn't understand science."

"What's your sign? You're born in the spring, right? But probably not Pisces . . ."

I shook my head.

"Aries?"

I nodded.

"'Course you are."

"What does that mean?"

Mina just folded the magazine open after looking at the date. "Okay, this is from August. 'Aries, it appears you are destined upon a doomed love this month. Be clear in your desire. Be honest with yourself.'"

I tried to smile. But the room felt hot.

Mina glanced at me with wide eyes, continued, "Well, um, mine says, 'Libra, you always need to work to keep your scales balanced, but now as great change approaches, you must turn toward yourself and meditate on the impermanence of the world.' Hm, makes sense. College, great change."

My eyes couldn't focus.

"So what do you think about fate, anyway?"

But before I could tell her that astrology is based on the sun passing through constellations at the time of your birth two thousand years ago and things have moved since then, my name was called by a woman in a white lab coat with a bobble-headed witch pin on the lapel.

Mina came with me. It was blood pressure cuff, weight check, peeing in a cup, and sticky paper covers on the bed. A ponytailed doctor with a gentle smile, noticeably lacking seasonal accessories, ordered my feet into stirrups for the exam. The doctor said that because I was so unsure of the dates, they should do an ultrasound. When I asked if I couldn't come back for this, she said that the sooner she could get an ultrasound picture, the more accurate the date, and the more accurate the date, the more closely they could track my pregnancy, and "the more aware you'll be of your timeline for choices."

"Isn't ultrasound used to coerce women into not having abortions?" Mina said, stepping closer to me.

The doctor smiled a false smile, then said, "Not in Maine. But if you're worried about that, if your friend knows for sure what she wants, we can schedule an abortion. But, if she isn't sure, this will give us a better timeline to allow her to decide. What do you think, Scarlett?"

"Do whatever," I said, my eyes on the ceiling.

"You sure?" Mina said, leaning toward me.

I nodded. "Whatever" meant they wheeled this small monitor into the room and turned on the little green screen. Early ultrasounds are done with a wand, and not a magic wand either. It was highly uncomfortable and hopefully never-to-be-repeated. I tried to turn my head away. I heard the doctor making little clicks on the machine. When I looked I saw an alien life-form that pulsed.

I didn't feel a surge of connection. I didn't feel anything. It was a strange in-between thing, something that could become something else, but didn't have to. The choice was mine. I turned my head away again and thought about the blue sky, high and unreal above the Great Divide.

Then I was asked if I had questions. I shook my head and was handed a paper that listed my due date as May tenth and a stack of pamphlets about everything from dental health to abortion services. The doctor offered the ultrasound photos, holding them toward me between gloved fingers.

"Um, no way," I said, and the doctor clipped them to my chart, clicked her pen, and said, "Have a nice day."

NOW

HENRY COUNTY, ILLINOIS

I guess I've made it pretty clear that David Warren had some serious assholic tendencies. But he always made it seem like he was in on the joke. Or maybe I was always giving him the benefit of the doubt because he was David, always there. Cody's best friend.

I was slow to realize that underestimating David is like underestimating a comet bound directly for earth. Just don't. But I did. Again and again.

Anyway, over the course of the year, I've been letting Mina know more about David. Little bits of the good stuff, and then some of his assholery, and finally the pills, the orange bottles of force. But what I'm going to tell you now, I've never told Mina. Maybe I never will.

TEN MONTHS AGO, AUGUST

SOMEWHERE, NEW MEXICO

After we'd stopped for gas, David pulled onto the highway and, a few minutes later, turned onto a dirt road. It climbed up a plateau lined with barbed wire fences that restrained horses and marked ownership of the parched earth, trailers, and adobe houses.

"David? Where are you going?"

"Driving on."

"Okay," I said as dust drifted in my window.

The road twisted up and we could see for miles—the horizon in every direction was a line of far-off mountains, the sky streaked by scudding clouds. David carefully steered around rocks and potholes, sometimes driving on the wrong side of the road to keep the car from bottoming out. Eventually rocks jutted up alongside the car, and we'd dropped into a narrow canyon. I could hear water but couldn't see it. Then suddenly David inched the car around a curve and the world widened. We were right next to a slow-moving brown river. A stone picnic shelter stood lonely near the banks, and a barbeque pit rusted in the sage. The only other sign of people were some car tracks in the mud.

"Time for a swim," David said, and jumped out of the car, dropping his clothes as he ran. I walked around from the other side and watched him splash as the afternoon sun made tiny rainbows through his kicks. I wondered how he knew there would be a river here. Had he been here before? Did he actually know where we were? Or was this just another one of his lucky breaks—try a road you've never been on before and find something wonderful?

I wanted to ask but said instead, "Remember when you had that swimming party when we turned eight?"

"What?"

"Your birthday party—you had swimming and it was on the same day as mine. Was that on purpose?"

"What?"

"Did you plan your party so that no one would come to mine?"

"Are you coming in?" he said, treading water.

"I am in." I was standing up to my knees, holding my dress out of the water. "So did you?"

"Did I what?"

"Make it so no one came to my eighth birthday party?"

"Scarlett, you're so beautiful right now. Won't you please swim over here and kiss me?"

"David, stop changing the subject."

"Your subject doesn't interest me. I was eight. It was a party. I think my mom was completely in charge of things then. Come on, let's swim to the other side."

"You really don't remember?"

"No, but apparently you do. You coming in or what?"

I looked around to make sure we really were the last people on earth, and then I slid out of my dress and swam into the cool water across to the other bank. We sat there, on the stony ground, drying, watching the clouds pattern the sky. When the evening sun was beginning to be too much, we swam back and gazed across the river. I leaned on my hands and rolled my head toward David's shoulder. There was something so beautiful about the way his neck met his collarbone. I wanted to curl up there. I wished all of me could fit. I turned my face into that hollow and breathed in the scent of dust and river and mint soap. David pulled back.

"Time for a nap," he said, and went to the trunk of his car. He pulled out a brown plaid sleeping bag; did he always keep a sleeping bag in the trunk? Why? I didn't ask as we made a nest on the floor of the shaded picnic shelter, curled together, and fell asleep.

We awoke to the whitening sky and a chorus of crickets and birds. It must have been only about four in the morning. My shoulder and hipbone ached from sleeping on the concrete and my skin was raw, burnt. David sat up and rubbed his temples, blinked at the light, shed his clothes, and splashed into the water. I watched his muscled arms surfacing one after the other. What was I doing, waking up here in the wilds of New Mexico with David Warren? To say this was out of character would be an understatement. But when I looked at him, my body warmed, and when I thought about how no matter what, in a few weeks this would be over, I wanted nothing more than for this day to last forever. Or at least as long as it possibly could. When David got out of the water he shook his head like a dog, then looked at me and said, "Ready?"

"For what?"

"To drive on," he said. I smiled and responded only by walking to the car, opening the passenger door, and climbing in. David drove back up the twisting dirt road, and when we were spat back onto the highway, he turned south. Hours passed as we watched the sunrise bring color to the landscape. We drove and drove. Mostly in silence. Sometimes I reached my hand to that hollow of David's collarbone. Sometimes I traced my fingers from the crescent moon scar on his hand up the muscles of his arms. He didn't reach for me, but he smiled. After a few hours we reached the end of our road: the US border at Antelope Wells. I'd expected David to turn the car around, to head back north, but instead he drove up to the border kiosk. When the agent asked for our passports, David lunged toward the glove box. "D—I don't have a passport."

He looked at me, stunned. "You don't? I thought I told you to put them both right here?" I watched openmouthed as he pulled his passport out of the dash box and flipped it open.

"No, you didn't," I said, confused. Of course David didn't tell me to get my passport when he showed up spontaneously at my window in the middle of the night. I don't even have a passport. I didn't think we would actually drive this far. But we'd just kept going and going.

David shrugged at the agent. "Look, sir, I told her to grab both our passports, but—"

The agent fixed his gaze on us and shook his head at me. "I can't help you. Even if I let you across as a favor, you wouldn't be able to get back easily." He shook his head as if this was the greatest understatement he'd ever made.

"But me and my girl just drove the Great Divide, and we're headed to college in a few weeks on opposite coasts— Can we just cross into Mexico to say we did? This is our goodbye—can you please help us with it?"

"I'm sorry, kid. You'll get in more trouble if I let you across. But over there, that's the spot where the bikers always take their picture after they've ridden the divide. I'll snap one of you as proof you made it this far." He gave David a genuine grin.

"Thanks, man." David smiled and turned the car around. We got out and stood in front of the sign that read BORDER INSPECTION STATION: ANTELOPE WELLS NEW MEXICO. David tried to put his arm around me. I shook it off.

"I'm not your girl," I said between clenched teeth.

"Smile!" said the agent.

"Smile, Scarlett!" David said, and I did. Why? I don't know. Maybe the same reason the border agent was so polite when

David tried to get me across without a passport, or why the cop let us go. David was genuine, even when he was lying, if that's possible.

As we got back in the car, I slammed the door.

"What the hell was that?" I said. "'My girl,' and 'Didn't I tell you to get the passports?' I'm not your girlfriend, D." David flinched. "And you know as well as I do there was never any talk of passports."

"Look, I was just trying to see if I could get us across. I figured he might have sympathy for a guy whose girl forgot to pack her passport. The guy's border patrol, he's a meathead."

"Nice way to be open about a stranger who was totally respectful of you. Especially one who probably thought you were abducting me and selling me into prostitution. Given that, he was a complete gentleman and even took our picture." I could feel the vein in my neck straining. I didn't care. I didn't even try to breathe.

"Ever dramatic, Scarlett."

"I'm not being dramatic, D. You're being an ass. Claiming you're only an ass because you were stereotyping a perfectly nice guy who was doing his job proves you're a *real* ass."

"I wish I'd kept track, Scarlett, of the number of times you've called me an ass over the years," David said.

"Ass! Ass! Ass, ass, ass, ass, ass, ass, ass, ass, ass, ass, ass, ass, ass, ass, ass, ass, ass, ass, ass."

David turned up the music. An hour later we were in Deming.

I was hungry and really thirsty. We stopped at a restaurant and ordered Cokes and breakfast burritos.

"Look, Scarlett," David said in a low whisper, "why don't you just stay here for a while. I'll go across and score some goods and be back in a couple hours."

"Wait. Are you serious right now? You can't just do that."

"Sure I can. A buddy of mine does it all the time. I've got a number." He tapped his phone.

"Ass," I said, then lowered my voice. "Did you seriously just bring me with you on a drug run? And pretend we were on some random adventure together? Really?" I took a long drink of soda. I hadn't brushed my teeth in what felt like forever, and I could feel the sugar sticking to the plaque. I pointed my straw at him. "Ass, ass, ass, ass, ASS!" I said.

He raised his hands in the air. "Okay, calm down. I was being impulsive, but I do have this standing offer . . . you know, if I ever wanted to be impulsive enough to take it," he said in a hushed whisper.

"I don't want to know any more."

"Scarlett, returning to the speed limit, are we?" David said, standing up, keys in hand. "I'll be back in three, maybe four hours."

"Seriously? You're not even going to eat your breakfast?"

"Save it for me. Come on, I'll make a killing when we get back to Graceville." David reached toward my shoulder. "I'll split the profit with you and we'll both head off to college flush."

I shook my head.

"Think about the debt, Scarlett. This could help."

"Ass," I said. He lifted his arms as if in surrender.

"Here." He handed me a twenty-dollar bill. "Breakfast is on me. I'll be back for lunch."

"And I'm just supposed to sit here until then?"

"I'm sure you'll find something to do," David said. "I bet there's a library. Ask the waitress." He leaned toward me. I slunk low in my chair to avoid him but he managed to plant a kiss on the top of my head anyway. I took a long sip of my soda as I listened to the bells jingle on the door, and David Warren left me alone in a border city, drinking soda through a straw. *Ass*, I thought, is not a strong enough word for this.

KAMPGROUNDS OF AMERICA · ROCK ISLAND, ILLINOIS

Maybe it wasn't David I underestimated, but the forces that pulled on him. He looked like he was dancing on his own, but really he was a marionette magnetized by what I could never understand. Just like David never knew what it felt like to be lying on my narrow Colwyn mattress, nauseated, thinking about how Einstein didn't have to deal with the practical parts of his unwanted child. Einstein flitted around trying to find a job, acted as if all was well while his girlfriend was alone, tending a baby they didn't keep simply because they weren't married before the birth. Biology. The unfairest of all sciences. But I was no Mileva Marić. I wasn't waiting for a wedding. I wasn't sure who the father was. And I needed, more than anything, to be like Einstein. I needed to not be undone by my mistakes.

Stuck in the breezeless air of an October heat wave, I listened to the sounds of my new landscape through the open window—someone practicing the violin, voices drifting up from the lawn. Beyond my door, the halls were silent. I lay on my bed, sweating in the heat as the supersized heads of Einstein and Curie looked down on me in the glory of their realized dreams.

"Oh no! You're staring at Einstein and his freaky puppet again!" Mina said, scuttling in and slipping off her platforms.

"Einstein's first wife was a physicist," I said.

"Was she also the reason he could work holding a baby? She cooked. She cleaned. She physic-ed?"

"Did you just turn physics into a verb?" I pulled myself up on my elbows.

"Language is flexible," Mina said, tongue appearing between her lips. "Can we not talk about Einstein for a minute?"

"You brought it up!"

"True."

I tapped the dictionary app on my phone. "It's just that the verb *physic* already exists, and it means something else."

"Meanings can change. *Scientist* doesn't just mean *white dude* anymore."

"*Scientist* only meant *white dude* in Europe and here, you know."

Mina touched her toes, then flattened her hands on the carpet and kicked up her feet.

"Um, Min?"

She walked across the room on her palms, her toes pointed, and then with complete control she arched her back, touched her feet to the rug, and slowly stood.

"What are you doing?"

"Distracting you with insanely cool tricks."

"Oh."

"I mean, you're still an undecided, knocked-up girl worried that this baby daddy is going to go on to do great things and you'll be like a footnote in history books."

I narrowed my eyes. "That just eliminated any progress you made distracting me with your bodily contortions."

"Oh come on, Scarlett. Get off Einstein. Curie didn't play with puppets of herself. She's a better role model."

"But—Curie, she's like—too perfect. She would've known exactly what to do if she was in my situation. She doesn't even believe in being afraid." I pointed to her words emblazoned on the poster: *Nothing in life is to be feared, it is only to be understood.*

"You're misunderstanding the quote," Mina said, flopping onto my bed and smacking the wall under Curie with her hand. "She means by understanding, you eliminate fear, not that she *has* no fear." She paused and tapped her neon nails on my elbow. "And yes, I did just prove why Comp is an important class for you to show up for."

I tried to smile but it must not have been convincing, because Mina sighed, stood back up, inhaled, and back-flipped right in front of my bed, sticking the landing, her hands poised in the air.

"Um? When did you become a gymnast?"

Mina tucked her lips under her teeth and dropped her arms.

"I'm not. Anymore."

"Could've fooled me."

"Yeah, well, I placed at state twice. And then. I fell." She shrugged like it was no big deal. "So I'm thinking of changing my major to English."

"Hmm," I said. "Why's English better than psych?"

"'Cause I'm good at it?"

"Okay, but practical reasons?"

Mina sat down next to me. "Um, do you have practical reasons for not making *your* choice?"

"Unanswered texts?" I pointed to my phone.

"You don't need him to decide, Scar."

I shrugged her off. "So your reason was?"

"Maybe it's a better path to law school?" She rubbed her chin, fingers coming away with a smudge of foundation. "Hey! The Society of Physics Students meeting is tonight. Aren't you going?"

"How'd you know about that?"

"I am Mina, the All-Knowing," she said, sitting up very straight. "Get your butt out of bed!"

"Fine." I rolled away and slipped on my shoes. "But I might toss my crackers all over Harold."

The meeting was in a midsize classroom in the Physical Science building, a mostly glass box at the edge of campus. Courtney and Sora were already there, up front. When they saw me, Courtney patted the chair next to her, then slipped her hands back in the pocket of her Colwyn sweatshirt. The AC was cranked in here.

"When do you think it'll snow?" she asked as I sat down, trying not to think about the burn in my stomach.

I shrugged. "Not today. It's like eighty-five degrees out. Next month? Who knows?"

"I can't wait." She looked out the window.

Sora smiled. At the back, a dozen or so guys, including Bert, stood clumped around a laptop, and I realized—Courtney, Sora, and I were the only non-male people in the room, lined up like ducks in the front row. Sora folded their arms across their Deadpool shirt. Courtney kept pulling her phone out of her sweatshirt pocket. Maybe she was checking the weather. Then Harold burst through the door, all smiles and high fives.

"Welcome!" he said, and I remembered running Step-up to STEM, how even when I felt I had to put on a show of having more energy than I did, I was thrilled to be there. I wondered if that was how Harold felt.

"Today we extend membership into the Society of Physics Students to our ten incoming majors." This was followed by clapping and hooting, but I still thought of the phantom crowd of MIT kids, the class I'd turned down. "Physics," Harold continued, "while it might be the best major on campus, loses about half of our ranks in the first year." He looked at us like he was the professor and we the likely-to-fail students. "We know it's tough, and we don't want to lose you. We want you involved. We want to help."

Courtney ran her hand to the ends of her shoulder-length hair. Sora took off their gray beanie. Put it back on. Took it off. Bert fiddled with his buttons. I counted my breaths. Everyone wondered who wouldn't be around next year.

"Is there a secret handshake?" I blurted, trying to cut the sudden thickness. Harold just shook his head and kept talking. I glanced down at my phone and was greeted by my lock-screen image, the cold stare of the girl in the painting from New Mexico, her eyes warning that life does not always go as planned.

I could feel the hair on my arms rise.

Unplanned.

Me coming to Colwyn.

This pregnancy.

David.

I could not be dropped from the major. Lose my scholarship.

But half. Half? And those were people who weren't pregnant, who wouldn't have turned down the number one physics program in the country to save money, who hadn't made choices so bad, they might as well have placed themselves inside a particle accelerator. I gripped my chair and let go, leaving wet residue on the plastic.

Harold's voice remained cheery. "The society provides extra resource money for travel, study, and connections to internships and graduate school. Chaun spent part of his summer at the Hadron Collider at CERN. He'll tell us about it in a minute. But first, we need to figure out our fall fund-raiser. Any ideas?"

The room went quiet.

"Bake sale?" I offered.

There was scoffing from the back of the room. "You going to do all the baking?" one of the guys called, and laughed.

I shook my head, inhaled the scent of chalk and chlorine. It was comforting. I liked classrooms. They were a landscape I understood.

"I've been 3D-printing gyroscopes," another guy said. "But they're complex, so we'd have to sell them for maybe twenty-five bucks."

Cool idea. Gyroscopes are fun, I used them at Step-up to STEM. They got kids excited.

"Huh," Harold said, hands on hips, "but selling anything for more than five or ten dollars to students is hard."

"We could print key chains with Curie's image on them," I

suggested. "They'd be cheap and easy to make a lot of. People would totally buy them."

"Yeah, but Curie," some other guy from the back of the room said. "You think people would recognize her?"

Was he for real? I pretended my teeth were glued together.

The guy continued, "Why don't we do little atomic models or something?"

"Yeah!" someone shouted. I looked sideways at Courtney, but she gazed placidly at Harold, and when I looked to Sora, they were just balling up their beanie into tiny twisted knots.

"Atomic-model key chains. Was that a motion?" Harold said, gavel in hand—where did that come from?

"I move we make atomic-model key chains," one guy—the same who asked if I'd bake—said from beneath his Red Sox cap.

"I second," said another.

"Scarlett, do you want to work on that design?"

"It was his idea," I said, pointing at the guy who'd spoken first.

"Chaun is a senior. He doesn't have time. Courtney can help you."

"Of course. When do you want us to be finished with that model for you boys?"

Harold's face blanked, as if realizing how he'd just passed off the work to the new girls.

"Okay then, Bert will help too once you get the model done. You know how to 3D-model, right?"

"Harold, I ran a STEM program for kids. I can 3D-model in my sleep," I said, like it was common knowledge and not the complete and total lie that it was. I did once write a grant for a 3D printer, but Step-up to STEM didn't get it. "We're on it. Right, Courtney?" I said. Courtney nodded and put a hand up to the locket she always wore, rubbing her thumb along the back before plunging her hands into her pocket again and pulling out her phone.

"This won't be like the scavenger hunt all over again, will it?" Harold said quietly to me.

I didn't answer.

I'd dropped out of the scavenger hunt after the condoms clue.

He turned back to the group. "So we'll sell atomic key chains in December? Can we vote?" Every hand in the room went up, mine halfway.

Classrooms were a landscape I thought I knew. But Colwyn was different.

I looked to Courtney, hoping to share a moment of . . . something, but her eyes stayed glued to her phone. I glanced at her screen. It showed a search for 3D-modeling software.

NOW

KAMPGROUNDS OF AMERICA · ROCK ISLAND, ILLINOIS

What did I want? For everyone at Colwyn to see me as the star I'd been in Graceville?

Maybe.

I think it's how David needed me to see him. Maybe that's why, for so long, I did.

Even now, when I look at the only picture of David and me alone together, the one taken in Antelope Wells, I see him as a kid running wild, me cutting loose beside him.

In the image, we stand close together, and David gestures with his arms out as though celebrating the fact that we made it to this place. As if our being there was planned. On my screen, I see a me that's irritated but smiling, unaware of how far out David had already spun, the latent receptors in his brain ignited, sparking. Pulling him on and on and on and on.

By the time the waitress brought our breakfast burritos, David was gone. I asked if she could wrap his to go. The corners of her mouth raised and her eyes flashed something that might have been sympathy as she took his plate to the back and handed it to me a few minutes later wrapped in tin foil. I sat with my back to the door, looking at the paper flags on the ceiling with their tiny decorative cuts. I remembered the same flags at Cody's birthday parties. Teri would hang them across the porch, and I loved to watch them in the breeze, blue, yellow, and pink.

The place was quiet. No music. No other customers. But it wasn't actually any mealtime. I decided to chew each bite thirty-two times before swallowing, a theory Mom had adopted and I was skeptical about. I didn't think it was supported by any data. The number thirty-two seems completely arbitrary. Still, I took the pen from my purse and recorded my bites. Considered my method. Made notes.

The waitress refilled my Coke. After two hours of incredibly detailed reporting of my eating, mentally making up every possible word combination from the letters in the vinyl beer poster on the wall in front of me, and my third refill of Coke, the waitress came to the table.

"Can I get you anything else?" she said, her eyes searching.

"Just the check, I guess."

I paid with the cash David had given me. Slipped his foil-wrapped burrito into my bag and left. Heat radiated from the sidewalk, glinted from the rusted cars. Everything was coated in dust. When I came to the end of the sidewalk, I stayed on a dirt path along the road. I felt like I was in some old western movie, where the stranger comes to town, so everyone stays inside and eyes him from their windows. I even thought I caught people peeking at me from behind the barred and curtained openings of the houses. Probably I was being paranoid and it just felt that way because I was not in my landscape. Not of this place. I pushed my hands along the sides of my dress, remembering—wishing I'd worn something with pockets.

Eventually, I came to a large brick building with a sign: THE DEMING LUNA HISTORICAL SOCIETY. I climbed the steps slowly. It looked dark inside, but the sign on the door said OPEN. My head hurt. It was hot. I walked in and was greeted by the musty scent of a faintly mildewed basement. A woman, the docent, with a silver pouf of curls peered at me from behind a Plexiglas desk. "The museum is free, but we take donations," she said. A plastic box with only a few one-dollar bills and coins in it stood on the side of her desk.

"Oh great," I said, reaching into my bag for the change from breakfast. I only had a few dollars left from David. The docent's eyes followed me as I folded one with a nickel from the bottom of my bag and slipped it into the box. In my wallet was a debit card with fast access to three dollars and seventy-five cents, thanks to organized me, who had already set up a bank account at Colwyn and transferred everything but what I had budgeted for August into it. I took a map from the counter and walked down the whitewashed hall. The museum, I learned, was housed in the town's old armory. Enjoying the cool air, I glanced at cabinets of table settings, a red Japanese tea set, a two-sided serving tray separated by a porcelain lobster. I wondered if someone had come here from Maine, bringing these emblematic dishes with them. How many people on the earth had stood in this town and also on the coast of Maine? Probably not many. I bet I was the only one headed there who was abandoned by a friend I'd been falling for as he went searching for drugs. Statistically there's a small chance that it had happened before. Just like there's a chance that if I could observe the right bend of light, I could witness that time again, me in Deming looking at old objects. Alone. David alive. David somewhere. Me not-yet-pregnant, or maybe already pregnant. Me standing forever gazing at the china, wondering why people find place settings interesting enough to put in museums.

I turned and stopped. In front of me was a painting of a girl about my age; she had long hair like me, though hers was blond and in two braids slung over one shoulder. She wore a red shawl and leaned barefoot against a curtained bedpost, which had the effect of framing her in white lace. At her feet, two potted plants brimmed with red impatiens. The look on her face and the way she leaned with crossed arms made her seem completely disdainful of the painter, or whoever she was thinking about. Her lover? Her father or mother?

Why was she so disdainful? And why did I find so much beauty in her disdain? *What happened to her?* I wondered. Who left her there? Had someone just loved her in that bed and gone? Run to Mexico? Or broken the law and been forced to leave? Who wanted to unfold her legs, her arms? Who led her to the bottom of the country and left her barefoot, hair a mess, and then ordered someone to paint her and call it beauty? Did she?

I stood motionless, gazing at her eyes, at the details of the lace, the shape of the flowers at her feet. Looking at her frozen-in-time beauty, I felt heat in my chest and my shoulders rise as my eyes went blurry. I don't know how much time passed as I let myself break there, undone by a nameless girl's stare. Eventually I heard a noise behind me and turned to see the docent eyeing me while dusting. I noticed her eyes, full of life. Though her skin was folded and loose, her hair silver, her eyes looked somehow young. She turned as I wiped my tears with the back of my hand, took a picture of the girl with my phone, and set it as my lock-screen before walking on.

The painting remained with me as I went alone through

the quiet rooms of red velvet chairs, silver tea sets, a shelf of brass bells. A plastic model of a cowgirl with a pool cue, a real meteorite, a painting of a burro delivering wood at an adobe house, a chuck wagon, displays of ornamental leather belts, a room of saddles, and another filled with porcelain figurines. One room organized as a historic hospital: two iron lungs, one adult- and one child-sized with doll heads sticking out of them, a wicker infant scale, arrowheads, shelves of Mimbras pottery, an old switchboard. I read every plaque, and that way it took a long time to walk each room. I thought about the girl, her white nightgown, her crossed arms and legs, her angered eyes. Sometimes I'd look down at her image on my phone as I held it, waiting for David to call. He didn't.

My stomach growled. David's burrito was in my bag, but I didn't want to leave the museum to eat it. I looked at my phone and the scornful girl glared back at me. It was quarter to four. If David had been right that his errand would take him only a few hours plus drive time back to Deming, he should have been back already. I walked through the museum and stood in front of the girl's portrait. I wished I could reach into the picture, tell her someone understood, but did I? How could I be sure unless I could unfold time and speak to her? I was staring, thinking about time, when I again heard the docent behind me. "We're closing in ten minutes." I turned. She held her feather duster in the crook of her elbow. "Did you find what you were looking for?" she said, voice dry as dust.

Her eyes stayed on me.

"I, uh, I don't know."

"One never does, do they?" she said, the corner of her mouth turning up and falling again as she turned to clean.

I sat on a bench at a war memorial next to the museum, waiting for David to call. I unwrapped his breakfast burrito and took out my notebook. The eggs were rubbery and cold. They squeaked as I bit into them. Thirty-two chews. Swallow. One bite after another. An hour passed. I arranged the letters of the war memorial plaque, "In honor of our veterans who fought in WWII," into 108 different words. Eventually, I must just have fallen asleep, because I remember jolting awake and the sun was low in the sky. A car of guys drove by slowly and held their heads out the window. Another. Was it the same car? Going even slower this time? Or was I starting to imagine things? I texted David:

"Where the hell are you? This is not my favorite town."

KAMPGROUNDS OF AMERICA · ROCK ISLAND, ILLINOIS

As everyone exits their RVs to make smoky fires over which they toast more marshmallows than any human should ever eat, I sit by bug-swarmed lantern light, wondering how many other people have found themselves at this very table. How many stories have been told, how much laughter has happened right here, in this place, as so many cars zoomed by?

How many have been so lucky to have a friend good enough to tell them to get it together?

I've had Mina.

David didn't have me.

EIGHT MONTHS AGO, OCTOBER

COLWYN COLLEGE · WATERTOWN, MAINE

Two weeks after the physics society meeting, my in-box presented me with a failure notice.

Mina and I had only one class together: Advanced Composition, designed for students with AP credit to meet the English requirement. For Mina, having to take Advanced Comp was pure joy. For me it was torture.

Not only did the eight a.m. class not jibe with my pregnancy-induced exhaustion, but I hated the assignments. One was "Write about a choice you made." I wondered, but didn't ask, if I could write about a choice I didn't *want* to make. Couldn't figure out how to make alone. Or how I chose to impulsively drive the Great Divide with a friend who was actually taking me on a drug run to Mexico. Somehow, I didn't think that would go over well with the Colwyn crowd, judging by how many of them wrote about their choice to come to Colwyn or why they gave up this or that sport. Hadn't anyone convinced their family to go to the basement during a tornado that knocked down their house? Or even just stopped for a homeless animal and ended up with a pet? Their choices frustrated me, and I was too frozen to be able to write about mine. So I didn't.

I was at Colwyn to study science. My goals in coming to college were simple: First to change the world and, second, to make enough money to pay back my loans. Why did English matter? I'd already learned to use a semicolon from Ms. O'Henry at Graceville High. Plus, I was pregnant; I wasn't supposed to stress. I had enough of that with my physics classes. It wasn't that I didn't study. It was just that I only studied for the classes I cared about. And I needed to stay in my major. When it came to English, I slept in. I skipped class. I just didn't hand in my essays. I figured I'd get through it somehow, but that morning, my in-box presented me with this:

To: scarlett.oliveira@colwyn.edu
CC: mmaudly@colwyn.edu
From: AcademicStandards@colwyn.edu
Subject: Mid-semester Failure Notice

Scarlett Oliveira has already missed six hours of class this semester. When she is in class, she does not participate in our conversation or appear to have done the reading. She simply neglected to hand in work and said not a word to me about the circumstances. It's likely too late to turn this around; however, I understand that Scarlett is a promising academic and a credit to Colwyn, so I am willing to help her provided she shows up in my office to discuss this matter.

Next in my in-box was a personal note from my advisor urging me to meet with Professor Bradshaw:

To: scarlett.oliveira@colwyn.edu
From: mmaudly@colwyn.edu
Subject: Mid-semester Failure Notice
Dear Scarlett,

I was surprised to see a failure notice come through for you today from Professor Bradshaw's Advanced Composition course. I urge you to meet with her as soon as possible to work something out in order to ensure your success in this very important course. I will remind you that failure to obtain at least a C- will result in your automatically being placed on academic watch for the spring semester, threaten the renewal of your scholarship, and may even result in your being dropped from the major. If there is anything I can do, let me know. In the meantime, know that Professor Bradshaw is a great professor and will figure out a way for you to get through this fairly. From your admissions interview, and your performance in my class, I know you to be a bright, dedicated student. Don't let yourself down.
Sincerely,
Morris Maudly
Professor of Physics

My vision was morning-blurry when I read the notice on my phone. 10:30. I'd just woken up. My eyes burned. How could doing bad in English drop me from the physics major? I pulled the blankets back over my head. When Mina opened the door and said, "'The world begins at the kitchen table. No matter what, we must eat to live,'" I flipped down my blanket, and she handed me some raspberry pastries and a coffee. "That's Joy Harjo, by the way."

"Huh?"

"The poet, Joy Harjo."

"Mina, I'm sorry. I can't deal with poetry right now—" A frown flashed across Mina's face. I waved my hands. "Just read this," I said, handing her my phone. As she read, I watched her face shift into concern.

"Oh shit, Scar." She sunk down on the floor next to my bed. "I did try to get you up this morning."

"I know." I flopped back on my pillow and closed my eyes. "I should've listened to you."

"Well, you can't go back in time, so go meet with her now. She'll be in her office. Always is. I've been talking to her about whether I should change my major and she's really nice." Mina pulled her knees up and dropped her chin onto them.

"But I worked my ass off to pass that test just so I wouldn't have to take this kind of annoying class."

Mina lifted her head. "You're angry."

"Of course I'm angry! Stop with the peer-leader stuff. I know what you're doing." I was trying to sound jokey but failing at that too.

"I get it—most colleges accept the AP exam. You don't think Bradshaw has anything to teach you. You're frustrated." Mina's voice was steady.

"I said stop it! I know you're trying to acknowledge my emotions so I'll feel better and calm down. It won't work. I'm pregnant and pissed."

Mina's eyes narrowed. She dropped her arms from her knees and rose to her feet. When she spoke, her voice was like I'd never heard it before.

"Oh right, you know all the tricks. You're above being helped by them."

Her words hung for a second before I spat back, "That's right. Now you're supposed to wait quietly until I offer up a solution."

"I'm not going to wait much longer," Mina said.

"Well then, you're right to reconsider your future. You'd be a shitty therapist. I'm pretty sure you're not supposed to raise your voice at clients. But, come on. I'm pregnant. I haven't really been awake at eight a.m. for two months! Even when I make it to class I'm not awake. Why can't I just write back and have that be enough? Why do I have to talk to anyone? Let alone some English professor?"

Mina backed toward the door as she spoke, waving her hands in the air. "First of all, you're not my client. You're my roommate and friend. Second, if you'd actually written the papers, that probably *would* be enough, but you haven't. And third, you're probably right—because you're pregnant and sleeping ten hours a day, I bet you're *way* more exhausted than the rest of us who are up until two a.m. every night studying, or even the ones who are up that late partying and still getting their asses out of bed for class. I'm not on your side with this."

I felt a sizzle under my ribs. I hadn't thought about how this place might be for other people. For Mina. I gripped my elbows. I don't know why the words that tumbled out of me were "You're not acting like a friend."

"Really? And you are?" I flinched under her laser stare. "Treating me like your therapist and insulting my dad's job? Not realizing that considering a change to my major is a big deal? I've wanted to be a therapist since sophomore year. Scarlett, just because I'm not pregnant doesn't mean I don't have stress. And that's true for everyone. College is hard. For all of us. I'm *trying* to be your friend because you don't really seem to have any others, and sometimes you're even fun—" I let go of my elbows as Mina's face changed for a split second before getting serious again. "But you aren't making it easy. Talk to Bradshaw. Just go. English professors aren't the lamest people on earth. Maybe they don't know about quantum mechanics or *solar super flares*, but they raise nice kids like me who bring you breakfast and listen politely when you complain about how you didn't read the graduation requirements and can't get out of bed."

"This is you listening politely? Really?" I said, feeling the sting of her words. The truth of them didn't matter. All I knew is they hurt.

Mina's hand was on the doorknob. Her voice was steady and her eyes charged.

"You think I'm being impolite, Scarlett, but I'm being a friend. When you figure that out, maybe I'll be around. Your chain of fuck-ups needs to end somewhere." She left and slammed the door.

"Mina," I said to the ring that echoed in the room.

I hate it when my friends are right.

I stood, afraid to climb the wide steps to Maine Hall, an old brick building at the campus's center, and home to Bradshaw's office. On a similar glorious, late October day a year—or possibly just a bend of time—ago, Cody and I stood gazing at Maine Hall. We whispered about how the campus seemed so calm, the opposite of MIT, which thrummed with city energy and seemed to bustle even in quiet corners. Maine was not what I thought I was looking for after Graceville, with all its quiet open space, but we convinced Mom we wanted to drive up to tour so we could miss another day of school.

I remember Cody whispering in my ear, "So this is what happens when you don't get into your top choice, huh? Looks pretty dead around here. I think *Graceville* might have more going on." I nodded. I didn't tell him I liked the smell of the ocean on the wind, or that the wide doorways and well-spaced maple and beech trees dotting the quad felt somehow familiar. I didn't admit to anyone that there was a part of me that loved the campus immediately. Not even to my mom. Not even to myself.

Still, when I decided to apply, it wasn't entirely a backup plan. Honestly, I didn't really think I'd get into MIT, but then why, when I passed it up for Colwyn, couldn't I admit that this place, this little school that not everyone in the world knew, was great and felt right to me from the start? At least until I arrived, and my body was occupied, and everything felt wrong.

I stood remembering that first feeling, wondering how different things would have been if I'd convinced Cody to apply to Colwyn too. Would he have gotten in? And if he did, would he be next to me now? Or would it have been one more rejection for him to punch pillows over? Cody. I did still miss him. But I couldn't tell him about this. Wouldn't. I didn't want him to have a say in it. So why did I keep hoping my phone would light up with David's name?

I pulled open the carved wooden door to Maine Hall, hoping I didn't look like a wreck. My eyes stayed red and my face was puffy for hours after I cried. I didn't want to look like I was seeking pity, and I could have waited, but I didn't want to lose the nerve. The thought of Mina coming to the room and finding me sitting there, not dealing, had me climbing the three flights of stairs to Bradshaw's office.

I knocked on Bradshaw's open door.

"Come in," she said, and added, not looking away from her computer, "Go ahead and sit down." She typed for a few seconds, then closed her laptop as I moved to a hardwood chair. Every possible space in the tiny office was lined with bookshelves. Light filtered in from the window and a lamp glowed above a stack of papers on her desk.

Bradshaw folded her hands. She wore her dirty-blond hair in a messy bun at the nape of her neck, and the style highlighted silver streaks from both temples. A chunky necklace in earth tones hung across her pale skin above a scoop-neck sweater. She seemed to radiate calm; it was immediately unnerving.

"So," she said, and then paused while she folded and unfolded her hands, "can you tell me what's been happening this semester?"

I looked out the window and noticed Mina, in her white pea coat, wave to two girls I didn't recognize.

I waited, Silent Scarlett, until she would say more. It worked.

"I've taught for a long time. The first year is a particularly difficult adjustment."

I took a breath, not even sure what to say but feeling like I had to say something. "I've just been having trouble . . ." But my voice trailed and my eyes went back to the window. Mina and the two unknown girls began stomping through maple leaves. I watched as they kicked them up into the air and imagined I could hear the crunch as they shuffled along. As if from very far away, I heard Bradshaw's voice:

"I'm sorry to hear that, but you need to know you're going to fail my class."

"Fail?" I said quickly. I'd done the math—papers were worth ten percent of the grade each, so even if I had zeros on the first two, a high C was still technically possible if I did the rest.

"Yes, Scarlett, fail. You haven't given me a single essay."

"I know but—"

She held up her hand. "I commonly see two kinds of students who fail Composition: Those who really can't cut it at Colwyn— but this is rare for an Honors Comp student. So you must fall into the second category: Those who found high school very easy and were able to get away with dashing off something last minute. Problem is, Scarlett, from you, I've not seen even dashed-off work. The reality is, the level of work required at Colwyn combined with the social distractions of college are difficult. Many students don't realize that papers must be written on Friday, Saturday, and Sunday night. And that, unlike assignments in some high schools, they aren't optional"—she paused— "for anyone." Then she turned her head toward the light of the window as if this were a speech she'd given many times before and even the body language was scripted.

I tried to count my breathing—*1, 2, 3, inhale*. But I couldn't focus on the numbers. I just kept thinking, Fail. Fail. Fail. Fail. Fail. I felt the tears behind my eyes and sunk my teeth into my lip to bite them away.

"I haven't been to one party," I managed to say. "I got an A on my physics midterm, and I've been recommended to work at the tutoring lab next semester by my advisor. I guess, maybe I've been spending too much time trying to learn 3D-modeling for the Society of Physics Students—"

"So, tell me, if physics isn't a problem, what is it about my course? And why haven't you come to me for help?"

Her classes weren't terrible. I just couldn't focus. I couldn't uncotton my mind at eight a.m. I didn't want to think about what was happening the way her class demanded.

Write about a choice you made.

Bradshaw rolled forward in her chair, leaned over the desk. "If you don't want to tell me, I can walk you over to Student Services. They're trained to assist students facing all kind of challenges."

"No—you don't need to— It's just . . ." I felt my eyes blur and I tried not to blink, but I couldn't, and the tears fell.

I took a deep breath and let the words "I'm pregnant" fall out. And as quickly as they did my eyes dried, as if the secret, now released, changed the elements around me.

Bradshaw nodded and tapped her pen as if she needed to recalculate who was sitting before her.

"I see," she said. "That's tough. Really tough, but not, Scarlett, something that hasn't happened before. You know, three out of ten American women will be pregnant before their twentieth birthdays. What happens with that pregnancy varies widely. You're not the first woman to sit in this chair and say those words to me, and it's unlikely you'll be the last." She paused. Her desk rattled. My foot was shaking. I uncrossed my leg and pressed my shoe into the floor to stop it.

Until that moment I felt like the only smart girl ever to get knocked up before heading to college. I wasn't one of those pregnant teens on reality TV. Girls like me got full scholarships. Girls like me changed the world. I couldn't imagine looking for the sensible skirts David kept saying I was doomed to. I wanted a life of living questions, a life committed to the quest for understanding. Until our road trip, I thought David did too.

I gazed out the window. David again. When I should have been in Bradshaw's office, trying to save my academic career. I breathed. *1, 2, 3. Inhale. 1, 2, 3, 4.* I heard Bradshaw say, "I want to help you if I can. There isn't enough time in the semester to make up all you've missed, but if you turn up for every class for the rest of the term, complete the final two essays and the exam, we can create an alternative assignment for the work you missed and you can pass the class. Does that sound reasonable?"

I nodded.

"Here is what we will do," she began again. "I'll issue an incomplete that will give you until the end of the spring term to finish the work . . ."

"But?"

"Just wait. I want you to start a journal, today, about this." She pressed a finger into her desk. "It should include any research you're doing as well as your emotional journey. Share as much of it with me as you're willing. You're welcome to write things you don't want to share in the journal, just turn down the corner of those pages and I promise to not read them."

"What do you mean, research?"

"Anything that gives you information, or helps you make decisions."

"Like if I read about the benefits of eating broccoli and stuff, for, you know—" I gestured haphazardly toward my middle.

Bradshaw blinked. "Anything that helps address your choices, so if that does, then yeah."

The room spun. I didn't want to think about decisions. Or make them. Or write about them. I just wanted to not screw up more. But Bradshaw was talking again. I gripped the chair and tried to focus.

"Then I want you to take that research and reflection and write it into a polished narrative. Do you have any questions?" It sounded like this was an assignment she'd given before. Maybe it was. Maybe I wasn't such a rare case after all.

"So, I just need to write a journal about this experience? And make it into an essay? Does it need to be an actual notebook?"

"Yes. I want you to be able to write wherever you are. Carry it with you."

I guess Bradshaw forgot laptops are portable.

Outside the window, Mina and the two girls were throwing leaves in the air now, letting them rain down. I didn't know these other seemingly good friends of hers. And Mina had so quickly recovered from our fight. It occurred to me, I was always saying no when she asked me somewhere that wasn't dinner or the cafe.

I realized the room had been quiet for too long and looked away from the window. I tried to think of something to say.

"I'd like to know if my plan for the incomplete sounds good to you? I wasn't sure if we had an agreement."

"Your plan, yeah. Yes. Whatever I need to do. I know I've screwed up. Bad pun intended." I half laughed, but the light in the room blurred. I dabbed my eyes, inhaled, and rose to leave.

Bradshaw smiled, then said, "And I can also help you find resources."

"For the paper or . . ." I gestured toward my belly again.

"Think of it as one and the same. I want you to do what's right for you, Scarlett. There isn't one answer in these situations." She looked down at her desk, and I had the feeling I'd just been dismissed, but my legs felt heavy. Part of me didn't want to leave.

"Okay," I said, and took a step toward the door, still confused by her calm, by her stoic transition from how to pass freshman English to my growing problem. No teacher had ever treated me this way, but then again, I'd never screwed up this badly before. I usually got extensions because I was presenting at a national conference on teen leadership, or had strep, but not because I'd actually screwed up.

And now I'd screwed up in a way that was difficult to correct.

And it seemed I was managing to screw up everything else along the way. I was in the doorway when Bradshaw said:

"Whatever you decide, you'll start to feel better soon. For me it was always around fourteen weeks. For some it's later, some a bit sooner. It won't be so hard to make it to the rest of class."

"Yeah," I said, "I read that too. Are those your kids?" I pointed to the picture on the wall behind her head.

She nodded. "Clara, William, and the little guy is Casper."

"How old?"

"Eight, five, and two, but the picture was last year." She paused. "I'll see you in class, Scarlett."

When I stepped into the hallway I knew Bradshaw was giving me something. I crossed the lawn now abandoned by Mina and her mystery friends. I kicked up leaves as I walked to the bookstore. Inside the too-bright shop, I navigated through sweatshirt displays to where school supplies lined the wall. I found a traditional composition book with wide lines for my Bradshaw project and splurged on a small black Moleskine journal for Mina. I left the Moleskine on her pillow and went for a jog. When I came back, she pounced on me the second I opened the door.

"Thank you! Thank you! Thank you!" she squealed, and then pulled back. "You are crazy sweaty, my friend!"

"Your friend?"

Mina smiled, full-dimple. "What kind of friends don't occasionally brawl?"

"Good point." I hugged her again, thinking of Hannah, how

many fights and makeups we'd had over the years. Once, I bailed on her to hang out with Cody, leaving her with nothing to do but devotions with her parents. To make it worse, it was her only Friday night off that month and even her little sister was out with friends. Ugh. I was so awful. I texted her a quick "How's it going?" before I went to the shower. I was keeping Hannah in the dark. But I missed her.

I carried my notebook around with me for a day, maybe two, without writing in it. Then I left it next to my bed, untouched. Mina had her Moleskine with her constantly and was always scribbling. Sometimes she'd ask, "How's the project going for Bradshaw?" And I'd say, "I'm bookmarking stuff on the computer." When I met with Bradshaw two weeks later to talk about all the research I was doing, she didn't ask to see the notebook. In fact, she never did.

So Mina would point while putting a record on and say, "What's that for? Are you collecting dust samples?"

"Yes"—I'd twist up my face—"everything's an experiment with me." Then I'd smirk and say, "I've got until end of spring term to make it look like I've been writing all along. I'll get it done."

NOW

IOWA STATE LINE

But, of course, I didn't. I gave up the notebook and went straight to my computer. I'm typing in my current now as Mina and I enter Iowa.

After the historical society closed, I began to fear my phone battery would run out and David wouldn't be able to find me if he returned. I heard an engine. I jumped up to walk back to the cafe where David had left me. It was the only place I knew. I waited, knowing he wasn't coming. Hands on my phone as the street shadows grew, mouth dry and palms wet. I tried to count my breaths. Couldn't. I texted my sister.

Scarlett: I think I need some help.

Jessica: Urgently? I'm in the middle of bedtime stuff here.

Scarlett: Maybe. Kind of. Yes, urgently.

Jessica: If you can hang on for five, I'll call you back.

When my phone rang five minutes later, I was pacing the sidewalk in front of the cafe, noticing myself being noticed by the waitress from the morning, her eyes questioning, or concerned.

I turned back toward the museum.

"What's up?" Jessica asked.

"Um, I'm in New Mexico."

"You're what?"

"I'm in New Mexico."

"What are you doing in New Mexico?"

"Look, don't tell Mom, she thinks I'm at Hannah's—"

"Scarlett!"

"Just listen, okay? My friend David and I were going for a drive and I don't know, Jess, we just didn't want to stop. But then—" I didn't know how to say the rest. It was hard to admit that David had left me alone in a town where I knew nobody, to seek drugs across the border. David, always walking the line between being an asshole and a saint. Still, this was really beyond him. It was the kind of thing people did when they no longer cared about friends, or whatever I was to him. My fingers tensed. How awful that must be, to be beyond caring.

"But then what?" Jessica said. She was angry.

"Then David decided to go across the border without me."

"What? What border? Do not tell me you mean the Mexico border."

"He had his passport. I didn't."

"Wait, Scarlett, did you just tell me that your friend left you somewhere in New Mexico and crossed the border without you?"

"Um, yeah."

"Holy shit."

"I'm okay," I said, but I was walking quickly, aware of how far apart the streetlamps were, far apart enough that whole swimming pools of darkness could swallow up any number of people waiting to do terrible things to an out-of-place eighteen-year-old girl.

"For now anyway! Seriously? Where are you exactly?"

"Deming."

"What? How long have you been alone?"

"Since about nine thirty this morning."

"Scarlett, that's like eleven hours. What have you been doing?"

"Well . . ." I looked down at the dust on my feet.

"Never mind. You need to get to a safe place. I'll figure it out and call you back. Tell me where you are exactly. A street address."

I turned back toward the restaurant, read the address from the door.

"Okay, Scar, sit tight."

"As if I could do anything else," I said, and hung up. I heard the bells on the restaurant door. The waitress held it open.

"Come on in," she said. "The water's free."

"Thanks, but I think I'm about to get picked up."

"You can wait in here," she said. I nodded and she disappeared into the kitchen while I stood behind the glass door.

A few minutes later the phone rang. My stomach dropped when I saw Jessica's name. It was what I was expecting, but I'd hoped for David.

"Okay, I've booked you a room in a hotel called the Desert Rose, and a cab should be there soon," she said.

"Actually, I think I see it now." A green cab was pulling up in front of the cafe.

"Everything is on my credit card. You owe me big-time."

"I know . . . Thanks." I turned toward the back of the restaurant to thank the waitress but I didn't see her. The bells sang as I left.

"If David's not back tonight, call Mom."

"Okay." I raised my hand to the cab, then slipped into the smoky interior.

"You're probably going to have to come clean to her about this, you know."

"I know." I covered the phone and mouthed a greeting to the driver.

"I'll let you figure that out, though."

"Thanks."

"You better be thanking me for the rest of your life."

"Right."

"The rest of your life, little sis."

"Yeah, Jess, I got it."

"Desert Rose?" the cabby said, and turned to me.

"Yep," I said, and then into the phone, "Thanks, Jess. I owe you big. Bye."

"Call me as soon as that jerk reemerges."

"Will do."

"And don't forget to double-lock the door and use the chain."

"Right."

"Seriously, Scar, you're in way over your head out there."

"I'm fine," I said.

"No, you're not. That's why I'm helping you."

"Right. Bye."

"Thank me again."

"Thanks, Jess."

"Okay, call me soon."

"Yep. Bye." A few minutes later the cabby pulled into the Desert Rose, a long rectangular motel painted pink with four cars spaced out in front of numbered doors. The windows had curtains pulled tight. The red VACANCY sign blinked.

In the empty motel lobby, there was a dish of mini candy canes on the counter and a bell. I stood looking at the brown carpets, the desk, and the Birds of North America clock on the wall, then rang the bell. An old man emerged from a door behind the counter, his pale skin pockmarked and sagging. He looked me up and down uncomfortably and said, "Oliveira? Here you go, room seven, all paid for." He took the key off a pegboard where it hung by a wooden key chain with the number seven written on it in black marker.

"Checkout time is eleven a.m.," he barked after me. I could feel his gaze on my ass as I walked out the door, and on my breasts as I passed the picture window at the front of the motel. It made me feel like I was covered in fleas. I locked the door to room seven behind me, bolted it, and pressed the chain into the latch. I kept one hand on my phone so I would feel the vibration if David called or texted. I texted again:

"Seriously, David, where are you?"

I held the phone. Nothing. I peeled back the polyester cover on the bed, lay down. It almost felt good, but I couldn't relax. I turned on the TV, flipped through the channels. I watched half an episode of some cop show where the girl is found dead the morning after her prom and everyone is trying to figure out why. I moved a chair in front of the door. I pressed call on David Warren's name. The robotic voice said, "The customer you are trying to reach is currently unavailable."

No surprise. David was out of service. The room smelled like Lysol. I was hungry again. I filled a plastic cup in the bathroom with water and took a gulp. It tasted like rust, but I drank three cups anyway. One by one I let the cellophane-wrapped peppermint candies from the pillows dissolve on my tongue until all four were gone. Where the hell was David? I stared blankly at the lights from the TV until my eyes lost the ability to stay open.

I woke to my phone ringing and vibrating David's name in blue lights.

"Scarlett I'm so sorry are you okay where are you?" he said in one breath.

"Where are *you*? You shithead," I managed to say despite my dry throat.

"Almost to Deming. You okay?"

"Yes, I'm okay, no thanks to you. I'm here where you left me, remember? Well, not exactly where you left me. I'm at a motel called the Desert Rose. My sister saved me."

"I'll be there in a few minutes."

"Whatever," I said. "I'm not going anywhere." I hung up.

I lay on the bed and watched the clock.

Five minutes later my phone rang.

"I'm here."

"Come to room seven," I said. I watched through the peephole of the door as David slumped toward the room. Something was wrong with the way he walked. I slid the chair away and undid each lock, keeping my eye to the peephole to watch David limp to the building. He leaned against the doorjamb as I opened the door. When he stepped into the room, he was not only limping. His face was cut, and he held his shoulder at an odd angle.

"D—" I wanted to say something harsh, something angry, but he looked broken. "What happened to you?"

"Oh, just a little run-in . . . some guys . . ." He trailed off.

"What?"

David shook his head, faked a laugh. "It's nothing, Scar, really."

"It doesn't look like nothing," I said. I hadn't forgiven him, but he was hurt. He reached up and touched my chin. I turned away.

"Hey, Scarlett," he said as I went to the bathroom and wet two washcloths. "I'm sorry," I heard over the noise of the water.

"You should be, you shithead," I said. "Now lie down." I carried the dripping cloth back to the bed, lifted up his T-shirt, and gently pressed on his shoulder where a cut had begun to scab along his collarbone. I ran the cloth along the hollow carefully and fought the desire to press my face there. *Why would I want to be close to him now?* I continued cleaning the wound. Then I unhooked his belt, unbuttoned his pants, and pulled them off to see the source of his limp. His knee was swollen to twice its normal size. "D—do you need to go to the hospital? I think—"

"I'll be okay." He grimaced. "Nothing my brothers haven't done before. I think the kneecap just popped out. I slid it back in."

"That can't be good." I dabbed the washcloth across his knee. He lay there, eyes half closed, teeth clamped hard over his lip. He was in pain. I pressed harder.

"I'm sorry," he said again.

"I don't forgive you, you ass."

He reached for my hand. "I'm surprised you let me in."

"I need a ride home."

"Still, you didn't have to."

"I know," I said. And I don't know why—maybe because I'd been alone and terrified all day, but I still wanted to be close to him. Even though he was the one who'd *left* me alone and terrified. It didn't make sense. None of it made sense. I managed to pull my hand from his. I went to the bathroom and ran the washcloth under water, trying to decide if I wanted to resist the gravitational field that was David or let myself be pulled in, momentarily obliterated.

I sat on the bed, my back to him.

"Scarlett, I'm sorry."

"Not enough, D," I said, and slid under the sheet, my back to him still. But once I was there, I could feel the heat of his legs, the weight of his silence. So I rolled over. I softly kissed the purple of his shoulder, and then his lips. He put his hands in my hair. It wasn't that I'd forgiven him. I hadn't. It was that—I wasn't alone. I was in a hotel room with him, and being near him, in bed with him, everything just—*surged*.

"I thought you'd—"

"Shh," I said, "you're an ass, but you probably know as well as I do this isn't happening after tomorrow anyway."

His face got dark then, and there was something in the corner of his eye that might have been a tear. I can't be sure.

And so an hour later, I finally remembered to call Jessica to tell her David had come back. That was really shitty of me. She was putting me up in a hotel, trying to figure out if she needed to get to New Mexico to get me. I should have let her know the minute I'd heard from David. Maybe it was the exhaustion and the drugs and the stress. I don't know—maybe I wanted to be worried about by someone just for a little bit. I felt a stab of guilt when I heard her voice. It was two a.m. and she was clearly wide-awake.

"Scarlett, are you okay?"

"Yeah, David's here." I stood at the foot of the bed, watching his eyes flutter closed.

"Where the hell was he?"

"Caught up at the border." David turned on his side and flinched.

"I don't get what he was thinking."

"I know." I turned to the window as David rustled again.

"Look—Scarlett, we're going to have to talk about this. But later."

"Right, we're going to sleep now."

"Okay. Leave as soon as you wake up."

"We will."

"Scar, this is the last favor I'm going to do for you for a very long time."

"Thanks, Jess. I get it."

"Just drive safely and get your ass back home."

"Okay."

"I love you, Scarlett."

"Love you too, Jess."

"So much that I stayed up half the night worrying about you."

"I know. I'm sorry. I really am." I dropped the drapes and turned back to the bed. David was breathing steadily. Asleep.

"You should be sorry."

"Got it."

"No, you don't, you have no idea what missing sleep means to a parent."

"I know, I know, but in fifteen years I will call you and tell you how sorry I am again. For now you need to accept my half understanding because that's all I've got."

"I guess I'll have to."

"Bye, Jess. Thank you," I said, and hung up before I could hear her own goodbye.

I set my phone on the nightstand. I watched David sleeping. I wondered if he'd gotten what he wanted, who he had a number from, and what had been going on all winter when Hannah and I were watching movies and David was off with Cody somewhere swallowing the dark.

TEN MONTHS AGO

DEMING, NEW MEXICO

The morning after David returned from whatever happened across the border, the light through the windows was bright despite the vinyl-backed curtains.

"It's better to travel hopefully than to arrive," David said.

I sat up in bed. "I think arriving in the shower is going to beat my traveling there."

David winced, peeling himself from the sheets. The cut on his head had seeped into the pillow and when he tugged, the crust stuck to the white pillowcase and fresh blood appeared across his temple.

"That looks like it hurts."

David just shook his head. "Funny thing," he said, "I should feel like shit right now. Shoulda felt like shit that morning we woke up in the picnic shelter too. Must be something about you," he said, not looking at me. "I wish there was more traveling. I don't want to arrive."

I know we should have started off right away, skipped the showers and everything. But we were two teenagers in a hotel room. I still had not forgiven him; I knew his leaving me was unforgivable. But we were leaving New Mexico that day, Graceville soon after. We weren't suddenly going to be boyfriend and girlfriend across the country. The storm that gathered inside me when I was close to him—despite what he'd done—I wanted to be in that storm for a while longer, that solar surge, every part of me, of him, lit up, suffused. So it's maybe not shocking we took our time leaving that room, and when we finally did, we were steamy, wet, and starving.

We checked out at eleven and went to the first drive-through we saw. David pulled up to the menu board, and said, "We'll take one of everything."

"One of everything?" said the voice through the crackling speaker.

"Yes, I can read them off if you'd like. David read from the top of the menu and worked his way down: "One breakfast sandwich with bacon on an English muffin and one on a bagel, one with sausage also on an English muffin and one on a bagel . . ."

"Okay, I got the idea," the voice said. "One of everything."

"That's right!" David looked at me and grinned.

"Pull up to the second window please."

When we did, David presented his credit card. We laughed as we were handed bag after bag. David passed them to me one after the other. I filled up the floor in front of me and then the back seat. When the last of the bags arrived, David started the car and said, "Hand me one thing at a time. I want to taste it all." I took a bite of a breakfast sandwich and handed it to him. He tasted a mouthful and then threw the rest out the window.

"Come on! What was that for?"

"The gophers." He held out his hand. "Next."

"No way." I held on to the bag.

"Please! I'm still hungry."

"Don't throw it out the window!"

"Scout's honor." David turned to me, two fingers raised.

"You are not a Scout," I said, handing him another breakfast sandwich as he smiled, stuffed it between his teeth, and rolled up the window. And though his look had made me laugh, and though the sky was azure-beautiful, there was a dead ache inside me. Still, I smiled as we drove and drove through the flat sage and on until we entered the mountains that once seemed so distant, and our ears began to pop and there were signs that pointed to views of the great continental divide. And an ache grew in my chest that counting my breaths couldn't stop.

So much of Mina's life is unknown to me—it took her till the end of October to hint at her checkered gymnast past. I just learned a few days ago that she only drinks fine wine, and a few weeks ago that she was born in Iowa. I only lived in one place until Colwyn, but Mina moved to New York when she was three. Now we're pulling into the city where Mina was born. Her mom gave her a list of landmarks to explore as we left their house, places that might ignite neural pathways locked deep in her brain—the Iowa City Public Library, their old University Heights apartment, the park with a merry-go-round.

When you grow up in a place like Graceville, so much about your friends is just a given. You know them, their parents, their sisters and brothers. And so to realize over and over that David had secrets more numerous than wallet-size photographs of himself, it meant maybe I never knew anyone at home like I thought.

New friends like Mina can unfold their stories slowly. The

people I know now, most of them will never see Graceville, my house, the trails behind it, the bench where I stretched, where we played. The people. But Mina will witness my landscape, minus David. Mina will know my great divide.

SEVEN MONTHS AGO, EARLY NOVEMBER

COLWYN COLLEGE · WATERTOWN, MAINE

About a month after I met with Bradshaw, I was in Elements of Electromagnetism trying to warm my hand, still cold from the snowy walk across campus because I'd only been able to find one glove. I was sitting there rubbing my hand on my jeans, trying to listen to Maudly's review for the midterm, when the lights blinked once, twice, and the classroom went dark.

It was strangely peaceful for one dim, snow-muffled second. Then:

"STORM PARTY!" Harold, the class TA, shouted from the front of the room, just as the emergency lights flickered on.

Maudly adjusted his bolo tie. "I guess we'll have to stop there. For those of you who don't know about Colwyn's Storm Parties, Harold will fill you in. Don't forget to save time to study. I'll see you Tuesday." Maudly clicked shut his briefcase and backed out the door, a goofy smile on his face.

Harold stood with hands on hips in front of the whiteboards. "The only time classes are canceled," he said, "is when the power goes out. We celebrate this rare-ish occurrence with a Storm Party held in the student apartments—so I'm a host.

Come on over." He walked to the door, and a bunch of freshmen and sophomores followed like he was the pied piper of Colwyn. Excited laughter punctuated the shuffle of backpacks and the clomp of boots. He held the door open to the hall, where a river of students chanting "Storm Party!" flowed. Courtney and I were the last ones in the room.

"You're coming, right?" Harold asked.

"I don't know," I said over Courtney's "Sure."

"I don't drink," I added.

"You don't have to. It'll still be fun."

I shrugged.

"Come on, Scarlett, what else are you going to do right now?" His nose crinkled. He looked genuinely confused.

"Study for the exam so I can keep my scholarship?"

"I can't allow it. The emergency lights are too dim. It'd be terrible for your eyes. Come on—come with me. Bert will be there. And Courtney just said she's coming. And your roommate too, I bet." His hand hovered in the air like he was trying to usher us toward the door without touching us.

"Yeah." Courtney set her red cloche hat on her head. "Storm Parties are legendary. Don't miss this, Scarlett." Her voice was almost scolding as she tugged on fuzzy mittens. This together with her long wool coat made her look like she'd stepped off a 1920s sleigh ride. She looked excellent. I pulled on my one glove. My stomach felt fizzy. Like I was starving, but no way would I dare to eat.

"They *are* legendary," Harold said. "Some years there aren't any. And now, the first one before Thanksgiving! It's epic! My first year, we had five Storm Parties, and one lasted two days." Harold's eyes shone.

"Okay, fine," I said. "But I might leave after five minutes." *Because I might have to vomit.*

"Bet you'll make it for at least ten," he said.

"Fifteen is the ideal brain break, so let's figure I've got about twelve-point-seven-five minutes for the party, then it's back to the books," I said, clutching my bag to the burn in my belly and following him out.

Harold took long strides into the thickly falling snow. I was determined to match his pace, but Courtney remained a few steps behind, turning her head up to the sky, or holding out a hand to catch snowflakes on her fuzzy red mittens. She was from San Francisco and she'd seen snow in the mountains, but she'd never actually been in a storm. Campus buzzed with the energy of a new, wild northern winter. We crossed the quad to the senior "apartments"–glorified dorms identical on the out-side to the brick housing Mina and I lived in, but inside they had real kitchenettes and living rooms attached to four single bedrooms. As Harold pushed open the door, I saw that they were redone with modern furniture and brightly painted walls. A small lobby opened into a hall already roiling with people chanting "Storm Party!" A wave of girls from Courtney's dorm swept her off, and I stepped closer to Harold.

He shook the snow from his hair and raised his voice over the din. "Because of my years on CRAC–"

"Why doesn't somebody *do* something about that acronym?" I shouted back.

"Ha! Too late—it's tradition. And Colwyn loves its traditions." His voice boomed.

"Right. It couldn't be Colwyn Campus Housing Community."

"CCHC? Who would remember that?" Harold screwed up his face. "Anyway, in case you're wondering how I ended up in the best suite of apartments, it was my years of service to CRAC. You should join. It has some perks."

"That would involve leaving my room for something other than science." And, I thought, maybe throwing up on someone's couch.

"I hate to break it to you, Colorado, but you're not in your room *now*." Harold reached the end of the first-floor hallway and pushed open the door. I swallowed hard.

"Welcome to the best apartment on the entire Colwyn campus," he said, bowing for me to pass.

Inside, there was a large living space already crowded with people.

"This is the best apartment?"

"Look," he said, leading me to the window by the kitchenette. "Ocean view." He pointed.

I squinted into the gray sky and snow. "I don't see anything."

"You'll have to come back on a clear day. I promise—it's the only room on campus with an ocean view."

"Wouldn't the room above you also have an ocean view?"

He smiled and leaned back to look at me. "Yeah, but they have to walk upstairs."

"*Hal!*" a guy shouted, squeezing by. Harold slapped his hand, and the guy smacked Harold's back, and I wondered why guys had to hit each other all the time.

"So I stopped by the 3D printer lab," Harold said, leaning toward me so I could hear him above the party, "and there weren't any atomic key chains running. Weren't you and Courtney going to have those printing by now?"

I peered out the window again, not looking at him. "We wanted to, but—" I paused, took a breath. How many things can I screw up in a few short months? "Isn't this party totally against the policies of CRAC?"

He squinted at me. "Beer is allowed in the apartments because most of us are twenty-one anyway."

"I don't see you carding."

"Well, the thing about Storm Parties is, it's so dark with only these weird yellow emergency lights, it makes it hard to check IDs." He looked at me for a second like he was going to say something else, but then he turned toward the kitchenette.

"Really?" I said, following him to the refrigerator. He pulled out a case of Natural Ice.

"Round of Natty Ice on the house!" Harold shouted, handing cans out. I remembered Hannah and me handing out beer at Graceville parties, parties where we knew everyone. Where we could call parents and friends if things got too crazy. My airway tightened.

When the box was empty, Harold tossed the cardboard in a corner and tapped the top of his can. Then he was suddenly waving, a huge grin on his face. "Hey Mina! Have a Natty Ice?" He offered her his can. Mina slipped between us to give him a quick hug.

"Urgh, no. Why do you buy the grossest alcohol in history?" Mina asked.

"Because I'm a classy guy," Harold said. "I believe you two know each other?"

"What are you doing here?" Mina put her arm around me and squeezed.

"Harold convinced me a Storm Party is legendary and not to be missed."

"Wow, he must possess talents of persuasion previously unknown to me."

"Mina, have you seen the atomic key chain demos? Scarlett keeps forgetting to bring me one," Harold said to her.

"Um, no," Mina said. "She hasn't shown me one either." I laced my fingers through Mina's and pulled her around me like a blanket.

"Why not, Colorado?"

"Weren't Courtney and I supposed to do this together? Why aren't you interrogating her?" I said.

"I wasn't interrogating."

"She only feels like you were interrogating," Mina said, slipping her arms off me, "because she hasn't made the key chains and feels guilty."

"Mina!" I turned to face her.

"Well, it's true. You need to tell him at some point. Break is coming up and you still need to take orders." She moved a half step in front of me as Harold said, "What happened?"

"Our girl here has had a lot going on," Mina said.

"If it's classes, you know I can help," Harold offered.

"I'm fine," I said. And Mina shook her head. Mouthed "No she's not" to Harold.

He swallowed hard. His hand, the one with the can in it, went to his forehead. "Oh, god, Scarlett. I'm so—dense sometimes. Taking on the fund-raiser your first year is a lot. Too much. You're even in Elements! Man, I barely passed physics 1 as a first-year. What was I thinking?"

"You weren't?" Mina said, tongue peeking between her lips.

I twisted my earring. The star physics senior had not only started in physics 1 but barely passed it? Boys. I'd had perfect scores on all my Elements quizzes so far and I was going to nail that midterm. I itched to study. And I needed some crackers. Quick.

"Aw," Harold continued, the can still pressed to his forehead. "I wasn't thinking. Maudly wanted me to help you guys get through the year, but in that meeting, it was only about how Chaun and me, and the other seniors, how all of us have grad apps due next month. Not what the first year was like." He took the can from his forehead and locked his green eyes on mine. "Scarlett, I'm so sorry."

"And maybe a little sexist?" Mina offered a smile.

"I, uh, try to fight the programming"—he shook his head—"but sometimes it's deep. Can you forgive me? I'll help you and Courtney, or I'll—I don't know. Damn. Why didn't you, like—" He waved a hand in front of him. "No." He shook his head. "Sorry again. You didn't need to do anything. I'm supposed to help you."

"Be careful or they might take away your Welcome Week pin," I said.

Harold tried to smile but looked down. We stood there for a second, watching our shoes, the toes wet from melted snow. Then Bert appeared and Harold took him back to the fridge to get a beer.

"Oh, a boy who recognizes he screwed up!" Mina breathed, grabbing my elbow. "And he likes science stuff. *You* like science stuff. He could be a friend. Or . . . *more*." She gave me her puppy eyes. "He's cute."

"No way."

"Oh. Wait." She paused. "You're really not into him?"

I shook my head. My stomach fizzed.

"Then you wouldn't mind if Harold and I . . . ?" Mina's forehead blushed pink.

"What? Hang out? *Date?*"

The pink grew.

"Hook up?"

She shoved me lightly, and I felt the contents of my stomach slosh. "Of course I don't mind, but"—and I tried to make my voice sound jokey like hers—"are you really into kind-of-sexist, clueless dudes?"

"He's trying," Mina said, defensive. "He apologized to you like six times just now."

"I heard twice, but yeah, if you're into him, I won't judge," I said, tipping my head down. "Maybe he's trying."

She smiled with both dimples, and the pink spread across her cheeks.

"And if he's fooled us, if he's just trying to *look* like he's trying, well, that's okay too. You know, we all get with an asshole from time to time. Look at me, still pining." Mina knew David still hadn't texted me back.

"Well, you, like, have reasons." Mina's eyes went to my middle. Reminding me I needed crackers. Crackers. I needed to get back to our room.

"So, what do I do?" Mina leaned close to my ear. "How will he know I'm interested? Do I just talk to him, or—"

"Just be yourself, Min."

She pulled out a tube of red lipstick and began to reapply.

"Yeah, you've got the idea." I smiled. "And now it's time for my cracker feast and solo study party."

Mina air-kissed my cheek, and I watched as she crossed

the room and leaned into the window, looking for the ocean between Harold and some brunette. Harold leaned away and turned to smile at me. I waved, pointed to the door. He gave me a thumbs-up.

The next morning, Mina brought me an atomic key chain taped to my coffee cup.

I gaped. "Where did you get this?"

She looked pleased. "As soon as the power came back on, Harold got Bert, Courtney, and a few people I never met to finish up the project. Dude feels genuinely guilty. Courtney and Harold designed the model, but we needed to make adjustments to it because the first print looked like a bird's nest. It took all night. Anyway, Harold wanted you to collect orders, but I know you don't really talk to people, so I can go around the dorms for you if you want," she said.

"Min, I'll get the orders myself. I should do *something*." A shiver went through me knowing Courtney stayed up all night to help. I should have been there. I was as bad as Harold if I let Courtney and the others do all the work. I rubbed my fist into my eyes. "So if you were with Harold so long," I said, "did you, you know, get anywhere?"

"Um, no." She turned to flip through her records. "But I did hear him apologize to Courtney like seven thousand times about saddling first-years with extra work. Also, I can recite seventy-eight poems to keep science nerds awake waiting for a 3D print."

"Well, baby steps," I said. "Who won't eventually get turned on by poetry?"

"Wait, did you just admit that you like the poems?" Mina bolted upright, purple nails shielding her unlipsticked mouth.

I just held out a packet of saltines to her and smiled. "Want a cracker?"

NOW

POWESHIEK COUNTY, IOWA

"So all this is corn, huh?" I say, looking out at the fields of end-less green sprouts. My teeth are filmed with syrup from all the soda Mina and I have been drinking. My laptop is open in my lap.

"Yep. And all these signs along the road?"

I look out at the fields. Nod.

"Those are the companies who own the seeds."

"Yeah." I let out a breath. "Science can be creepy sometimes— but the scientists, they're doing it because they want to help. It's complicated feeding seven billion people."

"Maybe you could figure out how to feed the world without splicing Roundup into everything we eat."

"I'm not going into Frankenplants. That's biology. And you know, I'd be more into lasers, or maybe time travel," I say, watching the seed signs blur together as we fly past.

"God, it would be so cool if you could figure out time travel. What would you do if you could go back?"

I inhale *1. 2. 3.* "I don't know."

Hours and hours after David and I had eaten so much fast food we nearly burst, we were driving through the purpling shadows of the mountains, the headlights just starting to show circles on the road. David put in a tape of classical guitar. We listened as the last of the honey-colored light dispersed into gray.

"This crepuscular light," David said.

"Crepuscular? Really?"

"You studied SAT vocab too."

"I did, but I try not to talk like it."

"You so talk like it, Scar." He shook his head. "Anyway, dusk— is that better?"

"Yep."

"Dusk always reminds me of when I was little and— You remember how I had asthma attacks?" David glanced at me.

"Yeah."

"I would imagine an angel sitting on my chest," he said, spreading one hand across his T-shirt, long fingers, sunken nail-beds, a couple fingernails bitten down too low. "I told myself

I couldn't breathe because my lungs were full of the feathers from her wings. The angel was there to keep me alive by pulling the feathers she'd lost out of my lungs. When she flew away, I'd be able to breathe again. I imagined it so often, it's as if it actually happened. And not having enough air—it's dusky, you know. To have not enough light or air. My angel of gray light and feathers, I called her."

"Your crepuscular angel, huh?"

David smiled. His skin was pale.

"I remember one time you couldn't breathe in gym," I said.

"There were lots of times."

"But this time you actually turned blue. They couldn't find your inhaler and finally Joey Trujillo gave Coach Keyes his. I remember him saying he couldn't give it to you because it wasn't yours, but kids started screaming—it really looked like you were going to die—and Joey grabbed the inhaler from Coach and pressed it to your mouth."

"Yeah, that time. The ambulance came. I imagined coughing feathers all the way to the hospital."

"But it doesn't happen anymore, right?"

"I'm one of the lucky ones. I outgrew it. No one can really tell you how bad it sucks to not be able to breathe. I don't remember my last attack, but I remember this dream I had right around the time they stopped for good."

"Yeah? What?"

"The angel was there. She was beating her wings and I

watched the long feathers. They sort of . . . shimmered." He swallowed. "She said she was sorry. She'd lost them inside me when I was very small, but she had them all back now and so she was leaving. Then she hugged me and suddenly I was awake; my blinds had been left open. I blinked into white light. A blur of white light."

"Weird."

"Yeah, imagination is a powerful thing," David said, touching the scab at his temple.

"So, are you going to tell me what happened?"

"When?"

"In Mexico."

"I did—just a run-in with some guys."

"That's not a story."

"Sure it is," David said. The guitar music stopped, so he popped in another tape. "This is my favorite," he said, and sang along, "Could you find me? Would you kiss-a-my-eye, lay me down, in silence easy to be born again."

NOW

JASPER COUNTY, IOWA

Despite the fact that I don't even believe in this kind of thing, there's a part of me that wonders, when he was alone in the dark on Mine Gulch, when he was taking his last dose, was his dream angel there? Was she watching? I know opioids impact the parts of the brain that control breathing; I know overdose victims' lungs fill with fluid. I have this image of David at dusk with an angel on his chest, cramming her feathers down his throat. His breathing growing slower and weaker, his lungs filling with water, fluid dripping from his nose and mouth. His punishing angel, all that medicine he didn't need.

SEVEN MONTHS AGO, NOVEMBER

COLWYN COLLEGE · WATERTOWN, MAINE

About a week after the Storm Party, Mina put both hands on my shoulders and said, "I'm not going to stand by until you strangle this thing in the dorm bathroom, so I made you an appointment at a pro-choice adoption agency."

"That's a thing?" I slipped out of her grasp.

"Well"—Mina cocked her head—"they said it was, anyway, and they rated top non-coercive according to this website I found."

"What coercive behavior will they not engage in?" I said.

"Apparently if you mention abortion, they won't say your soul is already burning in hell for thinking it's an option, which it is, until January. It also means, if you decide you want to parent, they'll support you."

"Well, that's something," I said.

"Yeah, I thought it was worth a try. Since you seem to not want one."

I pressed my palms into my eyes. "Mina, I don't. I don't know." The orange light behind my hands glowed.

"Why not? I see—" I felt her sit down next to me on the bed.

"I see you complaining about exhaustion, you can barely make it to class, and well, it seems if you wanted to end this, you'd know by now?" A question. Mina touched my shoulder. "But." Her voice was lighter. "What do I know about decisions? I can't even figure out my major."

"You will." I took my palms off my eyes and looked at her.

"You know, you can be pro-choice and *not* get an abortion, right? That's what the choice part's about?"

I nodded, didn't say anything.

"I'm sorry if I'm . . . rushing you or whatever. It just seems like you need help."

I didn't know what I needed.

"Anyway, I'll come with you—you know, to the agency—in case they have an agenda and try to shove lies down your throat for their cause." Mina put her nails in her mouth and immediately pulled them out, examining the yellow paint for chips.

"Thanks, Min," I said.

Should I know what to do by now? I wondered. Is inaction a choice?

I thought of the thing that was part me. Part-maybe-David-or-Cody. The little remnant of another life. My hidden child. Like Einstein.

No. Like Einstein's first wife, who had to hide their shame, their first child. Who never became the scientist she'd hoped to be.

Did I know my decision? Was it too hard to admit?

Mina made an appointment. She was trying to help. The

agency was on the outskirts of Portland, and Mina would skip class to drive me. It lessened the strain of gravity a bit to know I'd go and confront this with her there.

But I still wondered, had I already made my choice? And if I did, how?

"You know you're losing two hundred fifty-eight dollars by skipping this one class," I said as she drove.

"Some things are worth it." She eyed me sideways. "Did you run your loss totals on English?"

"Of course. I taped the number to my keyboard in case I ever want to skip again."

"See, you can cope."

"Maybe," I said. "The summer before sophomore year was bad. I'd stress about fall classes and Step-up to STEM. I felt like my lungs were operating at twelve percent capacity most of the time."

"Hey! Sophomore year sucked for me too! That's when I stopped gymnastics."

"Ouch."

"Yeah, it hurt. But I'm better off. Gymnastics destroys the body." She leaned over the steering wheel like she was hugging it. "But once I couldn't compete, I had nothing to do. No friends either."

"Really?" I said, having trouble imagining Mina without friends.

She shrugged. "They were always at practice and meets."

"That sucks, Min. I'm sorry. It was like the opposite for me. I had too much to do—Step-up to STEM every day, planning for it every night. Track. Robotics. I had no time for anything." I took a breath. Thinking about that time was still hard, which was funny because things at the moment were way worse. "I had a thriving nonprofit in my control, but I still needed to pass pre-calc."

"See, you're a superstar."

I shook my head. "I'd run home from talking science with ten-year-olds and sit in my dark room and watch the walls get bigger. Mom sent me to a therapist, but the most helpful thing came from Dad. He looked at me one day and said, 'Scarlett, you know how I can run into a burning building even though you and your mom are counting on me to come home? I take a deep breath. Then I charge.'"

"Your dad sounds fierce."

"He's well-trained. But I did some research, and his breathing thing is scientifically backed, so I started counting my breaths, and most of the time, when I feel my chest start to tighten, I can stay inside my body and the room doesn't shrink."

"See?" Mina said pulling into a parking space. "You got this."

She kept saying that. But I'd never faced anything like this. Before, all my stress came from the good things I'd done.

The agency was in an old brick Colonial-style house. If not for the sign out front, you'd think it was still a residence. There was a wraparound porch, complete with a white swing, and a plant stand housing a weathered mum. We skittered in through the storm doors and were greeted by a woman behind a table, a waiting room designed to look like a formal sitting room. My arm hairs rose.

"Can I help you?" she asked.

"This is Scarlett, she's here for a three thirty." Mina spoke for me. It allowed me to breathe.

"Scarlett?" A woman wearing a black skirt of sensible length and heels appeared in the hallway. I rose and looked questioningly at Mina, who stood next to me, arms crossed.

The woman held out her hand. "Hi Scarlett. I'm Sherrie," she said with a red-lipped smile.

"Hi." I shook her hand limply. "This is my roommate, Mina."

"You can both follow me," Sherrie said. At the top of the stairs she turned into the second room. It was furnished with blue wingback chairs and a broad oak desk. There was a bay window at the side of the room with a built-in padded bench.

"Have a seat wherever you'd like." Mina and I sat on the window seat. Sherrie rolled her wooden desk chair across the room to sit opposite.

"How are you?"

"Pregnant," I said. My stomach growled.

"I assumed." She smiled. "Hungry?" I nodded as she rose and brought out a box of crackers to place on a tray. "Tea?"

"No thanks," Mina and I said together as I took the crackers and turned my head to look out the window.

"So you're considering your options?" she asked.

"That's why I'm here," I said, my eyes looking out the window. I imagined I was cradled in the branches of the tree. I didn't even realize I might have sounded rude.

"Actually, I found your organization online and thought she'd benefit from talking to a professional. That is, assuming you're *actually* pro-choice. I don't need you feeding this girl lies about how if she has an abortion she'll regret it for all of her days, be unable to bear children in the future, and then die lonely, destined to burn in the depths of hell."

"Mina!" I said.

"What?" Mina put her hands out as if it was normal for her to be on the attack.

But Sherrie smiled, and a bell dinged on her bracelet as she said, "We actually will do none of those things here. Being pro-choice means supporting a woman in whatever choice is best for her at each particular moment of her life. Some women, over their lifetime, might make all three choices. It's individual. So Scarlett, tell me, how did you feel when you found out you were pregnant?"

"Um." The building creaked. "Frozen?"

"She really didn't want to face it," Mina said.

"Thank you, Mina." Sherrie turned and put up one hand like a stop sign as Mina's lips disappeared into her mouth. "But it's important that I hear from Scarlett." She looked at me, her face open. "How did frozen feel?"

"I don't know. I was . . . valedictorian. I never thought—I mean, first I messed up my birth control, but then, I don't even know who the father is." My cheeks burned. "This whole thing—being here. You. This isn't me."

"No known father is something we can work with, Scarlett. There are a few legal hoops, but it's not unusual." Her voice was calm and quiet.

"Not a problem?" How could she sit there not judging me when I judged myself constantly? "Well, it's not the Christ child," I said, "but I wouldn't know without a DNA test, and I'm not really in contact with the sperm donors right now. Could I *say* it's the Christ child?"

"I'm afraid not. I had a client do that once and it was too hard to track down God for a signature," Sherrie said, the corners of her mouth turning up.

"Damn, it would be cool for the kid to have my name on the birth certificate and then 'God.' It might eliminate some identity questions in the teen years."

"But it could complicate things," Mina offered. "Imagine having to live up to God as a parent."

"Hard to understand why God placed you for adoption too," I said.

"Nah, that would be easy—God always knows what's best." Mina smirked.

"You know, that's what Hannah always says. My best friend from home," I said to Sherrie. "But I never believed her." I felt Sherrie's and Mina's eyes trying to read me. I thought of Hannah cheering me up with brownies, urging me on when we ran together. I missed her, even if I would never tell her.

Mina cleared her throat. "I always thought adoption people were all religious," she said, eyes alight, "until I started doing research for Scarlett. It's true you aren't run by a church?"

Sherrie's bracelet jingled as she gestured between us. "We're one of only five percent of adoption agencies in the US that doesn't have a religious affiliation. Our employees and clients come from all different backgrounds. 'Adoption people,' isn't a type, Mina. Your friend is here. What type of person are you, Scarlett?"

"Not a religious one."

"So, why are you here?"

I knew she was trying to draw me out, but I felt like all of my words had dissipated.

"Because I made the appointment," Mina said into the quiet.

Sherrie's face remained placid, her eyes moved slowly between us.

I searched for my voice. "She did—but only because she's worried—it's hard to explain. I—I haven't been able to decide what to do because I don't want to parent. Now. Maybe someday. But not—now. Maybe it seems strange to go through with this, but I don't know. It's so, so"—I searched for the word, grabbed hold of one—"interesting?" My voice cracked. I must have sounded dumb. My hands trembled. I thought of David.

Of Cody. My life in Graceville. How I would never have that life again. Inside me, cells drained my energy as they multiplied. I couldn't stop thinking about them even when I tried.

Sherrie passed me some more crackers.

"If parenting is out, what are your feelings on termination? Are you aware of your timeline?"

"January," Mina said. Sherrie raised her eyebrows at Mina, who looked down to inspect her nails.

"The clinic had info about that. So I—I guess, can you tell me what I need to know about this?" I said, clenching my fists. The air suddenly felt too dense. I wanted to hurry things along.

Sherrie ran her hand the length of her sensible skirt. I thought of David. "What are your thoughts on adoption?" she said.

"My mom adopted my sister. But, you know, that's different because we have the same dad."

Sherrie dropped her hands to her panty-hosed knees. "It sounds like you have a positive experience with adoption in your family, even if it looks different from what your own options might be."

"I guess." I hadn't thought about that. My family was just my family.

"Well, most of our adoptions are open, but how open is up to the birth parents to decide."

"I guess I was thinking, if I went this route, then as closed as possible because this isn't something I'm really talking about.

My parents don't know. I thought I could just sign papers and move on."

"Some people do, but that's pretty rare now. Most placements are open. The child can have fewer questions about who they are and why they were placed. It works, and we keep relationships with our families to support them."

"That'd be more than I'm looking for. I'm ready to hand the baby over. I'd do it now if I could, but it needs to gestate a bit longer, so instead, if I do this, I'm kind of thinking of pretending I'm away at a home for unwed mothers or something. 'Colwyn College, the great destination for knocked-up girls whose potential was once celebrated.'" I tried to laugh, but no one else did. I rubbed my hands on my jeans, looked out the window. Could we leave yet?

"You don't need to decide now, Scarlett. But could you describe the kind of family you think would provide the right placement for your child?"

It was starting to snow. Big white flakes let loose from the gray sky.

"What do you mean?"

"Well, some mothers really want their child to have an adoptive family with a certain religion, or they want to make sure they have a stay-at-home mom."

"Okay, religion, I get that one. It's like a core value thing. But people really ask for a stay-at-home mom? Do they consider what might happen if the dad loses his job in another economic collapse or something? Because when my friend Hannah's dad lost his job and her mom hadn't worked in fifteen years, that pretty much sucked. They lost their house and had to move into the upstairs apartment in a duplex their friends from church owned." Sherrie nodded but said nothing. "And do they realize that families with stay-at-home parents divorce at the same rate as those with working parents? And that for women, not for men, the number one predictor of poverty in old age is if you have kids? Does no one read for their sociology class? Please, tell me, does anyone ask for a stay-at-home dad? Because maybe that's what I want. You got any stay-at-home dads?"

Sherrie's bracelet sounded as she crossed her arms. "As a matter of fact, we do. Scarlett, people have their preferences. It isn't a judgment on my part. It's my job to help you find the kind of home you want to see your child raised in. And not all my clients have access to sociology courses at Colwyn. So am I hearing that you would like a stay-at-home-dad?" She had that smile on her face again. She'd put one hand up to her chin like she was studying me. I wondered if she secretly thought my rant had some good points.

"I wouldn't really need a stay-at-home dad, but two dads would be fine. Do you place with same-sex couples?" The room felt like it was getting tighter and tighter. There wasn't enough air. I wanted to leave.

"Yes, we place with all kinds of families, LGBTQ+ are not excluded." Her face twitched. Or maybe she thought I was a privileged, self-important brat and wanted me out of there as badly as I wanted to go.

I breathed in. "It's just, if I do this, really all I want is people that aren't, you know, nineteen and complete wrecks." And as I said it, my voice cracked and my eyes burned, which just felt like another reminder of how I couldn't keep my life together. Mina scooted closer to me, ran her hand down my ponytail. I closed my eyes.

"You're not a complete wreck, Scarlett," Sherrie said in her calm voice. "You should know that. You're attending a great school. Your life took a bit of an unexpected turn, that's all."

Just an unexpected turn? I felt like I did in Bradshaw's office, like I was being told something that was dismissive even if it was true. These women seemed unaware of the excess gravity I felt. I knew this happened, to women, all the time. I tried to focus even though the room felt short of oxygen. I did have lots of unprotected sex for all of August. The facts added up. But believing my life could go on as planned, it was something I just—I could not—

I suddenly felt shrink-wrapped. I struggled, focused on oxygen, on *1, 2, 3. Hold. Exhale. 1, 2, 3, 4,* and after a moment, I managed to say, "Look, I'm open to all kinds of families." I breathed in again. "Single parents too, but maybe especially people in STEM fields. They can be religious, but they've got to believe in evolution."

"Okay, we can start there. Are you interested in looking at some profiles? Lots of people tell me that being able to visualize the adoptive parents, or not, helps them to make a clear decision."

"Okay."

"Good. So then I'll send over some profiles by the end of the week. You can take your time looking through them."

"Okay," I said again, examining her too-sudden, full-faced smile. It seemed practiced but genuine.

"Nice to meet you, Scarlett." She stood. "If you have other questions, don't hesitate to contact me." I inhaled deeply and locked eyes with Mina, and the gravity in the room lessened.

"Thanks," I said, and as we stood, I reached out to shake her hand. "You jingle." I pointed at the tiny bell on her bracelet.

She lifted it in the fingers of her opposite hand. "Bells are reminders to stay present. In this job, it's one of the most important things I can do."

I nodded. "So is this what you thought you'd be doing at nineteen?"

"Well, no," she said, "but I placed my son for adoption when I was twenty-two, and I realized I wanted—needed—to have a meaningful career. So here I am." And with that she turned to open the door. "I'll walk you down."

Snow swirled through the air, big heavy flakes that were starting to collect and whiten the road. Mina and I got in her car to navigate the slick route back to campus. When she clicked on her wipers to clear the snow from her windshield, they seemed to squeak, *Scarlett, Scarlett, you must choose. Choose. Choose. Choose.* I crushed Sherrie's card in my hand. Unfolded it.

"Any developments with Harold?" I asked.

Mina's dimple blinked but she shook her head. "You'd be the first to know."

We drove, listening to the windshield wipers squeak. Mina must have been freaked out too. She didn't even turn on music.

"Mina," I said, "do you think I really could do this? I mean, be pregnant, have a baby, and give it away?"

"Yeah"—Mina rubbed her fuzzy steering wheel cover—"if that is what you want."

Choice. Choice. Choice. The windshield wipers squeaked.

"But how on earth can someone pick a family based on some files? How can I?"

"Scar, I don't know. I don't know how you're doing any of this, except that somehow you are. Maybe that applies to the future too? Somehow, you'll do whatever you decide to do. Somehow you'll get through it because you already are."

I didn't remind her that she'd made the appointment for me, that without her I wouldn't be getting through this at all, that she was like some lucky stroke of fate, that I'd been pretending this wasn't happening and was only forced to confront it because she was making me.

What happened to the girl who started Step-up to STEM? What happened to me?

We rode in silence the rest of the way to campus.

Without the study of physics, Mina and I wouldn't be able to see ourselves as the blue dot on her car's screen, trekking across the heart of Iowa, calculating the approximate minute we'll arrive at our next stop—a roadside campground near a town called Walnut. All mobile technology is a gift from Maxwell's Equations. Without Einstein's Theory of Relativity, there'd be no GPS. But so far, even the best GPS cannot calculate what might jump in the road ahead of you and how you might react. Maybe that's what I want. To know everything before it happens. To not just flip back in time but forward.

TEN MONTHS AGO, AUGUST

SOUTHERN COLORADO

It wasn't long after David told me about his angel dream, we'd settled into a kind of half sleep, listening to his tapes. David was driving fast around a corner. There in front of us were two deer, a mother and her baby. They loomed like two graceful shadows. David slammed the brakes and swerved toward the mountain. For a half second the fawn froze, eyes reflecting our headlights before darting right at us. And some part of it—feet, neck, back—smashed the windshield. I covered my eyes and I heard something thump on the hood of the car as it spun sideways and everything stopped. I seemed to feel every cell in my body. Then David touched my hair, unbuckled his seat belt, opened the door. I could hear the sound of him crunching through glass. I moved slowly into the cool night air. The doe was gone. Probably watching from the shadows, waiting for her baby to join her. I stood brushing windshield glass off my shoulders and hair. When I looked up, David was leaning over the fawn, his hand on its sides.

"It's still alive," he said, and I saw the glint of a knife blade in his hand. Where the knife had come from I wasn't sure. It didn't seem out of place until I thought about it later.

David cradled the head of the fawn. He spoke softly. "It'll be okay, I'm so sorry, so sorry." He ran his hands across its jaw then down its neck. Then, quickly, without me realizing what he was doing, he slit the throat and held his hands to its nostrils. When its breath stopped he rose, wet with blood, and looked at me. His voice calm. "Come, on Scar. Help me pull her out of the road." I might have been crying. I don't know. I watched him struggling with the fawn's front legs. "Help me, Scar," he said.

I couldn't move.

Then: headlights. Another car. Two people got out. One came to me, asked if I was okay. Another went to David and helped him lay the body in the ditch. One of them asked if we'd called for help, and when we shook our heads blankly someone called. Someone lit torches and threw them on the dark highway. Cars drove by slowly. I couldn't see them, but I could feel them watching from their windows. Everyone loves to see an accident. They can't take their eyes off it. It's part horror, part empathy, part thankfulness it's not happening to them that they stare at the red lights, the darkness, the blood, at those of us standing there, needing help.

It wasn't until the medics arrived that I realized I was bleeding, or that there were glass shards in my forehead and arms.

David's cut from whatever happened in Mexico had burst open, and his shoulder looked askew. We rode together in the back of the ambulance, watching the darkness out the windows. Not touching. I remember watching him under the bright lights with the murmur of medics around me. His temple was bandaged, and his hair hung around it limp with sweat. He looked past me. It was like he'd entered a cloud.

"What happened to your head?" one of the medics asked.

"I hit it on the steering wheel, I think, I can't remember," he said.

"The abrasion isn't new," said the medic. David just gazed as if he didn't hear him. Nobody asked anything else until we were at the hospital, where David made up a story about defending me against some thugs. It wasn't a good story, and apparently not altogether believable, because they handed him pamphlets on domestic violence. I needed some stitches on my right cheek. Whatever they'd given me for pain as they dug the glass out of my face caused me to feel like I was floating four inches outside my body. I kept trying to pull myself back in. I squeezed the crinkly paper on the hospital cot thinking, *My hands are making this sound.* I felt detached from all of my movements. It was hard to believe my brain was controlling my fingers on the waxy paper.

"Hey, they're prescribing Percocet!" David said, reading his prescription. "Twelve days, not bad."

I shook my head. I knew I wouldn't take it, especially if it was what made me feel this way. Then we fell asleep on our separate hospital cots. When we woke, David's mom was there. She swooped him up and away with only a nod goodbye. Murmured something about his dad. It was only a few minutes later that my mom arrived and found out the doctor had issued me the same prescription as David.

"You don't give that to a teenager," she said, shredding the prescription in the nurse's face. Yeah, she's dramatic. She's totally my mom. "Are you people unaware of the market value of this stuff? Don't you know how addictive it is? The kid can take Advil; she has some cuts and bruises. What are you people? Getting some major handout from drug companies? Never mind. Don't answer that. I'm an NP. I know the scene."

"I'm sorry I— It's—" the nurse stammered.

"I know you don't prescribe, and it's shit of me to take this up with you. But question what the doctors are doing around here and why," Mom said, and we left. Then she pursed her lips tight as if she had to fight to hold in the stream of how-badly-can-you-possibly-screw-up-Scarlett-you-know-I've-always-trusted-you and opened her arms to hug me. When she unpursed her lips, it was to say she was glad I was okay. It wasn't her parenting technique to tell how much trouble I was in right away. I could look forward to that later.

I wonder if she even thought about David. Did she forget they probably prescribed him the same? Did she think to call his mom? Maybe she was so worried about me, it didn't occur to her. I've often wondered if things would have been any different if David's mom had been in the room to see mine flip out. If she'd had a real warning. If. If. If.

But probably not. His problem was already bone-deep. It began when Teri died. Maybe even before that. So much must have been going on with the boys I was closest to without my knowing any of it. David took me on a drug run, risked his life across the border, put me—put both of us—in so much danger. Is it just grief, imagining I could have rewritten the story? That I could have changed his ending, that I could have done something for him?

"CAMPGROUND IN A CORNFIELD" NEAR WALNUT, IOWA

Now, I have a small white scar on my right cheek. A line that reminds me every time I look in the mirror of how David and I crashed. And it was on that trip, in that crash, that I started to see him more clearly. For so long, it was like I'd been looking through an out-of-focus telescope at the blur of David. Then he started to come in and out of focus. And what I realized: I liked it better when he was blurry. Now, there's an ache where he's gone. Now, the only place I can find him is the past.

SIX MONTHS AGO, DECEMBER

COLWYN COLLEGE · WATERTOWN, MAINE

A few weeks after meeting Sherrie, I sat on my bed holding a thick envelope stamped PICTURES: DO NOT BEND. I texted David: "You there?" And waited for five minutes before tucking my phone under my pillow. I took a deep breath, imagined my father running into a burning building, and slipped my pen under the seal to rip it open. A letter signed in purple ink with Sherrie's bubbly script was followed by packets separated with colored paper clips representing different families. I glanced through the portfolios. The first page always had a picture of the couple or, in rare cases, a single person, seeking a child. Then brief information in a list:

Job:

Education:

Age:

Years Together (if applicable):

Religion:

Other Children:

Pets:

I didn't consider that some of these couples might be seeking a second child. I decided immediately and ungenerously to rule out anyone who already had one. Not because I didn't think they should get another kid, but because if I was going to give this baby away, I wanted to give it to people who really, really desperately wanted to be parents and hadn't had that opportunity yet. If I kept the baby, I'd be figuring it out as I went, so I wanted someone like me but who was ready. That was the difference. I could do it if I wanted to. I had a history of responsibility. I'd just slipped.

I counted fifteen profiles in the envelope with shaking hands. Four had another child already. I put them to the side, examined the remaining profiles. Caitlin and Jason were thirty-five and forty-one. He a computer engineer, she a freelance editor. They lived in New Hampshire. He commuted to Boston. Two cats and a fish. They liked skiing and kayaking. She hoped to have the baby at home with a nanny while she worked. They'd picked their neighborhood based on schools. Nope. Two cats and a fish? Isn't that inviting disaster?

Sylvie and Rowan, thirty-seven and thirty-nine, both Boston College grads, married zero to five years, both employed in the "financial sector," um, nope. Calvin Shanahan and Sai Reddy, thirty-eight and forty-two, married five to ten years, Calvin a biotech engineer, Sai a pediatric oncologist at Boston Children's Hospital. Their picture showed Calvin pale and smiling under his blue baseball cap and shorts, with arms wrapped around the slightly taller Sai, whose mouth was open mid-laugh under his red bucket hat on a white sand beach. "Annual winter getaway to the Keys" was the caption. The pictures that followed showed them splashing at a waterpark with their nephew Carter, and group shots from a family reunion in Yellowstone. They were willing to adopt any child under two, special needs acceptable, parental drug or alcohol abuse okay. I held their picture. I read the front page again and again. On the second page was a letter they'd written. It read:

Dearest Birth Mother to our Incredible Child,

I imagine this is a difficult time for you. Placing a child is a challenging choice. I want you to know that if you place your child with us, they will be raised in the most loving home possible. I hope you can tell from our pictures, Sai and I believe in the power of laughter. I spend my workday in a lab. I love my job, but when I get home I want to be with Sai and decompress. We don't eat out often because we get so much joy out of cooking together. Sai learned to cook from his ammamma in India, and her chicken biryani is a staple around our house. Sai is a master of recipe-less innovation, but I collect cookbooks. We love to make sushi, tacos, Georgian sauces, I could go on forever! You get the idea. Our love for food goes well with our love for travel. Because we're an interracial couple, welcoming a child into a home that values the cultural importance of food, family, tradition, as well as exploring other

cultures in our world is of great importance to us. Sai
is Hindu and does not eat beef, and so I never cook it
at home. It's our plan that, until our child can decide
for themselves what they believe, they will not eat
beef. We cannot wait to have a child join our family, to
laugh with us in the evenings, to learn with us on the
weekends. Education is very important to us, but not
just because of the economic benefits; we truly enjoy
reading, exploring, and solving problems together.
When we met we discovered both of us love to read
children's books for fun, and so now we sometimes read
them to each other. We have a full, happy life, but we've
been wanting a child for a long time, and of course,
biologically we can't have one together. We have so much
extra love and joy to share. If you choose to place your
baby in our home, you will never worry that they won't
be provided for in every way. We'd love the opportunity
to talk to you before you decide. We hope to hear from
you.

Sincerely,

Calvin Shanahan and Sai Reddy

Okay, maybe it was cheesy. And maybe it was the pregnancy
hormones, but the world went blurry as I read their words.
These guys understood not just how important it was for them

to have a child, but what it might mean to be given one. By someone else. And they were smart and sciencey and I blinked back my tears. I was still staring at their paperwork when Mina came in a half hour later.

"I think I found them."

"What?" Mina said, her eyes wide. "Wait—you mean, you're going to do it?"

"It's weird," I said, holding on to my own elbows. "But it's sorta like when I came to look at Colwyn, and it just felt . . . I don't know. Right."

Mina's eyes went comic-book big.

"Yeah, I know, Colwyn still doesn't totally fit."

"Come on! That feeling was right and you know it!" Mina actually cartwheeled across the floor. "Colwyn brought you me!"

"True." I tugged her down on the bed next to me. "So, maybe, this is the same. It won't be like what I imagine? But it's still what I want to do." I tipped a picture from the file up so Mina could see. "Just look at these two."

"Oh, they're cute. I love that hat. Is he Indian?" she said. I nodded. Mina read from the paperwork: "Pediatric Oncologist and Biotech—sounds perfect for you, Scarlett. Wait." Mina put her hand to my forehead. "Are you feeling okay? This guy Sai is Hindu. You *know* that's a religion, right?"

I slapped Mina's hand away. "Didn't you read the part about the kid getting to decide what they believe? These two people— they're really thoughtful. I think they're it."

"Are you sure? This is, like, a big decision. Did you try David again, or Cody?"

"Cody's not going to be involved. No way." I pulled my phone out from under the pillow. "And I just sent David my eleventh unanswered text." I breathed in deep. "I'll do the phone interview, at least, and if they're jerks or just really good at pulling off hype on a profile, then I'll pick someone else, because weird as it is doing this—somehow it fits."

"It's not just your religiously conservative best friend whispering into your subconscious?"

"No, it's my choice— It's—it's not like I think everyone should do it. Forcing someone to deal with all this—the exhaustion, not to mention all the stuff that's going to happen to my body"— I shuddered—"it'd be inhumane." I pointed to the photo of Calvin and Sai. "But they're, like, my dream dads. One helps sick kids and the other's in biotech. I'm going to assume he's in it for the right reasons—the save-the-world, heal-the-food-supply, manage-the-green-economy reasons. You know I'll be sure to ask. And they're into cooking like my mom is."

Mina considered this, then smiled at me. "And this way you still get to have your secret baby, just like Einstein."

"Right, because I'm just like Einstein."

"You are. Einstein didn't listen to his mother either."

"Oh Mina, nobody is as perfect as you."

"Hey, you haven't met my parents yet. Pretty sure I'm a failure when it comes to their social expectations."

"Then we're both failures in our parents' eyes, or I would be, anyway, if my parents knew anything about my life right now."

"You don't know that."

I shook my head. "You're not failing. You're completely social."

Mina laughed as she flipped through a psych textbook, then said, "I go to the parties I'm invited to, I bring my own seltzer water, and I leave as soon as everyone is shit-faced."

"Well, that's not so bad, that's like ninety-eight percent more social than I've been this year."

"You are not a fair comparison."

"Come on, you really don't have a circle of people to hang out with?"

"Um, wouldn't you know if I did?" Mina said.

I looked at her. All of Mina's running around, to study groups and parties—she went to them alone. Duh. If she had all these other friends, wouldn't she sit with them at lunch? Sure, she knew lots of people and studied with some of them, jumped around in leaves with others, but knowing people and having study buddies is different from having friends. I know almost everyone in Graceville. But how many were actually my friends?

"What about the physics kids?" I ask. "You said you had fun with Courtney and Bert 3D-printing all night."

"Mmm. I was mostly enjoying the view of Harold."

"Ew."

"Um, didn't you say he looked kinda like David?" Mina said.

"You've seen David's picture. They have the same sweatshirt and both are tall. It can look that way from across a field. The guy is totally not David. Go to his parties."

"I do. Or, you know, at least the ones at the apartment where he sometimes is. But I only stay until it's not fun to be the only sober person while everyone is falling down, shouting I LOVE YOU MAN at people, then pretending not to know each other the next day."

"Ugh, they really do that? Even Harold?"

"Well, maybe not him so much. Sometimes he just disappears."

"In Graceville everyone knows you. How you act at a party becomes you. You can't get away from anyone."

"Well, that's better! Here it's like people are completely different—make new BFFs at a party one night and then come morning, none of it happened. It's gross."

"Mina, you don't travel at predictable speeds. You don't."

She shrugged and placed a record on the turntable.

"You got your list?" Mina asked, sliding into the driver's seat.

"Right here, Mom," I said. "Dark clothes two sizes bigger than my usual—so ten, maybe twelve. One-colored outfits. Long open sweaters to layer, chunky jewelry, makeup, and 'body-shaping support bands,' whatever those are."

Mina smacked her lips. "They're like tight tubes to hide your imperfections."

"Well, I've certainly got an imperfection to hide."

Mina rubbed her hands on her fuzzy steering wheel cover. "One that you're choosing to hide. Now stop being sorry for yourself so we can have some fun? I'm pretty good at this. You're going to look like a new person when I'm done with you."

"I'd like to *be* a new person when you're done with me. Instead of *making* a new person."

"Oh, maybe we could make that happen! Is there a Hot Topic at the mall? What identity should we buy you? Goth? Skater? Punk? Cowgirl? Emo?"

"As long as you're picking out my outfits *every* morning, I don't care," I said.

Mina looked at me sideways. "With that long hair and freckles, I think you'd make a great cowgirl. Oooooh—punk cowgirl?"

"Uh, no. But if you actually make me into another person, I'll teach you to line dance later."

Mina's eyes got wide and she clapped her hands, causing the car to drift. I grabbed the wheel. "You really know how to line dance?" she asked.

"I thought everyone learns line dancing in gym," I said as a line of Subarus and trucks filtered onto 95.

"No, nope. No." Mina said. "Sorry I was judgey that you didn't know Emily Dickinson. Clearly there are ways your education was superior to mine."

Mina was talking excitedly with the woman at the makeup counter about how to layer eye shadow when I saw Bradshaw, hair down and being pulled through the department store by a small boy with something smeared across his cheek. She saw me and smiled.

"Oh, Professor Bradshaw, hey."

"Hi, Scarlett." She stopped, causing the child to lean forward, yanking her arm. "This is Casper. He really wants to get to the merry-go-round."

"Go! Merry-go-round!" the boy said to her.

"Hi, Casper," I said.

"Go! Merry-go-Mommy!" he said, and pulled her even harder. Her feet followed him.

"You like the merry-go-round?"

He coiled into his mother's leg in reply, probably wiping whatever was on his face on her pants. "Merry-go-go-merry-go," he whispered into her thigh.

"We were just on our way to the—"

"Merry–go-round!" Casper shouted. Then, "Daddy! Daddy!" He let go of Bradshaw's hand to charge headlong into a bearded man in a flannel shirt, who scooped him over his shoulder and strode toward us with two other kids, taller echoes of Bradshaw and this man, walking one foot in front of the other across the mall tiles.

"We are fixated on the merry-go-round," Bradshaw said to

him, over a chant of "Merry-go-go! Merry-go-go!" "And we've just run into Scarlett, a new Colwyn student."

The man nodded hello to me. "These two decided to join you," he said to Professor Bradshaw. "I'll grab us some coffee and meet you at the car after?"

Bradshaw nodded enthusiastically at the mention of coffee. She opened her arms to take Casper back. The other two kids continued their heel-toe progression along the tiled walk.

"Thanks, by the way, for buying those key chains," I said, not sure what else to do. I pushed my hands into my pockets.

Bradshaw smiled; the corners of her eyes crinkled.

"I—I, well, I found a couple, through an agency," I said. "I'm going to talk to them about adoption."

"Scarlett, that's great." She took a step forward as Casper bounced in her arms. Then she paused and met my eyes. "And brave." For a second I believed her.

I took a step after her. "So, how'd you meet your husband?" I said. Bradshaw looked slightly surprised, but then she set Casper down, took his hand in hers. She started talking to me as she walked, so I followed her out of the store and down the wide walkway to the merry-go-round. I listened. It felt good to listen.

On the morning of my flight, I dressed in black jeans, a black turtleneck, and a textured gray cardigan. After some debate, we decided punk cowgirl would call more attention than a more stylish me, one who "accented," as Mina said, with a multicolored beaded necklace and earrings so long I worried about them catching on my shoulders. Usually when flying I wouldn't waste time with jewelry, let alone makeup, but I darkened my eyes and colored my lips. Makeup and jewelry draw the eye away from your body's midsection, thereby hiding the baby bulge, or so the Internet claimed. When I examined myself in the mirror, the person who stared back didn't look bad. My hair was down, brushed, hanging past my breasts that swelled under my black sweater in a way I hoped was not suspect. My face had grown rounder. I was lucky, I supposed, that the baby weight was not appearing as a basketball I suddenly swallowed, but instead added thickness to all parts of my body, like my neck, which appeared to have doubled in size. Some days I felt like even my earlobes were bigger. Still, the person in the mirror looked pretty good. Her painted lips smiled back at me. Maybe she was even glowing. But she was not me.

"I feel like I'm about to step on stage," I said.

"Well," Mina considered, "you kind of are. Now, grab your bag. Time to go."

"Do you think I'll be able to keep this from Nurse Mommy?" I asked.

"You don't look knocked up to me," Mina said.

"She'll notice the weight gain. She'll think I'm acting weird. And Hannah . . ."

"You're nervous. Scarlett. That's okay. You can always decide to tell them."

"Um, no. No way. Nope. My dad—" I cringed just imagining the look on his face if I told. "Anyway, they would never think I'd be hiding this from them. Even if they suspect, I'm probably safe. You know, six months ago if you told me I'd be doing this, I would have laughed in your face."

"So what you're saying is, people see what they want to see."

"Thank you, Dr. Mina."

"Anytime. When can I start collecting my copay?"

Mina is snapping a shot of a sign that reads, NEBRASKA, THE GOOD LIFE: HOME OF ARBOR DAY.

Did you know that bits of our DNA look a lot like a tree's? DNA doesn't just link us to our biological parents and ancient ancestors, but to every living thing on the planet. When Nebraskans invented Arbor Day, though, they weren't thinking about that. Only the shade, or the beauty of the oak that would grow in their front yard, its leaves flipping over in the breeze.

In high school, biology seemed too practical to me. It lacked an interstellar vocabulary. But now I think how amazing it is to be connected to all the living things around me with a genetic code. Because of DNA, because of how living things turn that magic code off or on—a multitude of life appears. It's like physics but different. I don't want to study it, but we couldn't have one without the other.

TEN MONTHS AGO, AUGUST

GRACEVILLE, COLORADO

I dozed on the drive back to Graceville after Mom had rescued me from the hospital, and woke thinking I was still with David for a second. But then my mom's lavender body lotion entered my nose, and I saw her freckled hands on the wheel. And just like that I remembered the crash, and that David and I were moving away, and whatever had flashed between us was certainly almost done.

"Shower, then we'll eat," Mom said as we pulled into the garage. Her theory that no one should try to communicate when hungry was long-standing. By the time I finished my extra-long shower, Mom had piled the table with French toast, bacon and eggs, orange juice, and fruit salad. I ate, and ate and ate, knowing that when I stopped I'd have to answer to her. I wanted to keep eating forever. Mom poured herself more coffee from the French press and looked at me.

"Well?"

I set down my fork. "Sorry?" I said, then tried to smile.

"Not good enough."

"I'm really sorry, Mom."

"Really?"

"I'm really, really, really sorry."

"Scarlett, what are the four parts of an apology?"

Her tone was so calm, it made me want to throw things. My vein bulged.

She crossed her arms. Her long hair was ponytailed so the gray streak that ran from her temple made a silver line across her head. She stared, silent. I knew what I had to do. I took a deep breath. I counted *1, 2, 3, hold. Exhale. 1, 2, 3, 4.* I was sincere when I said:

"I'm sorry I lied to you, Mom. I know I was acting reckless because I'm scared about going to college, and David and I are going the farthest away. We got talking one night and then we were driving and we didn't want to stop. I shouldn't have lied and said I was at Hannah's. I should have called."

"You should have stayed right here is what you should have done."

"Mom, this is my apology."

"Go ahead." She twisted her tiny silver hoop earrings.

"Next time, I promise to let you know where I really am."

"Scarlett, there isn't going to be a next time. That's the point. You're grown up now. And this is the kind of choice you make? This is the kind of thing I get to think about you doing every weekend at Colwyn? Oh, sure, random guy, let's take a road trip down to Florida and see if we can swim with the sharks. And let's drive like maniacs on the way home until we get into an accident and see if we survive!"

"Mom, he wasn't driving like a maniac. It was a deer. It could happen to anyone. You know that."

Mom uncrossed her arms, sank deeper into her chair. I cleared my throat. "Besides, David isn't some random guy. He's my friend and you've known him forever."

"Scarlett." Mom's voice was sad now. "I know anyone could have hit the deer, but you weren't even supposed to be on that highway. It was the middle of the night. But more than that—you used to talk to me. I still remember the day you came home glowing because you sat next to Cody in math class."

"I'm talking to you now," I said.

She shook her head. "I don't know what's between you and David. You haven't told me that." But I knew she was lying. She knew exactly what was between David and me. The same way she knew something happened the first day of sophomore year. Still, my throat closed. I couldn't admit it to her. I didn't know how. Maybe it didn't matter. She already knew.

"I'm sorry. I forgot, my leaving isn't just about me. It's about you, and Dad, and Jess—our whole family will be different once I'm gone."

She reached for my hand across the table. "You have opportunities your dad and I never dreamed of. Don't lose them because you think it's romantic to be reckless."

"I don't think it's romantic to be reckless," I said, taking my hand away from hers.

"Then what do you think?"

"I don't know."

She stood and took two steps into the kitchen. "Dad and I are going to visit Jessica on Wednesday," she said, then turned back toward me. "Can we trust you with the house for one night?"

"Of course," I said, turning to look at her. "You always have before."

"That was before," Mom said. The room seemed to enter a slow spin. I felt all the hairs on my neck prickle. Maybe I destroyed something bigger here? But this drive with David, this thing with David, was just one impulsive move. In a whole life of responsibility. It was fine. I was still going to college. I was still Scarlett.

SIX MONTHS AGO

GRACEVILLE, COLORADO

I watched Hannah, pink-nosed, quick steps, coming up my front walk that first morning home for winter break, and I wanted to tell her everything. It would be like taking off a hair shirt. My throat tightened. She would look at me in her Hannah way, waves of green rising in her eyes, hug me tight and smell like comfort, like peach shampoo. She would think I was doing the right thing. But that's why I didn't want to tell her. I was doing this experiment, lending my body to cell-multiplication, creating something of me and David, or Cody, and letting it go. If I told Hannah, she might see it as a virtuous answer to a sinful error. I could crumble if she exalted or judged me. And what I needed most was to not crumble.

After several minutes of squealing and hugging in the way Mina and I had practiced—shoulders forward and butt back—Hannah passed me a folded green sheet of paper. "The program you wanted."

I unfolded the Graceville tree-lighting program. "Was Cody there?"

"No." She paused. "David wasn't either."

I let this wash over me. "Fourteen to one," I said.

"Math-MAA-tics!" Hannah sang, flashing her jazz hands. "Math-MAA-tics makes the world go round." It was a song we'd made up for an extra-credit project in seventh grade. "What does fourteen to one mean? Explain your Math-MAA-tics!"

I hip-bumped her. "Well, people bought more expensive lights this year than last, so maybe that's good."

"Economic improvement explained with Math-MAA-tics!" she sang. "I have fifteen thousand dollars less this year than last. Understand college loans with—"

She waited for me; when I didn't jump in, she finished on her own: "Math-MAA-tics!"

I smiled and gave her a side-squeeze.

Hannah touched the program and looked up at me. "I bought the light for Grandma this year. My parents couldn't."

"Oh, Hannah."

She shrugged, flashed a half-hearted smile, then sang, "Donating loan money is Math-MAA-tics."

Hannah's family had been in rough shape since they lost their house years ago. Her parents made her save half the money she made from her job bagging groceries for her car, then college, and the rest went to the food she was able to buy at a discount thanks to the same job. The store hired her little sister so Hannah could study at college without worrying that her family will go hungry. Between the grocery store, Step-up to STEM, and track, Hannah's high school free time had been even less than mine.

"Looks like Cody's mom had a red light, and David's grandpa—he died?" I said, looking up at her. I thought about the old man in the wheelchair David pushed around town, how he always asked how my dad was.

"At the beginning of the month."

"Ah," I said, turning toward the kitchen and trying to keep my voice steady.

"David wasn't at the lighting, Scar," she said again. "I'm worried about him. He looked like shit when I saw him at Rage's last week."

"That sucks," I said. I felt my face get hot. The unanswered texts. David, when I needed him, unreachable. We entered the kitchen and I gripped the counter, my hands sweating. Every year, Hannah and I spend an entire weekend baking sheet after sheet of cookies—spritzers, sugar, gingerbread—and each year we add a new recipe or two. If they're good they become part of the lineup. My parents order takeout as we fill the counters and dining room table with cooling cookies. Then we deliver them to the Graceville Retirement Center. We planned to continue the tradition even if we didn't actually live in Graceville anymore.

After a second I realized what Hannah just said, and turned to her with a half smile. "Wait, you were at Rage's? Spill it, what's going on—I thought you broke up in, like, September?"

Hannah curled her hair around her finger. "We did, it's just, we're still friends—and . . ."

"And what?"

"Friends can have other benefits-within-limits."

"Uh, not with you they can't."

"Oh come on, Scarlett, you know I'm not all straitlaced, but my limit line hasn't changed if that's what you're asking." She grinned.

"Yes, you're the baddest good girl I've ever met."

"That's right." She danced her elbows into the air. "I, um, really missed him. Even though there's this guy at school."

"What? You player!"

"Well, we just kissed once," Hannah said, and her eyes got far away.

"What? How am I just hearing about this?"

"Well, you haven't exactly been giving me a play-by-play of your life. But we had a study group together and, like, kept ending up at the same parties. He's just—cool, I guess?"

"That's great," I said, but my throat burned. Hannah was getting out there. And me? I was feeling sorry for myself all the time. "So where's Cody?" I said, changing the subject.

"The Keys, with his dad."

"Fancy." I was relieved I wouldn't be bumping into him around town.

"You still get all red and sweaty and the vein pops up whenever I mention Cody. Aren't you over him?"

"I'm over him," I said, but my voice wavered.

"Then why are you wearing the necklace he gave you for your anniversary?"

I put my hand to my neck. I wore the chunky beads but when I found the double-helix necklace on my old dresser earlier, I put it on too. I cleared my throat. "I just like it, always have," I said, opening the flowered recipe box in front of me. "Let's get going."

After a pause from recipe reading, Hannah said, "I heard David's not going back."

"What?"

"Leave of absence."

"Really?" I paused. Surprised. Not surprised. "But he *plans* to go back," I said.

Hannah shrugged. "He didn't look like he could handle a Stanford education in the state he was in at Rage's."

"Jesus," I said, dropping two sticks of butter in a bowl.

"That's who I've been talking to."

"Say a little prayer for me," I said, and Hannah held her hands in a prayerful pose before scooping the sugar into the bowl. "So weren't his brothers singing at the lighting?"

"Yeah," Hannah said. "He still missed it."

"Should I talk to him or something? He hasn't been in touch with me since August."

"Sounds about right," Hannah said.

I was melting like a polar ice cap, losing parts of myself just thinking about David falling apart. The urge to tell Hannah everything pulled—but a force real as gravity kept my mouth sealed. I turned the mixer on and we went quiet. I thought about David, the dropout, drug zombie, another lost cause of this sad town. I thought of the last time I saw him, dawn the day I was leaving for Colwyn. I had tried to reach him then; I guess it wasn't enough.

Still, I couldn't help wondering if what I was carrying might do something. Could I make this better or worse? If I told him, like I'd been trying to all along, would it change anything? My cutoff was soon, but I could still change my mind. I swallowed. I thought of that picture of Calvin and Sai. Their letter. If I told David, would I have to tell everyone, and if I did, would I be able to look at Hannah, my parents, my dad, the same way ever again? Would they be able to look at me? Would I be able to go through with my plans?

"Remember how David would come in late for an exam and smile as the teacher shook his head, and the next day we'd all find out he got the highest mark in the class?" Hannah said.

"That was maddening."

"It's like my mom always said—a small pond's big fish is the lake trout's dinner."

"Hannah, you used to complain that she only said that so you would feel better about your grades," I said.

"Yeah, well, maybe she was right," Hannah said. "I made the dean's list last term and—"

"And what? David and I are total screwups?" I said.

"No, but maybe it's so normal to see yourself as the best at everything that you're falling apart realizing you're not the next Einstein."

Her words seared. "Hannah," I said.

"What? Everyone needs a humbling sometimes."

"Pass me the flour. I need one and a half cups," I said. "And spoon and level it, please. I don't want these cookies to get all hard."

"Okay, bossy pants," Hannah said, dumping a spoonful of flour into the measuring cup. "Anyway, it changes people."

"What does? A *humbling*?"

"Well, that too, but I meant going so far to college. When I ran into David, his eyes were, like, dead. It was creepy," Hannah said.

"What does that have to do with going far away? Do I have creepy dead eyes?" I tried to slowly breathe through my nose.

"No. But you never told me what happened on your joy ride down the Great Divide. It's ancient history now—you should just spill it."

"Nothing to tell," I said, holding tight to the white tile countertop and hoping I looked like I'd been eating too many cookies all semester.

"That's not what David said."

"You can't tell a prank from a piece of news."

"Prank?" Hannah said, eyebrows arched.

"Um, hello. David's an ass. You're really going to believe him?

We were all playing a drinking game, and—and—I don't know, he was just being an ass!"

"You didn't deny it," Hannah said.

"I didn't have to."

"You're hiding something," Hannah said, pointing the spoon at me. "I can tell by the vein in your neck."

I inhaled *1, 2, 3. Hold. Exhale. 1, 2, 3, 4.* Then, clutching the countertop, I said, "Look, David and I have been friends since before I can remember. He had this idea that we should drive the Great Divide because we were headed east and west. It was silly but I went along with it. If David was having some sick fantasy about me the whole time, let him. It was just a drive."

"Really." Hannah didn't believe me.

"No, you're right, I'm totally lying," I said, deciding on a new tactic. "Actually, we had sex a bunch of times—all unprotected and now I'm pregnant with his baby or Cody's, I'm actually not sure."

"God, Scarlett. Melodrama. Maybe you should change your major to theater. You might do better in the classes. I don't care if you slept with him," Hannah said. "What you do is your business. I don't expect you to be like me."

"What you do is like speaking half a language, honey. It only gets you so far," I said, lobbing some dough at her. It hit her hairline, where it stuck for a minute, then fell to the tile floor.

"You wasted a perfectly good cookie there, Scar," Hannah said, trying to wipe the dough out of her hair.

"I thought you were about to evangelize again."

307

"I gave up on you long ago," she said. "But my point is, just watch out." She rubbed dough off her fingertips and shrugged. "Look, David's a drug-zombie dropout, and you barely talk about school, dress all weird, wear eye makeup, have gained a ton of weight. Scar, what happened out there? Did they brainwash you with boarding school etiquette and replace my 'I'm going to be like Marie Curie and wear one dress' friend with someone who suddenly cares about fashion?" Hannah eyed the green and purple beads of my necklace. I felt her stare burn into my outfit. Sizing up my long black skirt, loose turtleneck, and three-button cashmere sweater only half covered by my dad's fire truck apron, its soft sleeve now white with flour.

"Come on, Hannah. You know I don't like to stick out. Did you consider that people dress differently there?"

"Just don't get too serious. You science nerds already have a bad rap. And while you're at it, you might want to lay off some of the dining hall desserts too—or join the track team. The extra weight doesn't suit you. Neither does the new style."

"Wow. Did you go to college and forget all the lessons we learned in Fit Positive Girls? I don't remember you being so mean before. Do you really think I'd be doing better at State?"

"Maybe." But Hannah's eyes were on the counter. I'd touched a nerve.

"You're just jealous I got the package to go out there."

"Of course I'm jealous!" Hannah said, and I could see her eyes welling with tears. "You live in picturesque buildings, not block towers built to house five hundred drunk freshmen forever ago that might be infested with mice. But besides all that, I'm worried about you. You only text like once a month and you don't tell me anything. I'm glad to know you're thinking about me, but it's not enough. It was the end of our time here and you disappeared with David and you never talked to me about it, and you just got all pissy when he said you'd slept together, and now he's all zombie-eyed and you're not even staying home all break because you're doing some volunteer project. Scar, what am I supposed to think?" Hannah was red-faced, and there were tears dripping down her cheeks, but she didn't raise her voice at all. She took a deep breath and looked me in the eye. Damn that leadership training. Hannah was good. And I couldn't handle it.

"Um, perhaps you could have some empathy?" I snapped. "Maybe I gained weight from high-calorie dorm food and had to buy new clothes, and I go to school with a bunch of rich kids and have to try to look like them to fit in because you know I don't really love attention."

"Right," she said, turning away from me to wash her hands at the sink. "Unless it's for how smart you are. You never mind attention for that," she mumbled. When she turned back, she said, "I think I should go."

"What about your share of the cookies? What about going with us to hand them out at the home?" I said.

"The old people won't even realize I'm not there, and my mom made plenty, don't worry."

"Hannah, seriously, don't leave. Can we take a breath? It's time to practice forgiveness, okay? We've been friends since forever."

I heard Hannah slowly inhale. "I just worry about you," she said.

"I know, but I'm okay. I've missed you." I opened my arms and stuck my butt back as we hugged.

As I stepped away from Hannah, I felt a sensation like tiny wings inside my gut. My hand went to my belly. It was early, but I'd read there was a chance I could start feeling movement now. Still, I wasn't sure if that was it. I felt the wings again and I thought of a bird launching into flight. I thought of David. Of what I should do.

A year ago, I'd thought that Colwyn with its brick walkways, lined with smart boys outfitted in expensive outdoor gear, would cure me of my yearning for Cody. I'm not proud to admit it, but his dumping me was the hardest thing I'd been through. It almost seems laughable now.

Instead, August brought the cosmic collision that was me and David. And Colwyn became where my phone never lit up with David's name. I'd like to say I stopped hoping it was him when I heard a buzz, but I didn't. Not even when there wasn't a chance for any more messages from him.

Funny, because when he left me alone on our road trip, I began to see. All that shine and shimmer—it was David's supernova, the final flames, bright and burning. And when he came into focus, I pushed him off. Because he was an asshole, sure. Because what he was doing was wrong, yes. But mostly because I was afraid I was too close to a star about to flame out, and when it did, I'd get vaporized too.

SIX MONTHS AGO

GRACEVILLE, COLORADO

It ended up, the day after Hannah and I finished our cookie-a-thon, I ran into David Warren by accident. It would be the last time I saw him.

Mom and I were heading to Colorado Springs to see my sister and do some Christmas shopping, so we stopped to get road coffees. At first, I was just going to wait in the car, not wanting to run into anyone. But then I had to pee, even though I peed before leaving the house. Pregnancy, the pee-producer. I zipped up the giant parka my parents had bought for me assuming it was the kind of thing eighteen-year-olds wore in Maine—as if there isn't winter in Colorado! But I was grateful for the thing's oversized glory as I moved like a puffer fish into the cold air. I had a straight trajectory to the coffee shop and was moving fast when I heard "Scarlett."

I froze.

"Scarlett?" he said again, my name hitting with a gust of cold wind.

I shifted my boots toward his voice. He stepped closer. He

wasn't wearing a jacket, just his red-hooded sweatshirt, like Harold had, the hood pulled up against the wind. Black jeans and skate-sneakers sodden with snow. David's hair was cut unevenly short like he'd gone at it himself after downing a bottle of vodka. His skin was sallow. His clothes limp. Hannah was right. David in splinters. I tried to say hey or hi, anything, but the words froze in my throat. He stopped a few feet from me. "It is you. I wasn't sure at first," he said, holding my eyes. "Nice parka." Both of us almost smiled. I crossed my arms, dropped my gaze to the sidewalk, where puddles of early winter slush and snow wet the ends of David's too-long jeans. "So how is it? You know, Colwyn."

"Okay." My blood pulsed. David. David. David. I wanted to say *I'm pregnant. I'm so fucking alone. I don't know what I want to do. Or I think do but I'm scared. And I need you to see that something is wrong. I want you to know that everything sucks and I want to go back in time and I can't and you're standing here looking like a ghost of the boy that I, the boy that I.*

NOW

REST AREA · COZAD, NEBRASKA

It feels like the car is shrinking. I don't know— If I had said more— If—if if if.

Mina keeps her eyes on the road but touches my arm.

I'd like to think it's just Nebraska is so green my eyes hurt. But that would be like looking through a blurry telescope. When I focus, I know this hurt is for David. For me. For the world that lost him.

This rest stop hums with lawn mowers and retired couples walking their dogs. Mina is across the grass taking pictures of a historical plaque.

I got vaporized by David anyway. Did my trying to not get close undo me? I told myself I wasn't involved with his mistakes. But I was. Wasn't I?

"Wanna just stay here?" Mina shouts at me.

"No, Min. Rest areas are sketchy," I shout back, leaning out the car's open window.

Mina opens her arms and looks around as if to say *What the hell are you talking about?* In the late afternoon light, this place is completely tranquil.

"Things look different in the daylight. I'm not sure you want to be out here in the dark."

"You think there are less creepers at a KOA?"

"No. But I think at a KOA there are more grandmothers and families around if a creeper shows up to mess with us at four a.m."

"Point taken."

"Also, you should be congratulating me."

"On what?"

"On returning to risk aversion."

"Remind me to get you a grown-up pin," Mina says as she's getting into the car.

"I've been earning my grown-up pin all year," I say.

"You've earned more pins than some grown-ups," Mina says, "which is why this summer and next year you're going to be working on college-kid pins."

"What does that mean? Do I have to go to more parties?"

"More than one, yes. I'll be your wingman. Maybe you'll relocate your libido."

"I'm pretty sure that's sealed for the near future. Anyway, to be a wingman, you have to stay at parties past ten p.m."

"I'll try if you do. Who knows what the future holds. There are probably some pretty hot brogrammers at Google."

"I can't believe you just used that word, especially for someone you think I might be into."

"Well, I don't know who you're into. I only know you weren't into Harold for reasons beyond me."

"Um, isn't it good that I'm not into Harold because you are?"

"Aren't you supposed to be writing?"

"Aren't you supposed to let me make my own decisions?"

Mina wrinkles up her nose and clicks my picture.

"Surprise!" Mina said, pointing a nail-polish brush at me as I opened our dorm room door. She was sprawled across the floor in a bright blue, drop-shouldered sweater and black leggings.

"What are you doing here?"

"Painting my toenails to match my outfit," she said, flashing me blue-and-black-patterned toes.

"Cool, but I meant why are you back early from break?"

"I can't live without you. And Harold said I could volunteer with you guys." She capped her nail polish and flashed a sly smile.

"Wait, you're volunteering with the physics society? You aren't even a major. This is our community service project— Wait! Something's happened? With Harold?"

Mina almost dropped the bottle of nail polish. "Not yet. But I take this invitation as a positive sign. Plus you guys are running a warming room—it doesn't take a deep understanding of particle physics to make sure the coffee and teapots are full, or check the supplies of free mittens and hats." I shrugged. "Scar? Aren't you excited for all Mina! All the time?" Mina said, standing on her heels to toddle toward me.

"Of course I am," I said, and hugged her.

"Good, because after two weeks of endless family, I am beyond thrilled to see you, my Pregnant-Teen-Science-Snob-of-a-Roommate! Welcome back!" She released me from her tight embrace. "Did I successfully turn you into another person with our shopping trip, or did your parents recognize you at the airport?"

"Min, I've been texting you every day."

"True, but I could not see this!" she said, dropping her hands to my belly. "Oh, the black does hide it well, but people might notice soon."

My shoulders slumped. "I know. I wish there was something else I could do. I still can't believe my niece asked if there was a baby in my belly."

"And it only took sixty texts to calm you down after that."

"Fifty-two," I said. "But Nurse Mommy didn't seem to notice a thing, and Dad just said I looked nice. When Hannah told me to lay off desserts, though, my blood pressure shot up."

"That one only took twenty-four texts." Mina beamed. "I still have some templates from when I worked the text crisis line, so"—she shrugged—"supporting you through this was a breeze." She cleared her throat. "How'd you feel about running into David? You didn't say much about it. Did you tell him about—" She gestured to my bump.

I shook my head.

"Why not?" Then she sucked in her lip quickly and exhaled. "Did you get closure?"

I inhaled. I hadn't given Mina all the details about David. It was easy to talk about his charm, his inability to text, but his pills?

"No. I don't know. I guess I just realized this is my decision, you know? I don't need his—I can make the choice myself."

"Aw! You are finally listening to my wisdom!" Mina took an elaborate bow, one arm flung out to the side.

I tapped her head as she came back up. "There's hope for me yet, I suppose."

The baby could have been Cody's, sure. But I never needed him. I wanted David. From the minute we stepped off that bridge, David. I didn't want to throw him out. Though maybe I already had. That was part of the problem. But it was more than that too. Calvin and Sai, and how much they wanted a child . . . to think what I'd created could have a place. A footprint. A connection. But one that I didn't need to tend. For me, that felt right.

I reached into my backpack with both hands to pull out a wrapped package. "I saw this and thought of you."

Mina pounced and practically tore the package out of my hands. "For me?" She shredded the paper and got really quiet as she slipped the two-volume set of *Norton's Anthology of Modern and Contemporary Poetry* out of its case.

"How'd you know? My dad has a copy—I don't. This is so awesome. Thank you."

"You said you pick a lot of the poems to memorize from that collection and you didn't have a copy here, so I figured you needed one."

Mina swallowed me into a hug so engulfing, I felt like an octopus had me in all eight tentacles.

"Wait! Wait! I have a present for you too." She handed me a white manila envelope with a bow on it. What could be so flat? Inside was a printed PDF of an application for Google's summer internship program. My name was on it.

"I filled it out for you."

"Mina, that's illegal."

"Whatever, you going to bust me? Didn't think so. They should get back to you in a month or so. You have a good shot. My dad's friend hires the interns. You fit their profile."

There was a burn deep in my stomach.

"Um, thanks, I—"

"Come on, it'll be great. You know I've already applied to a ton of internships out there. We can great-American-road-trip it all the way out, like my dad did after college, and we can stay with my aunt. I've already asked her. She has a guesthouse. She teaches at Stanford but travels a lot during the summer, so it's not like she'll be another parent or anything."

"Wait, your aunt's a Stanford professor?"

"Yeah, so what?" Something about this fact made David feel so devastatingly and inescapably everywhere. I opened my mouth, finally said:

"It's just David—he was going there, but—never mind, it doesn't really matter— You shouldn't have done this."

"What?"

"Apply for an internship for me."

"Come on, what are you going to do this summer cooler than driving cross country with me?"

"I don't know. It's up to me to decide. The Society of Physics Students has some opportunities."

"That you haven't applied for—"

"The deadlines aren't for another month."

"Well, apply for them! Then decide what you want based on what you get."

I nodded as my vision hazed. I thought I was taking care of myself now, out here at Colwyn on my own, navigating the biggest mistakes of my life. But I wasn't. I was doing this with too much of Mina's help.

She got up, examined her smudged toes, and heel-walked back to her bed to uncap the nail polish. "Just because my dad knows the guy doesn't mean you'll get it. He's not unethical. There's still a big chance they won't select you. I just, you know, thought it would be fun. To do the road trip thing and be together all summer. We don't need to stop at all the state capitols like my dad did. I don't even know why he did that. We'd just have fun. You know, I missed you these last few weeks."

My face was tight, but I couldn't lie. "I missed you too," I said. "I'll think about it."

Mina cleared her throat. "So, you ready for the big phone interview?" She nodded toward the file next to my bed.

"Ready as I'll ever be." But I wondered, when liquids turn to vapor, if this is what it would feel like—parts of themselves floating off into the universe. "I think I'll go for a run, you want to come?"

Mina stuck out her tongue. "You want me to run?"

"Come on, I'll take it slow," I said, reaching for my running shoes. "Running isn't just good for developing fetuses."

"You sure it's good—shouldn't you stop at some point?"

"Mina, you know people train for the Olympics when pregnant! But, did you *also* know babies of people who exercise regularly have stronger heartbeats and better stress response? And, women who exercise through their pregnancies report shorter and less painful labors?"

"Well, thankfully I'm not planning to be pregnant for at least another fifteen years. I have plenty of time to start a new exercise regimen."

"Come on, you just admitted you missed me so much you committed fraud. Don't you want to join me?"

"No, thank you," Mina said. "I'll relieve my stress by listening to records and painting polka dots on my toenails."

"Suit yourself."

I went on an extra-long jog through the carefully shoveled and salted sidewalks of campus. I thought of everything Mina did for me. Everything I hadn't been doing. And still I managed to finish last semester. To get back to Colwyn. And David? Could he be headed to rehab? If so, I hoped it would work. Mom said most people have to go through rehab over and over. Seven times or something. I ran up the big hill in town where I could see to the ocean, farther than I'd run in a long time.

I thought about Calvin and Sai. Was I feeling intuition? Or did I just think they looked cool? Was picking a family for my baby something like the biology of attraction? On my way up the hill, I realized I was using their number as a mantra—310-555-2161, 310-555-2161, 310-555-2161. I ran and ran. When I got back to the dorms, I collapsed in a dreamless sleep. At six I woke needing to pee. And with hours until the phone call, I was wide-awake.

In the freakishly quiet campus cafe, I got a coffee and chocolate croissant. I sat with my hands around the hot cup watching the clock slowly tick minutes away. 6:35. 6:38. 6:45. 7:02. I kept hoping I'd run into someone, but campus was quiet. There was nothing to distract me. I took a bite, closed my eyes to enjoy the buttery chocolate taste, but as it melted away, I saw David, wet ankles and soggy sneakers, hollow-eyed in the gray Graceville day. Sipping my coffee, I thought about the warming room where anyone could sit because many can't afford to keep their houses comfortable. I shivered. I thought of my parents, asleep, not knowing what I was about to do. I felt so far from them. 8:15: Mina texted me to meet her at the dining hall. 8:35: Mina met me in the dining hall for rubbery eggs.

She slid into her chair. "You've totally got this."

"I feel like I'm about to split apart at the atomic level."

"Deep breaths, Scarlett, we can't have you spontaneously combusting all over our dorm room."

"Spontaneous human combustion probably isn't possible," I said. "Cases of it are so rare it's hard to tell if the person died or exploded first."

"Oh good. I really didn't want to have to wipe bits of you off the new record player."

"Yeah. I already broke one once," I said, letting my eggs slide off my fork back onto my plate.

"Come on, Scar. You know you've got this." Her words made my face flash hot. Did I? I hadn't done anything yet. If not for her, I'd probably still be pretending nothing was wrong with me.

"Min, I don't." I tugged my hair. "It's just everything about them will be tangible proof of how much better than me they'll be."

"Isn't that kind of the point?" Mina said, waving her toast at me. "That they're better than you now?"

I inhaled. *1, 2, 3. Exhale. 1, 2, 3, 4.*

"They are. Way better than me," I said, and pushed my fork around my plate. I imagined bursting open because of this pressure. The heat behind my eyes. The hunger I couldn't fill. Everything I wouldn't say, to Cody, David, Hannah, my parents. But these two men, they would know my secret. They would smile and take it away.

"I—" I said, and flattened my eggs with a fork, "hate it." I scraped them back into a pile. "I just. I hate it." I dropped my fork with a clang.

"What?" Mina said.

"That I have to admit defeat on this one."

"Scarlett, it isn't defeat. It's absolute sanity." The tip of her tongue appeared for a split second as she tucked her hair behind her ear. "Unless you want to make an appointment."

I sighed. "Min, I'm not going to change my mind now."

"You could. But a decision isn't defeat. It's just a choice. One choice."

"You make it sound so easy."

Mina shrugged, bit her toast.

9:58. I sat on my bed with Calvin and Sai's file spread out across my lap. I opened my phone—310-555-2161— I watched the clock change to 9:59. The picture of Calvin and Sai on the beach, happy in the sun, staring up at me. I glanced out the window. On the dirty snowbanks piled near the walkway, three girls climbed on a sled. They hooted as it flew down the bank and skidded across the concrete. 10:00. I pressed CALL.

"Hello!" an overly cheery voice picked up before I'd even heard a ring. Which one was it?

"Hey, um, this is Scarlett."

"Hi, Scarlett," two voices sounded together. "You're on speakerphone. I'm Sai." His voice was deep.

"And I'm Calvin." His voice was slightly higher.

"Hi, Sai and Calvin, nice to hear you." I closed my eyes and tried to picture them in their brick townhouse, but I kept looking down at them on the beach, sand on Calvin's knees.

"You too," Sai said, and I imagined him squinting under the brim of his bucket hat.

"So—" I was suddenly unable to form words.

"We were so excited when we saw your profile. How do you like Colwyn? My sister went there." Sai's words blurred together. Was he speaking fast or was it my nerves? Was he nervous too? I cleared my throat.

"Um, oh, Colwyn? Yeah, it's good, the classes are interesting, but—"

"Not what you expected, I guess, for your first year?" Sai said.

"Yeah, I um, never really thought this would be part of my college experience." My eyes landed on Einstein's puppet. Silence on the end of the line. I guess I needed to say more? I could hear some muffled noises through the phone, and I imagined these two men making faces at each other, communicating wordlessly, in the way that couples do. I wondered if they would like me. If I would like them. I inhaled. "I was pretty wiped out first semester. I had this eight a.m. English class I didn't make it to very often, so I have an incomplete to finish."

"Sai hated English," Calvin said.

"I was pre-med, and I passed the AP exam. Why did I have to take it?"

"Right? That's what I said!"

Sai laughed in three deep, easy waves, each tumbling into

the next. "And Calv knows something about incompletes, don't you, Calvin?"

Calvin guffawed. "What you hear is Sai mocking me for how I finished my incomplete in undergrad."

"Oh?" I said, wondering if this was what we should be talking about. Why weren't they quizzing me on my diet? Asking why I wanted to do this? Didn't they want to know about the father?

"I skipped too much of Spanish," Calvin continued, "and I never finished the term project. A presentation about a Spanish-speaking culture. The prof agreed to an incomplete that I could finish by the end of break, but I put it off until the last weekend, when I took out a credit card, flew to Nicaragua, took some pictures of myself on the beach, the food I ate, and the blanket I bought, then I wrote in bad Spanish about how I learned from the locals that my Spanish really did suck. And by some blessing of God, I was given a C minus in the class."

"And it only took you fifteen years to pay off that credit card," Sai said.

"Yeah, well, I would have done it sooner if it weren't for my student loans. Stay away from credit cards, Scarlett," Calvin offered.

"I tried to, but I had to get some clothes to hide the bump when I went home at Christmas."

"Oh," they said together.

"Well, I'm sure we could—" Sai said, and was hushed by Calvin.

I reached up and tried to fold back the dented corners of my Curie poster. I tried to take a deep breath, but then thought they could probably hear me breathe. I realized I might combust, just like Mina said, so I started speaking quickly. "My family doesn't know about this. I guess if you like me, you'll need to decide if you're okay with that. And you know, the drinking, drugs, and unidentified father part." My words were like a fast and icy wind.

"But the baby's healthy?" one of them said, so quickly I wasn't sure who. I was looking at a picture of them smiling. So perfect.

"So far, so good. I've been a model of purity since I got to Colwyn. I run like five miles a day."

There was a pause, a murmur. Then Sai's voice, deep and too loud:

"Well, Scarlett, if you decide to pick us, you'll need to be okay with the fact that—should we tell her, Calvin?"

"Oh go ahead, she deserves to know." Calvin's words were artificial, like he was saying cheese for a photo at the beach.

"We're gay!" they said in chorus.

I burst out laughing, and they did too, and it felt like we'd suddenly all entered zero gravity.

"Yeah, I know. It's part of why I wanted to talk with you."

"Do you think the fact that we're a nice, interracial gay couple will make it easier to explain to your friends why you didn't get an abortion?" Sai's voice, lilting a bit. Was he joking? He seemed like he was a straight shooter, but maybe this was his really dry sense of humor? I couldn't tell. My breath froze as I fell back into earth's gravitational field.

Before I could think of what to say, Calvin chimed in. "Look, Scarlett, we're so excited to be parents, we don't judge."

"Not true. We judge racists and homophobes," Sai said. "And people who think the earth is six thousand years old."

I wanted to say *me too,* but instead I found myself blurting, "My best friend from home might think the earth is six thousand years old. I'm not sure, because there are some things we just don't talk about, like me being pregnant and not knowing who the father is. So." I rubbed my fingers along the window sash, felt the cool air leaking in. I didn't feel like gravity had increased any more, but I wasn't quite floating either.

"What do you think your parents and friends would say if they knew?" Calvin asked. The line was silent for a while, and then I did a strange thing. I told the truth.

"I've spent so much time thinking about how they can't know, I've never really stopped to think about what they'd say to me if they did."

"*I'm here for you. Whatever you do.* That's all any good friend or family member should say. That's what I said to a friend who was pregnant in high school. I'm telling you this now," Calvin said, "because as much as I want a baby, I want to know the baby I'm getting is one that is meant to be with me. If you think telling people would change your plans at all, if their response is what you're worried about, you should consider it. We, well, we've had a baby fall through before and we just—really don't want to go through that again." So Calvin told it straight too. I liked that.

I looked up at Curie's face on my wall. She'd had two great

loves. The first died in a tragic accident. The second was married, but not to her. If you really boiled it down, I thought, life is discovery, love, and loss. The magic that moves us. The choices we make, sometimes impulsively, that pave our way through the world. I thought of David looking lost in his sneakers on the snowy sidewalk in Graceville. And I inhaled deeply, hoping that all mistakes were somehow mendable.

"It wouldn't change any decisions I make," I said. "I want this baby to go to people who really want it. But I—I do have a question. Um, Calvin—why biotech?"

There was a silent beat. Then: "You mean am I trying to destroy the world or save it?"

"Seems a fair question for someone I might allow to raise my spawn," I said.

"Well, you tell me." I could hear his smile radiating like it did from the beach photo in my hand. "Right now I'm working to develop regenerative tissues so burn victims can regrow their own skin."

My chest released from gravity again. "Awesome. So, what do you think? Do you want this baby?"

"Oh yes," Sai said, and Calvin jumped in for a chorus of "We do, we do, we do."

I'm pretty sure we were all floating there for a minute.

I'd just put out a fresh pot of coffee when I heard a voice call, "Scarlett!" I turned, surprised to see Professor Bradshaw coming through the door, dusting snow off her shoulders as she crossed the room. It was quiet in the commuter lounge turned warming shelter. A few people sat on the couches, stretching out, thumbing through magazines or the stack of donated paperbacks. Wet mittens dried on the heaters along the walls.

"I was hoping you'd be here. Maudly told me you were staffing the shelter with the physics society. Good for you," Bradshaw said.

"Yeah, we don't have these in Graceville, I don't think. Maybe some churches open up? I don't know. People must go somewhere. Yesterday, a woman told me that every winter she has the water shut off so the pipes won't freeze."

Bradshaw nodded like she'd heard that before.

"It doesn't seem like enough, you know? Just opening up the lounge and giving out hot drinks and snacks. Magazines." I gestured to a rumpled stack.

Bradshaw pulled off her hat. Loose hairs from her ponytail levitated, static-charged, above her head. "It is hard to figure out—how to do more help than harm in this world. I always wonder, is teaching enough? Trying to raise my kids thoughtfully? Was it selfish to have a third child?"

I thought of Casper pulling Bradshaw to the merry-go-go.

"Do you regret it?"

"Casper?" She choked back a laugh. "Oh God no, but I do wonder if it was selfish. American resource-use and all." She looked at me. "I always want to do more."

"You do a lot."

"Maybe." She shuddered as if shaking off a chill. "Well, I didn't come here to wax philosophical on the state of the world, but I was wondering how things were going, and if you needed help or anything?"

"I did talk to the couple I mentioned—Calvin and Sai. They seem great. We're moving forward."

"Good. Well, if you get bored or feel like you need a home-cooked meal or something, let me know. I can provide good food amid a messy house and screaming children."

"Thanks. That's really nice. Mina's here, so I'll probably be all right."

"Email me if you change your mind, Scarlett. My door is open to you." She gave me a sort of half smile, raised her shoulders, pulled on her hat, and turned to go.

I hadn't yet realized how important Bradshaw would be. I'm only just now kind of figuring it out.

I wonder if David ever had a chance to connect with any of his professors. Probably not. Stanford is big, and he wasn't there long. I wish he could have had that, though. I imagine he could have been like Harold, playing darts with the physics professors. But instead of escaping Graceville, he took all its demons with him, and they consumed him with a force so great, it dragged him back across the country and left him at the bridge to die.

I want to remember David alive at Mine Gulch Bridge, comforting me over the loss of Cody with snow falling around us. Or stepping into the air together. Or lying together on the bank. I want to remember David—so electric, all eyes had to follow him. And now, under this crushing blue Nebraska sky, I just want that. I just want to see him again.

TEN MONTHS AGO

GRACEVILLE, COLORADO

Two days after returning from the Joy Ride Down the Great Divide, sweaty from a day of discussing pond ecology with nine- and ten-year-olds, I answered the front door and found David, red-eyed but smiling, on my steps.

"You recovering?" he asked, touching the stitches near my hairline.

"Yeah, you?"

"Slow enough for some refills, I think." He smiled. I could have said, *Be careful*. I could have said, *Stop, David—stop messing around, especially with refills*.

He took a step closer to me. "You know, I tried not to hit it, Scar—the deer." His lips set tight, his eyes wide. "I'm sorry."

And I wanted him to be that perfect boy, suddenly, there, the one who had gone unnoticed my whole life. I wanted it so badly.

I ran a hand down his shoulder. "I know that was an accident— but Mexico? Come on, D—"

He licked his lips, inhaled slowly. We stood not talking. The ticking of the clock in the kitchen seemed loud. Neither of us moved any closer to the other. Eventually, I felt the energy gathering inside me and my breath became unstable. He stepped back toward the door. "I'm sorry about, you know, Mexico. Can we, just— I don't know." He touched my cheek. Cleared his throat. "Grab a burrito?"

"What?" I shook my arms. "I guess, if you'll talk more over food. Give me a minute to change." I left him standing in the entry, staring after me as I went down the hall to my room. I shut the door. Inhaled. Flipped through items in my closet and finally settled on a yellow maxi skirt and white tank top. I remember thinking—it's just David, why are you worried about what you're wearing? And what the hell? Why are you going anywhere with him after Mexico? But here he was, sorry, and what? Sad? Scared?

Just David.

I wiped down with a towel from the morning, and twisted up my hair, accidentally grazing the stiches on my cheek. I flinched. Just David? Was there really a "Just David" anymore? Was there ever? David was never really of the landscape.

And so after the river, the pool, the drive down the divide, we drove like the two old friends that we were (weren't we?) to get burritos and soda, endless chips.

"Let's skip the endless chips today," David said, and pulled into the drive-through instead of the parking lot.

"Oh, D. Terminal chips! Why?"

"Because, I want to go up Mine Gulch."

"Your urge to swim is keeping us from the best chips in the county?"

"Today, yes," he said, and dropped his hand to my leg. And just like that, I was electric. And afraid. I moved his hand away.

Our burritos and chips were handed to us in a bag. When we got to Mine Gulch, we ate in his car with the music on. Then David reached into the back seat. "I have something for you," he said. He pulled out a box wrapped in brown paper and an envelope that looked like it was depicting the big bang.

"David, I don't—"

"Just open it."

I ripped open the envelope to find a card that was printed with these words:

"One cannot help but be in awe when he contemplates the mysteries of eternity, of life, of the marvelous structure of reality. It is enough if one tries to comprehend only a little of this mystery every day." -Einstein.

Inside in David's blocky handwriting was written *Scarlett, every minute with you gave me some of that mystery. Thank you. Please forgive me for mixing physicists with this gift. Conserve your energy out there. You will do great things.*

"David—I—"

"Just open it," he said again, drumming on the steering wheel.

I ripped open the paper and read *Newton's cradle* in large red letters, and a picture of seven metal balls hanging still.

"Oh David," I said. "It's perfect." He leaned in as if to kiss me but I eased out of the car and pulled off my skirt in a quick movement, thankful that my boy-short underwear looked enough like swim shorts. I pulled David by the hand to the bridge. We stood for a minute, balanced on the trellis, looking at the water below us, then a whoosh of air and the slap of water as we went under.

I remember his hands. I remember coming up and how he reached for me. And we swam together, to the eddy, to the beach, where we kissed once and then lay for a long time, my head on his chest, his hand in my wet hair, combing the strands.

"You know that river with the picnic shelter where we slept?" David said.

"Yeah?"

"My dad, he would take me fishing there."

I remembered little David, hair always messy, and I imagined him there, rod and tackle in hand. I pulled his thumb to my lip to kiss his scar, but he pulled his hand away.

NOW

WYOMING BORDER

Now, Mina is out taking a picture of the WELCOME TO WYOMING FOREVER WEST sign. She's hoping to get all fifty states before we graduate. She keeps asking me if we should take the southern route back to Colwyn, Route 66 and all. But I'm not sure I'm ready to go to New Mexico again.

Mina's wearing a cowboy hat purchased at a gas station across the street from our campground in a cornfield, cutoff jean shorts, and six-inch heels. She has to hold on to the hat with one hand as trucks speed by, drivers pounding on their horns and catcalling out their windows. This appears to be making steadying the camera difficult.

Because I've been teaching Mina "science stuff," like she asked, when my hands need a break from typing, I've realized that the scientific method is not unlike writing. When you analyze your data, if you prove your hypothesis wrong, you go back and revise your question, revisit your research, think through your findings.

In school sometimes, science is taught with the idea that

getting things "wrong" is a problem. But I don't think it is. What matters is recording. What matters is thinking things through. Observing. Rethinking. Drawing a conclusion.

Then asking more questions.

FOUR MONTHS AGO, FEBRUARY

COLWYN COLLEGE · WATERTOWN, MAINE

Mina drove cursing and weaving between lanes to Sherrie's office.

"Scarlett, you're not even bitching about my driving," she said as she cut someone off crossing three lanes to our exit. "I'm worried."

"Don't be. I'm fine. Just about to meet the two people I'm going to entrust the life of my secret child to. So, you know, exactly the kind of thing I was well prepared for by all of those years of leadership training."

"Yes! Exactly. Plus, you love them. You felt like you entered zero gravity two times during your phone call—so they turned you into a poet and took you to space already. What could possibly go wrong?"

"You're right, I probably won't explode."

"Yeah, I have it on good authority that spontaneous human combustion is probably a myth."

We got out of the car and I watched Mina dodge puddles and drifts in three-inch platform heels. I followed, splashing through them in my boots. When we walked into the house, I could hear Calvin's and Sai's voices upstairs.

"Come on up," Sherrie called. Mina looked at me.

"I'll come," she offered.

I clutched the railing. Mina followed. Sherrie stood in the doorway, a bright red smile painted across her face. "Scarlett! Good to see you. This is Calvin and Sai," she said as I walked, trying not to tremble, into her office. I imagined maybe this was how David would feel if he decided to go to rehab, his mom behind him. The counselors trying to assess him. I imagined him clutching his arms. Afraid to be there. Afraid to be anywhere. But trying, trying to get it right. I shook my own arms loose and looked across the room.

Calvin and Sai rose in unison from the window seat as I entered the room. Sai's black hair was thick and wavy, graying at the temples, while Calvin's hair was shaved in middle-aged, balding-man fashion. They both wore dress pants that looked like wool, but Calvin was in a button-down shirt and Sai wore a turtleneck sweater. They looked like they'd stepped out of a Brooks Brothers ad. Pressed and dry-cleaned. They stepped toward me, arms open.

"Can we hug?" he said.

"We're big huggers, but we can respect if you're not," Calvin added.

"Um, yeah, we can hug," I said, feeling my belly pressing out, their eyes on it. The baby began to flail around inside me at that moment, like, *Get me out and give me to them!* And why wouldn't it say that? They were together, beautiful, wealthy, and shining with kindness. I was a pregnant teenager, missing a boy who needed rehab.

I opened my arms and stepped toward Sai, noticing that his socks had some weird pattern. I hugged him but I didn't keep my butt back; I let my belly push out, fill the space between us. Something about their hands on my shoulders gave me the shivers and calmed me at the same time.

"I'm Mina, the roommate keeping her from giving birth in the bathroom."

"Thanks for that!" Sai said, and hugged her too.

When all hugging was over, I turned to Mina. "Could you, maybe, wait downstairs?" I whispered.

"You sure?" She looked surprised.

"Yeah, I got this," I said. "Go text Harold or something."

Mina gave me the full two-dimple and grabbed my hands. A quick squeeze, and she slipped out the door.

We sat down. I found myself unable to digest a thing Sherrie said. I watched Calvin lean against the windows, and when Sai put his foot on his knee I saw his socks:

SpongeBob SquarePants danced around his ankles. I almost smiled. A pediatric oncologist who wore funny socks.

And they vibrated—Sai and Calvin. They wanted this kid so bad, planned for it, waited. I felt the ache I'd felt driving back to Graceville with David, that I was losing something I couldn't quite put my finger on; that I'd already lost it, and no scavenger hunt could ever help me find it.

"And we have some exciting news," Sai was saying. "My hospital's putting me on a bi-monthly call rotation for six months. It means I'll only be on call for one week every other month the entire first six months of the baby's life."

"And when he's on call, I'll be taking divided-up paternity leave," added Calvin.

"That means the baby won't go to daycare until they are six months old."

"Oh, great," I said, feeling like I should be interested in parental leave and daycare, realizing I wasn't. I looked for Mina, but remembered I'd sent her downstairs. I breathed in. I could do this. "So what are the next steps?"

"Well, if you think this is a fit, Scarlett, we go forward. You'll want to talk about how much you want Calvin and Sai involved at the birth and after."

"I think I'll wait until after it's born to give it to you guys, though it would be nice if you could take it now. It's getting a bit heavy," I said.

Calvin and Sai laughed. "You still think we're a good fit?" Sai asked, leaning forward.

"Yeah, I mean, assuming you do."

"We do, we do, we do," they said together, just as they'd done on the phone the month before. But this time, it didn't make me float away. I was just in the room with the slow knowledge that this choice I was making was the beginning of a family.

- - -

Later, when I was buckling myself into the Jeep, anticipating the hellacious drive back to campus with Mina at the wheel, there was a knock on my window.

"This might be unorthodox," Calvin said as I rolled down the window, "but Sai and I were wondering if you wanted to go to lunch because we drove all the way up here and conversations in offices, even ones that look like living rooms, always make me jumpy. What do you think?"

I inhaled. He hadn't seemed jumpy. His green eyes were hopeful. I looked at Mina.

"I've got to get back to study with Harold"—her dimple flashed—"but you should go."

"Hold on," I said, and, rolling up the window, whispered to Mina, "You have a study date with Harold?"

"Well, not exactly. He just said he'd be in the library later and hoped to run into me, so I figured I'd go work on my psych paper."

"Sounds date-ish to me." I glanced out the window. Calvin was looking away, hands stuffed in the pockets of his wool slacks. "So what's the deal with them asking me to lunch? Is it weird? It feels weird."

"Scar, even if it is, you should go, because dorm food sucks and you're pregnant. Plus this *whole* thing is weird. So—go. You'll love it. Well, at least the food part. The rest we can process later."

I nodded a bunch of times. "Okay. But only because it means

I won't have to be in a car with you any longer than I have to be."

"Whatever you tell yourself is fine."

I rolled down the window again. "Sure, but you'll have to take me back to campus, if that's cool? Mina needs to study."

"Great," Calvin said. "I'd love to see Colwyn. Sai's always talking about the time he was visiting his sister and the power went out—apparently there's—"

"Storm Parties." I laughed before I could stop myself. "Legendary Colwyn stuff." I turned to Mina. "Thank you. And good luck getting anything done in proximity to Harold." Then I clambered out of the car like a harbor seal. Two cars down, Sai sat at the wheel of a white Lexus SUV.

"Wow," I said, buckling myself in, "I don't think a car like this has ever driven through Graceville, Colorado."

"Aren't there all kinds of fancy people in Colorado?" Sai said.

"Not in Graceville. Graceville's on the road to nowhere, so fancy people don't usually pass through."

"Calvin saved for five years for this beauty," Sai said, rubbing his hands along the steering wheel.

"I'm responsibly fancy." Calvin pretended to polish his knuckles on his shirt.

It was starting to rain as we drove, and pedestrians hurried around, tugging up the hoods of their squall jackets.

"There it is." Sai pointed to a brick building with a large metal sign out front that read GOOD FOOD.

"Look for parking," said Sai.

"Dear Gladys, parking goddess, shine your little light upon us," Calvin said, and from the back seat I could see Sai shaking his head and grinning. "There!" Calvin pointed. "That blue Civic is about to pull out."

"Good eye!" I said.

"It's Gladys, works every time."

"Great, let the budding scientist know you're all about peer-reviewed documentation except in the case of city parking," Sai said.

"It's hard to do a double-blind study on appeals to Gladys. But if I had spare time I'd try," Calvin said.

"Luck does exist," I offered.

"And so does having a really good eye for people about to get in their cars," said Sai.

"And so does Gladys!" said Calvin, opening his door and stepping onto the street.

On the other side of the restaurant's heavy wooden door, an open dining room with exposed pipe running across high ceilings and down the brick walls bustled with a late-lunch crowd. The host immediately sat us at a table made from a wine barrel topped with glass. He handed us menus printed on thick paper. When you ran your fingers over the words you could feel them.

"Letterpress. Nice," Calvin said, turning the paper over in his hand. "But"—he lowered his voice—"maybe a bit extravagant for a daily menu?"

Sai shook his head and turned to me. "Get whatever you'd like, Scarlett, it's on us."

"Okay," I said, noticing that there wasn't a meal on the menu that cost less than thirty-eight dollars.

"And don't feel weird about it either, because half of the nourishment is going to the baby that we are going to take from you," he added, his fingers tap-tapping on glass tabletop.

"*Take* sounds so violent!" Calvin said.

I smiled. "It's accurate, though."

"I need a beer. Excuse me," Calvin said, and raised his arm. A waiter appeared. "A pint of your best pilsner, please!"

"Would you like—"

"Anything, dear, just quickly!"

"Nice, Calv, you're going to make her think she's giving her baby to some drunk."

Calvin showed off his mouthful of perfectly straight teeth. "Oh now she's *giving* us the baby! When just a minute ago we were taking it?"

"I don't care what word you guys settle on, but I wish you could have it soon. It's stomping on my bladder right now. Excuse me, but I need a restroom."

"Where you're no doubt going to reconsider giving your baby to bickering afternoon drinkers," Calvin said, raising the glass that was at that moment set in front of him.

"Calvin!" Sai said, but the smile never left his face.

When I returned, I found the two of them laughing with the waiter, who raised his pen, waiting for me to order.

"Oh, um, I guess I'll have the lobster mac and cheese with a pear and arugula salad."

"Good choice!" Sai said. "I got that too."

"Well, great minds."

The waiter left and then a long awkward silence settled over the table. It made me think of David. How would he handle this? What would he say? I thought about texting him again just to ask how he was, if he was getting help, but he never—

"So if you don't mind my asking," Cal said, "why didn't you tell anybody? Even your parents?"

I shrugged. "Einstein did it. I figured I could too," I said. How Mina would groan if she could hear me.

"Wait, what did Einstein do?" Calvin asked, the lines on his forehead deepening.

"He had a secret child," I said.

"And?"

"He'd promised his mom he wouldn't get his girlfriend pregnant, but he did. It was possible for him to hide it from his parents, though, and protect his soon-to-be wife and child from a culture that would have marked them all. I guess—for me it wasn't really any different? I've always been . . . capable. A rule-follower. That's how people see me. I didn't want this one thing to make everyone see me as a completely different person."

"Like a wreck, you mean," Sai said.

"That is . . . yeah, one—direct and accurate way of putting it." I tried to smile. Calvin swatted Sai's arm. "Yeah—a wreck is accurate. I actually *was* in a car crash last summer—"

"Really?" Calvin said.

"We hit a deer and got some scrapes and bruises." Suddenly my mouth felt very dry. "But other cars drove by. They looked at us with such—it was curiosity mixed with . . . thankfulness. That they weren't us. It made me feel sick, to be looked at like that."

Calvin nodded, his voice almost a whisper when he spoke. "Everyone loves a wreck. It explains most reality TV."

"Yeah, I guess. But I didn't want that—to be a wreck, to be stared at."

"I get that. It's part of the reason I didn't come out to my folks until I'd been accepted to graduate school," Calvin said.

"He actually called them and said, 'I got into Dartmouth and I'm gay!'"

I laughed, inhaling some water from my glass and coughing. "What did they do?"

"They said they had long suspected it and wanted to know if they could meet anyone special in my life."

"He was lucky," Sai said. "I came out my second year of college, and my parents told me I was in a phase for the next eight years."

"Oh, no," I said.

"Yep, it was awful. It was really our wedding that finally brought them around. For years, my parents thought they were liberal for allowing my sister to date white boys. They just weren't prepared for me to do the same. Some extended family are still uncomfortable around me, but I have hope for them.

Mostly I'm thankful my parents get it now. And I became a doctor, so I've met half of my obligations as a son." He smiled at Calvin and then looked at me seriously. "Don't get me wrong, I love my job, but it was expected. Now that I'm going to give them a grandchild, I think all is nearly forgiven. Still, I learned how important it is not to undermine a child's identity. I'll never do that. I know how terrible it feels."

I met his eyes. "I'm glad you'll accept whoever this baby grows up to be, whoever they love." And before I could stop myself, I said, "On the phone, you asked if it would make it easier to explain not getting an abortion to my liberal friends. Maybe you were joking—but I want you to know, I chose this on my own. Mina knew, but she didn't push anything. My best friend from back home, she's not liberal. But she'd be happy about you guys. Her particular brand of fundamentalism—it's different from what you see on TV. Anyway, I guess I don't want to explain my choices to anyone. Everyone thought I should have gone to MIT and I didn't. But it's my life. I can decide how much debt to take on. I can decide what to do with my body. This, I know it's a choice, but—" Suddenly I felt like I'd said too much.

Sai flattened his palms on the table. "Good for you. You don't need to explain yourself."

Calvin cleared his throat. "Your friend from home might have surprised you, if you told her. It's possible to support friends even when they do things we disagree with. I bet you supported her in things you didn't agree with."

His words hung in the air. I always supported Hannah's choices, even as I realized they were different from mine. Because I loved her. Had I been selling Hannah short? Keeping her in the dark because I didn't think she'd see any choice in my choice? Maybe she would have understood that, for me, there *was* a choice. I raised my shoulders. They felt so heavy. "You guys are going to be great dads," I said.

Sai leaned forward, one hand on the table. "We'll do our best."

The baby kicked and I put my own hand on my belly. Everyone stopped talking.

At last Sai said, "So you're worried if people knew, they'd stare at you and think you're a wreck, because they wouldn't see that you're actually calculating the Theory of Everything."

"That *is* hard to see," I said. Smiled a little. "So you guys don't think I'm a wreck? Why not? You barely know me. I'm a knocked-up eighteen-year-old. I've obviously screwed up somewhere along the line."

"Oh no, your reality show would be so boring," Calvin said.

"You think?"

"Oh, it would. Look at you—in your spare time you read theories about the universe and biographies of great physicists. I love it, but it doesn't make for good TV. Can you imagine? Here's a scene of Scarlett reading about Einstein again? Here she is, doing it still. Oh look, now she's applying for a job in the tutoring center. Gripping! Will she get it despite the incomplete in

English? She does! Thanks to those perfect scores in calculus! Now look at her helping struggling students with their homework. I'm on the edge of my seat. Wait, she's still intelligent despite the fact she is obviously carrying a child? You mean the minds of young women who are pregnant don't disintegrate under the impact of this biological process?" Calvin sat back.

I was still laughing when the server set the arugula and pear salad down in front of me. The pear was arranged on the plate like a flower and drizzled with balsamic. I lifted it to my mouth. I bit down; it was bittersweet.

Back in my room, under the paper eyes of Einstein and Curie, I thought, for all that Einstein is mentioned, how often is his secret child? How often his failed marriage? The fact is, no one was paying attention to Einstein when Mileva had their first child out of wedlock, because that was before he was Einstein as we know him now. He couldn't even get a job. He was working at a patent office when he wrote the paper that would change our understanding of the universe. He was Albert before he was Einstein. Toiling away. Just like I'm Scarlett. I'm Scarlett even before I do anything to leave my mark. Just Scarlett.

KAMPGROUNDS OF AMERICA · EAST OF CHEYENNE, WYOMING

"First the tent, then I'll get back to it," I say as a troop of kids with Nerf guns runs shouting past our campsite. They point their weapons at us and Mina sticks out her tongue. I wink and wave them off.

"I could do this on my own, you know," Mina says.

"Everything is easier with help." I set my computer down on the picnic table, my fingers still on the keys. I close my eyes for a second and see a flash of David, his soggy-bottomed jeans. His almost-smile.

Mina must be able to read my mind. Her voice is soft as she says, "What?"

"I wish I could have helped David more."

"Nothing you could have done." Mina's tone is firm now.

I look up at her. "But I didn't do anything."

"Self-preservation is the key to human survival."

And I want her to be right. I feel David's absence grow around me as I stand to help Mina pull our shelter together. I can't stop thinking that maybe if I had said more, if I had told my mom about any of it, if, if, if.

TEN MONTHS AGO, AUGUST

GRACEVILLE, COLORADO

"David?" I said, my wet head on his chest, the stitches in my cheek facing the sun. He'd just pulled his scar away from my lips. It was moments after we'd jumped off the bridge again.

"Seven stitches," he said, nodding to his hand.

"What?"

"Your scar"—he moved the hair off my cheek—"it won't be as big. But this one, the knife slipped. Dad was teaching me how to gut a fish. I screwed up."

"Ouch."

David shrugged. "It was my fault. I should've paid better attention."

"How old were you?"

"Five."

"What? Sorry, D, but that wasn't your fault. That was the fault of whoever put a giant blade in your hand. You were *five*." I could feel his heart beat faster.

He shook his head. "Tell that to my dad. He never took me fishing after that. Didn't want the trip to be interrupted by a hospital run. My brothers all seemed to figure it out."

"Yeah, no, D—that"—I pointed at the scar—"is your dad's fault. You don't give a five-year-old a knife."

I felt David raise his shoulders under my head, but he didn't say anything. We listened to the water, the birds, the voices of other swimmers upstream. I laced my fingers between his.

"I'm going to miss this," I said.

"Swimming?" His voice lilted.

"You know what I mean."

David raised himself up on his elbows as I pulled away from his chest. "Scarlett—I—I want to be—you know, with you."

"You're with me right now."

"Now's all we got?"

I kissed him. I didn't say yes. I didn't say no. I couldn't. The sky spun. I wanted more than now, but—our drive, his pills, his phones. He pulled away from me and spoke quickly.

"I'll be better. I won't—do so much—asinine shit . . . or be such an ass."

A splash in the water. Our eyes turned to the swoop of a bird. A heron. Long-necked and hopeful. Was this the same one as last time? It was less than two weeks ago. It felt like forever. We watched it lift into the air. And I wanted what David did—to be with him. But it felt heavy, impossible.

I squeezed his hand. "Come on. We gotta get back to my house."

Because my parents were leaving. It was time for our last party.

NOW

KAMPGROUNDS OF AMERICA · EAST OF CHEYENNE, WYOMING

If I was slow to get David into focus, I was even slower getting a clear picture of myself. I ran to the bridge with David. I fell with him into the water. When we stumbled to the shore, I kissed him first. I tugged down his shorts. I said yes to the pull of him. My mouth was greedy, my hands. I wanted all of him. I untethered myself. I entered that free fall, and I did it willingly. All of this. I did it.

About a month after I'd decided to place the baby with Calvin and Sai, I burst through the door after a run to find Mina lying on the floor of our room, staring at the ceiling as a record spun something in gloomy minor chords.

"Min?"

"Yeah," she mumbled.

"You okay?"

She pressed her palms into her eyes. "It's just, I've been studying with Harold, and sometimes he seems into me but then nothing—for weeks. So, I guess, just, you know, can't get a boyfriend and don't know what I want to do with my life."

"Okay. First, Harold is clueless. Second, boyfriends and knowing what you want to do with your life are both highly overrated."

"Easy for you to say, Ms. Physics Is Everything Since Fourth Grade."

"Come on, I'm trying to hold on to my scholarship." It was taking so much to study every day. But knowing that David couldn't stay in school was some kind of cold fire that kept me going. We couldn't both fail. "Come on Min, you'll end up with a boyfriend and a plan eventually. I promise."

"Not sure I believe you, but thanks." She wiped her eyes with the back of her sleeve.

"Hey, I have a favor to ask. And it's my birthday, so you have to say yes."

She popped up on one elbow, revived. "Really? Scar, why didn't you say anything? Now we don't have any cake!"

"Yeah, I'm not celebrating this year."

"But—"

"No, really."

"What pregnant lady in the history of the world says no to cake? Any kind you want. Let's go."

"No, Min."

Mina's smile dropped. She sucked her lips over her teeth. Nodded.

"But as a birthday favor, I was wondering, if you don't think it's too gross or weird or whatever—will you be my birth partner? I signed up for these classes—"

"On your own?" She sat all the way up, hair settling over her eyes. She blew it away.

"I know, look at me, refusing spontaneous childbirth in our dorm room. So will you or won't you?"

Mina flew off the floor and practically knocked me over with her hug. "Of course! Of course— Oh, you really are sweaty, is that a pregnancy thing?"

"No, just a running thing. You should try it."

Mina and I sat on the floor because it was better preparation for childbirth. This was what the woman in a nurse's coat and stethoscope around her neck said. We were in Childbirth 101.

"I wish they could just knock me out and take the baby," I said to Mina.

"That's called a C-section. I'm sure they'll cover it in this class."

"Welcome, everyone. I'm Nurse Lynne. Let's start by going around the circle. Mamas, tell us your name and your due date. And birth partners, tell us your name and one thing you especially admire about the mama you're supporting."

"I'm Kelly." Kelly smiled, wondrous. "I'm due April twenty-fourth." She leaned tenderly into the shoulder of the man next to her.

"And I'm Steven. I admire that Kelly's been taking such good care of herself and our baby through this pregnancy."

I was turning to vapor again. Bits of Scarlett floating off across the room.

I told myself taking this class was the right thing to do. It was. But why did I feel so aware of my edges? Why did everyone else's smile cut me like a scalpel?

I leaned toward Mina. "I think I might throw up. These people are pure cheese."

"Shut up or I'll elbow you in the baby," Mina hissed.

"Girls," the nurse said, looking at us sternly.

"Looks like we found a class I might fail, and it isn't English," I whispered to Mina, who put her finger to her lips.

"Did you want to go next?" Nurse Lynne said.

I felt my face heat. "We're college women actually, but sure," I said, the eyes of the room burning into me. "I'm Scarlett, and I'm due mid-May, but it could be off because I'm not sure when I got pregnant." One of the middle-aged men coughed and looked at the carpet.

"And I'm Mina. I put up with her."

"Mina, you're supposed to say something you admire about Scarlett."

"I admire that she's paying for her college education by being a surrogate for a nice gay couple," Mina said as I smiled at the group, patting my belly before leaning lovingly on Mina's shoulder.

About three weeks later, I was crossing the quad when I heard "Hey, Colorado!"

Harold was wearing the sweatshirt like David's. I kept walking, trying to remain invisible. "Scarlett!" he yelled, this time moving with his long quick strides toward me.

I stopped. "Yeah?"

"So, um." He looked uncomfortably toward my middle. I realized I'd unzipped my parka, that I wasn't hunched over, holding my arms across my bump. My hands began to sweat. I crossed my arms.

"Can you tutor tonight? Bert's got the stomach bug and we

need someone else who can do calc 1. People are freaked about the midterm Friday."

"Yeah, sure," I said, eyes focused over his shoulder on the bare beech and maple branches outlined against the gray sky. I started to step away but Harold said:

"I heard—well, some people are saying . . ."

"What?" I stopped, looked him straight in the eye.

"That—" His Adam's apple bobbed as he dropped his eyes to my belly, then the sidewalk. "That you're pregnant."

"Really?" I held each side of my parka away from me and looked down at my body.

Harold didn't see; he seemed to be inspecting his boots. "Yeah, I thought you should know."

"Why?" I said, recalling a lesson from Bradshaw's class about questions being the best way to deflect a subject, confuse your opponent. But Harold wasn't my opponent. I dropped my arms to my sides. This wasn't a debate. It was all pretty obvious.

"You don't want to know?" Had Harold had Bradshaw too? Or maybe he really was being kind. There was something in his voice, a faint waver.

"Not really," I said, taking a step forward.

"Is it, you know, true?" He said, putting a hand up to stop me—no, to reach for my arm.

I took a deep breath. I stepped back. Faced him.

"What do you think?" I said, pulling my top tight across my middle, my round belly exposed. Then I turned sideways so he could get a good look. "Is that the freshman fifteen or a baby?"

"Um." Harold looked back at his boots, their muddy tips. "You're never supposed to guess if a woman is pregnant. My mom taught me."

"Didn't she also tell you you're not supposed to ask?" I said, trying to make it sound like a joke; but by the look on Harold's face, it wasn't funny.

"I guess so."

"Then we have something in common after all. We've both done things our mommies told us not to." Harold paled. And my cheeks burned.

"Scarlett." He shifted onto his toes. "We have a lot in common." He held up his hand with a finger raised and listed: "We're both physics majors"—he raised his next finger—"and Society of Physics Students members"—a third finger went up—"we both work in the tutor lab"—and the pinky—"we both ski"—his thumb went out—"and we're both friends with Mina." He wiggled all five fingers. "It's enough for a high five." And he went for it, getting mostly air as our fingers collided but palms didn't slap.

I almost smiled. "Go ahead and tell the people who've been talking that they're right." I knew this would happen. Someone would notice and talk. But I didn't feel ready. Would people not want to be tutored by me? Girls who get pregnant are dumb. I'd heard it in high school every time it happened—didn't matter who she was, her grades, nothing. If she wasn't smart enough not to get pregnant, she wasn't smart. I shivered.

"Are you sure?" Harold said, his face open, green eyes flicking over mine.

Urgh, why was he sometimes so nice! It made me want to throw him and his big Adam's apple off the side of the clock tower.

"Isn't that why you asked me? Because you want to tell everyone?" I stuffed my hands into my pockets.

"No." His eyes widened and he tugged at the drawstrings of his sweatshirt. "No. I—I wanted to make sure you were okay. Because in the tutor center, the students really like you, and I just"—he pulled his sweatshirt hood up, pushed it off again, looked around and then back at me—"wanted to see if you needed help or anything."

I kicked a snow clump. "Oh. Okay. Thanks."

He met my eyes then, for the first time, swallowed, and nodded, cleared his throat. "See? My mom raised me well."

"Except you didn't listen to her," I said, and this time my mouth twitched into a real smile.

"Sit with us?" Courtney called to me in the dining hall a few days later. She was with Bert, Sora, and two girls I didn't know. I walked over. Might as well. Mina was meeting with her psych professor and was going to miss lunch.

"So you're pregnant?" Sora blurted, and all eyes around the table seemed magnetically attracted to my bulge.

"God, Sora, really?" Courtney said, lifting her fork toward Sora. "Way to make her feel welcome. Sit down, Scarlett. We're not going to interrogate you."

I inhaled, sunk into the chair.

"Why didn't you tell us?" Bert said.

"Bert!" Courtney said, her hands in the air.

"It's on a need-to-know basis," I said. I planned for it to sound strong, impervious, but it came out less than that.

The girl sitting next to Courtney shifted in her seat, adjusted her green cotton scarf that matched her glasses. "What's it feel like?" She gestured to my bump. "You know."

"Jackie! Oh my god. You guys, really, leave the girl alone. This is not why we asked her to sit here."

"She's a college woman, actually," Sora said, and smiled. Courtney shook her head.

"Thanks, Sora. I am a Pregnant College Woman. We're a rare species but not extinct." I smiled, then took a bite of a dry biscuit. The table stayed silent as I chewed. Bert looked at me sort of sideways.

"Okay, um." I sipped water and a little dribbled down my chin. "It's like a disease where I have to sleep all the time, and my back hurts. I'm hungry constantly, but the thought of some foods, like pizza, makes me want to vomit. My feet are swollen, and I've gained twenty pounds already and most pregnancy books say not to gain more than that in the entire time, which seems freaky and impossible, so it's not exactly an experience I plan on repeating any time soon."

There was an uncomfortable silence, during which Bert folded and unfolded his napkin, Sora tipped their chair back dangerously far, and Courtney took the world's smallest bite of food.

"Do you feel it swimming around and stuff?" Sora asked, dropping their chair onto all four legs.

"All the time. Sometimes I even see it too."

"Cool," Jackie breathed, leaning forward, squinting through her glasses toward my belly.

"What's your plan?" Sora said.

"What'd your parents say?" Bert asked.

"One question at a time, people," I said, fanning my hands out and trying to smile. "My parents don't know. Colwyn is my own version of a home for unwed mothers." I attempted a laugh. It was hollow.

"That's pretty hard-core," said Courtney.

"Well, I never want my parents to know I screwed up like this," I said.

Sora cocked their head. "I get that. My parents are cool about a lot, but if I do more than smoke weed or screw up in school? No way," they said.

Courtney clicked open her locket. "My mom thinks Colwyn is second-rate because it isn't Ivy League. My twin, Angela"—she pointed to her locket—"is at Yale." I leaned toward the tiny picture where two smaller versions of Courtney in French braids grinned arm in arm.

"I didn't know you had a twin."

"*I* didn't know you were knocked up." Her voice was dry as she clicked the locket shut.

I almost laughed.

"Why didn't you just get an abortion?" The other woman I didn't know asked, her voice soft. And when I raised my eyes to her, I realized this was the first time she'd spoken. She looked down and pulled her thumbs through holes stitched in her sweatshirt. "I mean, *I* did," she said.

"Via, that wasn't really a *just*. Remember?" Jackie said, touching Via's shoulder lightly.

"No, it wasn't—but if she doesn't want her parents to know, seems like it would have been—"

"Easier? Maybe, but—I dunno. 'Cause that's not what I did." But I smiled, and she nodded at me. "Thanks, by the way, for telling me—us. Most people don't."

"Sure." She twisted her earring.

"So," Sora said, "didn't you say something at orientation about how we need to stick together?"

I felt my neck grow damp. "I—uh."

Sora waved their hand. "Don't trip, you were kinda right. We do need to stick together. All of us. Physics is a hard major."

"Look, Scarlett," Jackie said, rubbing her scarf between her fingers, "Avia and I are the only girls who made it to the second year in physics."

"Um, oh, I didn't know you were majors—"

"We know how to make it here," Avia said. "Jackie's even been asked to replace Harold as TA for Elements next year."

"Cool," I said. "Congrats." Jackie smiled wide, revealing a small gap between her front teeth.

"We get together every Friday," Courtney continued, "to talk freaky mechanics and stuff. You should join us."

"Really? You weren't just harassing me about the bump?" I said.

"We don't really care about that." Courtney leveled her eyes at the group.

"Mostly I wanted to make sure you were going to be here next year," Jackie added.

"Where else would I be?" I said. "Of course I'll join you Fridays."

"Good," Courtney said. "We always have lunch, and we try to get this table, and sometimes also do other stuff. Like next week we're going to the Portland Planetarium for a lecture on string theory. If you want to come to that too?"

"Sure." I nodded, feeling a tingly warmth spread from my chest to my fingertips.

"Excellent." Sora leaned back in their seat, balanced the chair on two legs again, talked a touch too loud. "See, Courtney? You'll prove to your parents that Colwyn is awesome." Courtney's eyes flashed to the ceiling, like she didn't quite believe this was possible. "And Scarlett," Sora went on, "you'll prove you're not going to drop out just 'cause you're having a baby. We'll get into graduate school and go on to make amazing discoveries and have amazing lives and our biographies will talk about how back in the day, we all hung out at this table and went to string theory lectures together."

A beat of silence fell, and in that time, all of what Sora said crashed into me. "People are saying I'm going to drop out?"

"Yeah," Jackie said, hands on the table. "Pretty much everyone."

"Wow." I looked at my plate. "I expected stares, but—" My palms were sweating.

"But, you're not?" Courtney said. I think I managed a nod.

I wasn't sure what parts of me had liquefied, but I was pretty sure much of me was flying into the stratosphere. I nodded through anxious waves. *Inhale 1. 2. 3. Exhale 1. 2. 3. 4.*

Jackie cleared her throat. "So, good job making Harold feel so bad for foisting all the new work on first-year women."

I nodded.

Avia dabbed her lips with her napkin. "I could not stop laughing when I heard all that."

"Last year," Jackie said, "we spent hours and hours putting together this Cosmic Disco fund-raiser, and nobody even thanked us, and then they used the society money to fund summer stipends for their own work. That's why we aren't members."

"Maybe next year we'll give it another go. Apparently Maudly was pretty pissed about what happened. And since you managed to school Harold, Scarlett—well, maybe things will change," Avia said.

"Maybe." And I *was* hopeful. I wasn't sure I was the one who'd schooled Harold, but still, for a second, I'd felt like a beam of light, being invited into this circle. I knew it was a gift, because even at Colwyn, maybe especially at a school like Colwyn, pregnancy was still seen as a black hole from which no one's potential could escape. Could I avoid the pull of that? Could they help?

NOW

While Mina is Instagramming everything on the table one object at a time, I'm thinking about David. Specifically, his deadness, and how for the first time I will drive into Graceville and David will be gone. All that heat and light.

My lungs ache. The onion scent of the restaurant singes my eyes.

A baby at the table next to us screams and the mom picks it up, fixes it to her breast. There's a stab in my own chest as I look at my hands on the table. The baby. My baby. I miss the weight of her. Even though I was waiting until she was no longer a part of me, was itching to give her up, it's not easy to be so suddenly no longer part of her, an icy planet unattached to a sun.

SIX WEEKS AGO, APRIL

COLWYN COLLEGE · WATERTOWN, MAINE

"Wait—you're afraid of the records!" Mina's voice floated to me as if from very far away. I'd just returned from running, *David is dead* chant echoing in my head.

"I, uh." If I could have said anything it would have been that I was thinking about David's eyes, how they were like deep leaf puddles after a storm. How I would never see them again.

But Mina didn't know he was gone. She looked from my puffed face to my grotesquely swollen belly to the stack of records behind me. "Oh Scarlett, are you okay?"

"David—I." My chest ached. Fingers shook. "I—I just need help finding a song."

"David?" Mina said, the whole word a question. She cocked her head, put her finger to her lips. I must have looked completely off the rails. "Scar, what's going on?"

My shoulders rounded, as if curving into a ball could cover the words, keep them from being real. From somewhere that didn't quite seem my body came the words "He's dead."

Mina crossed the room and stood next to me. She put her arm around my shoulders, squeezed. "What song do you need?"

"I don't know."

"How'd it go?"

"All I remember is there were some pipes or something—and the lyrics 'would you find me?'"

"And you figured this song was so awesome that it must be in my record collection?" Mina said, half dimple blinking on her cheek.

I almost laughed; it came out as a hiccup. "Yeah, you have all the cool songs, and I um, I forgot about Google."

Mina passed me her laptop and I typed in the line. "'Astral Weeks' by Van Morrison" came up over and over again.

"Oh of course," said Mina. "That's from 1968. I can't believe I didn't recognize it—one of my dad's favorites. Here it is." She pulled out a faded record, where a man with chin-length hair was looking down. His image was superimposed with a tree. It looked like he was becoming a part of the branches. I thought of David walking ahead of me on the trail. David alive. She slid the record out of the case and put it on. I recognized it immediately. I had to inhale very slowly so I wouldn't fall over. *1, 2, 3. Hold. 1, 2, 3, 4.* It was like I'd time-traveled when I shut my eyes, felt the light through the windshield, saw the line of David's crescent moon scar as he held the wheel. I could feel his knee under my hand, taste the spruce of his skin where his neck met his collarbone, that little hollow that fit my lips so perfectly. It felt like if we drove off the embankment, the car would sprout wings and we would keep moving, fast and upward forever. It felt like whatever was between us had mythic energy, that planets could implode. When the song stopped, I asked Mina to play it again. I'm not sure how many times we did this. Me sinking back in time. Mina restarting the song.

"Mina," I said finally. "This is my playlist for labor."

"Just this song? You sure?"

"Yes."

"This is a really good song, and I know you're feeling a lot right now, but you've been at the classes. You know average first labor is thirteen hours long. You really want to listen to this song for thirteen hours? Assuming you're one of the lucky ones that doesn't go longer? Just this one? Not even this whole album? Because I promise you the rest is really good."

"No. Just this one," I said, tapping my phone to buy it. "The teacher kept talking about going to a happy place. Well, I didn't think I had one other than the bench behind my house, or maybe where we'd swim up Mine Gulch Road, but—" One of the last times I saw David was at the bench, and his body was found up Mine Gulch. So I said between sobs, "I forgot about this song." David would have said, *I forgot about the car, and the road, and that moment when you're suspended in air before you hit the water, the illusion of freedom before the present bubbles up around you, when everything is perfect and suspended—that flash in which you are unaware of life's crashing speed.* But David wasn't there. David wasn't anywhere.

I was alive and pregnant. I was expecting what was probably, maybe, most likely our baby any day. I was preparing to cast it out, like a rogue planet, untethered, alone.

NOW

LEAVING CHEYENNE, WYOMING

In biology we learned that if a woman has been pregnant she retains the fetal cells of her child and some of her maternal cells live on in her baby. These cells stay with her and appear to cluster around injured cells. Like stem cells, they can repair. But they might also cause damage. Either way, once your body has been occupied in this way, it's never the same. It changes you for better or worse. The cells I now carry could heal a cancer down the line or cause it. If an abnormality appears, they will go to it. They float inside me—the baby's genetic code, the father's signature. The cells we grew still morphing, still searching, always altering me.

"Scarlett!" David's coo through the screen woke me. It was my last morning in Graceville. My suitcase stood by my bedroom door. "Scarlett!" he whispered again.

David. I thought of the force I needed to resist David. His voice pulled me to attention, and I remembered David at our last party. His jealousy and how he drove, drunk, searching for drugs hours after saying he wanted to be less of an ass—and how I—in the bathroom for a moment—broke away from him and collapsed into the comfort of Cody. As if I could just roll back through time to before David and I tumbled into free fall.

"Come out for one last now?" David said, his voice cracking as I rose to the window.

Where did this strange energy come from? This sudden charge that repelled and attracted.

I motioned for him to wait as I pulled on a dress, slipped from my room, into my flip-flops, and out the front door.

David was leaning against his car.

"Walk with me?" I said. It would help if we walked. I could keep my own momentum.

I led him to the land trust trails behind my house. The sky whitened. He followed so close, I could hear his jeans rubbing together.

When we reached the bench at the overlook, David sat down. I studied his profile but stayed standing. The beautiful slope of his nose. His eyes, sunken. His jaw smooth. David unfolded a long knife. He scratched the wood with its blade.

"What are you doing, D?"

He looked up at me and my whole body felt the force of that smile, enough to launch rockets, enough to press me out of orbit. I planted my feet behind him, leaned over his shoulder. He'd scraped the paint off the bench to reveal: DW.

"You're carving your initials, D? What's this? Middle school?"

He grinned up at me, then focused back on the moving blade. He was etching a heart into the green paint.

"David." I watched his familiar hands, the scar from the knuckle of his pointer finger to his thumb as he pressed to make a slightly geometric S and O.

"David, this is very *Little House on the Prairie* of you, but—"

"Dammit, Scarlett!" he said, and drove the knife blade so quickly and fiercely into the bench, I stepped back. I was alone in the woods with this boy. His knife.

"David?" His eyes widened as he saw that I was afraid. His shock turned to sadness and spread into a slump down his spine.

He turned to me then, eyes streaming. "I can't believe you thought I would hurt you."

Maybe it was the early light, my mind fresh from sleep, maybe it was his jealousy at the party, his asshole comments, or maybe it was that this was really, finally goodbye, but in that moment, David was in sharp focus. His beauty, yes, but also his cracks. I saw how his nose ran. How he held one hand to his stomach as if a pain flamed there as he gazed out to where the sun was just starting to reach up into the sky. His eyes watered. I wanted to believe he was about to cry, for being here, for saying goodbye. But that didn't matter to me then. I knew for David, this wasn't just a crazy summer topping off our senior year. David was deep in another life.

"Remember when Teri died?" he said.

I felt dizzy. Why was he bringing this up?

"Cody was so fucked up, and we were all so sad, and everything should've hurt, but you know what I thought about the day after her funeral?"

I shook my head.

"How I'd stayed up all night talking to you. I was glad my friend had such a great girlfriend. I saw how worried for him you were. But I was also jealous because you were so damn smart. And I couldn't stop thinking about how we talked, about everything, remember? And I wondered, did you talk like that with him?"

My eyes burned.

"Cody and I, we talked, you know that—" But it wasn't the same.

David looked at the trees as he said, "Will you admit it?"

"Admit what?" I whispered. My question made his face go flat, and I was suddenly angry. Angry that he'd noticed something between us before I did. He'd felt it. But he was spinning out of control, and his trajectory had no room for me, or anything. His brain had been altered. What could I do about any of it?

I inhaled. "What do you want me to admit? You're an addict? Maybe I've helped you become this way because I've never said anything?"

David froze. He wasn't expecting me to say that. Maybe he thought I didn't know. I guess I hadn't seen it in full focus until that morning with the sun breaking on him. The blade in his hand. His eyes. His eyes.

I watched his anger grow as he tightened his hand on the knife. I flinched as muscles in his arms tensed and he stood. But he wasn't turning to me; he launched the knife toward the sun as if he could stick it in the eye. I listened as it hit the rocks below and skittered down the side of the mountain.

"David, you need help," I said.

"I'll be fine, Scarlett. Don't worry." He spoke softly. "Please, just tell me, why wouldn't you tell our friends? Why won't you ask me what to do now that we're leaving?" His face grew red. "What the hell kind of commitment do you have to Cody, who dumped you *nine* months ago? Why are you still sleeping in his T-shirts and pretending it matters if he's with Rachel or not? How could you—at the party—with him—" he stammered.

My hands shook. I didn't know the answers to these questions.

He looked me straight in the eye. "This summer, we've been together. You and me."

The sun was too bright. The day's heat crept over us like a blanket. I could have said, *I'm so scared for you. You say you're sorry, you say you're getting better, then you act like an ass in front of our friends and leave for drugs.* I could have said, *We both need to focus on school right now but maybe someday.* I could have said so many things.

"It isn't Cody. David. It's everything. The distance, the expectations, you."

The words hung between us and grew like the heat of the day. David wiped his tears with his half-moon scar. I remembered my lips on it. I remembered it resting on my thigh.

"I need to finish packing," I said. When David looked at me I knew he'd seen the suitcase in my room ready to go. He reached for my arm and with the force it takes to knock a planet out of orbit I shook my head, turned from him, and ran, flip-flops slapping down the trail to my house, where I slipped in the front door and closed it before I collapsed in the entry. I cried and cried and cried wondering if he was right. Maybe I hadn't really let Cody go. Maybe I wanted to be heartbroken from my fairy tale first boy and didn't want to admit that I could have possibly found something more, something bigger, with his broken best friend, because when I talked with David, sat near David, smelled David, there was no comparison.

I remembered that first time—after jumping the bridge at

Mine Gulch. How badly I'd wanted him, all of him. But even then, he was a secret. Had I just been too afraid? After Cody? Of going through all that again? I don't know. Maybe I'd been afraid of David—that someone could make me feel like that. A barrel going over a cliff.

Mom found me an hour later, knees pressed to my wet eyes.

"Oh honey," she said. She must have noticed David's car, the windshield replaced but the front end still dented from the deer, parked on the street where it stayed until we left for the airport, and who knows how long after. "Goodbyes are hard. Leaving is hard. But it'll be good for that boy to get out of this town and away from you."

"What do you mean by that?" I said, suddenly defensive.

She shook her head. "Here he can do no wrong, even when he does wrong. I know you're eighteen, but I still don't like leaving in the middle of the night." I wanted to argue with her but couldn't. She didn't like him and she had good reason not to. I felt the room start to shrink. I took a deep breath. "You want to talk about it?" she said. I shook my head. She gave me a tight hug. "All right. Coffee first, then before we leave for the airport, there's time for waffles with peaches and whipped cream." I nodded, unsure I'd be able to eat. "Thanks for using the front door, by the way."

"Mom!"

"Well, it's an improvement."

Mina is presently risking her life to get a good shot of the WELCOME TO COLORFUL COLORADO sign. I'm counting my breaths between every sentence I write. I'm getting sweaty and it isn't the heat. I can count my arrival back in Graceville in hours.

And after all this, I know, you've got to be wondering why I'm still unsure who the father is, when I could pretty easily do a test with Cody. I could. But I won't.

SIX WEEKS AGO

COLWYN COLLEGE · WATERTOWN, MAINE

The morning after Hannah called to tell me David had died, the whole world was emerging from the ice, as if overnight stands of daffodils had appeared at the edges of the buildings and waved yellow in the wind. Some trees were tipped with bright green buds. I talked to the baby as if she could hear me, wanting to believe the curtain between us very thin as Mina had said. "I lost somebody," I said. "He was important to me and I didn't do enough for him and now you've lost him too." I stared out the window at the snowbank flecked with dirt and mud. "He might have been—"

But even alone in my room I couldn't finish the sentence.

I did some research and found out that since David was dead his parents might have a right to the child, or they'd have a case anyway if Cody was not the father, and they could try to take the baby from Calvin and Sai anytime, even if they didn't find out for five years. They would have little chance of taking it from me. But that would mean—

Cody's number was still in my phone. He picked up on the second ring.

"Scarlett?" he said. He didn't sound surprised; he sounded like he had been waiting for me to call. It felt good to hear his voice. If I closed my eyes I could almost smell pine.

"Cody," I said, and the wet heat of my eyes was instant. I blinked tears.

"Are you okay?"

"Of course not. Are you?"

"No," he said.

"Good. I'm glad we agree on something."

"That's a start."

"It is," I said. "I need you to agree with me on something else. I mean, I really need your help."

"Okay?"

"But I need you to promise to keep a secret."

"Scarlett, what's this about? Aren't you calling because of David?"

"Well, I am but also"—I inhaled—"also I'm pregnant."

Silence.

"Okay." A pause filled by music in the distance, his breathing. "So what do I— Or, how can I help?"

I took a deep breath, focused on the picture of my family on my nightstand. *Inhale 1, 2, 3, hold. Exhale 1, 2, 3, 4.* "You can sign a paternal release."

"What?"

"Agree that we should give the baby up for adoption."

"We? What?"

"Don't you think we should?"

"Jesus, Scarlett, how pregnant are you?"

"Eight months."

"Shit."

"Yeah."

"Are you sure? That it's—it's mine?"

"No. That's why I need you to agree with me."

"Wait, what?" He paused. I heard him clear his throat. "Scarlett, god, now?"

"Look, I never wanted to tell you. I never wanted to tell anyone. My mom doesn't even know. Hannah doesn't even know."

"How does your mom not know?"

"Well." I paused, made my voice wry. "Einstein was able to hide his daughter from his mom. I figured surely I could too."

"Sarcasm, Scar? Really?" He sounded tired.

How stupid I'd been for thinking this would be simple. I dropped my head into my hands. "I'm sorry, Cody, I just, I don't know, this year was not what I thought."

"I guess not," he said, softer. There was a long silence before he spoke again. "So why didn't you just, you know—"

"Terminate? I don't know. Why didn't we use protection? Why do I need to answer all the whys here? Why didn't you ask for a condom?"

"Well, I wasn't really planning for that to happen, and you'd been on the ring or whatever."

"I was on the ring. Or I thought I was. I don't know. I messed up. We messed up. But can you just help me, Cody?"

"Why didn't you tell me before?"

"Because you'd been an ass, because I'd been an ass, because I wanted to do this myself, because I was handling everything just fine until David went and shot his final drug cocktail."

"David has a way of stealing the show no matter what."

"Had."

"What?"

"David had a way," I said softly as I watched Courtney out the window, snapping photos of daffodils in the snow.

"Look, Scarlett, why shouldn't I just say no way to your crazy plan. What if I want the baby? Or at least to know if it is mine? Do you really think I don't care?"

"No, Cody, it's just—I don't think you really want to know. And I know you don't want a baby."

"How?"

"Because you don't. I mean, *do* you really want to know?"

"I don't know."

"Do you want to be a father?"

"No. I mean, not now."

"And do you want to blow this up and make a big scene in Graceville with David's family?"

"No, I . . ."

"Look, I was going to declare the father unknown, but the one case in which declaring the father unknown can be challenged, even years later, is if the biological father is dead. Then there are grandparent rights. And I don't want to raise this baby, and I don't want David's parents to either. This is my choice. I found a family and they're awesome."

"You're asking me if I will sign off my rights so that no one will ever ask if the baby might have been David's."

"Yes."

"And you expect that I don't care, that if it were mine I would be willing to give it up too."

"She."

"What?"

"She. It's a girl."

More silence. Then he said, "Scarlett, you expect me to be okay giving her up if she *is* mine. And not only that but I need to keep this from my dead best friend's family, even if she might be his?"

"Well, when you put it that way, I sound like a real sweetheart."

"You do know this is messed up, right?"

"Yes." I wished my pillows could swallow me. "I do."

"And you know . . ." I heard his breathing change. He was starting to cry. "You know I'll do it right. For you. If this is what you think is best, I'll do it. Of course I will."

"I do. It is. She deserves it. Her own story, not Graceville." I cleared my throat. "I know you're doing this because you did really love me."

"Yeah, I did."

"Thanks—for all of this. You know I loved you too."

"And he did too—" Cody's voice cracked.

"What?"

"David. He loved you too." We held our phones in silence. The edges of my room blurred. I couldn't ask if David had said this to him, or if Cody just knew, in the way that I knew Hannah cared for Rage but wasn't crazy in love with him, that whoever this new guy was at college, he was now her main focus—all that from the few words she'd spoken. Part of me wanted to ask, but my voice evaporated. It didn't matter. Cody knew. I did too.

Finally he said, "So what's next?"

"I'll talk to my agency. They say it's just a signature. It can probably just be scanned and emailed."

"Okay."

"Cody."

"Yeah?"

"Thanks."

"Scarlett."

"Yeah?"

"I don't know if I'll ever be able to talk to you again."

"I know," I said, and for a long time we listened to each other cry.

Then he said, "I'm going to hang up now." Neither one of us said goodbye.

NOW

TEN MILES INTO COLORADO

It doesn't matter if it was OxyContin, or Vicodin, or Percocet, or loperamide, morphine, heroin, or fentanyl. It doesn't matter if it was snorted, swallowed, or shot. It matters only that the darkness came and took David's light away. Stole his nows. That he made a mistake. And another. And then all ways we can perceive him left.

But whenever, wherever David is now, I hope he knows that I forgive him. For making his terrible error. For breaking my heart. But forgiving myself for not saying enough, for not admitting my truth, this is much harder.

I've said so many times, "That wasn't me. This isn't me." But it is. All of it—messiness isn't erased by high grades and detailed plans. I'm still not used to mistakes. I'm just learning to keep going in the wake of them.

A week after my call with Cody, Mina drove home for April vacation, but I was staying in Watertown housesitting for Bradshaw. I found her book-crammed, drafty but cozy home awkward to be in, but maybe that was because I hadn't been working on the assignment I told her I'd started months before. Or maybe it was because of the Newton's cradle on Bradshaw's daughter's desk to remind me of the one from David I'd left at home. Or maybe it was that I was super-pregnant and in deep grief. I was sleeping in her daughter's canopy bed with the sun coming through the pink sparkles hung in the windows, lighting up the horse posters, the wall of books, the corner pile of stuffed animals and dolls, and for a minute, I'd forget everything. I almost felt like I'd entered another body, but then I would be hungry and see the lump of my abdomen, my swollen hands, and I'd focus on those seven metal spheres hanging motionless, remembering everything: David was dead. Gone. Just somewhere else forever. He'd never know how strange it is to wake up in his professor's daughter's bed to the sound of snow melting on the roof.

Every morning, to keep away the fear tugging on me since my call with Cody—that I might never feel again whatever it was I felt with David, that I could no longer leap and let myself drop—I kept a schedule.

I sat up in bed, set one of the balls in motion, and listened to them clack as I got dressed. I walked down to the front door and slipped on the L.L.Bean boots I'd bought because my feet were so swollen that I couldn't get wool socks and my old boots on. Then I'd head out to walk Bradshaw's dog. We'd stop for coffee at Barrow's Brew, where the lady selling it would eye my belly disapprovingly. On Friday, I tied the dog to the railing and almost ran into Harold as I turned around.

"Hey!" he said, and appeared to make extra effort to look me in the eye.

"Hey," I said. "Just getting something to wake us both up."

"Oh right, is that—"

"Just coffee, Harold," I said as he followed me up to the counter. "It isn't a problem. It's not like we were up late partying." A woman getting her order looked at me hard.

"Did you have a good break?" Harold asked as I gestured to the barista for my regular.

I looked at him, standing in front of me in the sweatshirt like David's and I thought how I would have loved David to be there. How I would give anything for him to be alive still. There with me. But there was only Harold, not David. I thought of David, of spruce and his leaf-puddle eyes, his hand in mine, a whoosh of air, my head on his chest, and then how he looked when I last saw him, wet ankles, sallow skin, jacketless in the December wind. My head went hot and dizzy and before I could count an inhale, my face was wet and I curved into my sobs.

"Scarlett?" Harold said. I just shook my head as I picked up my coffee, walked outside, and wiped my nose with the napkin handed to me with my cup. The rough paper burned. I untied the dog from the railing, blinked at the sunlight on the snow and the cold wind on my eyes. Thinking about David. Dead. Gone. And all I didn't, couldn't do to help him. Harold touched my arm; his body was stiff as he opened his arms and I stepped into them. I dropped my head onto his shoulder and cried. And every time I thought Harold is here, not David, my teeth sank deeper into my lip till eventually I tasted blood. Finally, Bradshaw's dog, who'd calmly sat next to us through this, tugged on her leash. I let go of Harold and took a step back.

"So, I guess break has been a little rough?" he said.

"Meh." I tried to laugh.

"Maybe the last weekend will be better?"

"Yeah, um, I guess I really miss Mina," I said. Harold turned a touch pink.

"Hey, me too. She's fun."

"I know," I said as he examined his shoelaces. "So, um, have a good rest of break?" I said, not quite knowing what to do with my hands.

Harold laughed. "Nope. I'm walking you home."

"Okay," I said. And it was.

"Can I do anything else? Bring you dinner?"

"I've got my schedule down. Usually it goes pretty well."

"But today you ran into me and I screwed it all up," Harold said, eyes on me.

"Yeah, this is completely all your fault," I said, and felt the corners of my eyes lifting.

Harold smiled. Harold. Not David.

TURNING OFF THE INTERSTATE AND ONTO THE HIGHWAY
TOWARD GRACEVILLE

I'm sure there was some time, maybe on a bus trip, that David and I were on this highway together. But I can't remember when. All I know is somewhere in time, maybe right in this ever-moving spot on the highway, David and I are together. And so, in some way, we still are.

I'm a scientist, so I shouldn't be so surprised that people like to ask why. Why does it matter if David and I drove this road before? Why did I have the baby? Hide her? Why did David die? But I'm human. And there isn't one answer. Every action doesn't result in an equal and opposite reaction. There are too many moving parts, too many factors to consider. In David's words, "It's quite a range."

Those last weeks at Colwyn, I felt separated from David by not only death, but miles and choices and billions of molecules of air. So to be somewhere David and I might have been together is comfort to this mind that replays every detail of the last time I saw him, as if stuck there, caught in a loop.

SIX MONTHS AGO, DECEMBER

GRACEVILLE, COLORADO

"I was hoping to see you," David said. My eyes ran from the glass door of the coffee shop and back to David. *Oh David, David, David.* The difference between hope and want. The difference between need and addiction. The way words slice our tongues. How we jumped together and fell through the air: two objects in free fall. Our trajectory different only because of a split second when I stayed on the rails.

"Yeah?" I said. I was trying to look at the sidewalk, or at the coffee shop for Mom, anywhere but at his pinprick pupils.

"I know what people are saying," he said, shuffling a step toward me, one hand holding tight to the elbow of the other arm. "And I know I'm fucked up, but I'm gonna be okay. I got—I got sent to the hospital at Stanford 'cause I'd overdone it there— but then Grandpa died and my first thought was I need to get the rest of his meds before anyone thinks to flush them. That was my first thought, Scar. I wasn't even sad. But everything runs out." His eyes clouded as he said, "Something's different about you—"

I inhaled. Could he see it?

His mouth twitched, he put a hand up to my face, his nails dirty. "Makeup. It's nice, but you don't need it."

I exhaled. "David—no one needs makeup. Some people just like to wear it."

His forehead softened and he made an almost-laugh sound. "Always keeping me in check, Scar. I've missed it."

I relaxed into a smile, then looked back at his wet feet. His too-pale skin. "You too. I've—"

"Wait," he said. "I want you to know, I talked to my parents. Dad got me into the best place in Colorado. I'm going to clean up, Scar. I'll go back to school, you know, I'm still going." He tried to smile, but the corners of his mouth couldn't seem to hold. "I'm going to save the world with shark genes." There was a hint of his joy. All his electric life.

"I know," I said. His words made me feel like my mass was both reduced and increased. David was getting help, but I couldn't tell him what weighed me down. Maybe it could help him—I had a sudden, perverse urge to just scream it into the cold, metallic air—but it could also completely derail him. Or me. I didn't know, I didn't know. I *did* want to talk to him, but I wouldn't. The risk was too big. Why should he have to bear that weight when he already had so much? I could protect him from this. I cleared my throat. "I'm glad. You know, I worried."

"I got your texts, I just—" He dug his hands into his pockets. "I didn't know what to say."

"I'm glad texts can travel three thousand four hundred forty-four miles," I said.

What would he want me to do with what I carried, my secret, ours? If I knew, would I change my mind? Would I vaporize, dissolve, be forced to let Colwyn go?

"Scarlett?"

"What?"

"I wish"—he looked down—"last summer—with you, everything was so perfect except me. If I could have been there. If I wasn't just searching for—you know—all the time . . . if you can forgive me, someday, I hope we get another shot."

Hope, Mina would quote, *is the thing with feathers.*

It was too much. What he didn't say. What I didn't say. All the forces between us. My tongue felt swollen. I made mistakes too—not letting go of Cody. Not admitting what I was feeling to myself. To David. Not wanting to look anything in the eye—David, the pregnancy, the ripples of my choices. And that day, I didn't take him in my arms, I didn't even say I knew he could do it, get better. Maybe I wouldn't have, even if I wasn't knocked up. It was too risky. Loving David was too much like free fall. I craved it, but it ended with a crash.

My breath was short. "David," I said. There was a hint of sparkle in his eyes. I looked toward Colorado Beans, and there was Mom with two cups in her hands and a bag of pastries. "Take care of yourself, okay?" I said. He opened his mouth. Closed it. "I gotta go."

That's what I said.

Then I turned back toward the car. My bladder burned, but I could pee later.

"David, hello," Mom said curtly.

"Merry Christmas," I added over my shoulder, the words dry. Forced. There was no way to fit inside them all I really meant. Be safe. Get better. Maybe someday. Someday.

He nodded, hunched his shoulders, and walked away.

The last I saw of David was the hood of his sweatshirt disappearing into the gray December day. How I felt about him—with him, the baby, these are things he would never know. These are the things I never said.

FOUR WEEKS AGO

COLWYN COLLEGE · WATERTOWN, MAINE

On the night of May seventh, I dreamed I was at the front door of David's parents' house. It was dark. The porch light was on. The planter of hen and chick cacti was full; the tiny succulents spilled over the edge of the clay pot. I inhaled rain on dry ground, crushed pine needles, a hint of wood smoke. Home. I lifted my fist to knock on the door, but just as I would have made contact I felt a wave of fear and it burst open with a flood of deep fast water.

When I awoke, I felt my abdomen tense, and I was wet. Waters. Labor. No. This wasn't how it was supposed to happen. This was a Hollywood beginning. I'd read my books; only fifteen percent of labor actually begins with water breaking vs. the probably hundred percent of labor on TV. I was supposed to have slow contractions, I was supposed to laugh, make pizza, and return my overdue library books before I needed to worry about leaking gross fluid everywhere. That was how the online birth narratives I'd read went. Mina and I learned there was no hurry in our birth classes because labor is generally slow and long. But, once water breaks, the hospital likes the baby to be born within twenty-four hours. But we weren't supposed to go in until several hours passed, or the contractions got real. I looked at the clock. 5:41 a.m. Mina had had a hell of an exam the day before and I wanted to let her sleep as much as possible. No one would be in the halls yet, or not many. I stole a pad from Mina's stash, changed my PJs, put on my bathrobe, and walked down the hall. Over time I felt a tightening like a low backache that spread from the center of my spine to my navel and back. Was that it? I decided to go downstairs to the vending machines and get a Coke to fortify myself for the long haul. But once in the stairwell, I discovered walking up and down felt really good. So, instead of going to the machines I walked the stairs. Up the stairs, down the stairs. The building was quiet except for the occasional shutting of doors, music from the water pipes as early risers showered and flushed. After a while these noises were more frequent, and then someone was on the stairs with me and I turned to see Bert.

"You okay?" he said, and gave me a worried look, like I might pop a baby out right there in the hallway.

"Just getting some exercise. You know—good for the baby," I said, grimacing through a tightening wave.

"You sure you're okay?" he said again.

"Just preggers." I forced a tense smile.

"Can I get you anything? Water or Mina?" he said.

"I'm okay, Bert." Between waves, things were calm. I looked at him again and noticed he was in the same clothes I'd seen him in the night before at our physics society meeting. "Hey Bert, where you coming from so early?"

He went bright pink and stuttered, "I—I—um, Courtney and I were studying and I—"

I laughed. "A likely story," I said, and would have chuckled but was swept up by another tightening wave.

"I, uh—"

"Time for Mina," I said. "If you want to feel useful, you can hold the doors for me." Bert nodded.

Mina was curled under her polka dot sheets. I placed my hand on her shoulder and then, seized by an untimely contraction, squeezed. She flinched, opened her eyes halfway. "Scarlett, what the . . ." But before she could finish, she'd jumped out of bed. "Holy, holy—Scar, are you all right? Is it crazy painful? What can I do for you? Get your bag? Put on the song? What?"

I laughed. "Calm down, Mina. I'm okay. Just getting a little freaky being alone."

"Right. I'll make coffee."

And guess what I learned from that. If I'm in labor, the smell of coffee makes me puke.

During birth I felt myself burn and stretch against my will. I thought there was no way I could do it, believed I would fail at bringing her into life. For a moment I thought the pain was death coming to collect her. I wondered if David went through withdrawal, if it was painful. I wondered if it was like this. I imagined his ghost sat down in the dark corner of the room and said, "I'll take her from here." I tensed. I was going to be punished for living, for forgetting, for falling from orbit, for crashing into David, for breaking, for swimming again to shore.

But I wasn't. If I felt David at all, if he had stepped into my time, it was only to be there. To watch as I went through a tunnel of pain to give life. It was hard, but I did it. I gathered myself and I squatted, balanced between the rails of the bed, I held Mina's arm until purple bruises in the shape of my fingers appeared. The midwife in her white coat leaned over me, measuring with fingers and nods, affirming, "Good. That's it, almost there."

"Just a bit more," Mina said, and I inhaled and then—one more knee-to-chin-grunt and a shoulder and body slid from me. And she was free.

And I was free.

They say babies look the most like their fathers right at birth. A kind of paternity certainty, a genetic check if you will, to tell the man who to protect, but she was pink, and small-eyed, cone-headed, nothing of David, or me, or Cody. Perhaps I was just her vessel. Calvin and Sai entered the room and held out their arms to take what was theirs forever, what was mine to give.

She was beautiful. She was like pure light, and somehow, I

felt good and strong. I felt her nuzzle toward my breast. And everything in the room disappeared around her, and everything I lost and was losing ran down my cheeks and onto her pink blanket. Before I started to shake I handed her to Mina, who passed her carefully to Calvin, and Calvin handed her to Sai, and maybe when they took her in their arms they said:

"There you are my baby, my girl, the one I've waited for."

Which is not what I could have said. But I couldn't hear them. My headphones were on. I closed my eyes. I stopped seeing their joy, but I could feel it pulsing through the room like waves as Van Morrison sang, "Lay me down, in silence easy to be born again," and eventually I fell asleep.

Hours later, Sai handed her back to me. "We want your thoughts on her name," he said.

"Mine?"

"Yeah. We were thinking Phoebe Divya."

"Divya?"

"It's Hindu," said Sai. "It means 'divine.' We figured if our white baby was being raised Hindu, then she should have at least one name to show that."

"It's too perfect," I said, and then whispered "Phoebe Divya" to the sleeping baby in my arms. She was red, wrinkled, and divine. My tears spilled silently as I tried to match my breathing with hers so I wouldn't shake. She was a warm little burrito of a baby. I ran my hand down the length of her. I wondered how I would ever say goodbye.

Mina slept on a chair next to my bed and brought me food from outside the hospital, things I hadn't been able to eat while pregnant, cold cuts and soft cheese. I felt drained but strong. I'd given life and for the first time in nearly a year, I felt I'd done something right. I was up, on my feet, I walked to the bathroom, down the hall, then with Mina to the cafeteria. This seemed to amaze nurses, which we found funny. We invented illnesses for me and pretended I didn't just give birth. We laughed. Nurses checked on me and gave me a shot to stop my milk from coming. But it came anyway, wetting my shirt as I cried. Mina held my hand.

For two days we stayed at the hospital with nurses in and out of the room taking my blood pressure, pressing on my stomach, peering at my body. While Calvin and Sai snapped photos and cooed, fed her bottles, and fretted when they couldn't get her to stop crying. Mina was wide-eyed as I held Phoebe and wondered if Cody and I had done the right thing. If there might have been a way to keep her. I thought of Cody at St. Olaf. I thought a Christian school would be supportive of a young couple with a baby—it wasn't Colwyn, but maybe we could make it work. I knew he didn't want to hear from me, but I ached for him, for the familiar. I texted him—

"Safe arrival. She's beautiful."

He didn't respond. Mina and I went for a coffee. He didn't respond. We walked the length of the hospital. And circled back. No response. No request for a picture. No "I'm glad you're well." Nothing.

We stopped in Calvin and Sai's room. Calvin was pacing back and forth, singing lowly to Phoebe. Sai was stretched out on the bed, his lobster socks crossed at the ankle reading something with a baby on the cover. I bet they'd already read a million parenting books.

"I ate broccoli," I said, too loud, and Phoebe started to cry. Sai put down his book and Calvin bounced but gazed at me. "Lots of broccoli. So, she'll probably like broccoli. I'm sure you'll give her lots of broccoli, right? Because it's really good for her. And when she's like four and figures out that other kids don't like broccoli, you know you can do that trick where you say 'Look, Phoebe, this broccoli is a summer tree,' and then you can eat all the florets off and say, 'Now it's a winter tree,' and then you can say, 'Now I'm chopping down the tree to keep warm,' and eat up all the stems. That's what Jessica did with my niece and it totally works. Kid eats servings of broccoli big enough for any grown-up. Phoebe will too, I bet, because of those studies that babies can taste what their moms eat. She'll probably also like bagels and clementines. And maybe coffee, sorry about that one, but I bet you can keep it from her until she's at least fourteen. I also ate peanut butter, which some doctors think keeps babies from getting the allergy.

Lots of peanut butter, actually, because the last few months I was always hungry and was trying to eat enough protein every day. I bet she'll like that too, what kid doesn't?"

Mina put her hand on my back. My phone buzzed.

It was Cody. "Sign the papers soon and leave me alone."

I read it and saw the edges of the room go soft. I backed out the door.

In my memory, I see myself exit, then double over as if I'd been kicked in the gut, slide down the wall, and bury my face in my knees. Mina placed her hand on my hair, and that brought me back. I could feel her hands, then the cold floor under me. I leaned on her. "Min, I want her. I almost started to think it was possible to not sign the papers. To take her from them, to run off with Cody to Minnesota and become a Lutheran teen mom."

"Of course you want her. She's perfect. But, Lutheran? No way."

I almost laughed, but the floor felt so cold, my body empty, and everything I had been trying to keep separate all year—Cody, David, my life in Graceville, the pregnancy—felt like it was crashing together and over me at once.

Mina tugged on my arm. "I hate to break it to you, but I wouldn't let you leave Colwyn if you tried. You're stuck with me now. You're going to need to help me with my new major."

"What?" I said, trying to bring myself back with steady breaths.

"Biology."

I could feel the room again. "You're kidding me."

"No. Really, it's the best major if I decide to become a mid-wife."

"You're serious?"

"I am. I'm lucky the midwife was on call for you. We talked and it's everything I thought was cool about being a doctor but with a different focus—one that really makes life better for women and children. I can't believe I didn't think of it before. I guess I needed to watch you get through this crazy, unplanned year, and somehow get stronger. You taught me when to help and when not to—"

"Min, I'm not stronger. I never wanted to do any of this. Not all of me even wants to go through with this."

"It doesn't need to be all of you that wants to, just most of you. You know, I wanted to stay home and go to a school where I wouldn't need to leave my parents or cats behind. Colwyn was the right choice, but Scar, it hasn't been easy. I've had this preggo science nerd for a roommate that I've had to look out for and it's really stressed me out."

"Yeah, that must have been real hard for you," I said, squeezing her hand.

"Ouch, careful!" Mina said, pulling her hand away. "That's still tender from the bones you crushed while in labor."

"I'm so happy you made it through that in one piece, Min."

"It wasn't easy, but I did it for you, and hey, I didn't even need to get X-rays! Plus now I might know what to do with my life." I dropped my head to her shoulder. Mina's voice was full of energy. "You know, I think I finally understand why my dad did that thing where he photographed himself with all of the state capitol buildings—it's like, not only proof that you were there, but a reminder that it doesn't matter where you go. You don't get away from you."

I thought of David's sloping shoulders, of Phoebe wrapped in her blankets, of Cody's voice on the phone. Of Hannah, and Mom, and everything that was my world in Graceville. I guess you also don't get away from who and what you love. Even if you want to. Even if you try really hard. Someday, everything you don't want to look at will be staring right at you—David's too-small pupils, Phoebe's swirling eyes, Cody's cool tone. And you'll have to admit your nows aren't individual. They are a stream, running and running. And until we understand the universe more, we'll never be able to go backward. All we can do is experience right now.

Mina pulled her head away from me so she could meet my eyes. She flashed one dimple, then said, "So, I have this idea to take a picture of every state sign on our trip."

"Every sign?"

"Every one."

"I'll try to keep you from getting killed."

"Thanks. Oh, one more thing. I kissed Harold."

"What? When?" I shook her shoulder. "Why am I just hearing this?"

"Um, you've been a bit busy lately," Mina said, tugging on my hospital gown.

"So what does this mean? Boyfriend? Or?"

Mina shrugged. "I don't know. He starts graduate school at UNE in the fall, so he'll be close by. You know, provided I'm still into him after all those West Coast guys we're gonna meet." I cut my eyes to her and she flashed a winning, dual-dimpled smile.

"Scarlett?"

I lifted my head. Professor Bradshaw was standing in front of us with a giant box.

"The end of all three of my pregnancies were just count-downs until I could eat sushi again." She nodded at the box. "I don't know if you even like sushi, but I figured you haven't had much of a chance to try Maine's—and this is the best sushi in all of Portland."

"Thanks," I said, standing up, "Professor Bradshaw." Mina took the box.

"She's with her dads if you want to see her."

"I came to see you, but if you want to show her off."

I shook my head. "Actually, I'm happy to not be with her right now. Wanna join us?"

Bradshaw followed us into my room and we ate right out of the box. She was about to leave when I realized I did want her to see Phoebe. I needed someone, other than Sherrie, Mina, and me, to know her. I wanted my worlds to overlap. I wanted proof. Sai opened the door with the baby on his shoulder. Bradshaw inhaled deeply. "Oh my, isn't she perfect?" My chest burned. I counted my breaths.

"She is," Sai and I said at the same time.

- - -

The morning I signed the termination agreement Sherrie presented, I felt like an actress, and with a shaking hand, I ended
my rights as a parent. I kissed her soft head. I took off the
double-helix necklace, the one Cody had given me so long ago,
and dropped it in Sai's hand. "Keep this for her. Tell her it's
from her birth parents. Tell her we tried our best."

Sai nodded and hugged me, Phoebe on his shoulder; I felt
her soft breath on my neck. I hugged Calvin. They raised
Phoebe's arm as if to wave. She was so small, she couldn't even
control her hands. She couldn't control anything. It's amazing
how much we learn. How much effort it takes just to wave, how
often we have to fall just to learn how to stand.

They told me I could be in touch, that we could have as much
contact as I wanted. I said maybe, but probably not. Sherrie
shook my hand and promised to give me a call in a few days. I
thought of how she'd done this too—somehow handed her heart
to someone else. Given away her moon. I didn't say so, but I was
glad she would be calling me. I was heading west with Mina for
my internship at Google in a few weeks. It was by far the best
opportunity for the summer, and I got it on my own. Mina's
dad's friend left right after she'd submitted my application. I
was continuing on my path, the one I was gifted for. I was going
to breathe in eucalyptus from the dew-wet trees as I jogged at
dawn. When I saw Phoebe with those two adoring fathers, I
knew what was real: Cody wanted nothing to do with her and

David was dead, but these men were ready and willing to give her everything. Sai kissed her temple as he held her gently on his shoulder. I'd done the right thing. I made two choices as a parent. They were the right ones for us.

Mina pulls the car over to photograph the wooden sign that reads WELCOME TO GRACEVILLE, MAY YOUR HEART BE FILLED WITH GRACE. I'm full of what is probably the exact opposite of grace. I'm terrified. Graceville will never again be home to me. Somehow, I always knew that, and still, now that I'm adjusting to a world without David, a now that cannot include him, a future where he will not be, the loss of Graceville, the town that built me, believed in me—it feels so much bigger. *It's all up to you now,* I imagine David saying. But he's wrong. There is a new star at Graceville High now, a new edition of the paper, seventeen new graduates to watch.

Still, I'm thankful. I know now is just my observation of this particular light, in this particular place. But if all of my nows are already lined up, that predetermination doesn't make me feel defeated. I can wait for that light to reach me. I don't want to know the future after all. Even with all I've lost, I still want as many nows as I can get. Maybe I can't share my nows with David, or the baby that might have been his, the one who stayed with me after David's death for a few more weeks, and then was born, and let go. Maybe my nows will be difficult, and lonely, and full of hurt. Probably they will. But not all of them. Mostly, they will be mine. Each now, a chance to acknowledge what is in front of me. To do my best. An inhale. An exhale. A chance.

Instead of directing Mina to my parents' house to rest and shower, I decide that since my folks are both probably still at work, we'll go straight to David. I point Mina toward the wrought-iron gates of the Graceville Cemetery, and despite the heat outside, I roll the window down to smell the cut grass, the dry air. I don't know where to look, so I lead the way to the little brick office, where a caretaker with dirty fingernails types *David Warren* into his computer and then circles an area in blue ink on a photocopied paper map. We walk into the too-bright day. The sun shocks. The wreaths of flowers are too fragrant. The buzz of life hurts. Mina holds me by the arm as we travel the dusty path that winds between the trimmed green rows. Finally, at the edge, near the fence on a little hill, we stop. "Here," I say, and Mina puts her hand on my back.

"I'll wait over at that tree," she says.

"David Warren," I read from the stone. Once. Twice. Three times. Four. I get down and touch the smooth engraving. I pass my palm over the dates. The stone is hot, but the ground cool. I sit down, and then lie down. I look into the sky, David's stone my pillow. "This is not what you see," I say. "You can't hear me. You're not here."

Still, like some romantic film, I want him to appear down by the edge of the field, a joint between his fingers, saying something like *I'm nowhere, where are you?* I lie there for a long time. The sun moves its slow arc. I press myself into the ground. Some people say if you listen, you can hear the earth's pulse. Bullshit. I hear nothing. I try, though.

In the sky, a pair of turkey vultures ride the thermals. Circling. I put up my hand. I point following their slow arc, all the places David is not. David, not here. David, nowhere. I remember David at Cody's mom's funeral across the lawn from where I lie. How he stood in his gray suit with a red carnation, his hands on Cody's shoulders. I thought, if Einstein is right about space-time, then we are all still there. It's just from where I sit, the light from that event can't reach me. I look across the grass; in the center of the cemetery are large stone crosses that widen out at the edges to flat stones. I wonder if wherever David is, if he cares about his stone here. Probably not. He's not here. He's there helping me to keep Cody standing, to hide the extent of his drunkenness from the throngs of people who've come to offer sympathy. How poised he was that day, how together in the face of it. I'd almost forgotten, but there he is. I can see him now.

Einstein is right. David's not really gone. He's still moving through space-time. He hasn't disappeared into a black hole.

He is somewhere, just outside my sight, in the past or taking on forms I can't recognize. I can't reach him again. I'll never be able to do that, but I know he's there. I lie on the ground, watching the vultures, pointing at the sky. I touch the soft folds of my stomach. I think of Phoebe, the weight of her, the pulse of her forehead, how fragile she was. I was glad I wasn't the one who had to bathe her, change her diapers and clothes.

Mina was right. It wasn't easy, but it was the choice most of me wanted to make. Mina reminded me I was entitled to my sorrow. And so, in those last blurry weeks at Colwyn, I cried and cried, for Phoebe, for myself, for David and Cody. I ate with Mina, Courtney, and the group of physics kids who waited for me at the entrance to the dining hall each day. Bert gave me notes from every class I'd missed and covered my hours in the tutoring center when I would burst randomly into tears and needed to return to my dorm, where Mina would make me tea and play records until I calmed down or fell asleep. Harold tutored me through everything I missed, especially happy to help now that he and Mina couldn't seem to get enough of each other. On rainy days, I went to the gym and ran the treadmill while I cried. When the sun was out, I ran with my tear-stained face off campus and into town. I ran and ran. First five, then ten miles every day. Sometimes fifteen.

I felt like I was a black hole running through campus, ready to suck out all the light of anyone who got too close. The weeks were a blur. I was not prepared for how much I loved her. Stupid, probably. I'd been worried about her from the start.

I'd even feared miscarriage, as illogical as that was. But I knew, even through the pain, that her dads could give her more than I ever could, and by letting her go, I was not just freeing myself for my own future, but releasing her into a better one.

I lie on David's grave thinking about how, despite everything, I didn't want to return to the unknowing Scarlett, the one before Cody dumped me. Last summer, last year, I unraveled, and unlike David, I had survived. I couldn't go back. All my life I'd been told I was destined for big things, and I believed it superficially. I knew I wanted to help the world, and I thought that my grades were proof that I would be able to. I wrote off Einstein's lack of care for his own as the male's ability to do that, when girls have to work twice as hard to prove ourselves. In high school, I made perfect grades. I served my community as best I could. But I didn't consider the things that might interrupt my direction, the collisions that would force me to recalculate my route, myself. Thinking back on all that happened during the last year, I know Curie was right: Life is not easy and with each error we make, each accident that sends us spinning, we must redirect ourselves. It's in that redirection that we confirm what we are gifted for, and what we truly love. My future will not be the sensible skirt and working-to-death-to-meet-my-bills life that David always feared. I will do work that matters to me and the world. I'll have my own story. I already do. I am surviving. It hasn't been easy, but I can do it. From now on, I will carry this story with me. I will know that despite great loss, I can still move toward the future's light.

In the cemetery, full of loss for David, for Phoebe, and Cody too, I cry and I look over and see Mina under the tree. I take out my phone and text Calvin and Sai.

"How is she?"

And I wait. My hands stay on the phone to feel it vibrate. It only takes a few seconds.

Calvin writes: "Scarlett! So glad to hear from you. She's great. You ready to see a picture?"

"Yes."

My palms sweat as I wait for the phone to vibrate again. I roll on my belly, shade the sunlight from the screen, and there is Phoebe sleeping, legs curled, arms splayed, a zebra-striped three-tiered skirt on and a blue T-shirt with black-and-white-striped flowers, blue headband to match. The caption reads, "See? Just perfect."

Scarlett: "Yes. Perfect. When I'm back, maybe we can schedule a meet up."

Calvin: "We'd love that. We're all so happy to hear from you Scarlett. Sai sends his love."

Scarlett: "Thanks. Tell him I'm going to send him the perfect pair of socks."

Calvin: "Please do."

Scarlett: happy-face emoji, sunset emoji

Calvin: eggplant emoji, sushi emoji

I trace the letters on David's stone with my finger. Then I reopen Calvin's text. I click the picture, set it as my lock-screen, resetting it from the painting of the scornful girl in Deming. I know that girl too well. I don't need her like I did last summer. My face feels stiff from crying as I walk to Mina.

"Look," I say, and hold up the phone with the picture.

"Oh, Scarlett . . ." She throws her arms over me, pressing her cheek into my sternum.

"Let's get out of here," I say. "There's more to Graceville than this graveyard."

I can't see David, but I know he's here, helping me get Cody into the car, getting behind the wheel of the Volvo, popping in a tape. I can't reach around the bend to him, but I feel him, and for the first time in probably a year, I feel peace. As I slide into the leather seats of Mina's car, the wind raises all the hairs on my arms. Hannah is in my front yard waiting for us to pull in. Mom is leaving the hospital, getting in her car, sanitizing her hands, checking her rearview mirror. Dad is watching the clock at the fire station, anxious to get home and see me. David is everywhere and nowhere. For me, Cody is too. I am shivering with life and Mina is smiling. And now, it's time to go. I've got myself in focus, and that means I've got Mom, Dad, and Hannah to catch up on all this too. It's clear I don't travel at a predictable speed. But I'm not on a crash course. I'll be okay. I really will. I'll email this right away. I guess you know I never got the journal done. You understand we all make bad choices sometimes. Thanks, Professor Bradshaw, for the extension.

ACKNOWLEDGMENTS

I am grateful to all who provided emotional, material, and practical support to make this dream of a book come true:

In particular, to my agent, Elizabeth Bewley, of Sterling Lord Literistic, whose dedication to this book and my career have remained stalwart, sane, and ever-encouraging, and who got the book into the hands of my tireless editor, Jessica Dandino Garrison, whose commitment to Scarlett and her story kept me from kicking my computer to Canada. Jess and Elizabeth, it's become a life goal to keep making you cry.

To the entire team at Dial Books for Young Readers and Penguin Young Readers for your excellent feedback and enthusiasm, especially Ellen Cormier and Nancy Mercado, and Regina Castillo for your copy-editing magic. To Leah Schiano, Kara Brammer, and others in PYR Marketing for your fandom and feedback. And to Maggie Edkins for cover design, to Mercedes Debellard for cover art that brought Scarlett and David to life, and to Cerise Steel for the beautiful interior design.

To Elysia Roorbach, my first teen reader, whose feedback

was as good, if not better, than any grown-up's. Thanks to the Maine Writers and Publishers Alliance for supporting writers across the state. To Kathleen Glasgow for welcoming me to the YA community with open arms, and being a model of kindness and generosity in the community. To Sheryl Scarborough and Rachel Lynn Solomon for encouraging feedback early on. To Julie Schumacher for advising on my agent search, adding to the list of why U of Minnesota's MFA was one of the best choices I ever made. To Mythyli Sanikommu for your expert read, science read, and good conversations. To Shane Breaux for your expert read and helpful perspective, and Éireann Lorsung and Dickinson House for the residency where I discovered the form of this story. To Gretchen Taylor for answering questions about Colorado. To Ginger Kent for answering questions about drugs with an NP's knowledge and for actually having a record-listening room. To my friends and students at the University of Maine, Farmington, for bringing joy to work and helping with this project in many ways.

Thanks to Sonja Ljungdahl, my sister, who has remained a strong supporter of my writing since I was in high school and who read the book for science content. Please don't blame her if Scarlett or I got anything wrong. She has taught physics, but she is mostly a biologist! To Beth, for proving every day that friends can be family. We're connected at the root, my friend. To Mom and Dad for never telling me my dreams were too big or too wild, but instead urging me to go for them. You guys are the best.

I'm lucky to have married my best reader. Nathaniel Teal Minton, thank you for your knowledge of story, thoughtful insight on craft, and help in making this book all it could be. Your role goes far beyond the countless weekends you were alone with our two kids, but for that I am also grateful. Thanks for always believing in me. I love you so much.

Finally, thanks to Adelaide and Elodie, for whom I write because if I gave up on my dreams, what would I be teaching you? Thanks for your understanding, support, and help in keeping the family running when I work. Keep believing in your own magic, and never stop.

ABOUT THE AUTHOR

Shana Youngdahl is a poet and novelist who teaches writing at the University of Maine at Farmington and has directed the Longfellow Young Writers' Workshop. One of her greatest joys is helping people embrace the stories they need to tell. Shana lives with her husband, two daughters, and two cats in Maine. *As Many Nows as I Can Get* is her debut novel.